-Sarah K.

Map of the Plane

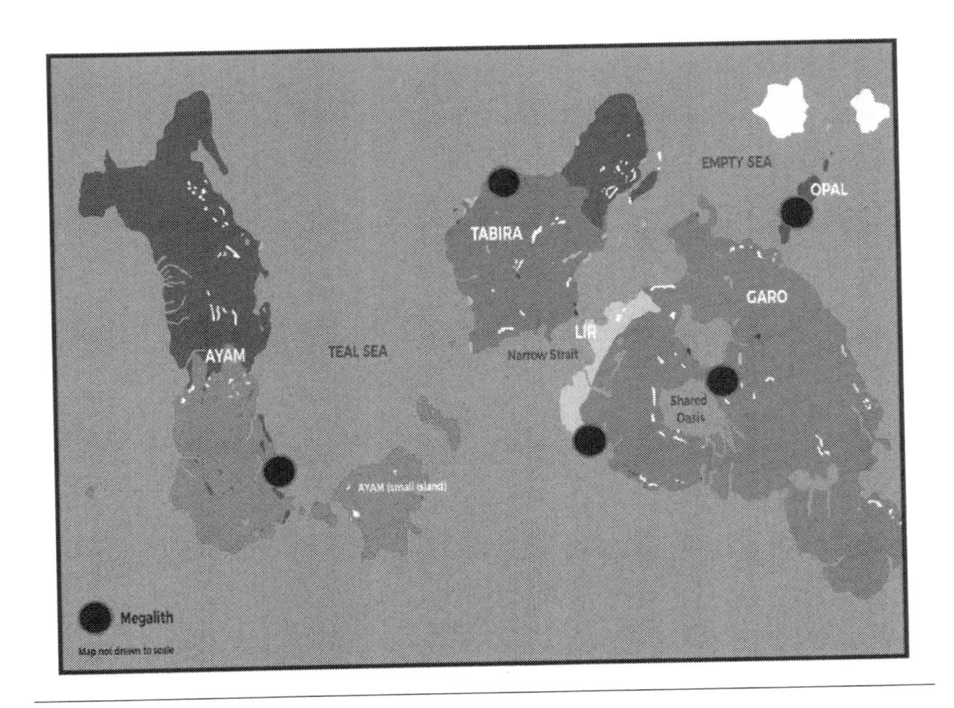

Glossary of People, Places and Things – page 246

Chapter One

Fire.

Flames of raw energy that fueled the very beginnings of all civilization across the Plane. With a life of its own, this beautiful yet dangerous light was as destructive as it was mystifying. Always safely controlled, the white-hot force gave rise to all power in known existence.

Now, for the very first time in recollected history, fire was uncontrolled – and falling from the sky in the form of flaming rocks.

Cascading torrents of orange and yellow soared through the day and night skies to plummet to the surface on all faces of the Plane. On every continent and isle, chunks of fire slammed into the soil, rocks and water below.

The barrage of rock and dust obscured the sun in the sky above.

The lead scientist had just given the final signal to retreat until further notice. With the violent shower now going on for eleven cycles, most survivors left on the Plane had already made the descent.

The scientist palmed the surface of the rise to make one final attempt at contact with the Star Unit.

"*Star Unit, come in. Do you copy*?" the scientist shouted over the commotion overhead.

No response via either voice communication or Field message. Why wouldn't they *answer*?

Just then, another communication reverberated through the Field:

"Warning – final evacuation now in place. Repeat, this is the last call for evacuation. Storm phase has gone from critical to fatal."

As if on cue, a deafening crash sounded from not far beyond the rise, nearly making the scientist cry out. If no one else from the Star Unit was attempting to make contact, the chaos must have become so cataclysmic as to interfere with signal between not only Plane and Void but across the Plane's surface as well.

As the scientist descended beneath the solar rise to enter the tunnels, several questions flooded forth.

Had the Star Unit survived? Why hadn't they warned the Plane?

Would the solar rises hold against the storm?

What would a life in the Void be like?

More importantly, would the Field be destroyed?

For the first time in eons, death was becoming a reality once again…

The scientist's thoughts were cut short soon after sealing the entrance against the maelstrom overhead – just in time for the greatest crash of all, a horrifying commotion that rocked the very tunnels and utterly eradicated the ground above.

Date – 12,042 YAS (Years after Storm)

Nasin moved through the crowded streets, carefully weaving her way amidst the bustling shoulders pressing by.

Even back when the rail tube had entered the purportedly poorest district of Tabira, people seemed to be rushing to and fro from various lines of work. The older woman marveled at how many adults simply pushed by begging children.

High overhead, police aircraft surveyed the city, the sound of their engines having replaced the familiar call of the temple song that still graced Nasin's home nation of Lir. Somehow, Nasin suspected the only remotely musical aspect remaining in Tabir culture was its national anthem.

Nasin had departed the tube about half a kilometer from the Capital Center. Only several meters ahead began the stairway leading up to the new government building, a smooth, silver structure dwarfed only by the cylindrical, glinting black megalith that stood directly behind it. Both architectural pieces gazed out over the entire region from atop one of the only grassy knolls amidst the otherwise flat green plains of Tabira. As the twilight faded away to dusk, the strange dark material of the megalith began to give off the iridescent glow that always came with nightfall.

Passing beneath the final overpass en route to the Capital Center, Nasin tried not to focus on the large motion picture broadcasts that replayed the same pieces of news and spectacle advertisements over and over. Meanwhile, if the traffic on the streets below the tube rail overpass were any indication, the majority of Tabir drivers found the large image display highly distracting.

The conditions of the peace treaty between Lir and Tabira had been threefold. First, provided Lirian adoption of certain forms of Tabir technology, Tabir officers would monitor the border between Lir and the neighboring Garo nation to ensure that Lir avoided unnecessary brutality when responding to Garo terrorism. Second, aircraft would begin transporting Lirians still living in Tabira back to their newly re-established homeland. Third, Lir would continue trade with Tabira.

Not a moment later, Nasin caught a glimpse of an elderly woman with braided locks and anxious eyes ushering two young boys into a nondescript entryway in the wall of the alley adjacent to where Nasin had just passed.

Moments before retreating back inside behind the boys, the woman reached down and snatched what appeared to be a figurine no larger than her hand.

The door shut with a thud, and Nasin quickened her pace. Harmless as the woman and children likely were, she had to focus on the mission at hand. Although she couldn't deny intrigue as to the social impact of the ruthless Kano police force, the affairs of Tabir citizens should not concern her.

Already, Nasin noticed the white-blossomed trees that lined the narrow walkway to her destination. Soon enough, she found herself at the exterior intercom outside the Capital's main entrance.

Once she had palmed the speaker panel, the Inquirer's questioning face greeted her from the small screen just below the flat caller surface.

"State national designation," he requested blandly.

"Nation Lir. Designation, First Lasha Nasin."

Nasin didn't miss how her title finally evoked the man's eye contact, his gaze flitting surreptitiously over her form before returning to her face.

"Your purpose for council with the First of Tabira?"

"Trade negotiations," replied Nasin smoothly.

"Very well," returned the Inquirer following a brief pause as he raised a communicator to his lips. "The First Lasha of Lir has arrived for trade negotiations."

Nasin was grateful for the brief opportunity to observe as two security guards escorted her upstairs. They passed no fewer than five levels of administrative workers, all typing furiously on keypads or barking orders at their data cubes while on telecalls.

Inwardly, Nasin excitedly anticipated her first meeting with the new Mak. As a matriarchal society, Tabir news had swiftly reached the Lir and Garo regions. For the first time in over a century, a male adversary had challenged a Mak's rise to office. Following her failed implementation of a socioeconomic system in which the government aimed to ensure every household was fed by equal distribution of resources in return for a clean criminal record of all inhabitants, a brief coup d'état had many suspicious of this new Mak's ability to govern.

No wonder security seemed to have hardened since her visit five months prior. Still, this Mak didn't seem to harbor any genocidal intentions toward Lirians, as had her predecessor. For that alone, Nasin was willing to put her best foot forward.

As soon as Nasin approached the entrance to the Mak's office, the guards stepped back about a meter.

Familiar with the drill, the Lirian pressed her palm against the panel beside the door. After a moment's pause, two doors slid apart and Nasin stepped into the room.

There she stood, before a large, silica-based window that demonstrated an impressive view of the entire cityscape, skyscrapers and aircraft silhouetted against a backdrop of golden twilight.

Eta. Tall enough to look Nasin in the eyes, the Tabir woman had a sharp hazel gaze and dark brown tresses pulled into a braided bun. That amber stare stood out against the soft bronze of her skin.

Nasin spoke first. "Mak Eta. Please excuse the late arrival. Our first meeting pleases me."

"Does it?" Eta retorted, perhaps poking fun at the formal greeting.

Nasin was quick to catch on. "Agreed. Shall we dispense with the formalities, then? The rail ride here was stifling, and I'd like some refreshment. Water, if you have some?"

Eta seemed a bit taken aback by Nasin's boldness, before breaking into a grin. "Water, it is."

"So then, First Lasha," Eta began, as Nasin sat across from her at the large wooden desk, finishing her water rather hastily with thirst. "How are the Network towers functioning?"

"Quite well, thank you." Nasin smiled politely.

"That is good to hear," Eta replied. "You've given some thought to my offer?"

Nasin released a steady breath. "You wish to partake in our hydrotechnology."

"Naturally." Eta smiled, as if they were discussing the weather. "Tell me, what capabilities do these devices provide? Are they primarily designed for irrigation?"

"Of course." Nasin retained her smoothest of negotiating expressions. "While we've come a long way since our return, the Lir homeland remains very much a desert beyond the city walls."

"And what about desalination?"

"Yes," answered Nasin. "I take it Tabira could make use of such a capability given your proximity to the sea."

"In fact," Eta began, "my sister, Vata, and her husband, Hak, have recently relocated with their two children to live on the Ayam islands across the Teal Sea. They plan to build a life there. You see, the Ayam natives still hold the archaic belief that someone will take care of them from above. They accredit the megaliths to the Zaam deities and still worship. This prevents them from progressing as a society in areas of science, such as medicine for their sick."

Nasin replied, "Perhaps the Ayam don't need missionaries discouraging their faith. Their beliefs have no impact on the rest of us."

Eta's gaze grew frosty. "Our informants along the Lirian border report a similar consensus from the Garo."

"We remain neutral regarding the Zaam and the megaliths," Nasin countered benignly. "The Garo choose to worship earnestly, painting their faces daily. We do not oppose this practice."

"They are bequeathing their gods for a gift similar to the Lasha, no doubt," replied Eta, evenly. "The Lirians worship water, unless I'm mistaken?"

"Our faithful choose water as our sacred symbol, yes," Nasin said plainly.

"How many believers?"

"Roughly one quarter." Nasin frowned slightly at the relevance of such a question.

"Then your nation retains religion, if only through the worship of an element." Eta nodded. "You have more patience than me, I'll give you that. The Kano officers employ their highly advantageous investigative talents to track down the last faithful Tabir. There's no room for such frivolity in a nation that still suffers poverty. Only education and hard work can pull you up. Belief only encourages laziness and stagnancy. The way I see it, in the face of all that science has given us in recent years, how can we attribute such discovery to anyone but the people of this Plane?"

The Mak's words brought to mind the woman and boys Nasin had witnessed hurrying to conceal the idol in the alleyway not an hour before.

"Mak Eta," Nasin said, not unkindly, "I mean no disrespect when I give my stance that although inhabitants of newly discovered territory deserve knowledge such as advancing medicine, there comes a point at which a power should stop expanding at the expense of another's freedom…there must be a limit to the power one empire can reach. Lest a *mission* turn quickly into an occupation."

"Certainly." There was that smile again. "I'd expect similar ambition from Lir. While we seek to salvage these people from their ignorance, yours continually develop technology that arguably creates a glaring advantage over those with whom you share a border."

"What about the children…begging in the streets?" Nasin ventured.

"An unfortunate result of the Code's failure. When the Center could no longer ration each household and institution accordingly, Tabira reverted to its prior three-tier socioeconomic structure. Many citizens from the third class are left wanting, a situation which the Oligarchy currently seeks to mitigate. At present, we fund all willing to perform in entertainment spectacles. As far as the streets, our priority as of late has been reining in the stray hounds."

"What I aim to know, First Lasha…" Eta began again.

"Please," Nasin held up a hand, "Nasin will do."

"Nasin," Eta's stony smile was unwavering, "this technology of yours, is it purely environmental or has it been weaponized?"

Think fast. Show no weakness.

"Unfortunately," Nasin smiled herself now, "the recent years of harsh drought on our arid soil has left little time for developing water-based weaponry."

The Mak's smile faltered then, only just.

"Our drip irrigation facilitator now works flawlessly in the recycling of natural underground water," the Lirian followed up. "We'd be happy to trade a shipment of five units. No currency exchange necessary."

That was when the high-pitched drone of an alarm sounded throughout the building.

Several moments later, the doors to the Mak's office opened and the same two guards who had escorted Nasin reemerged.

"Mak, we beg your pardon, but we've caught Hazard 14," one of the men huffed, short of breath as though he'd run up the stairwell rather than taking the lift.

Though Eta's eyes narrowed, Nasin detected a slight increase in her breathing. She was anxious.

"Where is it being contained? The lab?"

"Yes, Mak," replied the other guard hastily as his partner barked an order into his communicator. "It's being held in a gamma containment field. So far, it's made no move to escape."

"Will you tell them to shut off that noise?" the Mak requested irritably.

"Escape?" Nasin finally spoke up above the siren. "From gamma confinement? What could possibly get past that type of field?"

Just as suddenly as it had begun, the alarm stopped.

Sparing a fleeting glance at the Lirian, Eta quipped, "You've been out of the loop since the revolt five months back."

Nasin tilted her head. "The male opponent…he's—it's not vulnerable?"

"Is that a habit of the Lasha or the Lirians at large?" Eta tossed back. "Such cryptic terms. Everything is vulnerable, First Nasin. You simply have to know where and how to strike."

Well, the atmosphere of this exchange had certainly gone from congenial to frozen sooner than Nasin had expected.

"This *hazard* you speak of?" prompted the Lirian coolly.

When it became apparent that Nasin wasn't about to drop the other's gaze, Eta continued, "It took the Kano police force nearly two months to quell the first uprising under the rogue officer Joleh. In its wake, twelve others attempted to take on the goal of usurping my command, each put down in under a day."

"What made the first attempted overthrow different?" Nasin wanted to know. "Superior numbers?"

"You might have heard the news of another rebel having walked at the side of Joleh," Eta went on. "A powerful…creature, though it looked like one of us and barely older than a child. Once the creature fled, Joleh couldn't fend off the Kano on his own. His followers didn't take the initiative to step up until after his arrest. Our forces have swept the streets each night for the months since the uprising, searching for this accomplice. We've caught him, but he usually escapes not long after."

Then this entity must truly pose a challenge. According to recorded history, the Kano remained the most brutal law enforcement and military unit to ever grace the Plane.

"Well then," Eta suddenly seemed eager to change topics, "I'll show you to your quarter for the night."

While settling her mind for rest, Nasin couldn't help but think back to the 'hazard' from earlier.

Chapter Two

Unlike the sweltering sands of Lir, which didn't begin to cool until the sun approached its next ascent, temperatures in Tabira dropped about an hour after nightfall.

Grateful for the large window in her quarter, Nasin struggled to find sleep despite the soothing breeze flowing into the room.

Outside the Capital Center, the air grew cool and dry as lightning emerged from out at sea.

The Lirian intelligence unit hadn't learned anything significant regarding accomplices to Joleh in his attempt to seize control of the Capital Center. Who—or *what*—was this entity they had confined down below?

After several more minutes of pondering the risk of insulting Mak Eta should she be found out, Nasin decided she would see for herself.

Changing from her nightclothes back into her travel suit and shoes, Nasin crept quietly out of the sleeping quarter.

The lift ride to the lab below was smooth enough. The Center was dead quiet, the air still enough to hear anyone who might be approaching once she stepped out into the hallway.

Fortunately, the lab had been easily identifiable from the lift, with the button showing a beaker symbol. Down at ground level, the monotonous whir of large generators permeated the silence.

Following the dim lights overhead and keeping a careful eye out for security cameras, Nasin came to a door marked for Center officials only.

Although she was fairly sure the intrusion detection panel to the right of the door frame was the access key, she decided to try the handle.

Locked.

Nasin sighed. If the beaker symbol on the door was any indication, the lab was on the other side.

Then she felt it. A warm, prickly feeling on the surface of her skin, contrasting with the cool floor beneath her feet. As if the air had grown thicker.

Unsure if this static feeling simply seemed keener due to her acute senses or if the atmosphere had actually changed, Nasin decided to explore further.

Turning from the secure door, the Lirian crept quietly toward the other end of the hall. The lights seemed to actually grow brighter as she continued forth, glancing around in curious confusion at the several large panels of silica or some other translucent material. These panels lined one side of the corridor, and each section opened into a small space with three white walls. The static feeling was growing to the point of making her limbs ache.

As she came to the center panel, Nasin nearly took a step backward.

Before her, on the other side of the large lucid frame, a boy sat on the floor in the middle of the room.

Seemingly no older than seven, he had dark skin, the color of palm bark after a rainfall. Under the bright lights, splotches of dried dust stood out on his cheeks. A mess of black curls swept his forehead, which currently hung bowed over his crossed legs.

Nasin resisted the urge to rub her temples. As the boy slowly raised his head, the Lirian nearly started as brighter lights shot to life in the corridor where she stood.

Nasin's mouth went dry.

The child before her had a face like death. His flesh looked almost dark grey with a strange glint across gaunt cheekbones beneath the lights.

"Well, well," Eta approached from the main entrance to what Nasin now realized was some sort of holding cell, "you never mentioned the Lasha also acted as intelligence agents."

Slowly, Nasin pulled her gaze away from the child in the cell, just as her eyes met a dark brown stare. "Mak Eta. Please pardon the intrusion. I found myself unable to sleep and decided to explore."

The Mak broke into one of her eerie smiles again. Nasin could see she stood flanked by two guards.

Where was security when she'd first entered this area? If any cameras had been present, they must have been small enough to blend in with the shadows of the upper walls.

Moreover, why hadn't this area been closed off along with the lab proper? Had Eta *wanted* the Lirian to discover the cell?

"Naturally," replied the Mak. "In fact, I was considering whether to show you myself. First Lasha, this is Hazard 14 or, as my late opponent Joleh referred to him, Rohem. Mind the panel though, the containment field is designed to keep life forms out as well as in."

Rohem. The Tabir term for 'tree thing'.

"You found him in the trees?" Nasin asked inquisitively.

The Mak laughed dryly. Under this harsh light, her weariness was apparent in her haggard expression and the bags under eyes. "He favors anything close to the sky. To the sun. Treetops, buildings..."

Eta had stepped up to the cell panel now, beside Nasin, peering in at Rohem. Rohem dropped his gaze almost immediately.

"Look at me, boy." Eta's voice was sharp, and yet, Rohem remained still as a statue. "I said *look* at me."

Still no response.

The Mak palmed onto the pad beneath the panel and tapped a graphic on the resulting screen.

In the next moment, the entire area fell black as pitch.

Nasin's senses were struck next by the shrill, horrified cry of a young boy. He sounded so similar to Avithia that the Lirian nearly shouted at the Mak. And then she registered the words behind the sound.

"Please! Bring back the light! What do you want to know? I'll tell you anything, just please let the light come back!"

"Do you promise to be a good boy and tell us whatever we ask?"

"Yes!" the young voice broke, and Nasin's head was assaulted by a searing ache that shot down her spine, accompanied by a moment at which the very atmosphere seemed to blast with heat.

A second later, the lights returned full force. The boy was now standing so close to Eta and Nasin that he could have reached out to touch them.

"Good boy." Eta tapped another graphic on the pad screen. "Security rays at full force."

Rohem's gaze flitted briefly to Nasin, just as her breathing was beginning to calm.

"Our guest Nasin was quite impressed to learn of your resistance to gamma ray," Eta stated simply. "One might wonder how you'd respond after some time in the shadows…" She trailed off briefly, her eyes never leaving those of her prisoner. "Now show good grace and tell me, have you aligned yourself with anyone else since we last saw each other?"

"No," Rohem mumbled, looking like he'd rather do anything but hold Eta's stare. A steely resolve, indeed. Especially for one so young. "Joleh was the only one. I have been on the streets. Please let me go. I don't care about your Capital, and I will not hurt any other Kano officers."

Eta turned to Nasin, her face beaded with perspiration from the effects of the heat surge. "We suspected he could have been Lasha at first—until he showed no need to consume water—or food. My opponent Joleh was originally employed with the Kano forces, along with his brother, Samed. Samed eventually discovered Joleh's treachery in harboring a child—particularly one with…*unique* abilities. Despite claims to want to use the child's power for Tabira, Joleh's level of secrecy was suspect, and he went to prison for six years for having hidden the boy for so long.

"Meanwhile, Rohem spent time in orphanages, wherein he would protect children from being beaten, and keep some warm at night while on the streets during the cold season. As the dark makes him weak, Rohem lived as an ordinary Tabir child and refused to leave those he protected. Until Joleh broke out again and enlisted Rohem for an actual revolt. The boy's hardiness is what makes him the perfect accomplice. He can set traps in trees and on rooftops where no one else could go and risk the fall. Mostly, he distracts the Kano troops with that static heat trick he just pulled on us."

"But all under Joleh's orders?" Nasin inquired.

"He's generally compliant. Never actually killed any innocent people. A few Kano officers died here and there—usually from a bad fall whilst pursuing him in one of his lofty escapes to a rooftop."

Nasin thought it odd how Eta spoke as if Rohem wasn't right in front of them.

"The Kano succeeded this time?" Nasin asked plainly.

"Only thanks to the little waif he was harboring. The other orphan was hit by an automobile while trying to run with stolen food. Hazard 14 wouldn't leave the boy's side while he lay dying. Once the child died, Rohem allowed himself to be taken."

A pause.

She finally settled on a neutral question. "There is no immediate danger, then?"

The Mak hummed again. "Many citizens of Tabira smell danger. When we first captured Joleh, he ended up spilling the backstory of how he had first acquired Rohem. He'd found him on the streets. Somehow, Joleh figured out there was more to him. The officer sustained a nasty burn on his arm that left several fingers unusable, yet both he and Rohem claim that it's not the boy's doing. Since Joleh's capture, our agents have utilized particular means to compel him to share more information about the boy, and still the officer remains silent."

"You would leave all the children on the streets to the Kano…"

One look stopped Rohem mid-sentence.

"Come now." Eta glanced back at the boy in the cell. "You prefer it here with us to playing weapon for a man who cares nothing about you."

Rohem didn't answer.

"Good then." Eta turned to Nasin after a pause. "First Lasha, are you satisfied?"

"Yes."

Nasin couldn't recall a night when she'd slept more fitfully. Any dreams she dozed deeply enough to have were wracked by images of that child's desperate face. No tears. Only unadulterated fear in a deep black stare.

That child couldn't stay here.

Upon returning to her quarter, Mak Eta decided that sleep was out of the question.

Nasin—First Lasha and head of the Lirian autocracy—had caught Tabira at a weak moment.

Moreover, she had stumbled upon the hazard itself. That blunder had stemmed from pure carelessness on Eta's part. The holding cells should have also been under maximum security, just like the lab.

Granted, the containment field seemed to drain the hazard at night, and yet that wouldn't stop intruders from accessing that sensitive area. Intruders who were already inside the Capital, that was.

Even now, Eta felt both disdain and infuriating fascination towards that boy. She despised the very real possibility that the monstrosity could kill her if he truly desired. That, if he chose to rebel even without Joleh at his side, an entire force of Kano officers wouldn't stand a chance.

Eta set her jaw, staring up at the ceiling of her quarter in the dark. They had to either figure out a way to destroy him first, or he had to disappear. The fact remained that his presence at the Capital, and even in Tabira, at large, greatly endangered her reputation among the people.

Shutting her eyes, Eta willed away the simmering doubt that plagued her day in and day out. Both Tabira and Lir strove for democratic voting systems in which the people elected their leaders—and yet, despite working with a plethora of intelligence and military officers, these decisions always ultimately fell upon Eta.

She despised the pressure, and yet relished in the power all at once. Somehow, she had to wonder if Nasin's nature as a Lasha—an individual with enhanced physical strength and longevity—provided her an advantage in managing the stress of politics.

Tall and slim, Nasin had reminded Eta of a watchful bird of prey. The fact that the Lasha's hair showed streaks of silver suggested that Nasin must be at least sixty, despite her features not looking a day over forty.

Mak Eta rolled over with a sigh. Despite any benefits that might accompany being Lasha, she refused to let herself envy Nasin. Eta had always excelled on her own merits. No special gifts, simply she and her sister Vata with a mission to introduce the rest of the Plane to all the possibilities of advanced civilization.

Returning to the issue at hand, Eta hadn't missed the sympathy in Nasin's gaze upon seeing Rohem. The Mak could use this to her advantage. With any luck, the Lasha would accept an offer, or perhaps even volunteer, to take the boy away from the Capital.

Eta smiled to herself. Surely, Nasin would see herself as a heroine once again, taking in a lost child. So be it. Anything to ensure that Hazard 14 posed no further risk to Tabira's trust in Eta as their leader.

The following morning, the Lirian would have given anything for some tea. As always though, water would suffice.

Sitting across from Mak Eta during their departure briefing, Nasin was certain the Tabir hadn't gotten much more rest.

"So, Nasin," Eta's smile was definitely forced this morning, "I've stated our import requirements. Please sign here, including your tariff quote."

Nasin began speaking almost as soon as she picked up the pen to sign the parchment Eta had placed before her. "It's a simple tariff. I want the boy. Rohem."

The Mak went so still she could have been made of ice. "What would you do with him?"

"You already mentioned how the people view him as a threat. Besides, he clearly wants nothing to do with Tabira. He's got no one here. Lir, however, can give him the opportunity to eventually enlist in our defense efforts – counterterrorism and otherwise."

"A soldier?"

"In time, if he so chooses." Nasin nodded slightly. "For now, he is a child."

"First Lasha, for the past several years, Tabira has aimed to serve damages for the atrocities committed against the Lirians by the previous oligarchy under Mak Kerad. Therefore, we have refrained from interfering in how you choose to run Lirian affairs. However, something—*someone*—like that would provide you quite the unfair advantage..."

"You have my word in this agreement that Lir will not use Rohem nor any other resources against another nation, unless they strike first. You know from the Tabir overseers surveying the Lirian border that the Garo very rarely experience collateral damage due to our retaliation. If the scales tip at any time, we both know that they will inform you."

Once again, the two women entered into a staring contest, broken only when Nasin signed her name to complete the agreement.

"It's done then." The Lirian smiled.

"Right." Eta rose in time with Nasin. "Let's go get your tariff. I do hope the farming technology and cotton will be worth it. Remember, Nasin, he only looks like an innocent child."

After ordering the release of Hazard 14, Eta arranged for Officer Samed to take an indefinite assignment as the Central Oligarchy's head informant for the Lirian and Garo border. Freshly trained and something of a prodigy among the officers recommended for first assignment, he seemed the ideal candidate for the post. If the Lasha did somehow manage to gain enough control over her new ward to become overconfident despite Lir's flourishing commercial relationship with Tabira, Eta could not be too careful.

In any case, the presence of such a potential threat in the region would present all the warrant necessary to secure a full-time patrol around the Lirian perimeter. And who better to keep tabs on such activities than the very officer who had sold out his own elder brother for using the hazard in the first place?

The Mak had to marvel at how rapidly her initial panic upon security's report of the feed showing the Lasha wandering down to the science wing had given way to opportunistic excitement.

At least she no longer felt like flogging herself over the stupidity of not enlisting an all-hours security staff down there.

Most importantly, the Lirians taking the creature off her hands and away from her frightened constituents would undoubtedly improve her rapport with the citizens of Tabira.

The entire rail ride back to Lir, Nasin tried not to dwell on how suspiciously quickly Eta had agreed to let her take Rohem. Instead, she decided to focus on the boy who was now in her custody.

As she looked more closely, Nasin was taken aback by how normal Rohem appeared. Still dressed in tattered street clothes, he followed behind her silently and sat quietly beside her on the rail tube.

During the trip, Nasin marveled at the look of sheer joy and relief that had graced Rohem's features once security had released him from his cell to be led outside by Nasin.

Outside into the bright sunshine.

Once on board the rail tube, his dark brown eyes were curious—nearly hungry—as he gazed out the tube's large glass window at the passing trees and high hills that rose once they'd left Tabir capital territory.

When the tube entered onto the Strait Bridge, the boy's mouth opened slightly at the dark blue water that surrounded them on all sides.

"There is a lot of water," Nasin explained. "But only for a little while. We are safe in here."

Eventually, the Strait gave way to brown marshes and, soon enough, to the tawny dunes of Lir.

Nearly six hours had passed, and Rohem had politely refused the bread offered him by the attendant passing by. Nor had he taken a sip of his water.

"For you," was all he said as she insisted he stay hydrated.

The famished, almost skeletal look had disappeared from his face, leaving only healthy dark brown.

As the tube approached Lir territory and the sky grew violet with sunset, Nasin spoke up. "Don't be afraid, Rohem. You'll be safe where we're going."

"How long will I be there?"

Nasin pondered this carefully. "For as long as you like. I don't want you to be frightened. There are other people there your age, and we have animals there. Dunehorses. A mother who just gave birth to her foal."

"They always talked about animals in Tabira." Rohem's eyes widened. "We only ever saw sick hounds on the streets."

Then it was true. Industrialization had driven all of the local large and small game to extinction.

"We're calling the baby horse Yeni," Nasin added a moment later.

Though the boy remained silent, the light touched his eyes with his next smile.

"You will not need to run from the Kano anymore," Nasin said, following a pause.

Once they arrived at their stop, Rohem looked wary about disembarking the tube. Nasin gently took his arm and guided him down onto the sand. At first, he seemed perplexed at how the granules covered his shoes.

"Sand," Nasin murmured softly, gingerly assuming this was his first time seeing or feeling this sort of terrain.

Then, without a word, he bent over and removed his shoes, proceeding to carry them.

Nasin was about to caution him that the sand might be hot, before he started walking across its surface beside her with gentle plodding steps.

As the sky overhead darkened to dusk, the evening temple song rang out from both Lir and Garo with the third and final prayer of the day.

When they reached the newly installed electric gates to the inner city, Nasin noticed Rohem take a small step back to stand slightly behind her. Perhaps the key panel to the left of the gate reminded him of the holding cell's panel back in Tabira.

In that case, Nasin felt like the choice to forgo electric lighting in favor of traditional torchlight by night had proven favorable. No need for Tabir technology to mark every centimeter of the Plane.

The first stop before home was the medical facility. Nasin felt grateful that the head doctor, Gether, Avithia's father, had agreed to take such a late call.

"Pardon the late hour," Nasin replied to Gether's salutation of palm-over-heart as she entered, guiding Rohem by the shoulder.

"No worries at all," Gether assured her good-naturedly. "It's been a slow day at the office."

"Rohem, this is Doctor Gether," Nasin explained softly in Tabir. "He will examine you now to make sure you are healthy."

"Hello there, Rohem," the doctor greeted cheerily, also in Tabir.

"Will you stay?" Rohem asked Nasin.

He didn't quite look frightened, only somber.

"Of course." Nasin smiled.

The physical exam went fairly smoothly, with Rohem calmly and curiously observing the white room around them as the doctor set about listening to the child's heartbeat and looking in his eyes.

"Well, all sounds good inside," Gether announced with obvious interest. "Healthy heart."

So the boy had normal organs, Nasin pondered. She wasn't really sure why she'd ever suspected otherwise.

"Did they feed you well?" Gether asked.

Tilting his head ever so slightly, Rohem spoke. "I don't need to eat."

Frowning softly, Gether sat on his stool and rolled closer to the exam table. "How is that?"

"I don't eat food. I just need the sun. Then I don't feel hungry…or even tired."

"But you *are* able to eat?" Gether pressed.

Rohem nodded slowly.

Nasin could see the wonder written plainly all over the doctor's features.

"Indeed. I'd suggest an x-ray, but it's a bit late for that." Gether continued, "Wouldn't want to overwhelm him. Rohem, will you please remove your shirt. I'd like to hear how you breathe."

Gether posed his request in Tabir, and Rohem grew very still.

"I promise to stay," Nasin squeezed his shoulder.

Without another word, Rohem removed his patched shirt.

Nasin could almost hear Gether's breath hiss through his teeth. Before them, Rohem sat kneading the shirt fabric between his fingers and staring at the floor.

He had the normal body of a young boy, no doubt. Except that his torso was completely smooth, devoid of either nipples or navel.

"The Capital Center had him?" Gether asked, and Nasin was thankful Rohem couldn't yet understand Lirian. "Do you know if he's been genetically engineered?"

"Like the Eta's niece and nephew?" Nasin asked.

"Perhaps." Gether gingerly placed gloved fingers on Rohem's upper back, the boy's eyes remaining on his own lap. "Though the Flightless children inherited that trait. I have yet to see an instance of actual genetic engineering."

A pause.

"He keeps so still," the doctor remarked. "Breathing sounds entirely normal. And we are certain he isn't Lasha? Avithia also displayed normal vitals, though I can't explain this physical difference."

"He doesn't need food or water. He seems to…produce heat. When he feels threatened or stressed," Nasin explained.

"If he truly doesn't require nutrients, then any digestive organs would be vestigial. Fascinating. He must draw all sustenance from another source." Gether made his way over to the cabinets by where Nasin stood.

"Sunlight, perhaps," Nasin offered.

The doctor hummed in reply, and Rohem shifted ever so slightly on the exam table.

"Small pinch," Gether warned in Tabir, pressing a tiny syringe to Rohem's shoulder.

The boy did not flinch.

After withdrawing the small tube, Gether went still.

"What is it?" Nasin didn't move away from Rohem's side.

"No blood." The doctor breathed out his words in Lirian. "He doesn't bleed. I'd really like to see an x-ray right about now. But all in good time. Now you mentioned he sometimes gives off heat…"

At times like these, the First Lasha felt especially grateful that Gether had taken his medical schooling in Tabira. Fluency in the Tabir language and sciences always proved helpful.

"One of the better parts of trade with Tabira." Gether pulled a grey device from one of the cabinet drawers. "Small medical supplies. This is a radiometer, it will detect radiation for some of the larger imaging equipment we hope to manufacture ourselves."

Rohem seemed relieved that this new object only scanned the air before him, rather than needing to touch him.

"I'm getting only trace readings," Gether mused. "Extremely minimal, not harmful. I suppose if he's to stay here, you just have to make sure he remains as calm as possible. Other than that, he is in completely normal condition for a boy of his age. Speaking of which, do we know for certain how old he is? He looks about seven."

"Seven is what I planned to go with," Nasin affirmed.

"Nice to meet you, Rohem," Dr. Gether murmured in Tabir to the young boy. "Welcome to Lir."

As they reached the home compound, Nasin was relieved that Avithia and Oria were asleep. The written message she'd sent would have at least prepared them for the new arrival. The rest could wait until tomorrow.

"This is your room." She showed Rohem to the guest quarter after retrieving some of Avi's extra clothes for the new arrival to change into. "You should sleep now. Please let me know if you need anything. I stay in the room down the hall to the right of the window."

"I don't need to sleep."

Nasin nodded. "You're afraid of the dark?"

Rohem made a sound in the back of his throat. "Maybe. But I don't need to sleep."

Nasin frowned. "They didn't let you sleep at the Capital Center?"

"No, I just never sleep. Wherever I am."

"I see." Nasin's own eyes felt like sandpaper. "Well, it's been a trying day for all. Can you perhaps rest?"

Rohem seemed to ponder this for a moment. "Yes."

With a smile, Nasin turned to leave. Best to keep him calm and spare anyone else a literal headache.

"Wait...First Nasin?"

She glanced back with another smile. "Nasin will do. Yes, child?"

"I *am*...I am afraid of the dark."

"It's not all dark though," Nasin cooed gently, settling her hand on Rohem's shoulder. "Look out that window."

She pointed to the window, at the gently glowing megalith.

"It's pretty." Rohem breathed timidly. "But it's not the sun."

Nasin sighed. "I will stay with you tonight."

"Thank you." Rohem settled on the floor, "I'll rest. Please, sleep on the bed. I don't need the bed. I like this...this here."

"The carpet," chuckled Nasin. "Very well. Thank you. Good rest, Rohem."

If Rohem did breathe, his form remained so quiet on the floor beside her that it took Nasin mere minutes to fall into a dreamless sleep.

Nasin came to what felt like hours later.

At first, she couldn't tell what had roused her—only that her mind had registered a feeling unlike any she had ever experienced.

A sense of pure euphoria traveled in a tingle through her fingers, up her arm, and throughout her torso down to her feet.

Opening her eyes blearily, Nasin rolled over to see Rohem lying on his back on the carpet, holding her left hand clasped in his own.

Outside, the sky flashed with lightning from a dry thunderstorm, followed closely by a deep rumble.

"What...what are you doing?" was all she could manage. Her entire body felt like liquid lead.

"Is it too strong?" Rohem asked with a curious tilt of his head, concern evident in his voice. "I wanted to make you feel good. The Mak called it energy flow. Joleh's friends always liked it this way, during sleep, but I can try…"

Nasin's mind put the situation into focus faster than lightning. Still, best to tread carefully.

"Rohem..." Gently as possible, she withdrew her hand from his fingers, and the strange feeling vanished immediately. "You don't have to do that here."

"But to say thank you?" Rohem's dark eyes shone in the glow from the megalith outside the window. "Didn't the Mak tell you? If I don't do this after dark, I will end."

Nasin fought the compulsive urge to swallow, her mouth suddenly very dry.

"Mak Eta told you this?" she asked carefully.

The boy on the carpet shook his head. "Joleh knew. He told everyone. It's always been like this."

"Do you hurt during the night?"

"…No," replied Rohem thoughtfully. "I just feel…more tired."

Somehow, Nasin knew at her core that this couldn't be true. Simply a sickening ruse to justify perverse activities with this child. To keep him docile and fearful of the night.

"The first night we met," Nasin tried carefully. "How long had they kept you down there in the cell?"

Rohem pursed his lips. "I don't know. Time seems the same below ground."

That made sense.

"How many guards came in and out this past time?" Nasin asked, hoping that the lack of overnight guards was a constant.

Then she could possibly determine the number of days he'd been locked away.

"About five, maybe six," Rohem answered.

Right. Two guards per shift, so roughly two or three days. With even that small calculation, her brain felt sorely in need of rest.

"Rohem," Nasin began again. "I am Lasha. Lasha are different, much like you. We are strong, and do not require such thanks. All Lirians use words only for thanks. Besides, the sun is always shining on Lir—the desert sand keeps in the heat."

"The tower looks taller here," remarked Rohem, fiddling with the carpet fringe. "We are closer to it than in Tabira."

She supposed that, when entirely surrounded by flat desert, the Lirian megalith must appear even larger.

"And it watches over you." Nasin smiled in the pale light. "Though we do not go near it, same as in Tabira. Best to keep your distance. If you ever feel unsafe, you can always come to me—beginning tonight."

"I am frightened now," Rohem murmured, sitting up on his knees to face Nasin.

"I'll tell you what," Nasin replied. "I will hold your hand for the remainder of the dark hours. Only holding. In the morning, I promise, you will face a bright new day."

After a lengthy pause, Rohem ran a hand through his hair and curled up on the carpet by Nasin's bedside. He reached up to take her hand.

"Rest now, Rohem-*tha*," she finally soothed as she softly grasped his fingers, settling on a Lirian diminutive, her Tabir sounding idly scratchy to her own ears in her tired voice. "That is the only thanks necessary."

Once she'd settled back down, the little voice in the back of Nasin's mind spoke for the hundredth time that day.

Is he dangerous?

Quite possibly.

If he was lethal, would he have already made a move to kill and escape?

Most definitely.

Is he a child? Yes.

He deserves the chance to experience a safe environment. One where he is not threatened or used as a weapon and whatever else against his will.

The events of that night were never mentioned again.

Chapter Three

Date - 12,060 YAS

"Here you are, mother," beamed Ara proudly, setting the slightly charred morsel on the surface of the small bark table. "I thought you might like a bit of the rainbow fish for a change, with the ceremony coming up."

Vata granted the gift before her a feeble glimpse before rolling her eyes and settling back in her seat. "I see what you're trying to do."

Ara caught himself just as his face began to fall. "Aren't you hungry? It's fresh, I promise. Just caught it not even one hour ago today."

"The rainbow bit," his mother replied tersely. "You mean to persuade me into letting you parade around during the ceremony? Cover up."

"Come now, mother," insisted the young man before her. "You know I've been keeping it concealed, as always."

"And the fish?" Vata pressed curtly.

"Is just that—a fish," her daughter Inad chided as she entered the scene from behind Vata's makeshift lounging dais under the mighty palm at the canopy's edge.

Vata's eyes narrowed slightly as Inad handed Ara an item wrapped in cloth. "You've spent the better part of the morning fishing. Here's some food for *you*."

Inad's tone and momentary glance at her mother did not escape Vata in the least. She laughed coldly as Ara timidly accepted the wrapped gift from his sister.

"I see your stealth has improved. I must admit, I barely heard you coming this time. What have you been keeping busy with today?"

"Teaching," Inad answered, fiddling with the small dagger at her hip.

"I hardly understand why you pass so many hours with the children. You should really be honing your own skill."

"You can't remain the only Tabir teacher. Besides, they all must know how to defend themselves. Not everyone lives on the small island, Mother," Inad retorted, purposely avoiding their mother's scolding gaze.

Of their parents, Inad knew it was their father, Hak, who had truly held the passion for teaching. Vata simply continued in his stead, under orders from Tabira.

"They have their canoes, Inad," Vata pressed. "So what of us? Your father is gone, and I can only handle one at a time. We both know that when it comes to life talents, your brother's end with his looks. Who's to defend *our* unit? And I mean with actual weapons, not primitive knives."

Vata had barely finished speaking before the dagger impaled the palm's trunk a hair from her right ear.

"Guns aren't everything."

With that, Inad strode over and wrenched her blade from the tree's bark, disappearing up the rope ladder into the canopy above. Her brother followed not long after.

"Mind if I join you?" came Ara's voice from beside her.

"Go ahead," his sister replied, settling into her favorite lookout position on the rope bridge.

"Have you eaten today?" Ara asked pointedly.

Inad didn't answer. He knew how much his questions about her eating habits frustrated her.

"Think you can throw that dagger far enough to hit an *onn* beast?" he asked.

"Depends on how far it was," Inad replied simply.

She seemed distracted. The sun was slowly beginning its descent, and they both knew what that meant—for all in these parts, but more so for the two of them tonight.

"You know…" Ara started carefully, unwrapping his sister's offering - some bread with honey. "It won't necessarily be you."

Inad didn't realize how white her knuckles had grown as her fingers tensed around her dagger. She turned it over in her hands idly. "In all of Ayam's history, there's only been one male chieftain who's chosen a man."

"So about time for another then." Ara tried to lighten the mood as he pulled off the netted scarf he wore when outside their tree shelter. "Besides, Mother said it herself, I'm irresistible."

Inad spared her brother a glance and smiled weakly. He was a sight to behold, she supposed—for those who hadn't grown up with him, perhaps. The sharp contrast between his soft facial features and the vibrant colors of the many feathers that naturally adorned his crown never ceased to amaze the people amongst whom they lived.

These colorful features had proven more of a curse, however. Ara's striking resemblance to their father fueled their mother's disdain for her son's presence. That on top of his relentless clumsiness with all kinds of weaponry, as well as an innate struggle to read and write. For most of his life, he'd been the bane of her existence, permitted on the mainland simply for the sake of keeping the Ayam locals enthralled by walking among them once per day and singing both Ayam and Tabir hymns. Singing was a talent even their mother couldn't deny Ara possessed.

A good thing, too. According to Vata, so long as these savages still believed in their Zaam, she could use Ara's likeness to the jungle birds to ensure that the natives would believe in her splendor. In her immortality.

The woman from Tabira who had given birth to a Flightless. Well, two Flightless if you included Inad, whose own far plainer quills remained hidden at her nape beneath her thick, dark braid.

The rest of the time, Ara busied himself with finger-painting the tree bark with Inad's pupils during their rest from lessons.

"They've every right to hate us," Inad pondered aloud. "We've not only forced our language on them, we brought the Curse here."

"Only to show the Ayam that their precious *Zaam* are capable of sitting back and letting such horrors befall them," Ara reminded her bitterly, sounding disturbingly like their mother.

"But the Curse isn't the work of the Zaam," Inad shot back. "It's Tabir science. Isn't the whole point of this *mission* to prove that we don't need the Zaam to create miracles? To stop the Ayam believing in the Zaam altogether? And who's to say the Zaam ever existed? Instead, we use our own technology to bring destruction."

A tense silence ensued as the siblings backed off each other and returned their attention to the sunset. The glowing rays settled over the white sandy beach of their small island and onward, across the glittering blue strait of sea that led to the mainland.

The sun hadn't yet set, and already the clicking night song of the trees had begun all around them.

"Seems pointless to base an entire mythology—a whole religion—on a couple of structures," Ara observed quietly. "I mean, let's face it, if the Zaam ever existed, the megaliths are all that are left of them. Otherwise, power probably wouldn't end with Aunt Eta and her capital."

"You have to admit, it's odd though," Inad pointed out. "That the Ayam and the Garo—cultures separated by leagues upon leagues of ocean—both call their gods by the same name. Zaam. Even the most familiar of them, Echil the Hopebringer, is called such by both nations."

"Mother was always fond of the idea of an ancient land bridge that once connected Ayam land with the old Opal territory," Ara reasoned.

"In any case, fables aside," Inad replied, "I don't like this kind of imposition. Even if Mother and Eta won't admit to it, the disease is Tabir, and it's our fault. The scientists at the Capital Center developed the serum that cures the cellular growth disease. The fastest killer of all. Here in

Ayam, even the small inventions such as cellular regeneration serum seem like a miracle. The Ayam are still thankful for our sharing it. Mother has used that trust to her advantage."

"Ironic," Ara muttered. "They trusted us, and now they have not only another plague to deal with, but the burden of those infected eating nearly all the wildlife."

"Except the birds and the fish," Inad agreed quietly.

"And the snakes," Ara added. "For all the good they are."

"This is why I'd never want to leave the rainforest for Tabira," Inad huffed. "She makes it sound like such an advanced, amazing city. The birthplace of the *Illumination*. Advanced isn't everything."

Ara grinned. "Well, according to Mother, we do speak Tabir with Ayam accents."

"Ayam feels more natural. Must embarrass her." Inad almost chuckled. "Children of such an esteemed Tabir figure raised among *savages*."

Ara said nothing.

"Their trust in us is fading though." Inad spoke up again. "That's why Mother's arranged this marriage in the first place. Why else would she initiate a union between Ayam and Tabir when she views the islanders as such unworthy primitives?"

"Such a joining would show that we consider our fate tied to theirs," Ara reflected.

"Why don't you fly? You could get away so easily."

Ara started at his sister's sudden question. "Fly? You know that Mother forbids…"

"*Mother* forbids, yes," Inad cut in icily. "Mother this, Mother that. Promise me, if I am taken tomorrow, you'll start to look after yourself, learn to *think* for yourself better."

Ara heaved a deep sigh. "I promise, sister. On one condition."

At that, Inad glanced again at her brother, avoiding the urge to blink at the brightness of his crown in the approaching sunset.

"Your bones are hollow, just like mine," he continued, replacing the hair cover over his crown. "You're a light weight to lift. I won't use my wings for any purpose besides helping you escape."

***

Telo stood overlooking the great Maw, its depths inky black despite the soft white light of the Great Stone overhead.

Tales of the great chasm's origins had always been his favorite before his father's death. Thoughts of his father caused anger to bristle and nerves to rise simultaneously. Tonight he would become Chief of the Ayam—or at least his age and birthright provided him the opportunity to try.

First he had to survive a night at the lip of the Maw.

When his first warrior, Dato, had insisted on accompanying him, Telo had steadfastly refused. He must embark alone on the quest to chiefdom.

Yet it wasn't tales of the Flightless, or even the Zaam that plagued him tonight. Instead, the far more recent threat of the Cursed loomed for anyone who remained outside after nightfall.

Dark brown hair tied back in a softgrass ring in an attempt to cool the sweat from his back, Telo almost wished he had no locks.

Already, the warning call of the grass shoot seemed like an age ago. The darkness had fallen soon after. Telo moved cautiously, guided only by the light of the Stone, the night clouds beyond faint in comparison.

He'd stayed awake nearly the whole night, and thank the Zaam none of the *onn* beasts had befallen him yet.

Drawing a deep breath to steady himself, the young Ayam looked upward to the Great Stone that towered above the jungle canopy, several dozen footfalls from where he stood by the Maw. For just a moment, he allowed himself to close his eyes, and uttered a silent prayer to the now glowing form of the usually black structure. Circles of brighter white created a design like a winding river down its length.

Here by the Maw, the absence of dwellings meant a lack of light even from the modest home lanterns.

Behind him, the rainforest seemed alive with the song of nocturnal insects and tree frogs. If he hadn't known better, the night would have seemed almost peaceful.

A rustle in the shadows to the right caused him to stiffen. Mustn't make any sudden movements…no movement at all, if possible. They were attracted to motion. Beyond that, it was said they could *smell* fear. And yet Telo mainly wished to avoid the need to encounter one of them, should the creature turn out to be a familiar…

Staring into the chasm before him with shallow breaths that he kept as silent as possible, the young man only wished his people knew more about this Curse. For eons, the legends of unseen light that dwelt within the Maw had fed the fears well enough for soon-to-be chieftains. These days, it was what dwelt *around* its edges—and all throughout the jungle—after nightfall.

How much simpler life had been for Ayam when the people still felt safe after the forest came alive with the gentle sounds of the dark. So long as they avoided the gaping pit just beside the quietest part of the forest stream.

After sundown, however, the darkness itself meant the entire terrain was off-limits, and all Ayam must withdraw into their tree shelters.

The near pitch dark threatened to disorient him. Telo found himself wishing that the once-often seen lightstreams would grace the skies above.

As soon as the heavy rasps reached his ears, Telo closed his eyes. They had weak sight, he knew. Yet, despite years of warrior's training, Telo's own eyes could barely make out how close his feet stood to the edge of the abyss before him.

Equipped to move at the same enhanced speed as an afflicted in man form, the beast's only weakness remained its eyes. Telo would have to think fast, the hot breath of the creature behind him now close enough to feel on the nape of his neck. The stench was rank with rot. It could surely smell him as well, but shouldn't be able to determine exact distance…

Screwing shut his eyes tighter, Telo chanced a nimble leap to the left. He held his own breath at the quiet grunt of the creature as it processed its prey's change of position and rattled quietly. The only noise that followed was the sound of tiny pebbles as they slipped off into the oblivion that now lay directly beyond his toes.

How silent it was besides the breath and that light scuttle…Telo hadn't even heard its footfalls. Which was why he needed to use every sense he had at his disposal. Drawing in a quiet breath, he opened his eyes just as a long, moist tongue lapped at the air centimeters from his bare shoulder. The sheer proximity shot through Telo like a flame, spurring him on.

Got him.

Whirling around to throw his opponent off guard, Telo took care to maintain his balance so as not to go tumbling off the ledge behind him. He kept his eyes trained on the vines before him, just visible in the weak light and swaying from the treetops around the creature.

The one feature he allowed himself to note was the beast's eerie eyes, reflecting the soft glow of the Great Stone overhead. Silver orbs, like two scales, only slightly lighter than the black scales that adorned the rest of its hulking form. Barely visible in the dark, the locks of the person the creature had once been trailed its broad shoulders.

Setting his jaw, Telo resolved not to allow any more thoughts on how these monsters lived as Ayam villagers during the day. Not when their form by night posed such danger to their people.

As it tore open its mouth wide to reveal multiple rows of fangs as sharp as any spear, Telo took this opportunity to dart away again—this time to the right—narrowly avoiding the creature's long, scalding tongue.

The beast licked a sizzling path along one of the thick hanging vines, swaying its large head in Telo's direction. Jaws snapping noisily, those teeth just missing the flesh of Telo's left cheek.

For a fleeting moment, he regretted not bringing the small weapon the Flightless Hak had given him—the gun. No need. Going back countless years, the spear had always sufficed for his people.

Rolling behind the monster, Telo drew back his arm and released his spear with a mighty force that would have easily slaughtered a palm cat from a far greater distance.

But then again, the *onn* beasts had wiped out all the jungle cats—and the spear fell to the dirt with a clatter.

Those scales were too thick.

Now too far away to retrieve his spear, Telo again moved slowly toward the lip of the Maw. Both to his apprehension and relief, the creature followed, the low rattle sounding again from its throat.

The monster charged.

By the time those jaws opened again, Telo could feel a stroke of hot breath caress his arm, and chose that moment to leave his precarious position at the edge of the chasm, maneuvering beneath the beast's right upper limb.

The creature before him hadn't a moment to right itself, and went tumbling over the Maw's lip into the yawning abyss below.

Perhaps the most chilling part was the sound that accompanied its fall. A sheer, rattling wail.

After retrieving his spear from the ground, the Ayam collapsed onto his back. Still panting slightly from the thrill of the fight, he closed his eyes.

The first luminous fingers of dawn were approaching over the horizon, causing the glow of the Great Stone to gradually recede by comparison.

Zaam willing, no others would attempt an attack before sunrise.

Braku, a young woman recently afflicted, fell to her knees at the center of the circle of warriors.

"Where is Telo?" she demanded, glancing around, determined to conceal her fear.

Or perhaps she truly had none.

"The new chief has more important matters than listening to a Cursed boast of her own plague." Dato, the chief's head warrior, placed the tip of his spear on Braku's right shoulder, forcing her to kneel to the ground.

"You've seen what I can do!" Braku slammed her fist down onto the quarter-meter-wide rock she'd carried here. The rock crumbled to bits. "During the day, I can fight!"

"And what about at night?" Dato challenged, sliding the spearhead until it touched the side of Braku's throat. "Shall we let you roam free to consume our flesh?"

"You'll be in the trees!" Braku cried in earnest. "Just as you are every night. Safe in the trees. I can fight for you by day. I will be the strongest warrior of all. Is that what you fear, Dato? That I will challenge you?"

A tense ripple shivered through the circle of warriors at that moment. In the next fraction of a second, Braku moved quick as lightning, grabbing Dato's spear by the point and snapping the weapon in two.

Just as the Cursed woman dove for the head warrior, Chief Telo impaled her with a spear through the belly.

"Chief!" Dato shouted in warning, as Telo withdrew his spear as fast as possible with a sucking pop. "Aim for the eye!"

Anywhere to reach the mind. Anywhere else, and they would heal nearly instantly.

As Braku rounded on the chief, Telo drove his spear between the rabid woman's eyes.

"It almost seems a shame," Dato mused, looking down on the corpse before them, its eyes still open, staring into nothingness. "She always wanted to be a warrior, despite not having a man's power. When she finally gets the gift of speed and strength, it's thanks to the Curse."

Chief Telo wrenched out his spear.

Chapter Four

Once Nasin asked Oria to go track down Avithia and Rohem, the young Lirian woman didn't have to look far.

If the cloud of sand about a dozen meters from home base didn't speak to the young duo's whereabouts, the exhilarated shouting confirmed Oria's suspicions.

As the sand settled near the reservoir, Oria called out, "Hey, you two! Time to quit playing around. Nasin wants a word."

Though Rohem was the first to leap the meter and a half from the glider's passenger seat to the ground, Avi's face was the first to come into view for Oria.

Dark brown hair tousled and eyes bright with excitement, the sheen on his swarthy skin was only just muddled by the layer of dust that covered both his forehead and cheeks.

Always the competitor, Avi made sure to hit the ground before Rohem circled his way around the glider to stand beside him.

"So early!" Rohem mock protested as Avi stepped forward to gratefully retrieve one of the two water canisters Oria had ready. Oria modestly averted her eyes at Avi's shirtless presence.

"Early was when you two decided to take out the glider at dawn—again!" Oria exclaimed, using the hem of her skirt to clear the sand from her spectacles. "This is why Yeni never gets her exercise anymore."

"You're on about that dunehorse again," Avi quipped. "She'll thank us for not using her anymore to scout the border. Times have changed. She's old. Best to use the glider for making sure the Garo are on their best behavior."

"It's true," Rohem agreed. "The Garo can see a dunemobile or Yeni coming by ground far easier than when we're in the air."

Oria scoffed, still rubbing at her glasses. "Overusing that glider, spreading sand all over the compound…"

"So get the laser optic treatment," Avi suggested easily. "My father will do it for free."

"No need," Oria replied, wary as most observant Lirians regarding technology brought by the Illumination. "You two will piss off the border patrol again…"

"They're not even supposed to *be* here. It's the Lirian border with Garo. Call it Garo territory too, if you like, but it's definitely *not* Tabir. How come they get to stick their noses everywhere?"

"May have caught a glimpse of Samed today," Rohem added.

Oria paled. "The rebel's brother?"

"Yes," murmured Rohem, securing his pistol to his belt. "The telltale brother."

"Still think he's after you?" Avi teased, and Oria threw him a look.

"Rohem," Oria quickly changed the subject. "Why do you carry that pistol? It's not as if you need it."

"You two know I fight to defend Lir. Lirian technology is all we've ever needed here."

"Though the hydrotech is the *serious* weaponry." Avi grinned, earning him another look from Oria.

"Avi!" she whispered loudly. "You never know who might be listening."

"Ah, yes," Rohem chimed in. "Never know where Officer Samed might have ears. If I didn't have priorities like the medical exam to worry about, I might pay him more mind."

Once inside the compound, Nasin wasted no time in her briefing.

"I'm already running late for the meeting with Governor Par." Nasin hastily finished her water. "Oria, tell me, any signs of militant activity within Lirian territory?"

"Not as far as my people tell me," Oria replied.

"Her people." Rohem smiled, and Avi snickered.

"You two," Nasin turned to the young men, "if you're going to take out the glider instead of go on foot or with the horse, the least you could do is take your post seriously."

"It might be time for some new informants. Someone I can actually rely on," Oria muttered.

"Oria," Nasin said, not unkindly. "Intelligence head Tarel left only last week. I've still a while to go helping you take over."

"What's the meeting about anyway?" Avi interrupted Nasin, to Oria's relief. "I thought Par was just here last week."

"He was," Nasin replied. "We are negotiating terms of water supply. They want access to the reservoir, following their own side of the oasis finally drying up."

"Now we're trading water?" Rohem asked, incredulous.

That was when a deafening boom sounded not far from the compound, seemingly nearby the megalith.

Sure enough, a billow of smoke was already forming between Nasin's group and the megalith, shielding the great structure from view. A few meters away, the glider had caught fire.

"The glider!" Rohem cried, running over to the tattered piece of equipment.

Out of habit, Nasin called out to Rohem to be careful, though she knew it was hardly necessary.

Once he'd gotten close enough to touch the glider, Rohem was able to see straight through the tower of smoke. No one was in sight.

That meant the militants had taken to the tunnels once again – likely just beneath the glider landing pad.

Taking a deep breath, Rohem reached out a hand and began drawing in the fire's heat with his fingers, until the flames gradually dissipated into harmless wisps of smoke.

After about a minute, he had absorbed all heat from the flames, still leaving the glider a singed mess.

"Show-off. Why do we even bother with the hydrotech?" Avi asked, shaking his head.

Oria scoffed. "When your neighbors are terrorists with the inconvenient tendency to set everything on fire, themselves included, you need all the help you can get."

"No one in sight!" Rohem informed, returning to the group. "Nasin, I take it this will be in your meeting with the governor today? Tell him to keep his 'freedom fighters' above ground where they are visible and under control."

"Honestly," Avi put in as Nasin shooed them back inside, "to think the Tabir see these people as the victims."

Once inside, Nasin announced the next steps. "Avi, you've expressed interest in partaking more often in intelligence gathering. Although we both know that's more Oria's area, we could always use more border investigation, as well as scientific research on the hydrotechnology."

"Nasin," Avi implored their mentor. "I've been saying for ages now how I'd rather take on training or even weapons testing than straight science. All that research business is Rohem's fascination. I like to be out there on the ground."

"Besides," Oria added, "it's not as if Rohem needs help."

Rohem chuckled. "Oria, you might be the only one of us not able to self-insert so easily *as* a science experiment."

"Quiet, all," Nasin stated briskly. "I truly am late now, and I've quite a word for Governor Par. So, Avi, listen carefully. I've been unable to negotiate with the Mak a way to leave the Lirian police force in power. The rank has all but dissolved to Captain Kari, and he's still not permitted beyond the border. So as Second Lasha, you will go on a mission to track the Garo. Not like the last few though. During your first assignments, I've been trailing you. I'll need to hang back this time. An elder needs to be on call at the base, especially following the talk I'm going to hold with Par following this little scene today."

"What's the mission?" Avi's brown eyes sparkled.

"Infiltrate their tunnels. If it's anything like their last venture, it will be accessible through our reservoir. The old crawl space behind the sealed stones."

"Right," Oria drawled. "Setting the glider alight was likely a ploy to distract us from infiltration attempts on the reservoir. Rohem's next invention idea should concern keeping those brutes away from our water."

"We provide them enough water." Rohem shook his head. "They shouldn't need access to the reservoir. Avi, if you do find a tunnel connected to our supply, we should take it to the governor—assuming he'll do something about it, that is."

***

"I assure you, First Nasin," Governor Par smiled, stroking the beige-colored snake that sat coiled about his neck, as if it were the most natural thing to pet such a creature, "the men of the Evaporation are warriors, not cowards. They fight only above ground."

The Evaporation, indeed. Garo's ongoing, terrorist uprising to oust Lirian presence from the entire region between the Strait to Tabira and the former Opal territory.

Although Nasin had managed to at least make herself understood beyond simple greetings in Garo this time around, she was still grateful for the Garo native Lan who served as interpreter, filling in where Nasin fell short.

This governor was stubborn and reputedly refused to learn any Lirian. Nasin had to admit that she partially understood his spite. Several years ago, three religious Lirians had gone behind both her regulations and those of the Kano and attacked the governor's home. In the chaos, Par's young daughter had perished, an incident that Nasin considerably struggled to define as collateral damage. Monetary reparations had done little to move the governor's scorn.

Still, diplomacy called for civility at all costs.

"Then I ask," Nasin replied as calmly as possible, "what set our aircraft alight? There was an explosion..."

Just then, Par murmured something over Nasin, and Lan quickly explained, “Governor Par suggests that perhaps the creature you adopted from your Tabir friends…is the one who staged the fire.”

“In fact,” interjected Nasin frostily, “Rohem helps us put out fires more than starting any. If we are speaking of friends—Tabira trades with both our nations.”

Upon hearing the translation of this latest statement, Par smiled slightly and resumed caressing the serpent that had begun to move ever so slowly, never leaving his neck.

“No one was injured in this fire, were they?”

“No,” Nasin replied tightly. “Though plenty have been in such events. Particularly those carried out by your martyrs when they set themselves on fire.”

Thank Echil or whichever powers reigned or had once reigned supreme, this latest attack had occurred at their outpost rather than nearer to the city of Lir proper. No doubt targeting the Lasha’s base and her wards.

Par remained silent, suddenly quite interested in shifting his pet’s position.

“The steppeviper is venomous, you know,” he drawled, as Lan interpreted. “Though its bite is only a risk if the snake is untamed. This one trusts me. It is necessary to tame all creatures that sprout unexpected from these lands.”

Nasin suppressed a sigh. She knew the animal’s very presence to be an intimidation tactic on the governor’s part.

“Our regions hold enough heat as is. Let us drop the subject and turn to one we both favor. Water.”

“We’ve provided you with six months’ supply of electricity through the shared network lines, and sixteen units of irrigation ploughs, as agreed upon last month,” Nasin stated. “I am afraid the drought has deprived our water supply as well. We will try our hardest to provide you another several units next month, dependent of course on favors from the Tabir engineering unit.”

The tan viper hissed ever so quietly, and Nasin forced herself not to drop her gaze from Par. Beside the Lirian’s seat, Lan shifted a step away from where her governor sat with his pet.

“Very well,” Par spoke. “Tell me. We know your lot can go without food for weeks. It is no secret anymore. You are like dunehorses. However, the rest of us are not. We do not have your strength, and we cannot switch between male and female. This is a curse, surely. Yet it makes you strong. We know you Lasha enjoy your water. Do you truly leave enough for the rest of your people and for your neighbors?”

Nasin stiffened. “I wouldn’t know, Governor. Does Garo use its Tabir petrol imports for automobiles and hearths during the cold season, or does it all go towards staging protests?”

Lan looked like she’d rather be anywhere else at that moment than interpreting this latest question. Nasin could practically see the woman’s face glistening beneath the muted gold paint designs.

Once he had heard the translation, Par’s fingers stilled in their caress of the viper.

“This meeting must adjourn,” he replied next. “I have important matters to attend to. Lan, that will be all. Lady Nasin, may fortune always find Lir, and may Echil be with you always. These are dangerous days on the border between dune and steppe. One must take care not to lose their way.”

“Indeed,” Nasin replied smoothly, rising to her feet. “May Echil grant you ease in your affairs. Lan.” She nodded at the Garo woman who averted her strange green gaze, gold-painted slender face framed by sand-colored locks that fell over one shoulder in a neat braid.

In her own private opinion, Nasin rather wished that the face-painting custom applied to the Garo leader as well. Even as she steeled her gaze, his dark eyes bore into her in a most uncomfortable fashion as the snake settled comfortably on his protruding belly.

“One more question,” Par added after Lan had exited and Nasin glanced back, incredulous.

He had just spoken in Lirian.

“They say you stay man or woman if you choose—what man did you choose, Lady?”

“Forgive me,” Nasin quipped back in Lirian, not bothering with his title. “I’ve forgotten. Must have been all that water I drank. Muddles the memory.”

“It’s decided.” Nasin bristled as soon as she stepped inside the base, where surprisingly all three of her wards sat waiting since she’d communicated her approach. “Oria, you’ll be taking the next diplomatic discussion with Par. I don’t trust myself not to do something foolish—starting with that ridiculous pet snake of his.”

“Did he at least admit to the bomb?” Rohem asked.

“No,” Nasin replied coolly. “Seems now they’ve adopted underground tactics. They’re up to their old tricks again.”

“Good thing I’m headed on this mission, then.” Avi grinned unceremoniously.

Oria, for her part, beamed unabashedly. Although she'd never openly admit it to Nasin, she'd longed for a chance to represent the non-Lasha side of Lir. Training with the ground informants was a fine aspect of intelligence operations, though did grow somewhat monotonous.

Now she would finally have the opportunity to converse with a Garo face-to-face.

***

Officer Samed chose to use the stairs rather than the lift. Following a six-hour tube ride back to his home nation, the lengthy stairwell to the Tabir prison provided exercise he gratefully accepted.

Still, despite the long period of time sitting, he had to admit that rail was a vast improvement upon the ferry ride that once served as the sole way of passage across the narrow Strait between Tabira and Lirian territory. Ever since the construction of the Tabir rail bridge, the crossing time had been reduced from one day and night to a mere six hours.

Escorted by a guard from the Capital Center following successful admission by the Inquirer, Samed nearly chuckled at the odd feeling—the notion that this time someone else was escorting *him.*

Strictly for security purposes, of course. By now, Samed knew the route to the prison like the palm of his hand.

However, the sight that greeted him upon entry into the panel room that harbored his brother felt altogether unfamiliar.

In the year since his last visit, Joleh's face had aged considerably. Streaks of white now graced his once gradually silvering hair, deep-set wrinkles lining the weathered skin of his face. Samed couldn't help but notice the resemblance his cheeks and forehead now bore to the ragged red scars of his left arm—as if the old injuries had spread up the left side of his body, right across his face.

Dark green prisoner attire in tatters, Joleh smiled a nearly toothless grin, the dried blood visible on his chin.

"His mouth…the teeth." Samed caught himself stumbling over his words. "Did they put someone in there with him?"

"This prisoner remains in solitary, as he always has," the guard replied gruffly. "Though perhaps he thought the wall was an enemy. He's been regularly biting and gnawing at the cell wall for weeks now. Sometimes, he even runs at it like an attacking animal."

"I know you think I'm an animal!" Joleh's voice pierced the dank air around them, shrill against the hushed voices of Samed and his escort. "A pet gone rabid! No need to whisper about it. The boy was the tree critter, while I crawled on the ground like a lowly..."

"Joleh," Samed managed a smile as he stepped up to the edge of the containment barrier, "your mouth all right?"

Samed never did believe in sugarcoating the obvious.

"It's better to fight back when it's solid than when it's hot," Joleh murmured, running his tongue over his remaining top teeth. "*This* is the real beast."

He indicated the containment barrier with his good hand, the sour smell seeming to waft outwards with the gesture.

Samed nodded. "It can certainly fry the best of us."

"Still doesn't hurt as much as this did, though." Joleh raised his mangled hand, wriggling the fingers briefly. "I ever tell you how I got it?"

"It's a different story every time." Samed sighed. "Always figured you got hurt hanging around that boy."

Samed inwardly cringed at the very memory of his brother harboring the child—how he didn't even know the details of what had transpired, only that the boy had made Joleh quite popular for a time. That alone could have easily implied facets of his older brother of which Samed would have gladly never gained inkling.

"It wasn't the boy or the Opal war," Joleh replied, now averting his gaze and beginning to compulsively rub together the thumb and forefinger of his left hand. "Still though, this sight must be a far cry from what they all expected of me back then. A vision dashed. The great Kano—the great Tabira—well, at least we've come far as a nation. Perhaps the greater glory comes after death."

"Tabira has brought great things. They don't call it the Illumination for nothing."

Samed wearily wished he didn't feel the need to treat his brother like a child—even though his mental state of recent years clearly called for it.

"You did the right thing." Joleh's soft tone brought Samed's attention squarely back to the present. "Ratting me out."

Running a hand through his dark hair, Samed contemplated whether he should just admit to his selling out Joleh.

"You still think it was me," he settled on.

Joleh grinned. A grisly sight.

"No need to pretend after all these years. You were always too observant for your own good, whether engineering computer viruses or catching criminals."

Silence.

Joleh sighed. "It wasn't right what the Maks order us to do – Kerad and her vendetta against the Opal. From what I hear, it's no different with Eta and the Ayam. And with Rohem…I tried. I did care for him. It's just that—people *respected* me. You can't know how that feels, after years living in your shadow."

"Don't put that on me," Samed answered coolly. "That was abuse. Your brothers from the street, as you called them. Complete scoundrels that you let near that child."

"Not just men." Joleh glanced up at Samed then. "Even leaders get curious."

Seems they truly were being honest now.

After Joleh didn't break his gaze, Samed suddenly realized the previously unnoticed piece of the puzzle.

"The Mak?" Samed asked, horrified.

Just then, the communicator at his ear chirped. Pressing the button, the officer at the other end spoke. "All officers on leave are asked to return to position as soon as possible. An investigation requires all hands. Lir, exterior base."

As Samed turned to apologize to his brother, Joleh spoke up again. "Do you enjoy your work over there? Are they still called dunehorses here at home?"

"By many." Samed nodded. "The Garo and Lirians alike."

Joleh scoffed. "As if these plains are any better than the desert."

"I'm on my way," Samed replied into his communicator, then to Joleh. "I promise to return again by the week's end."

"Go ahead." Joleh waved him off. "They need you more than I do. Hope it's not too great an emergency."

***

Avi suppressed a groan as his back hit the wall with a thud, having just narrowly skidded to the left to avoid the pool behind them.

Training in the rejuvenation quarter certainly had its advantages. One could easily take a dip to bathe and cool off after a session...

Or one could take a less consensual splash when shoved into the water after a particularly strong blow.

"You were aiming for the pool that time." Avi managed not to wince as he sprung to his feet once again.

Rohem grinned, a mischievous gleam in his dark eyes illuminated by the mirrors in the room that reflected sunlight from above. "You said no holding back."

As Rohem charged again, this time Avi made sure he was ready.

Darting first to the left to throw off his opponent, Avi made a sudden, unexpected dash back to the right. The rapid change in maneuver stunted Rohem for the fraction of a second needed for the Lasha to duck down and tug harshly on Rohem's calf, knocking him off his feet and pinning him down with an elbow to the throat.

Rohem's eyes sparked as he finally smiled, a slight gash visible beneath the curls on one side of his forehead where his head had hit the stone floor on the way down.

"Brute strength doesn't stand a chance against tact." Avi smiled shrewdly, fixing his opponent with a mock-malicious stare before letting up and getting to his feet.

Rohem stood up as well, the shallow wound healing almost instantly without a drop of blood. "Brute strength? You have the power of over five grown men."

"And you of at least that many."

When Avi stripped off his trousers and headed for the shallow pool, Rohem chuckled and followed suit.

"I remember first seeing this place," Rohem remarked softly, wading over to a corner to sit on the submerged ledge, leaning back on his arms.

Avi laughed. "How could you forget? I was in the middle of a change. Even Nasin had to come down. What an introduction."

"I found it fascinating," said Rohem. "You changed—and yet you stayed the same. Boy and then girl. All in one person."

"Thanks for summing that up." Avi quirked a smile. "I'm just glad the process has gotten easier over the years. Sometimes I imagine what Walar would think if he saw me during the change."

"He knows what you are." Rohem stated the obvious.

"Of course he does," Avi returned offhandedly. "He understands the concept, but—I don't know—sometimes I wonder if he likes to pretend that this half of me doesn't exist. Only the Thia half."

"I certainly related to you more as another boy when we were children." Rohem tried to lighten the mood.

"Must be easier with no one placing labels on you," Avi murmured, staring into the pool. "You're neutral."

Almost immediately, the Lasha regretted that last statement. Though the two of them had often seen each other change while playing by the pool as children, Avithia hadn't brought up that aspect of Rohem before.

"With Joleh and Hazur as main company, I adapted to that label," Rohem said with a subtle smile.

A pause. Both took a moment to submerge beneath the water's surface.

After reemerging, Avi lifted himself from the lukewarm water to stretch out languidly up on the ledge and begin drying off with a towel from the pile next to the pool. Rohem had already risen, dripping onto the stone lip of the pool as he stretched out a bit.

"And now?" Avi pressed, gazing idly at the reflected ripples from the pool on the upper part of the wall he faced.

His eyes fell pensively on Rohem's smooth chest. He couldn't help but wonder if Walar would prefer him if he were hairless all year round, just like the man sitting before him.

"Now it's all just *you*. One and the same for me and for Oria. I'm different, you're different, and she is different from the both of us. Then there's Nasin, who teaches people to accept such difference."

"We're just a group of misfits," Avi said lightly. "Fitting for our work."

He tossed Rohem a towel, as the latter rose from the water.

"Feeling rejuvenated?" Rohem asked, ruffling his dark hair with the towel to dry faster.

Avi smiled. "You know, even as much as our faithful have come to almost worship water on the Lasha's account, I'm not sure I believe it holds any mystical healing properties for us."

Rohem inclined his head. "Then I suppose it's the thought that counts. The people need to believe in a power that protects them. We can give them that, at least."

Chapter Five

Inad awoke that morning to the sparse cries of jungle birds. The birds whose shrieks and calls alerted the Ayam to the returning safety of the dawn and a new day.

Birds whose exquisite colors matched those of Ara's crown and her own quills usually hidden at her nape.

If she was being honest, however, Inad sometimes envied the varied design of Ara's crown. Her own few feathers were a dull brown that matched her eyes, often barely discernible from her hair, even when she did twist up her braid in the traditional Tabir style.

Still, she much preferred helping the village wisewoman, Maru, with the children to masquerading as a 'creature of the Zaam' for the locals.

This thought brought Inad back to reality like a leaping fish that flopped back onto the unforgiving surface of the cold river.

Today, one of them would be chosen.

The grass shoot sounded then throughout the village, carrying across the small strait to the island where her mother usually slept.

Like many nights before, Inad had chosen to spend this one apart from Vata. She wasn't sure where Ara had slept, though she'd taken peaceful bliss in what would likely be her final night alone.

Drawing a deep breath, Inad vacated the small hammock and descended the trunk steps as slowly as possible.

Sunrise. For the first time, that notion held very little joy for her.

Turning around the wide trunk of one of the last trees before entering the village proper, Inad bumped into Ara.

"Ready?" He grinned, also making his way to the colossal black megalith that rose far beyond the treetops, into the blue sky above. Always chipper, her brother, despite the shadows under his eyes.

"Trouble sleeping, too?" she asked, willing some cheeriness into her tone.

"Not too bad," Ara replied, resting a hand briefly on her shoulders. "Let's see what this chieftain is all about."

"Bright morning, children." Maru greeted the siblings from where the villagers had already begun forming a circle. "Wonderful news. The gods have smiled on the chief in his dance with the *onn* beasts. This morning will be one of celebration. Your mother and Chief Telo have both agreed to let me escort you during the ceremony. Please, kneel, both of you."

They knelt. Inad swallowed hard, her stomach making its way into her throat.

"You are both full of light. Inad, child, please raise your hair."

Taking another breath to steady herself, Inad swiftly ran her fingertips below the back hem of her shirt to ensure the dagger was still hidden between her shoulder blades, secured in her upper garment. Once she felt the hard hilt, Inad took to tying her braid atop her head, revealing her nape.

"We now say our prayer for the lost ones who have fallen to the Curse. To those of you among us this morning, Echil guides us to bring you a healing gift. We now only ask to see the lightstreams once more—the dance of the Zaam watching us from above."

Silence befell the crowd, the only sounds those of the surrounding rainforest.

It was no secret that by day the Cursed walked among the villagers as if they were still Ayam. Indeed, they were—until nightfall, when they either attempted self-restraint in hardgrass cages or gave up and roamed the jungle.

Ara and Inad felt fairly certain that the identities of the Cursed Ayam escaped even their mother. Those who still lived, that was.

"No tricks, Inad, please." Ara breathed without looking at his sister. "Just this once. For your own safety."

Inad nearly grinned, despite herself. Her brother knew her too well.

"You have your wings to escape. Use them if you must, and let me use mine."

Metaphorical wings on her part, of course. Sharper and no quills.

It wasn't moments after seeing their mother's scrutinizing gaze from the front of the village crowd that Ara and Inad heard the chieftain's voice as he approached from behind and circled around to stand before them, joining his warriors who stood, flanking him with their hardgrass and bone spears.

As the chief stepped forward, his first warrior Dato joined him, holding his own spear at rest.

"Fine ones, both of you. How is your health this day?"

"Good health, Chief Telo," the siblings replied nearly in unison, hands raised with palms facing inward in the traditional greeting.

"Your Ayam flows as easily as the river. I honor your mother, and all the village." If Inad didn't know better, she would have thought Telo sounded like he was just going through the motions as well. "You are well aware of my father's passing to the Curse. The plague took him, and my mother before him. I stand before you now, ready to take a partner to walk by my side and continue the chiefdom, as I lead this village to brighter times. May Echil, the bringer of hope, smile upon us."

A resounding hum echoed from all around as the villagers marked the conclusion of this prayer.

Ara released a quiet breath. Beside him, Inad resisted the urge to scratch her toe, which suddenly itched awfully.

Turning from the semicircle of villagers back to the Tabir siblings, Telo continued, "I've seen how you both care for our village children. You take to them and us all as if you've walked among the Ayam for generations. It is my great honor to make this choice."

Then he stepped forward and reached out. Inad bowed her head, shutting her eyes, as Ara looked to the dirt ground before him.

"Such beautiful light shows through you to the surface. The gods have blessed you well."

That would be about Ara. Inad felt equal parts afraid for her brother, and rising relief that Telo might be the odd man who didn't prefer a woman at his side.

She kept her eyes closed.

"It is my great joy to join the strength of the Ayam and the Tabir into a power unlike any warrior has ever held. Ara, as the last surviving man of your line and the final holder of the gift of flight, will you grant me the honor of your sister?"

Inad's eyes flew open, angry tears pricking them instantly.

What followed was a silence so thick, even the villagers began to rustle around, many of them sensing the uncomfortable tension. Behind the siblings, Maru shifted from one foot to the other.

Softly, Ara reached out and grasped his sister's hand in his own. "My chief. Will you consider me instead? I can train at your side as a warrior. I shall pledge my undying loyalty to you and charge at your side into battle."

Inad thought her mother's face would have exploded, were that possible. To her relief, however, Telo gave a slight smile.

"I admire your fealty to your sister, Ara. However, I must decline this offer. I already have many strong and loyal warriors. What I seek now is a partner with whom to continue my family and that of my father."

A female partner. The former chieftain who had taken a man at his side had been swiftly assassinated and replaced by his uncle's son. Anything to carry on the chiefdom.

Ara remained silent, lightly squeezing Inad's hand. His fingers felt clammy.

"Inad," Telo began, and Inad's head snapped up to look him in the eyes. "Rise, please."

Steeling herself, Inad avoided her mother's drilling gaze as she rose and traded her brother's hand for the outstretched palm of the chief.

"Do you choose to walk our path together?"

Although he phrased the question as a choice, Inad knew there really wasn't much of an option. No one refused the marriage proposal of a chief.

Inad's heart was racing. All around, the gentle voices of the Ayam warriors sounded from all sides as they began the wedding celebration chant, the softer sound accentuated by the louder hum of the women wailing softly through the holed trunks of the trees lining the space beside the base of the Great Stone.

The humid air wafted over her sweaty forehead and face, making her feel as if she were drowning.

She could try to fight—and risk Ara getting caught up in whatever punishment would likely befall them both, once she was outnumbered. She could make a run for it—only for the chief or one of his warriors to catch her.

For now, it seemed she had only one option. However, that did not mean she would go down lightly.

Inad looked her chief directly in his light brown eyes. It was decided.

"Yes."

Upon the ceremony's conclusion, Telo's younger brother, Finu, was the first to greet him.

"Echil smiles on you." Finu grinned brightly with the customary half-embrace and joining of cheeks between two siblings. "She is a warrior at heart."

"She has strong light, yes," Telo nodded, falling in step beside his brother as they moved along slowly within the procession of villagers away from the megalith and deeper into the forest toward the village.

"I don't think I've ever seen her feathers before today. She always wears her hair long," mused Finu, twirling his spear.

Telo sighed. His brother had never wielded the warrior's weapon with true ambition. Finu cared far more for the charm of words.

"She will make a proud new member of our family," Telo finally settled on. "Her way with the dagger is no secret."

"She'd have to be both proud *and* strong to match you," Finu shot back good-naturedly, with a smirk. "If she truly does capture your attention and respect, she already has all the respect I can give. Likely the surprise of most of the village as well!"

Telo simply gave a half-smile and continued alongside his brother as they approached the first tree homes.

Inad was no stranger to the way of the warrior.

In fact, she committed more energy to training alongside Braku and the boys deemed too young to be warriors than she did teaching.

Only now, Braku was gone—taken by the Curse mere days after her husband fell to the disease. Though initially a shock, Braku's affliction and death passed easily for Inad. In retrospect, the Ayam woman had always frowned at Inad's desire to fight. After all, what use could a Tabir have for a spear or dagger?

Still, Inad remained determined to dedicate herself to the light of battle.

In contrast to what her mother had always seen as pandering to a 'feral sport' once a spear came into play, Inad often spent all her free time on the mainland, watching the warriors train from the treetops.

Even without palm cats to hunt, the battle cries continued throughout practice, lending an air of ferocity to every movement.

She had seen Telo plenty a time. He and Dato often trained together, and each had a graceful form. She'd idly noticed how the chief's practices had increased, following the death of his mother and father.

Even as Maru placed the white-shelled marriage necklace over her head, Inad's mind raced. She would play along for now, but how long could she stall? She steeled against the now constant urge to dry heave.

Traditionally, the village wisewoman guided the children in learning of the Zaam, whereas the chief and his warriors trained the boys in battle tactics from a young age. As long as the stories had been passed down, an Ayam chief had always chosen his wife from among the sisters of his warriors.

Yet this wedding had been symbolic. A beacon of unity between Ayam and Tabira, meant to exonerate Tabir intentions to help rid the island nation of the Curse.

A union upon which an entire people placed its hope.

Thinking furiously about how she would play the next few hours, Inad pondered if she could bide her time. Although she'd heard some of the young women talk of their husbands seeking to bed them immediately following the vows' ceremony, Telo seemed somehow…withdrawn.

"Inad." He glanced at her pointedly. "If you wish to visit with your family for a time, please do so. I will wait here by the river."

"How long?" Inad wanted to know.

"Until the sun has moved behind the Great Stone." The megalith.

Right, she had about a half hour.

Taking this opportunity, Inad decided to toss aside all history with her mother for one slim chance at civil conversation.

As soon as Vata saw Inad coming, her daughter could already see the storm billowing behind her mother's eyes.

"What's wrong now?" Vata hissed lowly, so as not to rouse suspicion from the village women who still went about gathering ingredients for the afternoon meal and washing pieces of clothing, while Vata sat there feigning to sunbathe beneath the forest canopy.

Leave it to her mother to relax while the so-called *savages* labored around her.

"Most of them can't understand us," Inad snapped a bit louder. "You can relax about your reputation. I wish to ask for passage to Tabira."

"What makes you think Telo will want to leave his people?" Vata asked.

"Alone."

Vata's eyes narrowed to slits. "You can't be serious."

Throwing all caution to the wind, Inad felt her heart thump almost painfully as she voiced what her mother likely had never fathomed her children to know. "The Curse spreads by lying together. You know this."

"The illness spreads by the bite and exposure to a tongue stroke. Just how *stupid…*"

Although stomping her bare foot in the mud didn't have quite the effect she would have liked, Inad's sudden step toward Vata's seated form had the intended effect, silencing the older woman instantly.

"Let's not pretend you don't know this," Inad snarled.

"The chief is healthy," Vata bit back.

"I am asking you as my mother..." Inad could feel the angry tears welling up once again. "Did it truly take you by surprise when father fell ill? Or had you expected him to be immune when he played around with the natives?"

The side of her mother's hand struck her cheekbone so fast Inad almost didn't know what had happened.

Setting her jaw against the sharp sting, Inad inwardly cursed her slow reflexes. Hollow bones and light build aside, she trained nearly every day as well. This woman should not be able to strike her so easily.

"You get back to your husband *now*," Vata growled through gritted teeth as Inad already began to back away. "And *eat* something. No curves, it's hideous. I feel like I have two sons."

Fighting the urge to scream curses when she took her leave from Vata, Inad briefly pondered if she should take a detour to the Maw. Save the village the trouble of either slaying or being mauled by another *onn* beast.

Inad found Telo at the small clearing on the way back to his tree hut, his back facing her. The chief's voice pulled her from her thoughts.

"Please bathe now," he stated simply, turning to her.

Moving to the water, Inad carefully avoided his gaze. As she stooped to remove her trousers, Inad felt on the verge of panic as she realized that the dagger would soon be revealed.

Telo seemed to notice her falter, and spoke up again, nearly startling her even more. "You may leave on your underclothes."

Gingerly removing her shirt so that the blade would not be disturbed, Inad used her fingertips to surreptitiously push the hilt as far down as possible into the undergarment.

"Will you bathe too?" she asked.

Best to play along for now.

"I will prepare the mid-day meal from the hunt last night," Telo explained. Seeing Inad's disbelieving glance, he added, "Dried tree snake, Inad. Nothing more."

Well, at least the mighty chief refrained from cannibalizing his fellow villagers, even if some of them did grow murderous after nightfall.

"It was a good hunt," Inad allowed, as Telo nearly managed what would have been the first smile she'd seen from him.

He turned to go, ascending the wide rope ladder into his tree home.

So then, this was where the chief lived.

Once he was out of sight, Inad drew a massive breath of moist morning air. Far overhead in the trees, the birds called to each other.

Momentarily distracted by a cloud of watermoths passing over the river's surface, Inad focused on the gentle green dappling of the large jungle leaves in the water's reflection.

Even if she somehow managed to avoid the Curse, she refused to resort to a life chosen for her by Vata. Her mother would not have the last say.

She thought of her father. Their mother had known Hak was unfaithful. Somehow, all those years ago, Vata had known that his death was due to a love affair.

After the first several years of learning the customs of the Ayam and gaining proficiency in their language, Vata and Hak had persuaded a group of those who had fallen ill with an incurable growth disease to submit to a pricking by tiny spears.

These tiny spears were needles. Those afflicted with the disease were cured overnight.

Having gained the Ayam's trust and near reverence, Vata and Hak then informed them that the Zaam had not created the gift cure, but the missionary's own people, the Tabir who lived across the sea. Both Tabir assured the locals that they need not worship the Zaam any longer, as the Zaam did not exist.

The Ayam refused, insistent that the cure must have come from the Zaam.

Taking matters into her own hands, Vata feigned acceptance of the Ayam decision to maintain faith in the Zaam. She then promised the villagers eternal life, if they would only submit to another kind of Pricking.

Though most of the locals shied away from the Pricking, those courageous few that participated fell to the Curse in a matter of days.

The excuse of the Tabir missionaries to the then Chief was that those chosen had been unworthy of the Pricking of eternal life due to their unwillingness to rescind faith in the Zaam, and thus had been cursed, rather than blessed.

To this day, Inad considered it a miracle that Telo's father had not slaughtered her family.

From there, it spread—through blood, Inad had always reasoned. Though surely, not all of these people were sharing blood. Then, several years after her father's passing near her twelfth birthday and the brief but frightening burst of rage from her mother blaming him for his own death, Inad had realized that Hak wouldn't have taken part in whatever strange blood swapping rituals the Ayam may have had.

By now, Inad floated lazily on her back, treading water rather than actively washing herself. The gentle ripples lapped languidly at every inch of her partially submerged flesh.

It was around her fifteenth year that she came to realize the natives didn't have a blood swapping ritual at all. They simply slept together—married and otherwise—and somehow, this spread the Curse as surely as exchange of blood.

Thinking of it now, Inad was fairly certain that one of Telo's parents must have been unfaithful. For, although neither had participated in the Pricking, they had both fallen to the Curse—the disease, as the Tabir knew it to be. Though Vata had never fully explained its process to her children, Inad had deciphered enough from what she'd seen.

Inad's blood ran cold, beginning in her chest and spreading to her feet beneath the lukewarm water. If the worst came, she supposed that eighteen wasn't a horribly early age to die. Not when the *onn* beasts had taken several children under ten years.

And she would rather die fighting off the chief than become one of those monsters.

Chief Telo had free reign over his own activities, especially following the death of his parents. She had overheard one of the girls gossiping about Telo's brother, Finu, so who was to say that the chief himself took precaution regarding with whom he coupled…or that he even knew how the disease spread? Surely, he would not keep Inad as his only lover.

Taking yet another deep breath to calm her leaping gut, Inad decided it was time to leave the refuge of the river and face her husband.

Chapter Six

“Doesn’t it seem strange to you?” Avi asked Oria, who sat poring over a book about the same size as the one he had open. “How fast the Tabir have advanced?”

“Just because it took us three centuries to fully develop the hydroweapon hardly means anything.” Oria sighed. “We were on the run first from the Opal and then lived in ghettos for over three centuries in Tabira…and that was *before* any of us began trekking across the wilderness for nearly two more centuries before finally starting to settle back here for good. That’s what has Nasin so convinced that you are all the result of some genetic mutation.”

“I know, I know.” Avi waved her off. “It’s less the time taken and more the...level of advancement they’ve reached. I mean, think about it. In just about twenty years, we’ve gone from simple electricity use and basic dunemobiles to developments like data cubes for computing, the Network and cures for the cellular growth disease. Plus, Nasin’s informants…”

“Hey, they’re my informants, too,” Oria grumbled.

“Not while you’re still a ward,” Avi pointed out. “But in any case, you said the Lirian informants have caught word of some sort of biomolecular pathogen on the Ayam colony. We haven’t even come close to anything like that.”

“Well, if Rohem has anything to say about it, it won’t be long now.” Oria chuckled.

“Nasin is still pretending he’s some kind of Lasha.” Avi laughed.

“What else would he be?” Oria asked. “Of all the things he tells us he reads in those science books, genetic mutations are not even that hard to swallow.”

“But he thrives on sunlight, not water,” Avi pointed out.

Oria shrugged. “Still a notable desert feature. He could have just adapted to his environment in a different way from the rest of you. Besides, who says there always only has to be one per generation? Or even that Lasha only turn up among Lirians?”

“I’m serious though,” Avi insisted, returning the conversation to its previous direction. “I think we should have people on the ground in Ayam.”

“I doubt they need any more invaders over there,” replied Oria, closing her book with a thump. “Well, I’ve officially read every page of every book we have on tactical operations. All prepared for the mission?”

“I suppose.” Avi stood up.

“You’re sure it’s not too close to the change?” Oria ventured. “You don’t need added stress making it any more trying…”

"Investigating terrorist operations tends to take top priority," Avi answered nonchalantly. "Can't be choosy about these things. Besides, Walar is catching a tube over within the next few days. Good incentive to clear out this problem quickly."

Oria nodded. Walar's visits always seemed to brighten Avithia's disposition.

"What about you?" Avi asked. "Plans for a partner arrangement at the temple any time soon?"

Oria barked in laughter. "Affairs of the nation come before romance. That goes for us of the faith as well."

"But I suppose it's always been easier for you, taking the oath of piety and all?" Avi's gaze had caught that gleam again. "No exploration outside of marriage?"

"As always." Oria nodded furtively.

"And the hair, too?" Avi prompted, nodding at Oria's dark rust-colored locks, which now reached her waist.

"When I join you in direct combat with terrorists, then I'll cut it," Oria quipped. "Until then, it stays untouched."

Avi had to admit he admired the pride with which she maintained her beliefs on a Plane that was becoming quickly godless.

Just as Avi was exiting the base's study room, Oria squeezed his hand. "May Echil bring you light," she wished him.

Avi smiled. Despite the copious amounts of time spent with him, Nasin, and Rohem, through all their scientific babble, he sometimes forgot that Oria came from a religious Lirian background.

Turning out the lights to the study, Avi made his way over to the exit, eyes adjusting quickly to the darkness.

He'd just stepped out into the warm night air when he was tackled from one side.

Instinctively reaching out, the Lasha felt for his opponent's hand. Once he'd grasped it by the digits, Avi spun his assailant around to face him.

Oria panted, her face flushed in the soft white glow of Lir's megalith.

"I almost had you!" she protested indignantly, tugging her hand free from the grip of a maneuver whose next process would have been to break all her fingers at once.

Lucky that Avi did not consider her a true opponent.

"Come from behind next time, not the side," Avi reassured her. "I would have been much more helpless to find your hand."

"Sure, sure," Oria grumbled as he gave her a farewell clap on the shoulder. "Let's hope those militants come at you from the front."

Avi was no sooner out of sight that Oria realized how dark the outskirts of Lir now were.

The darkness was velvety thick, the shadowy sand appearing almost inky in places where the megalith's light didn't touch.

The last signs of natural light faded quickly in the sky overhead, the faint wispy clouds graying to dusk with the dying remnants of sunset.

It was then that Oria remembered it had been easily two years since she'd been out here alone after dark. Even then, she usually only stayed out around the base that late if Rohem or Avithia were around.

She nearly uttered a prayer that the lightstreams—last witnessed centuries ago—would grace the black night once more.

That the Zaam would dance overhead once again.

The silence of the night and the thick shadows instantly made her mouth run dry, as she realized how utterly vulnerable she was out here.

Hand shooting to her communicator, Oria decided against calling Rohem. She wasn't going to let this fear of the dark rule her forever.

By the time Oria realized she'd been striding, she'd already left the base several dozen meters behind, approaching the inner city.

Now just to reach the dunemobile lot…

Though she knew it was silly, Oria felt inwardly elated. After spending most of adolescence and early adulthood at a weight significantly above that of her fellow wards, her tri-weekly jogs with the others had definitely paid off. She was barely even winded.

Ultimately, Oria was happy that Nasin had encouraged her to participate in the Lasha training sessions. It helped set her apart—not as a Lasha, but as a regular Lirian.

As always, she made sure to set aside at least one hour per day to visit her grandmother at her small home near the temple. Of course, Oria couldn't usually bring herself to reveal to the elderly woman just how dedicated to the intelligence cause she had become. Ever since Oria was born, her grandmother had stood adamantly by the conviction that women of their family line must continue the tradition of pieties, as had her daughter, Oria's late mother.

With Oria's grandmother having gradually grown infirm with age, the duty fell upon Oria to make three daily visits to the temple for each of the prayers. Personally, she never understood why she couldn't manage both a career in intelligence and remain faithful to the Zaam. After all, it wasn't as if the two had ever been mutually exclusive.

Still, Lirian women of the faith were often expected to commit to a livelihood of teaching their children and others' children the ways of worship. Moreover, as her grandmother never failed to remind her, respectable Lirian men sought after women with a healthy figure and a strong desire for many children of her own…

Stopping briefly to fan out her torso beneath her sleeveless but thick top, Oria took a moment to glance up at the skyflame. Glowing just a bit softer than the megalith below, the flame shone as shattered, bright pieces of white strewn across the black night.

Closing her eyes, Oria took a long, deep breath and fingered the wave pendant of her necklace. She had trouble understanding how, despite both the skyflame and megalith, the darkness still pressed in like an inky ocean.

In truth, she couldn't fathom the reason Tarel had given for leaving the intelligence initiative.

Taking the exact opposite direction of most Lirians, Oria's former intelligence mentor had chosen to join the Kano forces in Tabira proper in the *science* division, no less. Oria dearly hoped the woman realized that strategic investigations and scientific experimentation were two very different fields. Not to mention, provided the lingering distrust the Tabir held toward Lirians, every day she spent there would likely place her life on the line.

Though apparently, Tarel's father had worked at the Capital's science unit during the time of the Illumination. Educated in Tabira, she had immigrated to Lir upon his insistence, following the Cleansing. Now, years later and after his recent passing, she had finally chosen to acknowledge her guilt enough to return to Tabira.

With Tarel having left Lirian intelligence for Tabir science, Oria resolved to stand by Lir, no matter the drawbacks.

That included suffering through a courting process arranged by her grandmother. Anything to remain in her true nation and protect the Lirian people from the terrorists who sought to annihilate them from the map.

"Trouble seeing in the dark?"

Oria couldn't say later which struck her first at the sound of that voice—the cold shock that shot down her spine fast as lightning or the sensation of her stomach leaping into her throat.

It had come from almost directly behind her. Not good.

Whirling around, Oria instinctively held up both hands, palms facing out in a gesture of feigned submission.

Throw your opponent off guard. In this case, the would-be opponent happened to be Samed, Joleh's brother.

Thank the Zaam she had her pistol concealed in the loose pocket of her slacks. Now if she'd only have the opportunity to retrieve it…

"I asked you a question," the man continued to speak in accented Lirian.

A border patrol officer.

"I'm headed back to the city," replied Oria in Tabir. Having left Tabira at age three, the language had never come naturally, though Nasin had ensured that Oria retained it for these types of encounters.

Show them compliance, and they will be more likely to leave you be.

"I see," replied the officer, also in Tabir. "You know, it's not very safe out here. I will escort you to the gates, lady—"

"Oria," she blurted, fairly certain that he would recognize her as one of Nasin's wards.

Surely, even if she did go missing, Nasin wouldn't be far behind on her trail. Sometimes, she truly thanked Echil for Nasin having taken her in. As a group, the older Lasha, Avithia, and Rohem could be an unstoppable force.

"Thank you," she finally answered. "Officer…"

"Samed," came the officer's voice again, as he stood his ground a meter or so away, half of his face illuminated in the pale glow of the megalith.

Here he was. Throughout all of Samed's years in their territory, Oria had somehow managed to avoid crossing paths with him.

Just play along, Oria decided, eyeing the rifle slung over his shoulder. At least he had a gun, in case any terrorists were about.

Following slightly behind Samed, Oria nearly jumped when he spoke again.

"I'm escorting you, Oria," came the gruff tone. "You should walk in front of me. Don't worry, no need to watch your back. I won't leap."

Oria almost shivered. He'd caught on to her precautionary tactic learned from years of watching her back. Never let a stranger walk behind you.

Her grandmother would have likely had a heart attack seeing Oria walking with a Tabir.

Though this time, a stranger was asking to walk behind her — and said stranger had a weapon.

Fiddling with her necklace once more, Oria sped up her gait until she was striding in front of Samed.

At least they had nearly arrived to the city gates. Only around ten meters to go.

Up ahead, the city lights twinkled in the otherwise dark night.

"It's come a long way," Samed remarked from beside her. "So many have come to settle."

"Thirty-thousand now," Oria stated shortly, proving her own knowledge of the population numbers.

She was also well aware of Tabira's current population of over five hundred million.

"Excellent comeback," was all the officer replied on the matter. "Your Tabir is impressive."

"My family were Lirians of Tabir." Nearly as soon as she spoke, Oria wished she hadn't brought it up.

"The Cleansing." Samed nodded curtly. "No doubt the worst blight on Tabir history."

Oria kept silent, pressing her lips together.

They would reach the dunemobile lot soon.

***

Rohem felt restless.

Re-entering the compound after a final test run of the hydroblaster, he carefully set the folded weapon atop the cube charger and used a finger to call up the blueprint model on the monitor.

The image didn't hold his attention for long.

His skin tingled, as if the very flesh were riddled with millions of tiny needles. Hot needles that seared at the surface of every centimeter just enough to almost hurt, but not quite.

He had been working with Avithia's father, Gether, on new methods of radiation. Gether had been absolutely giddy about showing him the new imaging equipment they had imported from

Tabira. Apparently, the most recent trade agreement had included large medical supplies, the terms allowing for products of a far greater size than usual.

These machines were nearly as high as a doorway, and rumbled loudly when connected to an electrical power source.

Although the radiation-related risks of long-term exposure to such equipment was no secret, Rohem knew himself to be immune to even gamma rays— during the day, that was, when sunlight was readily available to replenish one's energy levels.

He'd made sure to take just as many breaks today as any other day, leaving the machines to go bask in the light of day.

And yet…despite the run-in outside with an ejected stream of cool water from the hydrogun, his skin smarted. While he never actually produced sweat, he could suddenly barely tolerate the heat.

Or perhaps it wasn't so much heat as—a sort of *itching*. The insurmountable urge to keep moving around gripped him like an iron fist…

Throwing himself into work to abate stress had become habit. Only tonight, he had puzzled for nearly two hours straight—and succeeded in using the data cubes graphics tool to design the finishing touch on the hydroblaster. Their strongest weapon yet.

Twice the size of the regular blaster that Avithia wore on missions against the Evaporation, this hydroweapon would be capable of releasing a tidal wave powerful enough to easily wipe out fifty men at once from the ground as well as in an airborne attack.

At last, the prototype matched the graphical blueprints provided to Lir's engineering sector by Tabira's Capital education wing – designs for a fireblaster that the Lirians had adapted to eject water. In the past ten years, they had succeeded in securing the aluminum container and perfecting the trigger to activate the electric solenoid valve, ejecting the pressurized liquid contents in a controlled stream at a speed of roughly one hundred kilometers per hour.

Although Gether had initially questioned his interest in constructing a larger hydrogun when Lir's engineers prioritized civil infrastructure, it seemed Rohem's side endeavor in assisting the engineering team had paid off.

After months of toil over testing the very limited supply of imported Tabir aluminum as a grounding mechanism, Rohem had finally managed to replicate a larger weapon that was still light enough to transport via small glider for counterterror missions.

Now Lir harbored their largest hydroweapon yet, and Tabira need not find out. The Advisory would use the blaster sparingly, after all.

Only several moments passed before he realized he no longer had any tasks to keep his mind and senses occupied.

So he deactivated the cube monitor and trudged back out into the night, unbuttoning his shirt.

Once he'd gone to check on the dunehorse, Yeni, he decided to continue his stroll. He couldn't fathom the idea of resting just yet.

The night was quiet and clear, the more rapidly cooling sand signaling the dropping temperatures as the cold season approached.

Behind the megalith, the milky skyflame and stars beamed softly in the night sky.

Despite the still air, every slight breeze or rustle of sand beneath his feet sounded deafening to Rohem's ears, his senses on exceedingly high alert.

Soon, the desert nights would grow so cold even the snakes and scorpions would burrow beneath the sand when dark came.

Glancing up, Rohem closed his eyes and let the soft light of the Lirian megalith soothe his heated face.

Never having shared the religious fervor of Oria, Rohem had grown somehow more *at ease* in the presence of their megalith.

In fact, even now he felt his gaze drawn to the not so distant gleam of Garo's megalith some sixty kilometers beyond the border. Although no aircraft had yet ventured the journey to one of their peaks, those who had come close reported a height of roughly thirty-thousand meters. At roughly two-thousand meters in width, the megaliths stood tall and bright over the residential lights of both cities, against the vast expanse of pitch-black sky.

It was then that Rohem realized he had already approached the general spatial birth Nasin declared for the megalith.

The older Lasha's reasoning held that, although the structures did not possess any clearly paranormal nature—or celestial, as Oria would argue—they were likely highly radioactive. Perhaps from a natural source. A glow that bright would seem to indicate such, if Rohem consulted his knowledge on the subject.

Still, he'd never been one to shy away from a challenge, or even danger. Although he felt immensely grateful to Nasin for the wonderful life he now had here amongst the Lir, he wasn't one of them. Not truly. Even Oria, who often felt different due to her status as the only non-physically gifted of Nasin's wards, still knew from which family she came, to which nation she belonged.

He would not commit to an indefinite medical career in Lir. The need to explore and heal beyond this city was too great.

From seemingly nowhere, a shape flitted across the lit pathway of the megalith, vanishing as quickly as it had come. Far too large to be a moth or even a night bird.

The tingling spread then from his torso to his toes and fingertips almost immediately—in reaction to his natural fight or flight instinct or external stimuli, he couldn't be certain.

The unbidden flashback hit him like a wave of sand thrown out from behind a veering dunemobile. A long-buried memory unearthed from over fifteen years ago, before he left Tabira.

Of hands caressing him in the oddest places, while he performed the energy transfer that he'd spent the first seven years of existence thinking determined whether he lived or died.

Of eyes looking at him with what he had come to realize over the years that followed was perverse admiration. Almost reverence for the pleasurable sensations he could bring.

Joleh, on the other hand, had always surveyed Rohem with a sort of cold detachment. Even in his innocence, Rohem had always understood the importance of keeping his head down and doing exactly what he was told.

For so long he had harbored the conviction that unless he performed the energy transfer on at least one recipient each night, he would die. Meanwhile, he'd come to learn that carrying out the transfer in the absence of sunlight actually drained him.

The worst of his dynamic with Joleh was the inability to understand what he'd done to evoke his former guardian's resentment. While the man assured everyone that his brutal scars were not Rohem's doing, Joleh felt he must have been somehow responsible.

Why else would he have threatened Rohem nearly daily with the danger of the dark?

When the tingling increased to a vibrating, Rohem forced himself to shake his mind of these thoughts. That part of his life had long since passed. He'd left it behind for a life of purpose, science, and comradery in Lir.

Indeed, he remained grateful for how much the others treated him like a fellow Lirian.

While Rohem's difficulty with paying attention during weapons training had subsided following adolescence, the urge to venture outside of Lir grew ever stronger.

Still, despite the large shadow he'd seen up ahead, the pull to cross that boundary and approach the megalith—to *touch* its very surface—now felt like a palpable push from an unseen hand. Almost as if he could *hear* a voice both taunting and soothing, daring him to experience the colossal obelisk in all its glory.

Now he might not have to wait much longer.

Closing the remaining distance to its surface, Rohem gazed up at the iridescent tower—so immense that he had to crane his neck back all the way to behold its skyward ascent, the width extending into the darkness to both the left and right. At this proximity, the winding, bright designs that typically stood out from the softer white blended with the rest of the megalith's face.

Over the past hundreds and possibly thousands of years, the five nations maintained legends surrounding the danger and mystery of these megastructures. Some fables held that contact with a megalith brought sudden death of unknown cause, while others warned of the freezing of bones with a single touch.

Yet such horror stories seemed somehow distant, as Rohem stood surveying the sight before him. Never had he been so close to an object so magnificent. And the warmth...

He could feel it now more than ever, somehow soothing the prickly feeling in his flesh while simultaneously filling him with a creeping sensation of...was it joy?

No, more akin to power. Strength. *Energy*.

Raising a palm up to the glowing face of the structure before him, Rohem extended his hand to touch the surface, to finally feel that unknown substance that so many only wondered about...

The sound of voices shattered the reverie.

Rohem tore himself away from the megalith and staggered back several steps, hurriedly re-buttoning his shirt.

Even from a distance of about fifteen meters, he could make out Oria's voice. And the male voice as well.

By the time Rohem stepped into view, Oria and Samed had nearly reached the city gates, stopping by the dunemobile park just outside.

"Well now." Samed's tone seemed to smile in the half-light of the two entrance torches. "Looks like this is where I leave you. Are you all right from here?"

Rohem nearly opened his mouth to answer for Oria before he remembered himself and shut it again.

"Yes," Oria replied furtively, "thank you. Rohem, this is Officer Samed. He escorted me back after Avi left to trail the tunnels."

Avi had left so close to the change. How had Rohem not known?

"Thank you, Officer." Rohem's expression remained neutral.

"Safe night to you both." Samed turned and left.

Oria turned to face her friend, and felt a chill at the look in his eyes. No, it wasn't a look exactly…as much as a hint of another color. Of dark blue in the dark depths, now clearly visible in the torchlight. The odd glow seemed to extend even to his forehead and cheeks, an ember's touch just visible in the dark.

"Is everything all right?" Rohem asked with that unique tilt of his head, once they'd started up Oria's dunemobile.

At least Rohem still sounded the same, despite looking definitively shaken.

"Yes, all fine," Oria murmured, starting the engine and taking out her communicator to signal the wireless gate opener. "Are *you* all right?"

Rohem paused. In fact, the tingling had entirely left his body, replaced by what felt like a leaden numb sensation.

"Yes." He smiled at last. "Let's get back. It's late."

Once the gates opened, the dunemobile headed for the inner city compound.

***

"Quiet," Kel ordered his three men as they stooped to a bent gait, accommodating the increasingly low ceilings of the tunnel. "We're near their reservoir by now."

"The oasis?" Rad asked, twirling his *tso* blade in one hand. "Already?"

Kel sighed inwardly. Rad had joined the Evaporation over a year ago, and still acted like an adolescent at times, overly eager to scout out the action.

"Satt," Kel turned to his other fighter, "you've made sure not to leak any petrol? Need me to take over again?"

If the extra sheen on his face beneath the gold paint was anything to go by, Satt, a man around Kel's middle age, looked as though the five liters of petrol he carried on his back were weighing him down a bit.

"Fine here, sir," Satt huffed out.

"What if they're expecting us?" asked Nok, the newest recruit.

"They won't anticipate another attack so close to the first." Kel was sure of it.

The dank air contrasted with the typically arid climate above ground.

Stopping abruptly, Kel held up his lantern. Confirming the thinner wall of soil before him, he gestured for Rad to give him the pick ax.

After hacking away at the loose dirt, sure enough, the remaining surface crumbled, opening into another narrow corridor, barely higher than a crawlspace.

All four men dropped to their knees, Satt sliding the canister of petrol in front of him when it wouldn't fit through the tunnel while on his back.

"No sounds up ahead?" Nok whispered a bit too loudly.

"No," Kel replied gruffly, emerging around the corner and standing up to look around at the large circular basin covered in tarp. Beneath the covering, running water rushed out from the several turbines surrounding the reservoir.

No matter what they encountered up ahead, the Evaporation would prevail, its men unscathed. Even if they lost their lives on the Plane, their sacrifice for Garo's freedom would grant their light acceptance into the Realm of Joy.

A place of perpetual warmth and happiness alongside the Zaam.

"Well, well," Satt panted, already opening the petrol container. "We've found the holiest of holies for the water worshippers."

"Do you think any of those La-*sha* monstrosities are around?" asked Rad, emphasizing the final syllable, as was common among the Garo.

"One against four of us." Kel grinned. "I wouldn't like those odds."

With that, he turned to Satt. "Prepare for flame."

Satt nodded, wrenching off the lid and turning over the metal container to release thick splashes of petrol all around the tarp-covered sphere.

"The time has come for these heathens to stop hoarding all the water," he growled, dropping the emptied container with a clang.

"The turbines will burn then?" Nok asked, clearly trying to conceal the shakiness in his voice.

Kel nodded.

"And then we can turn back?"

Kel glanced at Nok. "This time, yes. Setting ourselves alight for a non-public demonstration is a waste of resources. In this case, of men. However, you understand the risk once the room goes up. Now quiet down and watch the other entrance."

Now it was Nok's turn to nod as he visibly took a step back.

Rad, who had already knelt, listening beside the entrance, hissed suddenly, "Men, did you hear that?"

"What is it?" Satt asked, returning to stand beside Kel as the latter removed the flame gasket from inside his lantern and stooped to set the petrol-covered ground alight by the nearest turbine.

"Sounds like…splashing or some movement by the oasis. I heard it over the noise from the turbines."

"The rushing water all sounds like water," Nok chortled, never leaving his spot by the entrance through which they'd arrived, expression noticeably nervous even beneath his face paint.

"No," Rad snapped. "I'm serious. It sounded like…"

All four men were flabbergasted at what they saw next.

The moment the tarp corner was pulled aside to reveal a figure inside, Kel cursed himself for not bringing a pistol. Granted, a patrol officer had confiscated his previous weapon—yet he should have ensured another before setting out on this mission.

Taking out one of them with only a knife would be difficult, even above ground.

And as the person emerged fully from the reservoir and pulled itself over the rim to land on the ground before them, Kel became certain of two facts:

This was a Lasha, and it had come heavily armed. Sweating profusely, chest heaving, the man—or woman—still looked more like a man, carried a structure on its back, about the size of a small child.

"Am I interrupting something?" the person asked in thickly accented Garo, voice still deep enough to be a man.

Wiry frame moving nimbly and ear-length dark hair slicked back from what appeared to be sweat, he wore a full-body suit of what appeared to be protective plastic over a typical dark blue Lirian martial uniform, black gloves covering his hands. No doubt to avoid contaminating the water in the oasis. Surely, the Lasha would not risk bloodying its treasured supply…

"Commander!" Rad shouted, nearly giving Kel a heart attack on the spot. "Drop the flame *now*!"

Kel narrowly avoided the creature's foot as it slammed into the lantern, knocking it upward from his hand and grasping it again out of mid-air. From there, the Lasha swiftly leapt back and wasted no time blowing out the small flame inside.

"Apologies," it continued, voice slightly higher and posture indicating that something was askew.

That was when Kel realized the Lasha must be in the middle of a change. With any luck, it wouldn't be male much longer. Then they'd be able to take it down.

Nok chose that moment to circle behind Kel and try to grab the weapon off the Lasha's back, the edge of his dagger nicking a shallow, angry red line just above the creature's collarbone. Swift as a viper, the Lasha whirled around and cracked the young Garo across the face.

Nok skidded in the dirt before slamming his head on one of the turbines and falling to the ground.

Satt straightened his posture and smacked his lips. Before he even spoke, Kel knew his comrade had also surmised the situation.

"Well, what have we here?" Satt drew his knife and walked up to the Lasha until they were standing face-to-face. "You're a *woman* now? Never seen one of you up close, Lasha."

Surely enough, the Lasha appeared quite slight before Satt's hulk.

From his other side, Kel registered Rad withdrawing his own knife as he began to inch ever so carefully from his position behind the turbine closest to the Lasha.

The young woman suddenly looked as if the weight of the contraption on her back no longer burdened her. "My name is Thia."

Kel had already thanked Echil for their luck as Rad stepped up directly behind Thia, dagger raised.

"You know what the best part of being Lasha is?" she asked sweetly, reaching with one arm behind her head to clutch Rad around the throat so hard that he gasped.

In the next moment, Rad dropped his blade as the Lasha swung him around by the throat and, quick as a flash, smashed his nose into Satt's chin, knocking them both off their feet.

"I don't need to be a man to take out a group of terrorist scum."

Honor be damned.

If it would mean he'd live to lead another unit with an improved strategy, Kel had one more reason to escape now. He would see that this Lasha snake paid.

Moving faster than he'd ever thought he could manage, Kel leapt into the passage to avoid the brute force of the hydroweapon's initial spray.

Despite missing the fatal impact, his spine jolted with the fraction of the deluge that struck him.

Surely, a better plan would quell the guilt he already felt upon abandoning his comrades.

Zaam, give them many luxuries in the Realm of Joy, he silently prayed, entire back soaked as he bounded back through the tunnels toward Garo territory.

Chapter Seven

The moment she set foot on the bottom rung of the rope ladder leading up to Telo's home, Inad halted.

Biting her lower lip, she knew that she had to be smart about this. She couldn't kill him. In fact, she had no desire to kill anyone. But he would inevitably try to take her, which left her with little choice. She had to at least maim him long enough to somehow get away.

Glancing back into the forest behind her, Inad desperately wished she could transform into one of the small birds or insects that flitted between the treetops, unnoticed by her own kind.

Even as she began the ascent up the ladder, her limbs felt weighed down by liquid metal.

"How was the river?" Telo faced her from where he sat against the back of the modest shelter, slicing an *ur* fruit with a small blade.

Before him sat two basins of water and two platters of pale brown meat.

Tree snake.

"The waters pleased me," Inad affirmed, taking her seat on the wooden floor before him, though maintaining some distance from the food—and from the chief.

Telo gave a slight smile as he finished preparing the *ur* and distributed several pieces beside the meat on her platter.

"Tell me of your family. Do you and your brother enjoy the forest?"

Inad tried to feign a smile. This was at least a conversation topic about which she could be honest.

"Yes, Chief. As you know, Ara and I have lived here all our lives. In many ways, we are just as Ayam as Tabir."

Telo made a gruff sound in his throat. "Your mother might not approve of your words. Your grasp of our language is impressive, it is true. Yet your people surely think you belong across the water."

"Maru speaks well of you," Telo began again. "She says you handle the children with an equal amount of guidance and gentleness."

"They learn Tabir quickly," Inad replied, gaze flitting to Telo's face for a split second before returning to her meal.

She picked at her food.

"Tell me," Telo started, and Inad tensed, though resumed chewing the tough snake flesh. "Has your mother shared with you her reasons for poisoning our people?"

This time, Inad really did pause in her chewing.

When he said 'our', Inad wondered if he meant his people or that the Ayam were somehow her people as well.

Which, in a sense, they truly were. When they had left Tabira for Ayam, Ara could barely talk, and Inad had been little more than a toddler. Neither had any memory of life beyond the island nation.

The chief continued, "Don't you ever wonder—during the morning meal, when the people gather—which of us has just returned from bathing in the river after a night of brutality in the jungle? You and your brother seem to prefer eating with us rather than on the smaller island with your mother. I'm sure you've been curious which of us have fallen."

Inad's stomach felt painfully tight, the water dripping from her wet hair cooling the bone of the dagger concealed against her upper back.

"My mother and I don't get on," Inad finally managed. It wasn't a lie in the least. "She does not trust me enough to share her methods. However, I feel for the great loss the people have suffered. I truly feel this, Chief Telo."

She held his gaze now.

Finishing his food, Telo pushed aside his platter and downed the remainder of his water.

Inad idly noticed the color of his skin as his hand brushed her own, setting down his water bowl as she withdrew hers for a final drink.

Pale bronze just like hers, perhaps a bit lighter. Both of them raised beneath the canopy their entire lives. Both now living in fear of the same plague.

"Thank you." He rose then, circling behind her, and gently stroked her hair. "Please remove your braid and release the water from your hair. It's dripping."

Inad had to stop herself from instinctively recoiling under his touch, horrified that he'd discover the weapon.

Pulling the band from her braid, Inad began to very carefully drag her fingers through the knotted waves. Going for her still-filled water bowl to wring out her hair, Telo reached a hand past her shoulder and offered his own.

"Let me."

No wonder he hadn't moved from behind her. It was almost as if he didn't trust her.

Smart man. It terrified and frustrated her all at once.

The chill gripped her again, harder than ever, and Inad wasn't able to quell the shaking this time.

It was now or never. Just maim, don't kill.

"Forgive me, I have to scratch."

Maneuvering her hand around to reach beneath her moist shirt and upper garment, Inad just avoided nicking her fingertips on the blade. She hadn't anticipated withdrawing the dagger from this angle, but there was no time for second guesses now.

Grasping the bone weapon, Inad pulled free the small blade and leapt to the side, turning rapidly as she went. Telo's hoarse shout was all the confirmation she needed, before even laying eyes on his slashed forearm.

"You stay away," she commanded, willing the quaver to leave her voice. "You will *not* give me the disease."

Though Telo was clutching his arm, he never broke eye contact with his new wife.

"Has the light fled your mind?" he demanded, taking a step toward her, dropping his arms to his sides and widening his stance. At least he no longer held the knife he'd used to cut the fruit.

"I will not be punished for a crime I did not commit," Inad went on. "I've had nothing to do with the Curse!"

"You fear I have the Curse," Telo replied in a lower, cold tone. "That I roam the forest at night as a beast. So you choose to try and kill me with tricks—like an animal, rather than use your words and ask."

Inad backed further away while trying desperately to inch toward the threshold to the ladder outside. How she would be able to escape from this high up without him catching her, she had absolutely no idea.

"Why, Inad?" The chief's voice had grown almost taunting. "You believe that fighting is the only language the Ayam savages understand?"

Inad had to choke down the lump in her throat—not tears, but something that felt like her entire meal.

"But then, if you truly are your mother's daughter, savagery might just run in your family line. As true of Tabir as of our finest warriors. Perhaps violence is all that *you* can truly understand."

He was a mere step from her now, and the hut space was small. She'd fall to her death if she took one more step back.

That was it. This would be the end.

As Inad fought the urge to cast her eyes downward—perhaps even beg for mercy—her racing thought train was shredded as Telo grabbed her by her wet locks and spun her around, tossing her roughly to the floor of the hut.

Moments after instinctively springing to her feet, Inad's lungs deflated with the second blow to her upper back that kept her down. Her last spark of fight had emerged too late.

Even the fact that she'd miraculously managed to maintain her hold on the dagger was rendered moot when she felt the weapon wrestled from her grip.

A souvenir she had taken from before the large beasts became completely extinct following the onset of the Curse. Snapped from the femur of the last palm cat carcass.

Now she lay bent over before her new husband, completely at his mercy, unable to even see him.

By this time tomorrow, she would likely be cursed. By tomorrow night, she would become a monster.

Any terror of the future Inad may have felt gave way to the most excruciating pain she had ever experienced in her life.

Beginning as a cold stinging, a sharp throbbing shot down her spine as the quills on her nape were ripped out by the roots.

Gritting her teeth, Inad hissed and moaned, but refused to shout or sob despite the hot tears already streaming down her cheeks.

With that, she fell to the floor with a gentle nudge from Telo as he released her shoulder, her entire back still pulsating in a hot, dull ache.

"You will not become an *onn* beast," the chief murmured icily. "And you will no longer be a revered Flightless. You will be just like everyone else."

The moment the chief approached her dais, Vata suspected the worst. Then her eyes fell on the gash along his arm, confirming her suspicion.

In broad daylight, not even the *onn* beasts were a concern. No. Just as had been the case for many years, her own children were her worst fear. The liability keeping her from truly civilizing these natives—from releasing more of the pathogen by force. From destroying them one by one until they gave up their gods.

Instead, she had to water down her tactics for the sake of her children. Especially Ara, slow and fragile as he'd always been. Waste of time and space.

At least Inad's teaching skills were hopeful, yet that ridiculous penchant she had battle craft angered Vata beyond belief.

Her daughter had obviously struck out at the chief—Inad's husband in a union that served as Vata's last hope for establishing trust with the natives, that they might accept another Pricking to cure them.

Her hopes dashed, Vata gnashed her teeth even before Telo began to speak.

"You come today from the mainland," she stated in Tabir. Ayam had always sounded too guttural for her liking, particularly those horrid yip sounds that accompanied various syllables. "A long way."

"Yes, Vata."

His accent was impressive, she had to admit. Hak had taught him well as a boy.

"What is the trouble? Is it my daughter?"

"In fact..." Telo stepped forward, opening his outstretched palm to reveal about six brown feathers, the white root tips coated in a faint red. "She feared catching the Curse when I took her to my home."

Vata's eyes widened at the sight of the feathers. She couldn't deny the leap of joy she felt at seeing that, for once, someone had done the job for her.

"They were unbecoming anyway," Vata decided.

"I felt you deserved honesty," Telo went on, closing his fist once more. "As do I and my people. Vata—Inad's fear confirmed how the Curse spreads. You wish to punish us by transforming us. Punish and torture, but for what? Not giving up belief in the Zaam? By now, half of the adults on Ayam have fallen. We cannot bear children if the plague spreads further, until too many are infected to contain."

"Perhaps you should refrain from mating like wild animals and control the rate at which the population grows," Vata bit back. "Try putting on some actual clothing and learning to read."

"I can read Tabir," Telo replied flatly.

"I meant the rest of the Ayam," Vata bristled. "What is your point, *Chief*?"

"Is that how you teach your children to fear what is natural—the very experience into which you have sent your daughter? Blinding them with stories that lying together turns people into monsters?" Telo spoke up, closing the distance to Vata's dais and turning over his hand above Vata's lap. "It ends now. From this day on, you will never lie to or touch the girl again. You hide out here on your small island as you have always done. She stays with me. She is *mine*."

Vata's breath hitched in disbelief as the bloodied feathers fluttered down onto the lap of her beige slacks. Beside the thick trunk of her dais, the two Kano officers that flanked her at all times shifted, but made no move to intervene just yet.

"I am going to restore safety for my people." Telo turned to go back to his canoe. "Whatever it takes. If I do not see a cure within the next twenty suns, my warriors will take things into their own hands."

Even after the boat and its wretched occupant had faded from sight, Vata's heart still beat so fast it pained her.

His presence, towering over her as she sat, had brought up far too many memories from when she and Eta were children at the mercy of their father.

Twenty suns, indeed.

Rising from her seat, Vata gathered the two guards present to alert the Kano troop lead by Officer Doreh. Vata would show that savage brat. If taking away his precious bride would show him who wielded the power, then so be it.

In the tree high above his mother's dais, Ara waited for the chief to retreat to the shore before setting out silently after him. For the first time, he'd evaded his mother's careful eye. It was for a good cause, no doubt. An essential mission. His mother wouldn't have to know.

"Is leaving wise?" Officer Doreh asked Vata, as soon as she had laid out her plan in a seething tirade. "Might the natives run wild?"

"Not if your watch is secure," Vata retorted. "Should I doubt your ability to control these people?"

Doreh sighed, avoiding the urge to shift under Vata's livid gaze. The woman simply *never* broke eye contact until she broke you.

"No, Mak-*ke*," replied Doreh, "You can count on me."

"My name is Vata, I am not the Mak, nor am I bound to my sister. As long as we are in Ayam, my word is just as good as hers."

"Of course, Vata." Doreh had to wonder at her eagerness to be addressed by her given name as opposed to any title.

As Vata turned to depart the Kano base by the Network tower, Doreh turned to finish his afternoon meal. Although he had long since grown accustomed to the jungle diet of tree snake and fish, just then, he found himself longing to relax and watch a stage spectacle back in Tabira.

Docking his canoe back on the mainland, Telo smiled to himself.

Although he had brought the handgun given to him by Hak, he was happy he'd no cause to waste it on the likes of Vata.

Moreover, he had no intention of invoking any more pain upon the girl. In fact, he doubted she would be a threat any longer. Not following this incident. In any event, he needed Inad at his side for leverage against Vata. Assuming that the woman cared for her daughter enough to make that leverage worth anything.

Ashamed as he felt in torturing her, he could not risk her trying anything with him. Even something as simple as forcing her blood into his mouth. He had no idea how many ways the Curse could truly spread. For all he knew, Inad could even be engineered with the plague in her blood. A carrier.

It was times like these that he was thankful to have not been graced with the urge to take anyone to bed.

All of his light had always gone into the warrior's journey. Although he knew what he had to do next, and it pained him greatly, sacrifices like this were never enacted in vain.

The afflicted were no longer Ayam. Though they looked normal by day, they were suffering. The time had come to ensure the people could defend themselves.

***

Having never used his wings, this was one of those times when Ara wished he at least knew whether they actually worked.

Even if his wings did function properly, he had no idea of his own carrying endurance while in flight.

Clutching the side of the trunk and avoiding the rope ladder to remain as concealed as possible in the dense foliage that grew intertwined around the tree, he remained determined to reach the chief's hut before nightfall.

Truly, he considered it a miracle that the chief hadn't rolled up the ladder before making his descent—lest Ara have no backup hand and foothold.

That also likely meant that Telo planned to return before sundown. So where was he? Ara supposed he should consider himself lucky on that front as well—as long as he could reach Inad and roll up the ladder before any of the *onn* approached.

Swatting at the relentless parade of insects that seemed to hover in the humid evening air, Ara moved around toward the front of the tree to adjust his balance on the side of the ladder.

That was definitely a spider by his left hand—quite a large spider, the tips of its legs extending out as far as his fingertips.

The tree spiders had surely begun to breed again, despite the cold season having set in. Already, he could hear the subtle clicking of billions of tiny eggs throughout the treetops. Miniscule translucent beads that jumped of their own accord.

It was quite fascinating to see and hear—until they all hatched.

Keeping his torso as close to the tree's surface as possible, Ara inched just enough so he could avoid the spider, not really caring anymore that he was easily identifiable from the ground.

He would rescue Inad. He would only ever use his wings to escape with her. She needed him now more than ever.

Emerging from the shade of the vines just enough to clutch onto the second-to-highest rung, Ara nearly jumped at a rumble that grew closer.

He had seen Telo leave about an hour ago, and had left not soon after, making sure to avoid the chief's radar. He'd figured Telo had gone to train with the warriors after speaking with Vata.

No, this was the sound of a machine far beyond any technology used on Ayam.

Moments later, the humongous glider swam into view from over the graying sea beneath the dusky sky.

Bright flashing lights momentarily blinded Ara as he pressed himself closer to the rope ladder. Loud engines roared, drowning out the hoarse cries of the Cursed as they slowly and painfully transformed deep in the forest below.

Idly, he wondered where Telo could be hiding out now that the Cursed had already begun to roam the land.

Squinting up at the huge silver shape hovering just above the canopy, Ara remained hidden amongst the large palm fronds. Even as three men barking at each other in hurried Tabir swung down from the glider on grey ropes and entered the chief's dwelling.

Although he had seen images of such gliders on his mother's data cube, never had he imagined they caused such immense noise.

As soon as the second one descended the harness onto the roof of the tree shelter to climb into the hut, Ara moved.

Even as his sister's indignant shouts began, Ara leapt on the man nearest the entrance.

"Get off me, freak!" the man shouted, swatting at Ara.

How he wished he'd untied the wings. Just this once.

Maneuvering off the man's back as he approached his sister, Ara dove onto the floor to grab Inad and block her with his body before they could reach her.

They would make it out of this.

The final sound to hit Ara's ears was his sister's loud curse—before a searing shock wracked his entire body and darkness fell.

Chapter Eight

Determined not to drag her feet, Thia willed away the urge to trudge along, despite her aching limbs.

For a weapon comprised of the thinnest sheet metal coating, the collapsed hydroweapon weighed her down like a boulder. Of course, the skirmish forcing her to fend off four men at once while wielding said weapon surely contributed to her soreness.

Struggling to maintain upright posture, the Lasha drew two fingers gently along the paper-thin slit where the terrorist's blade had pierced the flesh of her collarbone.

Within a few moments, she withdrew her hand. Hopefully any bleeding ended with the few red droplets that came away on her fingertips—as she still walked within the border region, any lingering Garo might well mistake her injury for a much greater weakness.

Thia's thoughts dissolved at a rapid scratching sound up ahead.

Even in the welling dusk that followed sunset, her eyes made out the shape of a man dressed in filthy rags, the front of his shirt torn diagonally all the way across his torso.

As soon as Thia approached, she used her peripheral vision to ascertain the source of the scratching sound. The man dragged his right foot backward and forward through the dirt in front of him.

Thia's jaw clenched. A Garo beggar no doubt, judging from his pallor and bloodshot eyes surrounded by grey shadows.

Just as she made to stride past him, he reached out a hand toward her.

Preparing for the worst, Thia made a step to the left to put some distance between herself and the beggar. He could easily be hiding a knife in those rags.

"Stay where you are," she barked in Garo as he finally went to stand, swiftly falling back to his knees with a groan and a hacking wheeze. "Save your requests for someone who carries der or the Kano will hear of your begging on Lirian territory."

"I ..." the man rasped and managed to suppress another cough. "I am Lirian. Please, my sister, I need the herb..."

Thia's blood ran cold as she caught herself just in time to keep walking rather than stop short. Sure enough, the man had spoken fluent Lirian without even the trace of a Garo accent.

A Lirian beggar.

How could a Lirian be begging for grass on the streets? She had never seen or even heard of Lirian addicts. All the dance venues that sold the herb had a strict policy against serving patrons who visited more than three consecutive days per week.

Moreover, Nasin had recently confirmed that Lir had maintained a homelessness rate of zero percent for several years already.

Pursing her lips and ignoring the man's persistent pleas, Thia sought to distract herself with Walar's approaching visit.

***

Rohem sighed with relief when the text arrived from Thia reporting a successful mission.

The news provided a welcome break. So far, he had been alternating between poring over his books and staring at the common area data cube for several hours.

After four months of studying, he had nearly completed the second radiographic imaging textbook lent to him by Gether in preparation for his final exam at the Lirian Medical Academy.

Although medical studies in Lir still required a great deal of independent study due to a shortage of classroom instructors, Rohem simply couldn't muster up the initiative to pursue medicine in Tabira. Gether had been immensely fortunate, having graduated and returned to Lir a mere half year prior to the Cleansing.

Rohem preferred to keep a safe distance from Tabira—as cautious as any Lirian. While Tabir technology and education might produce stellar advancements and experts in various fields, he would much rather take longer to complete his training in a safe atmosphere than speed along in an unsecured environment.

His attentions were so absorbed by the current image of a bone mass that Rohem started when the knock came.

Speaking into the microphone that connected to the intercom by the door's exterior, Rohem requested, "State your name and purpose."

"It's Walar," came the voice of a young man. "Is Thia in?"

Rohem sighed and stood up, pushing the imaging cube away from the desk's edge. Thia hadn't mentioned that Walar was visiting. He had to wonder if it was on family or personal business.

"Walar," Rohem greeted politely. "Come in. Can I bring you some water?"

"That's fine, thanks." Walar smiled, holding up a water canister as he sat on the sofa opposite the desk. "I'm all set. The rail tube does seem to be getting faster."

"A smooth ride, then?" Rohem really preferred to return to studies than make small talk. "Thia should be coming back soon. She's out on a mission."

"Mission?" Walar asked. "Hm, she never mentioned it to me. What kind?"

"It's the Garo," Rohem replied, taking his seat back at the desk. "The Evaporation fighters have started tunneling again."

"Do you know if she's all right? The change would have just happened…"

"Of course," Rohem retorted. He didn't know why he felt increasingly irritable lately. "She wrote me via communicator. She should be back soon."

Walar suddenly looked like he wanted to keep quiet. Rohem instantly regretted his brusque attitude.

"So," Rohem began again, swiveling around slightly to face the man on behind him. "Have you been well?"

"Yes, thank you," the lanky young man replied tentatively.

"Staying long?" Rohem wasted no time. Not that he actually expected Walar to indulge any information regarding his long-term intentions with Avithia.

After a brief pause and shifty glances between Rohem and the front entrance, Walar spoke. "Just a couple of days. I've an important exam coming up to qualify for a legal apprenticeship back in Tabira."

So it appeared he had no intentions of setting down roots in Lir. At least not for a while.

Rohem contemplated taking his blueprint designs outside to the upper level veranda for some fresh air.

"Well," Walar finally moved from his position between the front entrance and the desk, "I think I'll just wait in Thia's room, if that's fine with you."

"Go right ahead," Rohem replied, eager to return to his studies.

In truth, Rohem felt Walar looked awfully pale for a Lirian, lanky with dark brown shaggy hair that always looked like he'd just woken up. Rohem had to wonder how he handled Thia, especially in one of her moods or close to the change.

Just last month, Avi had been complaining about how he longed to spend time with Walar more than every fourteen weeks.

Rohem couldn't imagine managing such cycles. Although Arin, his former classmate at the medical academy, often spoke of the sleepless nights involved with apprenticeship, Rohem simply felt grateful that none of them had to balance an entire change of form as well as a strenuous career, such as medicine or martial affairs.

Moments later, the front door burst open.

"Thia!"

Rohem stood just as the Lasha stumbled in through the threshold to the home compound's back entrance, nearly tripping under the weight of the hydrotank on her shoulders.

"It's fine, I got it." Thia swatted at Rohem's attempt to relieve her of the contraption, struggling with the straps until she managed to drop it to the floor somewhat gracefully.

A shallow cut glared from right above her left collarbone.

"So glad Nasin isn't here." Thia said with a sigh, bee-lining for the couches and grain chair at the room's center. "I almost didn't stop to call my father. Didn't want to waste time, but I'd promised to check in after finishing up."

As expected, Gether had been beside himself after learning she'd survived a solo encounter with four militants.

Especially given the death of Avithia's mother at the hands of the Garo.

"What happened?" Rohem insisted, going to the cooler to retrieve a canister of water for the Lasha.

Once she'd managed to rummage her way out of the protective suit, Thia slumped onto the soft grain chair.

However, once the usual comfort of the chair's malleability began to gnaw at her aching limbs, she soon opted for the floor instead.

"It's as we suspected," Thia grumbled. "They've reopened the tunnel down by the reservoir."

"I thought we agreed to finish the hydrotank before using it in the field," Rohem pointed out, taking a seat in the grain chair.

"I won't tell Nasin if you don't," she panted.

"Never happened. How'd the mission turn out down there?" Rohem asked.

"I took out three of the four terrorists," Thia grumbled. "The leader who actually aimed to spread the fire—pretty sure it was Kel—escaped."

"Next time." Rohem nodded, then grinned. "You did well, Thia. You deserve a reward. Walar's here. He's waiting in your room."

If her back hadn't started to protest, Thia would have shot up even faster than she did.

"*What*?" she exclaimed, dropping her voice just in time. "Right now? Did he say why?" Then even lower. "Why is he in my room instead of out here?"

Rohem shifted a bit in his seat before replying with a slight smirk, "He says he knows the change just happened."

"No." Thia slapped a hand over her forehead. "Why is he telling *you* these things?"

"He's waiting for you," Rohem replied, also keeping his voice low.

Thia had barely left the front quarter when Rohem added, "Oria's still out with the informants. I'll keep an eye out for Nasin. Till then, you have my permission to make all the noise you like."

Once Thia had left Rohem with a look of utter disdain written all over her face, Rohem took a moment to enjoy the peace of the afternoon.

Nasin hadn't yet returned from an intelligence training session with Oria, and he hadn't the stamina to sit any longer fiddling with that radiology equipment at Gether's office.

Instead, Rohem found his curiosity drawn toward the activities of Thia and her…partner, Walar.

He'd heard them on the nights Walar had snuck over. Not sleeping had its drawbacks, especially when his quarter shared a wall with Avithia's.

What intrigued Rohem most about the entire situation was how Walar only ever seemed to visit every fourteen weeks—when Avithia lived as Thia.

Why the Lasha's other half seemed not to appeal to Walar, Rohem wasn't certain. They were the same person, after all.

Then again, Walar remained one of the very few Lirians whose family hadn't fled Tabira following the Cleansing of eighteen years past—the deadly, three-day government air raid on the Lirian quarter of Tabira that had killed Oria's parents before she could barely talk.

Between a passing knowledge of the night the Cleansing occurred and his own experiences on Tabir streets, Rohem found it little surprise that a man such as Walar wouldn't have his oddities after living his entire life as a Lirian in Tabira.

Thoughts returning to the sounds Thia often made during Walar's nightly visits, Rohem questioned the latter's intentions to actually relocate to Lir. After nearly five years, he still always returned to Tabira. Thia, for her part, didn't seem to mind. When Rohem would ask if they planned to become true partners, Thia would scoff and explain that the Lasha experienced stronger emotions—and urges—than most people of the Plane, and that Rohem could not understand.

In fact, he realized with a start, particularly following that encounter with the strange force around the Lirian megalith, Rohem felt he was beginning to understand that sort of unexplainable emotion. An ache. A *yearning* that defied description.

Or at least that seemed akin to how Avi described physical intimacy. Avithia always had seemed to open up more to Rohem while in male form.

"So…when do classes begin?" Thia wouldn't admit to herself the growing deflation she already felt.

"Well, if all goes well and I pass, in a couple of months," Walar replied. "I'll have my own flat in Tabira's old quarter and everything. Education and housing are covered in full by the Mak's reparations for children of Cleansing survivors."

"Housing near the former ghetto." Thia managed to muster a bittersweet smile. "Congratulations, you've worked so hard."

Walar just smiled in return, averting his eyes more than usual.

"You're welcome to relax here in the meantime." Thia had already stood up to start arranging the pillows on her bed.

"Actually," Walar interjected, "I am in a mood to lay with you. Just relax, maybe. I'm sure you're tired after your trip."

"And sweaty." Thia wrinkled her nose as she stripped off her sleeveless top.

"Is there always so much hair if you don't shave?" Walar asked suddenly. "Your arms, I mean."

The Lasha nearly froze before she resumed tossing her shirt in the wash basket.

"I didn't have time to shave before the mission, and just recently changed," Thia muttered. "You caught me on an off day. Let me go shave and shower. I'll be back."

Running her face under the cool water first, Thia took her time in shaving under her arms as well as forearms and legs. It was no secret that Walar aimed only to be with Thia, and not Avi. She cared a great deal for him, and admired his driven personality. He had been there for her after many a mission…and yet, something stung at her core. Something that felt like disapproval on his part.

In a way, she preferred the space she had to train when he wasn't around. Yet she had also begun to consider how they might see each other less often one day if he didn't end up settling in Lir.

It seemed that time had finally come. She felt confident they could work it out.

Returning from the washroom, she was surprised to see Walar hadn't quite undressed all the way. He still wore his shirt, his trousers the only item removed.

"Come rest with me," he beckoned, already lying beneath the thin coverlet.

Thia obliged, and Walar put an arm around her, capturing her lips in a tender kiss.

"We smell similar," he remarked.

There was that gnawing feeling again.

"It's close to the change," Thia explained again. "Happened just this morning."

"Mm." Walar seemed to ponder something.

"Are you hungry?" asked Thia, "Want to go to the eatery across the way before getting comfortable?"

Walar half-smiled. "For spiced bean stew?"

Thia giggled softly, as Walar reclined rather rigidly.

"Come on." Thia turned on coy mode, rolling over to caress Walar, her hand moving south. "I know what you're like, coming back here after a couple months. You like…"

"I guess you'd know what I like," Walar finished. "What *we* like."

Thia's hand stopped in its tracks. "What do you mean?"

Silence.

"Because half the time, I have what you have." Thia dared speak the words aloud. "That's it, isn't it? It bothers you."

"No, of course not," Walar rushed. "It's just…would you still want to do…what we do if you were the other way?"

"You mean would I want you in my male form?" Thia clarified. "As Avi? Yes, Walar, I would. I do."

"Thia, this has been going on almost six years now," continued Walar, speaking faster. "I feel you are owed a promise. We don't practice marriage in Tabira anymore, yet you deserve a commitment. A long-term commitment. The kind where you share a bed with someone nightly. And I…I want to be completely honest when I say that I am not sure I can do that. Share a bed with another man."

By this point, a flip had switched in Thia's mind, the tingling deflation transformed into numbness.

"Thank you, Walar," she stated simply. "I appreciate your honesty. I think you deserve a commitment too. With a proper Tabir woman who remains a woman all year-round. Or perhaps another Tali such as yourself."

"Come on, Thia," Walar groaned. "That's not a nice term."

"It's true though," Thia pointed out. "Your family stays in Tabira instead of moving back. You are a Talirian. Do your Tabir friends even know who you're seeing?"

"It's called diaspora," Walar shot back. "It happens. All Lirians don't have to live in Lir for us to remain a united nation. And yes, those back home have known for a while now, as have my family. A nice Lirian woman."

"Just a woman," Thia quipped. "Not a Lasha."

"Details," Walar brushed off. "Most Tabir may not fully understand the concept of Lasha or consider Lirians as their own people, but I grew up there. Tabira is where I will always feel most comfortable."

"And that is where we truly differ. You act as though another Cleansing can never happen." Thia rose from the bed. "Look, you can sleep on the sofa in the front quarter. I think I need to be alone. Still jittery from the change."

"It's fine," Walar insisted. "I should probably go. I just wanted to discuss this in person."

Always the formal one.

The tube return trip was easily booked. Within the next hour, Thia bid farewell to Walar as he left once again for Tabira.

Once he had departed, Thia felt two parts grief and relief. Sorrow for his obvious discomfort with an aspect of her person over which she had no control, and relief over the fact that she now only shared the space with people who welcomed her the way she was.

In particular, Rohem, whose playful yet diligent personality never failed to offer cheer even during the greatest of challenges. Arguably more different than even her and Nasin, he never seemed to fret over his unique nature.

Perhaps his secret was avoiding romance at all costs.

Although Avithia and Walar had never agreed to exclusivity throughout their long-standing, long-distance relationship, the dynamic had fallen into a sort of comfortable understanding. Space when needed and affection when necessary. Not only physical intimacy. Thia could get that easily enough either in her current form or as Avi, and didn't shy away.

The Lasha smiled, remembering the time she had asked Rohem to accompany her one week as Avi. A man's night out. Rohem, for his part, had agreed to come along—only to ruin Avi's chances with one girl by pouring a grasswater cocktail over the Lasha's head mid-sentence.

Several weeks later, she had tried Oria just to see what the latter would say. Of course, the answer was a blatant and nearly horrified refusal. So most nights, Avithia went out dancing alone.

Yet Walar had always been the constant. The space would take some getting used to.

Now Thia suddenly found herself recalling Rohem's prank at the dance house—as if he wanted Avi to himself. Or perhaps she was reading too much into it.

"Can I sit out here with you awhile?" Thia asked, approaching to sit on the couch near the desk. "I'll just read and stay quiet, promise."

"Of course," Rohem returned warmly. "I'm always happy to have your company, Thia."

"Sorry if it was strange for you earlier, with Walar." She sat down with her data cube.

"Strange is what we do." Rohem smiled wryly. "May as well wallow together."

Mutual understanding at its most genuine. Of course, she soon inwardly berated her wayward emotions, putting them off to the recent change.

Still, it was all Thia could do to quell the tears that threatened to spill forth as she fought the urge to embrace the man before her.

Soon enough, Oria and Nasin returned for the evening and delighted to hear of Thia's successful mission in the tunnels.

Later that night, even after Nasin had gone to sleep, Rohem did hear a sound from Avithia's quarter.

Not of ecstasy, but of sadness.

***

Telo resisted the urge to scowl as Maru dressed his arm with small fronds and soothing herbs.

Kindly as always, she had taken to fussing over him as soon as she'd finished the hardgrass flute call of dusk.

Although he had intended on tending the wound himself, the wisewoman had insisted, complete with Finu grinning over his shoulder.

Suddenly he regretted ever coming to consult Maru on how he should proceed with Inad.

"Proud, indeed," Finu teased lightly, taking a bite from a honey melon as they all took shelter for the night in Maru's home. "I'm sure she won't miss you tonight."

Just then, a rattling cry broke the usual clicking song of nocturnal insects.

A cry from just beyond the dwelling entrance.

Peering out from the entrance, Telo and Finu took in the hulking form of an *onn* beast struggling to climb the trunk.

"He's at it again," Finu scoffed. "I'm sure this is the same one that was scratching at my tree the other night. Only he looks somehow different…"

Just then, the rattle became words. A plea. "I beg you…wisewoman. Help me!"

"He is still turning," Telo breathed, squinting to make out the creature's features in the dim glow cast by the dangling lantern by Maru's home entrance.

Finu had never witnessed a transformation.

A boy of only twelve at the time, he had stayed with Maru, while Telo—who had been seventeen, and therefore a warrior by right of age and parentage, had snuck out to watch his mother change one night before a group of women gathering breakfast discovered her mangled, once-again normal body several mornings later. She had evidently lost a fight with a fellow beast.

He would never forget the piercing mewls of pain, or her tears as she cried out for her sons and for the Zaam.

He had run for the safety of Maru's tree the moment his mother's voice ceased to be recognizable.

It wasn't long after the affliction of his mother so closely followed by that of his father, that Telo put two and two together. The Curse spread through lovemaking.

Fewer than fifty suns following Telo's mother's death, his father threw himself into the Maw, thus forfeiting his position as chief. By tradition, Telo had taken on the title of chief, to be confirmed upon the slaying of an *onn* beast on the eve of his twenty-fifth year.

His brother, however, still refused to believe that something so seemingly trivial could be the cause.

"I thought it was instant." Finu's expression grew grave.

"The rising of the beast causes great pain," Maru murmured sullenly.

The creature's next cry turned into a full-blown rattle as the villager finally succumbed to the beast, transforming beyond the ability for speech. "The powerlessness to help them is a sorrow unlike most."

Just as Finu touched his brother's arm to speak again, a dark blur obscured the nearly-turned villager from sight, followed moments later by a sickening crunch. One of the other plagued villagers who had already transformed must have claimed the first as this night's meal.

Even the insects in the trees seemed to have ceased their call.

A large chunk of tree bark snapping off under its next blow nearly made Telo jump, the hanging lamp swinging slightly from the movement down below. Beside him, Finu shifted uncomfortably and pulled the dangling lamp toward him to blow out the flame inside and decrease the risk of fire. Finally, Maru muttered a prayer to the Zaam and pulled the grass covering over the entrance.

Not that any thin covering could silence the rattling bellows or atrocious scratching that soon sounded once more from the shadows below. Nor could it shield them from the ear-splitting rumble that came next.

Like a roll of thunder that manifested in a terrifying roar from overhead, the signature sound of the Tabir air machine permeated the Ayam forest.

In his haste to squeeze by and glance at the dark sky, Finu nearly pushed Telo over the edge to the ground below.

"Why have they come?" Finu shouted.

"Come back inside, please, Finu," Maru urged him.

"No, he is right," Telo yelled, his voice nearly drowned out by the racket above. "They have no right to come here. No one told me they would fly over the canopy!"

"Look where they're headed!" Finu called as the giant machine hovered over Telo's home dwelling, about twenty meters away.

"Does she seek to escape back to Tabira?" This time it was Maru who spoke.

"Perhaps the alliance is off," Finu mused as they all watched helplessly while three men descended into the chief's home and then returned to the flying contraption within minutes.

Under any other circumstances, Telo would have thanked the Zaam for taking such a rebellious woman off his hands. However, knowing with full certainty that Vata had taken such action this time only made his very blood boil.

With a second glance downward past the grass curtain, Telo saw that the ground was clear—at least far as he could see from up here. The beast had left, likely distracted by the motion of the giant flying machine.

"Where do you think you're going?" Finu shouted as his brother's retreating form slipped past the entrance.

"The beasts will follow the glider!" Telo insisted. "I can track from behind."

"Telo, come back here right now!" Maru protested as soon as the chief began climbing down the rope ladder.

"She is my responsibility! I have to see where they're taking her," Telo said, more to convince himself.

He knew very well that the glider would likely take off across the sea before he could sneak aboard, leaving him soon for the Onn.

Once his feet hit the ground, Telo took off sprinting into the brush, eyes darting back and forth for any sign of the beasts as he followed the well-known trail from Maru's to his home.

After several strides along the seemingly clear path, the chief stopped short and nearly fell over when he collided with a solid object that seemingly fell from above.

Telo hadn't time to right himself before falling backward and gazing up into the lethal stare of a palm cat, the creature's lips drawing back in a feral hiss.

Impossible. The people knew that the beasts had slain all the palm cats.

As long as Telo was tall, slick brown fur shone in the light of the Great Stone that dappled the canopy leaves, its pale green eyes following the chief as it slinked towards him…

Rising before the once-worst predator in the jungle, Telo raised his hands and released a battle cry, making himself seem very large, as typically remained the only strategy to stall one's demise when facing one of these animals.

With another harsh hiss, the cat leapt at the chief, narrowly avoiding his shoulder, and immediately launching itself onto the *onn* beast that had silently crept up behind Telo.

Transfixed at first, Telo took off toward his home, taking a moment to realize that the glider's roar had begun to fade.

His wife was gone.

Clenching his fists in anger at his own cowardice, the chief decided this battle was not yet over. Still, he ran for his home as fast as the swift wind amongst the palm fronds.

***

Mak Eta stifled a groan as her communicator buzzed sharply from the bedside table.

"Yes?" she inquired curtly, pressing the receiver button on the edge of the small device.

"Forgive the late message, Mak Eta," came the officer's voice from the other end. "Commander Vata from the Ayam outpost has requested emergency transport of her daughter to the Kano prison hold in Tabira."

That got her attention.

"Inad? What has the girl done?"

"Evidently, she has attacked the Ayam leader," replied the officer. "Vata sees fit to confine her for the time being. Her brother was taken into custody as well, following his assault of a Kano officer attempting to escort the girl."

Eta sighed. This truly wasn't her issue, and yet she still had to wonder what kind of trouble her sister had gotten into this time. Or her niece, as it seemed was now the case.

"I authorize the subject's transfer to confinement. Both of them."

"Then they are not a hazard?" the officer asked.

"The girl is not a threat to me, and while you are around she's no threat to the people. Therefore, she is not a hazard. The boy couldn't cause harm even if he wanted to. End call."

Rising steadily, the Mak arranged her hair atop her head and dressed to look somewhat presentable.

During the descent downstairs, the air grew sluggish and cold. Despite her heavy cardigan, Eta wrapped her arms around her torso. The tepid weather on the plains would soon give way to a brisk cold season.

If Eta felt ragged, her sister looked even worse.

Sitting in the guest chair in front of Eta's desk, dark hair strewn about down her shoulders, Vata's sharp face emanated fury. Kohl liner streaming in faint trails down her cheeks, for the first time since Eta could remember, her sister looked as though she couldn't be bothered with appearances.

The Mak took her seat at the wooden desk, facing Vata head-on.

"It's raining outside, I take it." It wasn't a question.

"What do you think?" Vata shot back.

"I think you might want some tea." Eta went to rise again.

"No tea, thank you," Vata replied shortly. "I am here to officially state the reason for my presence, nothing more."

"Why would I assume there was more?" Eta ventured. "An officer has already given me the official report, and I have ordered both your children into confinement for as long as you see fit."

"Both?"

What had Vata missed while riding up front with the officers during the flight? Did Ara really follow his sister at every turn?

"Yes. Ara put up a struggle and struck one of my officers. He should share at least some of his sister's penalty, don't you agree?"

"If it will keep him off my back about my brutish daughter, so be it. Sometimes I truly think you made the right decision never having children."

Eta had to admit this level of flippancy from her sister surprised her.

"Should I set up a quarter for you tonight at the Center?"

"That won't be necessary," Vata quipped. "I've a colony to manage. I won't be staying the night. Now that you've given your permission, I'll be on my way. Thank you for your time."

"Vata," Eta nearly reached out a hand for her sister's wrist, "you couldn't have troubled a six-hour flight to Tabira to tell me something you could have messaged via communicator. Tell me, are the natives giving you trouble?"

"That's just it," Vata stormed, leaning forward in her seat, "you question our mission. *My* mission. You always have."

"In fact," Eta's voice dropped an octave, "I seem to recall the conversion of the island as my idea."

"An idea that I sought to realize!" Vata nearly cried, then too dropped her voice. "Which I have been carrying out for over two decades. It's my ability you always question."

"Vata, it was your decision to send the girl into confinement…and her brother too, apparently." Eta sighed. "I'm really not sure what else you want from me at the moment."

"She did ask for it…" Vata steeled her gaze as Eta raised a brow. "To avoid marriage, she requested passage. And quite frankly, Eta, no one has given you the right to question everyone's actions. After all, it's meant to be an oligarchy, isn't it? Not a monarchy of ages past."

"Indeed," Eta replied curtly. "I simply have veto power over any oligarchic ruling. The people have elected this process, and me as their leading representative. You know this."

Vata hated this part. That moment when she must back down and accept the fact that her sister truly did make all the rules.

"I believe we need ground officers in Ayam," Vata replied.

Eta quirked a brow. Outside, lightning struck the skies over the Teal Sea. "Are the Kano security officers not sufficient? Have the conversion methods gotten out of hand?" Eta asked.

"Not at all." Vata sat back again. "We and the natives take to our dwellings at night. The afflicted don't climb."

"I see." Eta fiddled with the communicator by her right hand. "And if the affliction is spreading so quickly, why would we require ground officers?"

"To intimidate the locals. They still *refuse* to acquiesce belief in the Zaam, and remain utterly uncivilized. They haven't abandoned the tradition of marriage, yet do not practice monogamy. They are a hypocritical nuisance, especially that spoilt *chief*!"

"Seems to me they will submit one way or another." Eta rose to prepare her own cup of tea. "The affliction will frighten them into agreement, believe me. Though their methods were brutal, the previous oligarchy intimidated the remaining Lirians straight out of Tabira with the Cleansing they carried out."

Vata pondered. "If not ground forces, an economic investment could be beneficial. Ayam children, both male and female, become physically fit from a very young age. Awake at the crack of dawn to hunt, fish, cook, build and weave. The women are expert weavers of diverse materials, and the men can lift heavy loads."

"You're considering setting up a factory?" Eta probed.

"Why not?" Vata almost smiled. "The construction of the island's first Network tower has gone over without much interference at all. The locals actually kept out of the engineers' way when they built it."

"I'm glad to hear it. However, the factories here in Tabira manufacture plenty of clothing for our citizens. Lirian cotton has always sufficed for material."

"I'm sure they do," Vata nodded. "Yet think of what profits could be made from the exotic materials of rainforest greenery."

Eta averted her gaze, seeming to reflect.

Vata spoke up again. "Your first strategy for order with the Code of Decency…was admirable, if unsuccessfully implemented. People need to be controlled in order to thrive. They will fight each other not only for food, but for power as well. Even if properly fed, they will find reasons to skirmish for success and individuality. It is our way. It's a dangerous trait among the masses, and one we must keep in line. In the case of the Ayam, institutionalized labor might just be a necessary addition to the affliction."

Eta finished mixing her tea and returned to her seat.

"Forgive me," Vata went on, "those primitives have me on edge."

"Empires are not built overnight, sister," Eta cooed. "In the case of Ayam, there is only one direction this can go—the same way it went with Lir, Garo, and Opal. With the first two under our constant watch and the third wiped from the face of the Plane—their national identity assimilated into nothing. From the plains to the mountains to the desert to the steppes to the jungle, we have dominated."

Vata almost smiled. "We've come a long way, haven't we? I suppose that Joleh was good for something in the end. Let's just hope we can trust his brother."

"No trouble yet with Samed's work over in Lir," Eta replied. "Nor with Tarel."

"The intelligence officer under Nasin?" Vata frowned.

"She's defected," Eta said. "Or at least that's how I would phrase it. She's now working to gather intelligence for the Kano science division. Needless to say, we're keeping a close eye on her. We could use someone with insider knowledge of Lir—a primary source closer than that of a Tabir Kano officer."

For once, Vata stayed silent, pondering.

Eta continued, "All in all, women have carried Tabira to great heights with this newfound knowledge and order. It's turning into a true golden age, Vata. A power apex with no signs of weakness—not from the other nations, and certainly not from the farce of religion."

"And Father always used to talk of women's lack of importance beyond roles in servitude and pastime." Vata's expression lit up then. "If only he could see us now."

It was decided. Vata would leave the children here and return to Ayam. Until the situation on the island was resolved, even prison proved a safer place for them. Telo wouldn't get back his trophy bride, if Vata had any say on the matter. Ara, well...who knew how his Flightless genes might prove useful in the future, now that the Tabir monarchy had long fallen and with it, the alienation of Hak's kind. Not to mention, she was finally willing to admit to herself the soft spot garnered by years of unconditional love from Ara - a devotion she had never received from anyone else.

With her children secure for the meantime, she would arrange return to the jungle island. She would see through this mission, whether it meant the end of her and every last Ayam native. While Tabira may belong to Eta, Ayam remained entirely Vata's responsibility.

Chapter Nine

Hissing at the sharp twinge in his lower back, Kel turned the corner to the herbal shop.

After nearly a week of suffering a deep ache where that damned Lasha's wave had struck him, the leader of the Evaporation relented and decided to retrieve herbs to soothe the bruising.

"Ah, Kel," the shop owner Edo greeted. "Come by for more goldleaf?"

"Not today." Kel nearly grimaced at the thought of coming clean. "I…I need something for pain."

Edo's wife, Tsal, appeared from the doorway to the back area, carrying a jar of goldleaves for face paint.

"Deki's not here, by the way," she stated bluntly. "He left earlier this afternoon. Did the latest mission fall short?"

Kel frowned. "I'm only here for the pain herbs. And I'm not at liberty to speak about missions. The battle against the water people goes on."

"The grass, then?" Edo offered, turning to the shelf behind him. "Diluted, of course. Not pure."

"Yes, thank you." Kel withdrew two der bills from his vest pocket.

Kel had barely entered his modest flat and closed the door behind him when a pair of bulky arms ambushed him from behind.

Nearly starting, Kel sighed with relief when the grip let up and he turned to see Deki's smiling face, the gold shining softly in the glow from the gaslight.

"Deki!" Kel cried, embracing the other man heartily. "You can't sneak in here, someone might see you!"

"Then let them see!" Deki grinned, placing a shameless kiss on Kel's mouth. "You survived an encounter with the Lasha! You can't simply send a communication like that and expect me not to pay you a surprise visit. And it happened nearly a week ago! Took you long enough to spill the news."

Kel slumped in his chair by the window. In truth, he'd wanted to recover, physically at least, a bit before seeing Deki.

"The mission was unsuccessful," murmured the leader of the Evaporation. "We lost three fine men."

"Fine men?" Deki seemed skeptical as he took his seat in the chair beside Kel's.

His steps shambled, Kel noticed.

"You're using the grass again?" Kel asked bluntly. "And yes, fine men. Or promising anyway."

"Mm," Deki contemplated. "Those of us who are unworthy of the Evaporation must find other means of amusement."

"What happened with the grain business?" Kel wanted to know.

"Those Lirian bastards built their blockade too strong to let any of our men reach Tabira anymore, even on honest business," Deki huffed. "I'd swear, it's as if the border officers are all Lirian these days, the way they guard the checkpoint."

"No luck persuading the Kano patrol?"

"Who knows where their loyalty lies anymore," scowled Deki, turning slightly to face Kel and leaning his chin in his palm. "The water people lived among them for centuries."

"Before they killed a chunk of them and all but exiled the rest," Kel pointed out. "Listen, I'm sure you can convince an officer to take pity. Show him your product, if necessary."

"It's all been tried, believe me," Deki replied with a sigh. "Speaking of which, have you gotten in good with the Kano lately?"

"Hardly," Kel scoffed. "Why?"

"You left the door unlocked," Deki chuckled. "You'd have to have some important people on your side for that sort of confidence."

Kel began to retort that he'd done no such thing, when Deki looked like he wanted to interject something further—before several dark red rivulets poured from his open mouth.

The gas lamp flame revealed the sheen of the blade that had so neatly sliced across Deki's throat, blood pouring from the wound like a small waterfall.

As Deki's still choking, gasping form toppled to the ground, Kel leapt backward from the figure that rose from behind the corpse of his lover.

Belim. Husband of the interpreter Lan and treasurer of Garo. The same man who provided every member of the Evaporation with their weekly, government-funded salary.

"You truly should shed more light in your home." Belim stood perfectly still despite Kel's backing up slowly toward the window nearest to the chair he'd sat in.

Kel steeled his visage, even as furious tears threatened to spring forth.

"Your lover is not the brightest." Belim still held his ground, practically grinning as he cleaned his dagger with a tattered piece of cloth. On his face, he wore no paint.

"When he tries for weeks to bribe the Kano for passage to the west so that he may collect his narcotic products—and then has them escort him back to this very location when Garo curfew comes each night—information like that tends to get back to the treasurer. And a man so often sleeping at the same home that's not his own speaks for itself. Don't you think?"

"You can't prove anything," Kel murmured through gritted teeth as he fixed Belim with a livid stare.

"Kel..." Now Belim did step forward, until he stood directly in front of Kel, not much taller, but enough to loom. "I *am* the one to whom such things must be proven."

"Then why get your hands dirty?" Kel inwardly winced at referring to his own lover's murder so flippantly.

"It seemed like a rich situation," replied Belim nonchalantly, replacing the dagger in the thick belt at his hip. "Pious leader of the Evaporation laying with another man. Forbidden within Garo society since before the written word. Yet you choose willingly to engage in such illicit activities. What will Governor Par have to say?"

Suddenly, Belim drew very close to the freedom fighter, taking his chin in one hand. "I'll let you in on a secret, Kel," he cooed, his shirt still reeking of fresh blood. "Lan is beautiful. It's why I chose her. Those eyes. If the Opal left us with one good thing, it's the influence in the faces of those special few among our women. Surely, even someone like you would have noticed those exotic fair features during your Tabir lessons with her. Even after Garo swore the oath of one woman per man, the decision between my first wife and Lan was simple.

"But even with Lan, I've never been fond of looking at her in the midst of it. They're much better with face flat—where they can't see what's coming next. Completely at your mercy. Were you and your man the same way? Did you make him lie flat while you showed him how a true warrior fights for freedom?"

Belim's reputation for intimidation didn't precede him, Kel had to admit. Then again, neither did Kel's reputation for resourcefulness.

The fact that the treasurer stood close enough for the hilt of his belted dagger to press against Kel's hip provided the necessary leverage.

He now knew the exact location of his new weapon.

In one swift motion, Kel suspended all self-doubt and raised his hand to grab the wide knife by its handle, stepping back a stride before holding it outward at the ready.

"A fighter, indeed." Belim simply raised a finger to the communicator at his ear. "You should really thank my sparing your little friend a slow, humiliating death on a spectacle stage."

Kel didn't move.

"I've caught the terrorist." Belim's lazy smile as he released the button on the communicator instantly chilled the freedom fighter. "Surely you'll also have a plan for managing the backup I've brought?"

In the next instant, a team of five men burst through Kel's front door.

Kano officers.

If there was any justice in this world...

"He murdered a man!" Kel shouted as loud as he could, even as the officers raced to take hold of him. "Look for yourself!"

One of the officers went over to check the body. "How did this happen?"

"Most unfortunately, this zealot seems to have sacrificed him to the Zaam." Belim turned gleefully to Kel. "For luring you to him for temptations of the flesh, isn't that right?"

Kel had a fairly solid understanding of genetic evidence collection at crime scenes, and was about to shout at the officers again...before he laid eyes on Belim's gloved hands.

In all seriousness, Kel doubted that Tabir would have bothered with a criminal investigation involving a Garo murder, anyway. Best keep quiet for now and wait until he was rid of the sight of Belim's horrible face and could think more clearly.

"Thank you for reporting this, treasurer," the officer who had examined the body acknowledged. "Let's get him out of here."

"I do not fear your Tabir prisons," Kel murmured, though in truth he knew little of them. He was still reeling from the shock of Deki's death to even form any truly coherent thoughts at the moment.

"We don't get involved in the skirmishes of steppehorses," one of the other officers said as he went to grab the knife from Kel, who raised it to his own throat. "I thought fire was more your suicidal weapon of choice," sneered the officer, raising a pistol to Kel's forehead, until he finally dropped the knife with a clatter.

All because those wretched Lasha had the Kano under their thumb. He somehow suspected that if a Lirian had been murdered, the Kano would have investigated. The 'civilized' Lir from whom the Tabir imported useful technology.

The time had not yet come to take his own life. He would wait for the honorable moment to do so.

He would handle Belim, and avenge Deki.

Governor Par often wondered if he'd have more pleasant dreams with the serpent at his side. His late wife had always cautioned him against it, especially with their young daughter in the house.

Then she had succumbed to the growth disease, before the Tabir found a cure. Never desiring a second wife even before the acquiescence of polygamy, Par's bitterness had begun to well after the death of his daughter's mother.

When his six-year-old daughter, Hiti, perished in a shootout at his home, not six weeks into his term as governor, the bitterness had simmered into a rage.

How he marveled at the way Lir called out the Garo as terrorists…

Following his daughter's murder, the name Hiti had gone to his pet snake. Having reared the creature from the time of her hatching, Par took great pride in having tamed the venomous viper against harming him.

This breed was native to both the desert and the steppes, feared by inhabitants of each region. These days, such a formidable confidant served well in putting dissidents off their guard during political discussions.

Par sighed.

The people had elected him, and still the Lir insisted that he sought only to sic the terrorists on them. Never mind that the Lasha's very presence deprived the lands of much of their water. Even their advanced hydrotechnology had more to offer than they shared with the Garo. Par was sure of it.

Barely a year into living as an established nation on Garo land, and the invaders still weren't satisfied. They expected the Garo to simply lie down and accept occupation. When the Lirians encountered resistance, they lashed out, killing a child—*his* child—in the process.

The sweat beaded on his forehead as his mind roused halfway from another nightmare of her horrified face, three tiny bullets having pierced her forehead. Her death had been quick, yet surely not painless…

No, it wasn't enough that they had the Lasha. For nearly two decades, they had also harbored that Rohem—a man with strange and terrible power. A man unhindered by flame.
More than the hydrotechnology and the Lasha, that *thing* was the true weapon. If only the Zaam would grant the Garo such a unique gift. Instead, his people had come to rely on the power—

even the worship—of fire. An element that could either help living things to thrive or kill them instantly.

Such ideas dawned on Par while he dozed half asleep—only this realization came as solid as a rock. The Garo had spent so many years fearing the creature immune to fire. With him out of the equation, the Lasha could be easily picked off. After all, that Nasin was pretty much an old woman by now, surely weakened by age.

Nasin. He nearly scoffed. She had approached him with an apology the day following his daughter's murder, insisting that her intelligence officers had acted against her knowledge.

How convenient.

But how to mitigate Rohem as a threat? He fed off of heat, off of light. So take the light away. Trap him in the dark. Trick him, if need be.

Nothing and no one was ever completely invulnerable.

The buzz of his communicator roused Par completely from his thoughts.

Within minutes, the governor had stumbled his way down to his office to receive the captive.

Kel.

"Why have you brought him?" Par asked sharply, now fully awake.

The officer he knew as Samed stepped forward, as his partner continued holding a pistol to Kel's head. Beside them both, his treasurer Belim beamed.

"Please Governor…" began Samed.

"Allow me, officer," Belim interrupted smoothly. "My Governor, I will avoid wasting any more of your rest time, and get down to the point. I have caught Kel red-handed in the arms of his fellow man."

Par resisted the urge to clench a fist as Belim's words settled in.

Stepping forward, Par closed the distance between himself and his best freedom fighter—the very leader of their great Evaporation.

"Do you deny it?" he asked roughly.

"I do not," Kel answered after a brief pause, eyes level with Par's. "As I do not deny that Belim murdered Deki in cold blood."

"Deki," Belim scoffed. "Your lover. The other transgressor."

The bastard didn't even try to deny it. Not in front of the proper audience.

"Leave us now," Par interjected at Belim and the officers. "All of you."

After nodding, the two officers exited the room, followed haltingly by Belim, who caught Kel's gaze a final time before his departure.

"You are my best fighter," Par hissed lowly. "The pride and joy of our struggle against the occupation."

Kel lowered his gaze.

"You deserve death for your actions," Par continued. "You have disgraced the Zaam and defaced your name."

Kel remained silent.

"Yet we both know the Evaporation cannot go on without you. Not without a regroup and retraining of many men, and we cannot afford such a delay in tactical procedures. Not with the creatures the Lir have at their disposal."

"My Governor…" Kel began, before Par cut him off again.

"You shall live, on one condition."

"Anything." Kel nearly brightened, hoping beyond hope for a mission into Lir. A chance to take out the Lirian weapons, beginning with those Lasha.

"You have the next two weeks to train a new fighter. A young fighter, worthy of taking their own life to liberate hundreds more."

"Of course." Kel inclined his head. "Thank you, Governor."

"Kel," Par started again, "I would suggest against any ideas of revenge. Belim is not to be underestimated."

"Governor." Kel nodded respectfully.

Activating the microcommunicator on his desk, Par spoke. "Two guards are needed to escort a prisoner."

Then, to Kel, "For tonight. Tomorrow, you meet your new ward."

The head freedom fighter set his jaw in an effort to maintain a stoic expression. With the new man assigned to him, Kel steeled his resolve to carry out a successful mission and redeem the disgrace upon both his and Deki's names—not only in the eyes of his governor but of the Zaam as well.

Once the guards had taken Kel down to his cell, Governor Par decided the night didn't have to be fruitless, after all.

"I require a sleep companion for tonight. Have her sent to my quarter," he ordered over his communicator to Yote, head courier of the provincial service.

With that, he rose to settle into bed with an air of decision.

Kel's new mission would invoke a greater response than any they had attempted before, he felt sure of it. Tabir and Lirians alike would finally understand how far the Garo were willing to go.

This called for celebration.

The following morning, the bright sun glaring into his eyes served as the first reminder that he hadn't slept in his own bed. The second reminder came in the form of the rock-hard surface on which he lay.

Sitting up shakily, Kel groaned against the flood of memories that assaulted him from the night before.

Deki was dead. Gone forever. Butchered by a fellow Garo. A death without honor.

And Kel had refused to let himself feel the full guilt of it until after he'd taken revenge on both the Lirians and Par's treasurer.

Kel's stomach gave a sour lurch as he struggled to sit up against the harsh light.

The third reminder of how much his life had turned upside down in the past half day peered down at him. A young girl of about six, large hazel eyes set in an unassuming visage.

"I am Unno," the girl spoke in a high voice, like a bell. "Forgive my face, they say I am too young for the paint."

"Are you throwing children in prison now?" Kel called out nastily to the guard that now stood just outside the cell.

The clinking of the lock must have been what had ultimately roused him.

"I am not a prisoner," the girl Unno uttered with an air of greater clarity than he would have expected from one of her age. "I am your ward."

"Sorry to wake you up," taunted the guard, as he passed Unno to take Kel by the shoulder. "The governor says you're free to go. Take the girl and get out."

Chapter Ten

Samed had barely a few hours to sleep before duty called him once again.

A man murdered one night and the very next morning, the same governor who called to have the body taken away now evidently required assistance with a monthly diplomatic meeting.

With the Lirians, of course.

If he'd looked tired last night, the governor looked haggard and somehow jovial all at once.

"Good morning, Officer," he greeted in accented Tabir, the incense still wafting off of him following morning prayer at his home shrine. "Thank you for your presence. As you know, Garo custom dictates that a woman shall not visit alone with a man who is not her family unless she wears the paint. Our young diplomat refuses, and thus, she requires an escort."

"There were no Lirian men to accompany her?" Samed ventured. "Is it the younger Lasha?"

"Thank Echil, no," Par scoffed, taking a seat at his desk as Samed entered close behind him. "From what we gather, martial activity is more the young Lasha's area of expertise. It's the other one. Nasin wanted to send that Rohem as escort, but I informed her I would only accept an actual man. But at least today's diplomat is succulent to the eye."

He murmured the last sentence, and Samed had to admit the extent of the governor's Tabir vocabulary impressed him.

Then the guest would be Oria, the Lirian he'd met not a week ago outside the city gates. He assumed Par's comment referred to the young woman's fairly round shape.

Samed shifted uncomfortably before taking up stance beside the governor's desk, turning to face the entryway just in time for their latest arrival.

Indeed, Oria walked through the doorway with an air of ease. Chin held high and back straight, she strode in and sat down before Par, as if she'd done so many times.

Samed had to wonder if she was putting on a show simply for Par or for both of them. A moment later, the interpreter, Lan, who stood beside the Lirian's chair, joined Oria.

Just as Par opened his mouth for a formal greeting, Oria held up a hand. "Greetings, Governor Par. I ask that you don't shower me with empty wishes from the Zaam. I intend only to express how things will go from now on. I am not Nasin, and I have no patience for diplomacy when the other side has malicious intentions. We know that you set our aircraft alight, just as the group of freedom fighters set themselves on fire at the border last month. Since one of our own discovered your men running around in terror tunnels leading to our reservoir, we now know for certain what your tactics are."

Samed tensed, and Par let out a low whistle. He almost wished he'd bothered to bring out the serpent. If only the sight of such a woman didn't contrast so hilariously with her words.

"Brave, aren't we?" Par drawled in Lirian. "If you don't mind, I will speak your language. Your Garo accent is harsh on the ears. Girl, you have a lot of courage, considering none of those creatures walk beside you. Have you perhaps been training?"

Oria replied smoothly, "This will not go down lightly. If it were up to me, I would dispense with the peacekeeping altogether. They are needless talks."

"Indeed." Par folded his hands before him on the desk and leaned forward. "Why talk when you can spend all day eating?"

Samed nearly rolled his eyes. That was perhaps the most childish comment he'd ever heard leave the mouth of a politician.

Oria seemed at a loss, but retained her masked expression.

"Then again," Par went on, "maybe you train with the Rohem. I bet even your Lasha fear him. Tell me, haven't you ever wondered what life would be like if the Lir didn't have such advantages? Such powerful individuals? Someone like you might even have a chance at assuming a position of power."

Oria pursed her lips. She truly hadn't expected Par to even speak Lirian so well, much less make a remark about her appearance.

May as well pretend it was a remark from her grandmother. Nothing more. Despite her minor setback, she had watched his features carefully. When she mentioned the attack, his eyes had flashed ever so slightly.

That was all the confession she needed.

"The Lirian people feel safe with Rohem, just as they have selected Nasin as democratic adviser for the past three terms. The Tabir have re-elected Mak Eta just the same for the past fifteen years. Meanwhile, Garo leaders serve terms of ten years."

Not to mention the Lirians had experienced more terror under Par than any preceding Garo governor.

Par's dark gaze was unmoving. "We are not speaking of Garo or Tabira. Though perhaps a sense of security comes with having a powerful leader," he conceded. "The Lasha may well be dependable, if also intimidating. The creature, however, is not of Lir. How can Lir trust an outsider of such immense power?"

Although her interpretation skills were clearly unnecessary here, Lan stayed. Samed wondered if the Garo woman wanted to see how the meeting played out. Under that gold face paint, who could tell? Still, the Tabir officer appreciated her interpretation for his own sake. Very possibly, the Garo wanted to give the impression of transparency, where Tabira was concerned.

One thing was for certain, however. Par had just admitted his intentions, a revelation he would have been unlikely to utter in front of Nasin.

Steadying her voice, Oria stated in no uncertain terms, "You want to take down Rohem."

After a fleeting stretch of expressionless features, Par's half-smile widened to a near grin.

"Your knowledge of tactics does impress," the governor allowed. "Fighting fire with fire. A strategy I would expect any intelligence professional to recognize."

"Burning innocents as you have done for years is no intelligence tactic." Oria stood up then. "It's a disgrace. It's murder. And yet you play the victim. How can a people of such allegedly solid faith commit such atrocities?"

"In fact," Par now rose in kind, "the Garo pray that the world be rid of occupiers such as yourselves. It will make a safer Plane for everyone. For all of us *regular* people."

"A prayer, indeed." Oria strode out of the room and past Samed, quipping in Tabir, "Good day, Officer."

Once she had departed the office, Belim emerged from the adjoining suite. "So you are intent on taking out that thing? Plan to lead another operation?"

"Attacking from underground right by their reservoir was foolish. We can use one of the old tunnels that burrow directly beneath the city wall. From long before the Illumination."

"Before the Tabir decided to civilize the world and share all their secrets with the Lir," Belim presumed to finish for the governor.

"Indeed," Par continued. "It's time for another plain-sight demonstration."

"Location?" Belim raised his eyebrows.

"Wherever *he* is," Par replied. "You know other men willing to self-sacrifice."

"A good several," nodded Belim. "They have trained with Kel, but he didn't deem them fit enough for the latest underground mission."

Par went on, "The girl, Oria, is religious, so we can count on her to be at the temple tonight at the same time we hold services. If we find her, the creature shouldn't be far behind."

"Governor," Belim cautioned, "what if the flame—even at such a high capacity—proves futile?"

"The fire will simply be a ploy," Par elaborated. "I want a group of men waiting behind the temple as well. Once the authorities are occupied with extinguishing the fire, the hidden group will capture the Rohem. Twelve should be sufficient for that role. Researching Tabir archives has its benefits. If he is kept in the dark, his power fades."

***

Later that afternoon, both Thia and Rohem joined Oria following her daily visit to the city temple. When Oria inquired as to the purpose, Rohem simply replied that he needed a break from studying. "And I need some time to reflect," Thia explained. "Perhaps I'll pledge to the Zaam after all. People of the Plane certainly aren't that wondrous."

Oria sighed. Although she felt for Thia regarding the parting from Walar, Oria truly believed that her friend deserved someone who didn't fixate on small details such as gender. In spite of the faithful's shared hesitance toward accepting two women or two men who loved one another, Oria respected the ways of those who chose such partnerships.

Closing her eyes and crossing her wrists over her chest so her palms touched her shoulders, Oria knelt in prayer to the Zaam, Echil.

As with many Plane people of the various nations who worshipped the Zaam, Oria considered Echil the most trustworthy. The tales of old bespoke of her kind lessons and guiding words to the first people of the Plane.

Every small statue—akin to the wooden idol to which she now prayed—portrayed Echil as a curvaceous figure with painted-on black hair and large, all-seeing white eyes. As with most renditions, she bore no limbs and her face stood out from her brown body with a dark blue hue.

"So..." Gether smiled as Rohem entered his office following the exam. "How did it feel?"

"If only I had a photographic memory, I could tell you for certain," Rohem replied. "The chemistry section took some time. Then there was a great deal of analyzing the fine details in the images, especially when it came to the brain. But I'm pretty confident it paid off."

"Excellent." The doctor handed Rohem a stack of paper. "Here's your application for the apprenticeship."

"Thank you, Gether." Rohem beamed. "I'll finish them here, if you don't mind. I'm going to meet Thia and Oria at the temple in a while."

"Has Oria converted you two?" Gether asked with a hint of mirth.

"We've been meeting her there every day this week after studies and training. I find the temple…peaceful." Rohem settled on the term.

Gether nodded. "You two are good for her. Nasin schooled you all well. Avithia's never had much patience for academia or the sciences—it's always been about the heat of the moment, the thrill of combat. I suppose it's not a setback for someone of her nature. It's a shame not everyone can see it the way you and Oria do."

"You mean Walar." Rohem felt it safe to assume the doctor knew. "I remember when they first met. He visited Lir to take a course in the sciences and see how he liked the atmosphere here. Avithia said he'd commented on the lack of resources for a proper education."

"I was a young man once," the doctor said almost wistfully. "We learn in time—both how to make the most of our environment and appreciate those we keep in our lives. Speaking of which, what about you?"

"Me?" Rohem asked, thinking Gether was again referring to the apprenticeship.

"Yes. Any romantic prospects?"

Rohem nearly laughed aloud. "Gether, you should know by now that there are so few of us in the medical course as is. Otherwise, it's just my family at the compound. I've never had reason to think of anything else. Medical studies leave little time for fun besides flying the glider with Avithia. And well, until our engineers manufacture new ones, our last glider's gone…"

"So all the more reason to find diversion elsewhere." Gether chuckled.

"Or more free time to ponder a specialty."

"Hm." Gether nodded. "The other lead physicians and I have compiled a list that we will begin implementing into the apprenticeship beginning within the next several months. Still set on radio imaging?"

Rohem smiled, then thought of the pressing question he'd been increasingly anxious to pose. "Of course. Speaking of imaging…Have...have the results of the x-ray come in?"

"Ah." Gether strode over to his large imaging cube. "The infamous x-ray."

Rohem followed the doctor's movement closely with his eyes.

Gether turned on the large imaging cube, displaying the graphic of a full-body skeletal frame. "Took us long enough, that's for certain. But as much as this might disappoint, you are completely normal, as far as we can figure. No abnormalities, at least not so far as our imagers show. Your weekly radiation output checks have cleared as well. Zero, as per usual."

"So no conjectures as to the cause of the heat absorption? Or the lack of necessity for nourishment?"

Gether smiled again, wrinkles gracing the corners of his eyes. "If I were religious, I'd say it was a divine gift against our fire-happy neighbors."

"I was so apprehensive about the imaging," Rohem mused. "Now it seems as if there's nothing to worry about."

"It's only been a few decades since the Illumination and emergence of all the technology from Tabira," Gether pointed out. "Currently, we don't even know what causes the Lasha gene. Only that Lasha biology can sustain bodily processes, heightened cellular immunity and remarkably enhanced muscular proteins for several weeks without food, so long as around half a liter of water is consumed daily. Like a dunehorse, as much as I hate to draw comparisons often used by the Tabir. With you, it seems that sunlight remains your sole source of energy."

"Like photosynthesis in plants," Rohem remarked. "And the physical strength, the healing..."

"Let's hope time will tell," the doctor replied. "A fine specimen and ripe curiosity to go along with it. You've certainly chosen the right field."

The temple sat quietly, a sparse number of occupants entering and exiting the spherical, flat-roofed building.

Inside, the shrine stood colorfully at the temple's center, awash in parchment streamers of vibrant red, gold and black.

Flanked by Thia and Rohem, Oria knelt at the man-high wooden platform that supported the shrine, topped by the last surviving copy of the Sen scripture, reputed holy word of the Zaam. Closing her eyes, she mouthed Echil's name in respectful acknowledgment of the Zaam idol figurine and placed the Lash, a small offering of water, at the base of the black streamer to conclude the evening prayer.

To the left of the evening offerings, other various morsels lay strewn atop the red streamer of sunrise and the gold of midday, all colors slightly dimmed by the soft glow of the ceiling lantern above.

Once Oria had concluded her prayer for the discovery of the Great Oasis, the three donned their shoes and exited the temple into the soft, twinkling torchlight of the quiet night.

Around them, a flurry of children scattered, laughing loudly.

Oria sighed impatiently. "Let's hope the temples keep better watch over the offerings this time. Yesterday, nearly all the food had been snatched between afternoon and evening prayer."

"Nasin's latest reports verify zero percent homelessness." Rohem frowned. "They shouldn't be hungry."

“Not hungry,” Oria huffed. “They have families, just no respect.”

Overhead, silvery clouds passed by the colossal megalith that stood overlooking the city in silence.

Just then, an utterly bizarre sensation befell Rohem, as if every nerve in his body stood on end. Rigidly, he turned first toward the darkened, wind-rippled dunes to the west, and then to the great obelisk in the east.

When he opened his mouth to ask if the two women had seen anything, his thoughts were interrupted by a buzz from his communicator.

“Rohem!” came Gether’s excited bass from the speaker. “The exam results are in! The academy has officiated you for an apprenticeship!”

With a garbled shout of joy, Thia leapt upon Rohem, and Oria soon followed suit.

“Well done.” Thia grinned. “Just promise us you won’t go off to some clinic in Tabira.”

“And miss the chance to work with your father?” Rohem smiled. “Never.”

***

Upon arrival back to the home compound one block over, Oria was the last to enter.

When someone spoke from behind, she nearly gasped aloud.

“I am sorry about earlier.” Turning, Oria wasn’t entirely pleased to see Samed for the second time today.

“Do you have business here?” Rohem asked, before Oria waved him off.

“Samed acted as escort for me today with Par,” Oria explained. “I won’t be a minute.”

Once they were alone, Samed took a breath. “You handled yourself well.”

Oria never broke his gaze.

“I saw you returning from the temple…”

“Why were you inside the gates?” Oria asked suspiciously.

“We walk the streets along with Lirian officers, you know that.” Samed replied, not unkindly. “I wasn’t following you, if that’s what you’re wondering.”

"You speak Lirian well," Oria observed.

"I make a point of studying the language of those with whom I work."

Oria smiled bitterly. "Don't you work with the Tabir?"

"On paper," Samed replied. "However, I've spent nearly the past twenty years in Lir. Besides, there's not much tying me to Tabira anymore. I've received news today—my brother, Joleh, has passed."

Oria opened her mouth to express condolences, and then settled on an inclination of her head.

"In prison, just one week ago. The news came late this morning. I expect Rohem will be pleased," Samed added dryly.

"I won't tell him," Oria quipped. "He doesn't need to know. I offer my regret for you, but it doesn't concern any of us, Rohem included."

"I suppose not." Samed nodded once. "Very well. Pleasant night, Oria. Echil lent you strength today."

"Impressive knowledge of the Zaam as well," Oria murmured. "You *have* lived away from Tabira for a while."

Samed smiled lightly. "Just a firm believer that we should draw strength from wherever we can find it."

Just then, a shrill scream sounded from the direction of the temple.

Not moments later, the scent reached them.

"Smoke! It's a fire!" Thia cried from inside. "Oria, get in here! It's already rising. Rohem saw it from the top level!"

Carrying the large hydrotank and nozzle buffer on her back, Thia brushed past Samed and Oria to re-enter the street outside.

Samed instantly regretted not having a dunemobile at hand today. Once they'd rounded the final block, they saw the men—it looked like a group of six—all alight. They wailed in pain, struggling to mask their mangled cries as praises to the Zaam.

"Death to the creature!" shouted the last one to burn before his lips melted beyond the ability to speak.

Before them, the foundation of the temple had begun to crumble. They must have doused the base of the building and themselves in petrol before igniting everything.

Though he'd cleaned up after plenty of staged protests involving auto-ignition, Samed had never seen such a demonstration up close—nor had he heard the agonized cries of both victim and martyr.

"Rohem!" Thia barked, as he ran to help. "Check inside. I'll let you know if I need any absorption around the perimeter."

With that, the Lasha made a mad dash around the back of the building as Rohem sprinted toward the still-flaming temple entrance to track down any civilians stranded within.

Thank whatever oversaw the Plane for the compound's proximity to the temple.

Even as Thia charged at the flames with her tank, Rohem grabbed Oria by the arm roughly, holding her at bay while she broke down in tears over the horrendous scene.

The group of Garo men who charged out from behind the flaming temple just then found themselves thrown backward in an unexpected deluge from the hydroweapon.

Gulping at the acrid scent of burning flesh, Samed spoke into his communicator.

"Requesting backup. Garo militants have breached the city perimeter. We have a Lirian temple on fire."

His brother Joleh had died by fire—in the electrical rays of the high-voltage containment field. Leapt right into the thick of the charge while the night guard had stepped out.

Once again, fire had been employed for suicide.

The Tabir officer knew he would see the peeling white, blood-red, and eventually blackened flesh of those men's faces for many a night to come.

Once inside the temple, Rohem glanced around for signs of movement amidst the roiling black smoke and flickering flames.

Already, the fire was licking its way along the rows of seats at the room's center, spreading quickly toward the idol of Echil on the far side by the temple's only window.

Rohem's ears registered the tiny whimper and cough seconds before spotting the small form crouched in the corner to the right of the idol platform. Huddled with his hands over his mouth, the young boy caught sight of Rohem with wide eyes.

Ignoring the slight sting of the smoke, Rohem repressed a blink as he closed the distance to the far wall as fast as possible. Scooting away from the flames that now covered the statue of Echil atop the podium, the boy watched in silent fascination as Rohem cleared a pathway through the blaze, absorbing the heat and dousing the fire with every step.

Raising his voice over the fire that raged even louder outside, Rohem swiftly knelt before the boy. “Are you hurt?”

With a slight gasp, the boy managed, “I can walk.”

The boy yelped, and even Rohem almost jumped at the booming whoosh from beyond the slightly open window. In the next moment, several streams of water sprayed into the temple, hinting at the deluge taking place on the other side of the wall.

Thia had activated the hydroblaster.

Once he’d stood up, Rohem clasped the boy’s shoulder and guided him urgently toward the exit, glancing around a final time. “Was anyone here with you?”

“I came alone,” the boy nearly shouted as they reached the temple entrance.

Rohem reasoned he must have visited the temple looking for food at the offering platform.

With a quick wave of Rohem’s hand, the thin layer of flame that surrounded the threshold slowly dissipated, and he gently pushed the boy out of the temple and back into the fresh, clear night.

Turning around, the child gazed up at Rohem, his mouth slightly ajar. Soot covered his dusky cheeks, eyes shining more with curiosity than fear in the lights from the businesses across the street.

Before Rohem could even ask after his health, the little boy took off down the street, disappearing into the sparse groups of onlookers.

Chapter Eleven

Ara's belly somersaulted dangerously with every sudden drop of the giant glider around them.

Trapped in nearly pitch black for what seemed like hours now, he assumed that the officers had tossed them into some sort of cargo hold. Their first time aboard the famed Tabir flying machine held no thrill—only fear and sickness.

Beside Ara, Inad seemed to fight to keep her own gut at bay, coughing here and there.

The miserable feeling had taken hold almost as soon as the sleeping fumes wore off about an hour ago. Queasiness and an ache throughout his entire body from whatever those officers had used to knock him out overwhelmed his senses.

This was one of those few times he supposed his sister's self-monitoring eating habits paid off—nothing to come up. Swallowing fervently, he shifted slightly against an uncomfortably full bladder.

"Are you all right?" Ara asked weakly, anticipating the response.

"He took my dagger," Inad grumbled just loud enough to hear over the humming engines. "If I'd had my dagger, they couldn't have taken us."

"Slim chance," Ara replied. "You're great with a knife and all, but there were three officers."

Inad screamed inwardly for not dragging herself free of Telo's dwelling as soon as the chief had left. Even given the dangers of nightfall, she could have surely sought refuge somewhere else. Instead, she'd lain pathetically on the hut floor and allowed herself to be captured.

"Any idea where they're taking us?" Ara asked, pulling Inad from her inner tirade. "Can I know what actually happened? They're taking me now too. Seems fair."

Inad sighed and rolled over to face the sound of her brother's voice in the dark. "I…attacked Telo. To stop him from taking me."

Inad hastily added the last bit when she practically felt her brother take a hysteric breath.

"You are truly afraid of him." It wasn't a question.

"It's how the Curse spreads," murmured his sister. "Through lying together. So yes, I am afraid—but not of him. Of becoming one of *them*."

"Then I guess we're headed to prison," Ara scoffed. "What a way to finally see Tabira."

He drew another deep breath, drawing up his knees where he lay staring into the blackness.

APEX FIVE

"Still think you can fly us out of this?" Inad sounded as if she were willing some mirth into her voice.

Just then, the glider took another small but sickening dip, and Ara gulped.

Taking a deep breath, Inad rolled onto her back as the belly of the airship began to produce a keening whine.

"Maybe, only this thing has wings that can fly," Ara muttered.

Every now and then, Inad hissed softly as each jerk and roll of the hard floor beneath them aggravated the ache at the back of her injured neck.

She soon realized she must have dozed off again, and perhaps hadn't fully woken yet.

Drifting in and out of a haze, Inad soon realized a melody kept playing over in her mind. An old Ayam lullaby Maru used to sing to the very small children during afternoon nap time.

As the bird sings,
So the palm cat growls
The river flows and the trees grow.
For all this life, we give thanks
To the Light.

The first sign of light she noticed appeared in the form of light green circles that slowly grew larger.

Two eyes with lined pupils. The eyes of a palm cat.

The palm cats were all gone…she must be dreaming.

Just then, the cat opened its jaws wide with a yowl, and Inad snapped awake to the dark cabin of the glider.

Within the next few minutes and several jolts later, the glider touched down onto ground once again.

As the machine came to a grinding halt, the engines died, leaving the two cargos in black silence.

"Where do you suppose Mother is?" Ara asked as the hatch opened and two of the officers pulled them out.

"If either of you puked in here," one of them stated, grasping Inad by her shoulder and pulling her out through the small opening, as the other followed suit with her brother, "I don't care who your mother is. *You* will be the ones cleaning it up."

Squinting against the bright light of first the glider's interior, and then swallowing her initial panic of venturing outside after nightfall, Inad glanced around wildly.

Once outside, Inad closed her eyes against the brisk, dry breeze that struck her face.

They no longer faced the dangers of the rainforest—of the Cursed. Yet the roar from countless aircraft, shrieking of automobiles, shouting men, and crying children could have driven her mad.

Overhead and several dozen meters away, an extremely long and loud automobile passed atop a road built on a high bridge. Above even the bridge, a massive cube of moving pictures stood bright against the black sky.

Even in the dark of night, she could see the crowded streets full of people wearing clothing like her mother wore. As they approached what she assumed to be the prison, she marveled at the great glowing megalith that extended high into the night sky, beyond even where the aircraft circled.

If anything, the many other lights from the city only added to that of the tall tower, so bright it barely seemed like dusk.

Still handcuffed, the Flightless of Ayam were hustled up the steps to the Capital Center and pushed through the sliding double doors.

Once inside, Inad's senses calmed a fraction, though her eyes still smarted terribly.

They had barely crossed the front area when she nearly cried out at a commotion to her right. One of the fabled hounds of Tabira barked ferociously in their direction, tied by its neck to a tall metal pole that was rooted to the ground. Inad turned away quickly, she and Ara sprinting to follow the guards away from the wide-eyed animal.

After turning several corners of drab grey, cold interior, the guards steered them into a tiny room. When one of the men pressed a button, the entire room lurched, and Inad fought the urge to grab onto her brother. Ara, for his part, clutched at the wall beside him, despite its completely flat surface.

The guards just chuckled.

Mercifully, several moments later, the doors opened. The men then shoved Ara and Inad across another hallway and into a room with a wooden desk at its center.

At the desk sat a slender woman with nearly completely silver hair. As soon as they entered, she eyed the newcomers like a bird surveying its prey.

"Good evening, children," the woman before them greeted stonily with a clearly forced smile.

Children, indeed.

So this was their Aunt Eta. Inad recognized her from the few images she had seen on their mother's data cube. Quaint.

"Where is our mother?" Ara asked insistently.

Inad resisted the urge to slam her face into the desk. Or transform into a palm cat and make a swift escape—only to get pummeled by one of those automobiles outside.

Best to stay put, if just for the moment.

"Your mother could not make an appearance," Eta replied.

In truth, the Mak contemplated whether to reinforce her nephew's wrist restraints with a straight jacket to encase his wings.

Although she'd never laid eyes on a person with wings, she trusted her sister with the possibility that the young man before her might just be the exception.

"Then she accompanied us here?" Ara pressed.

For Zaam's sake, give it up! She doesn't care about us! Inad wanted to scream, nearly verbalizing what would have been her first curse ever uttered.

"Do you know why you are here?" continued Eta, gaze shifting between her niece and nephew.

Just then, Inad decided to do the opposite of what her mother would have dictated, yet always chose to do herself.

She followed her instinct.

In a foreign land with no one by her side but her sibling, she decided to invite her brother to retreat to something familiar. *"Did you see those screaming machines out there, Brother?"* Inad turned to Ara as she lapsed into Ayam.

Initially at a loss, Ara soon grinned.

"Terrifying. And my wings ache terribly from the extra ties. I wonder when we can have true sleep in a soft hammock or bed. I suppose we will not rest well in prison."

By now, Eta glanced past the Flightless to her guard, who stood by the door.

"Nojeh, I've seen your linguistics profile. Translate please."

“Forgive me, Governor.” he averted his gaze. “Lirian was always a forte of mine, but the Ayam language eludes me. I only ever visited the island once, years ago.”

“Really,” Eta huffed. “They’ve grown up on that *island*—don’t we have anyone to translate this savage tongue?”

Besides her sister, of course. Vata had expressly refused to see either of her children for the time being.

Just then, the girl bolted forth, coming nose-to-nose with Eta and slamming one forearm on the desk, brandishing her shelled marriage necklace with the opposite hand.

“I am the wife of the great Chief Telo. The beasts that roam our home will come for you all like palm cats catching fish. Then our warriors will cut you down!”

Then for full savage warrior effect, Inad let loose with the battle call. The shrill, vibrating cry uttered through rounded lips, chillingly primal to any non-Ayam—if her mother’s opinion was anything to go by.

Inad hardly noticed the quick gesture Eta made toward her guard by the door, who withdrew a long black cylinder from his belt.

The look on her aunt’s face was definitely worth the bone-rattling current that shot through every fiber of her being in the next moment, rendering reality into darkness.

***

Samed slept restlessly.

Halfway between alertness and slumber, he recalled his last conversation with his brother—and what would now serve as their final interaction before Joleh’s death.

“She will come back,” he’d strained out through a gasp of pain as the field’s current shuddered through him.

“Don’t touch the field!” Samed had shouted.

Joleh let out an insane cackle, falling to his knees. “It’s a glorious field! The true field is one we can’t see!”

“You know mother is gone.” Samed had tried desperately to calm his brother who was now scratching at his own ear hard enough to draw blood. “She can’t hurt us anymore.”

“She *is* dead, isn’t she? Good thing, too.” Joleh had suddenly stared off into space. “Better fortune with beings not of this Plane. Of the great starry void beyond.”

Samed had to wonder if his brother's recent descent into madness originated from age, if it had always been there, or if perhaps they were feeding him drugs here in his cell. Ever since Joleh's second imprisonment, his ability to hold a steady conversation had drifted considerably.

"Joleh," Samed had whispered, inching as close as he dared to the force field barrier marked in red on the floor, "tell me. You can tell me—do they prick you? Do they give you medicine here?"

"No, Tabir medicine would be wasted on me." Joleh grinned up at his brother, who knelt down to look at him in the eyes. "Medicine, automobiles, all the technology of this new age. The Illumination! It won't be used to benefit the poor—a prisoner? *Forget* it."

A stark cold chill struck Samed just then. The realization that he might never be able to lay a hand on his brother's living body ever again.

"You always took the brunt of her anger," Samed murmured to himself more than to the man facing him. "I am...sorry for that."

"You were a child," Joleh replied, and such logic would have made more sense had Samed not learned what his brother had likely gotten up to with that orphan he'd kept. "Mother was a sorry woman. Always screaming, she was. The Kano command taught us to read and kill well, but they screamed too. Best thing to come out of it was me finally getting over that awful stammer. But still, that need for *prestige* seems to be everywhere. So I found better people—more subdued, worthy of attention...but they all expect unquestioning fascination, don't they? It's all about a person's self-worth in the end."

"Validation." Samed nodded, trying to quell the steadily rising ember of hope that he might succeed at a normal conversation with his brother—one that did not erode into delusional rambling of which he understood little. "Everyone on this Plane thrives on validation, no doubt about that."

Joleh fixed him with a stony gaze just then. "And beyond the Plane."

At Samed's inquiring frown, Joleh elaborated, "Everything must have its limit, they say. What if it doesn't have to?"

Then, Joleh glanced upward, seeing but not really seeing. "It's always there, isn't it? You always excelled. You and your data cubes. Practically *invented* the Kano's computing and satek initiative, all while still in training."

"There is still much we don't know about data systems," Samed pointed out. "Even less about satek and the potential of artificial intelligence. Besides, that opportunity exists for anyone who joins the Kano—the chance for a solid education, regardless of natural talent. Getting out of Mother's home and enlisting showed great promise for us both."

Joleh continued as if uninterrupted. "But for most of us, that need to excel when you don't match up…it eats at you. Like a jilted, unstable lover you can't shake. The need to conquer, to *improve*. It increases every day, grows stronger and stronger, rising every day with each new sun, reaching the heights of the megaliths and beyond."

"Have you taken up religion while here?" Samed asked, truly curious if Joleh had perhaps found an area of study that provided him some cerebral stimulation to help pass the otherwise atrociously dreary, gruelingly long days of solitude.

"Religion." Joleh smiled again, tongue poking ever so slightly through his remaining front teeth. "Religion requires something worth believing in."

Something about the whole situation didn't sit right with Samed.

Certainly, his brother's deteriorating health might have suggested that his death was a long time coming.

Yet there was something about the insistence of his tone when he talked about the cell's containment field—how glorious it was—as if he were referring to something else altogether.

And the mention of a woman, possibly their mother, only perhaps not. Samed certainly never knew of Joleh taking any lovers, at least none about whom his brother had revealed any information.

Then again, Joleh's brief year-long station in Opal prior to Mak Kerad's end of term had seemingly cured the then young man's stutter. His older brother should have embraced his soaring career and yet, insecurity had won out. Though admittedly, Samed had underestimated him, taking a whole six years to even piece together the fact that Joleh was hiding a child behind his back—and the backs of everyone on the force.

Samed still recalled clear as day the evening he had overridden Joleh's panel code. When his brother had refused to eat meals with him all days of the week following duty hours, Samed had grown suspicious.

Once he had gained access to Joleh's quarters within the Kano wing of the Capital Center, he first laid eyes on the boy.

Intrigued by the closet door that was closed all the way, Samed soon took notice of the padlock on the outside. After striking the lock several times with his duty handgun, the door finally swung open—to reveal the only child Samed had ever seen inside the Kano quarters.

No more than eight years old, dressed in rags and…his face. That face. Strangely silverish and matching the rest of his body, tiny points gracing every inch of his visible flesh. It almost seemed as though miniscule metal spikes covered the child from head-to-toe.

When the boy glanced up weakly to look at who had entered the room, Samed's stomach had lurched. The tiny dark silver spikes stopped just short of the boy's glazed, sunken eyes, casting his face in a skull-like mask.

Now ashamed to admit, Samed had never turned and run from anything so quickly in his life.

Of course, he wasted no time in alerting his superior officer, who had informed the then Mak Kerad and the entire science wing at the Capital.

Following Eta's rise to office and Joleh's attempt at seizing the Capital, circumstances of the revolt revealed that the boy required sunlight for strength. Mak Eta had seized such vulnerability as the perfect opportunity to control their child prisoner, and Joleh along with him.

Though Joleh attempted to escape in a small Kano glider, it wasn't long before an air unit had forced him into landing, lest he be shot from the sky by their much larger aircraft.

Now Joleh was gone and, Samed supposed, any secrets right along with him.

***

"They worship the Zaam just the same!" Thia cried indignantly, kicking over a grain chair so hard that a seam ripped slightly, tiny pellets scattering onto the floor. "How *insane* can one be to attack a place of worship to their own faith?"

"Insane," Rohem muttered simply, sitting on the windowsill with downcast eyes. "It's fire they worship now. Fire and destruction."

"I suppose you'll be going off to live at the medical academy soon, then?" Thia turned to him—or perhaps on him.

"They do want him gone." Oria sniffled, steadying her breathing as Nasin held her hand. The light from the shaded lamps in each corner of the room caught her troubled hazel gaze. "But we need all the strength we can get. Unless you'll object to being their primary target, Rohem."

"I can handle myself," Rohem added. "Even if I do end up living away from the compound for a while."

"This has gone on long enough." Nasin bristled, frustration nearly simmering over. "Rohem should not have to fear for his security—nor for the safety of anyone close to him. I will be honest, for the first time as adviser, I am truly considering declaring war."

"We don't have an organized military," Rohem pointed out. "And with all the Kano watching over every single move we make, we can't form one. Now with the Lirian police force also decommissioned, we can rely on only intelligence officers for land and air raids against the militants."

“We could easily have those willing train under us,” Thia suggested. “Back-up for what we can bring with brute force and hydroweaponry.”

“No,” Nasin spoke then, “we must begin with re-enforcing the ground beneath the city walls. Somehow, those men found a way in, and we must ensure it never happens again. Officer Samed already has the Tabir engineers investigating.”

Silence.

“Other than that,” Nasin continued, “you are enough. All of you. Strategic intelligence, martial strength, and science. Tabira won’t allow the establishment of a Lirian military, because they believe we would always have the upper hand against the Garo. We have always been enough to protect our people. If it comes to war, we can defend Lir with the strength of those inside this compound.”

“Can we really though?” Thia challenged. “Or should we just take more notes on Tabir methods like we always have?”

“The hydroweapon is all ours,” Rohem reminded her. “We built it.”

“*You* built it. Using armored tank blueprints from the Illumination,” Thia shot back. “Besides, it couldn’t have even been that difficult if we could manage without official engineering training. For all we know, the Tabir could have already developed the hydroblaster.”

“I mainly copied the design that our own engineers shared with Nasin for the smaller blaster,” Rohem pointed out. “You were with me nearly the entire time.”

“Thia has a point,” Nasin interjected. “The time has come to gather all the information we can.”

“Where?” Oria suddenly brightened. “Anything to take care of those Garo monsters.”

Thia raised a brow at Oria’s uncharacteristic nihilism.

“Oria, you’ll be best suited here to work with me, and perhaps Officer Samed as well, for as long as he leads the border patrol unit. I’d keep you local.”

“Because I can’t fight like…”

“Because we need you to stay alive,” Rohem cut her off. “You’re our main source of intelligence here on the ground.”

Oria looked away in a soft pout that she tried hard to conceal.

Thia glanced pointedly at Nasin. “Tell us what you know.”

"I've suspected it for a while," Nasin began slowly. "As I've told you, a suspicious sickness has spread throughout the colony of Ayam."

"The disease that took the last Flightless?" Rohem ventured.

"There are still his children," Oria reminded him. "Though I'm not sure they can fly."

"The last Flightless' children are fine, according to Eta," Nasin went on. "The mission, however, would be to diplomatically infiltrate the colony—offer help, as it were. And we truly will extend aid. Any way in which our hydrotechnology can assist."

"So we'd—or they'd—gather intel about this illness? How to use it as a bioweapon?" Oria pressed.

The light from Nasin's smile didn't reach the Lasha's eyes.

"Precisely."

***

Governor Par suppressed a shiver.

Despite the still warm days, nightfall brought a certain chill to the steppes he doubted even the Opal had handled very well. Such a shock the cold caused following a day on the heated steppe.

Pulling his robe about himself, he finished his prayer to the home shrine before the large window of his flat's main quarter.

Thirty more good men had been lost today, to no avail. This had to end.

Kneeling with arms crossed over his chest, he raised his face to the nearly featureless visage of Echil, the figurine's white eyes staring out at nothing.

All-seeing, indeed. If only the Zaam could see what was becoming of this world. That flicker of doubt kindled by the death of his wife and daughter grew at a pace he hesitated to admit even to himself.

Dunking the cloth in the bowl beside him, he finished cleansing his face as the prayer's conclusion left his lips.

The power of flame could overcome all. And one needn't be a god to wield a flame.

Only one prayer left. If any Zaam still listened, their flame would vanquish the Garo's enemy.

Lest Par burn them himself.

As the last of the incense burned away, Par drew a deep breath of the sweet smell and rose to his feet.

After replacing the basin in the adjoining washroom, Par decided he didn't feel like bathing alone this night.

Whereas the previous companion had barely moved a muscle or made a sound, he thought he'd request this next one come from the streets. Perhaps a less rigid training would add some originality to her style.

Once he'd placed the service call with Yote, the governor called off his security guard for the night. No need to risk his reputation as a pious leader.

Finally, Par retrieved Hiti from her heated glass tank beside the washbasin. She always kept visitors on their toes—business or pleasure.

And added an air of mystery, if Par were being honest.

The door call to his quarter buzzed. Impressive timing.

"Enter," Par called once he'd unlatched the door and turned to sit in the chair beside the bed, settling Hiti about his neck.

Yote had not disappointed tonight.

Par would have to send a request to Belim for a weekly salary raise on the courier's behalf. Thirty der seemed fitting.

The young woman who entered was modest-looking, if not unattractive. Black gaze set in an oval face, her eyes were so dark the whites stood out by comparison. Her gold-painted face was surrounded by sleek black hair that stopped just below her bosom in thick, wavy tresses.

Her body didn't differ drastically from the previous girl, perhaps a bit thicker. Yet the way she moved was…enticingly bizarre. It wasn't outwardly sultry, no. Her gait held confidence, yet mystery. Even the chest of her loose dark brown tunic came up higher to her throat, while the hem flowed lower to the knee and sleeves reached the wrists, leaving much to the imagination.

Best of all, as far as he could surmise from her face and hands, her body was entirely painted – just the way he preferred them. Par decided he favored the walk of a commoner to that of a trained companion.

"You keep a home shrine." the woman spoke in a voice that was both rich and low, almost quiet enough for Par to have to struggle to hear her.

Her lilt teased the mere hint of an accent he couldn't quite place.

He then realized she had spoken first.

"Yes." Par could already feel himself begin to stir within. "Do you believe?"

If the girl truly was of Garo, he already knew the answer.

"Tell me," she skirted the question, head cocking slightly to one side, "do you pray often?"

"Certainly." Par inhaled slightly as she moved ever closer, the gaslight catching her dark eyes in a soft sheen. "Such is…the way."

By now, she had lowered herself onto the arm of his chair, her left thigh mere centimeters from his lap.

Unlike Lan, and even the Lasha, this companion seemed utterly unfazed by the serpent that was lightly nosing its way over to investigate the newcomer, black tongue flitting out to taste the air.

The companion hummed softly. "What do you pray for?"

The governor nearly gasped as she reached a painted hand to caress Hiti, muted amber tunic brushing against Par's thigh with each rhythmic motion.

Now he knew he was sweating, no thanks to the fire burning in the hearth across the room.

"I pray…" Par began—and decided to speak the truth, speak it where no one of importance would hear. "I wish for my people's freedom. For the death of my enemies."

"Of Lir?" the woman asked pointedly, still petting the snake as the animal began coiling partially around her forearm, the majority of its body still resting loosely around Par's shoulders.

Hiti released a soft hiss, then, sounding more akin to a purr.

"Yes, the occupiers." Par's voice grew husky with both arousal and the relief of rare honesty. "And that *creature*. That sun beast. The people fear him. He is the only reason our fighters haven't burnt Lir to the ground. But most of all…"

He did sigh then, as the snake's soft scales brushed against his neck, adding to the anticipation of the companion's heightened proximity.

Still, she had yet to lay a finger on him.

After realizing he had closed his eyes, Par opened them and gazed up directly into the midnight stare of the woman he would soon have beneath him.

"From the earliest days when our people first discovered firelight on the cold steppe, fire has served as the Garo emblem of pride. Most of all, I pray for the Zaam to return and revive the power and glory of the flame."

The companion smiled then, her hand halting in its caress of the serpent about his throat, pupils taking on an almost soft blue tinge in the subtle light. Her expression looked somehow—*playful.*

Then that rich voice spoke once more. "Your prayer has been answered."

In the next moment, the tingling that had begun in Par's core gave way to disgusted horror, as the woman's gold face paint dissolved away into a gruesome visage. The Garo's fear gave way to fright, as the snake turned to blackened cinders at the beast-woman's touch, leaving a soot trail all the way up his arm.

No sooner had Par made to back away, that the white-hot heat—the invisible fire—passed beyond the incinerated reptile, engulfing the left side of his neck and ear in a scorching embrace that melted the flesh in a matter of seconds, searing straight through to his mind and beyond.

Within the moments that followed, both man and pet lay as ashes on the ground.

Stepping over the cinders, the other being sauntered from the room as unceremoniously as it had arrived. Glancing from the Senti text considered sacred to the idol atop the small bedroom shrine to its right, the one long referred to as Echil smiled again.

Such a form would once more suffice for those who called them Zaam.

Once outside, Echil's shadow passed over the darkened steppe, fading moments later into the pale glow of Garo's megalith.

Chapter Twelve

Vata barely rested beyond a mere doze. The heat from the radiator in her quarter did little to quell the draft seeping in from the crisp air outside.

Although she'd never admit it, Vata secretly cherished the rainforest humidity. On nights when her father would strike her or try to touch her painfully and she put up a fight, he would shove her outside and lock the door. He made sure to do this most often during the cold season, when the plains were particularly unforgiving.

Vata was clearly his favorite target—something from which Eta, for her part, tried her very best to distract him.

He would enter the washroom where Vata bathed or the bedroom where she slept, and Eta would see him. Moments later, Eta would push a flower vase or a fragile plate from the table surface, the shatter resounding so that he would hear.

Sometimes their father forgot about Vata and turned on Eta. Other times, they both bore the punishment. Her elder sister, Eta—the protector, the one who always seemed so in control—of events around her and of her own emotions.

Their mother never stepped in, as terrified of him as they were. Then, of course, there was the family's reputation to consider - the wife and children of an esteemed Tabir politician.

Thank Tabira's eventual dissolving of the ridiculous arranged marriage tradition—and all marriage, for that matter. Another miraculous change brought about by the Illumination, as more women entered fields of science and walked their own paths.

On the island nation of Ayam, they still practiced marriage. Yet, people slept around on their partners, and the locals refused any sort of civilization, including the establishment of paved roads or clearing of dense foliage.

Save for the hideous makeshift burial ground in that crater they called the Maw.

Still, the rainforest had that soothing moisture in the warm air, the calming humidity with the natural sweet smell of the many types of leaves. Vata could appreciate that much.

Rolling over, Vata exhaled as more memories surfaced from returning to this familiar environment.

First of the news that their father had perished from a heart attack. This was before the Illumination, of course—before medicine became equipped with treatments and surgical knowledge that could save him.

Their mother had passed not long after, her health finally succumbing to her longstanding weakness for grasswater. Perhaps it wasn't coincidental that both Vata and Eta had taken up careers in politics. In an odd way, taking after their father seemed quite fitting. To exceed everything that he had ever hoped to achieve.

Following the Illumination, Vata had spent time frustrated over the exact source of the sudden spike in unprecedented scientific information. In all areas—from using electricity for data cubes, satek development and the Network to gliders to medical advancements to finally even more extreme developments such as the Ayam pathogen—Tabira had brought the Plane to new heights of existence.

Yet she held a certain contempt for Eta's hiding the source. What right had she to conceal the truth from her own sister and, most importantly, where had Eta stumbled upon such a wealth of knowledge? Although Vata knew her sister to be the type of workaholic that quite literally *lived* at her office, such advancements couldn't have simply come to her at her desk.

Something to do with that officer, Joleh, she knew that much. But then, where had he obtained such facts?

Perhaps they had been lovers. Vata never would have known. While Eta had decided weeks following their mother's death that Vata would marry the final remaining Flightless, the now Mak had always kept her own personal life quite hidden. Avoiding scandal had perhaps contributed most prominently to her ultimate victory in the election for Mak nearly two decades ago.

Following along with her elder sister's actions as she had since childhood, Vata couldn't say that Hak had mistreated her. In fact, he was a jovial man, if rather vain at times. The feathers of his vibrant crown had fascinated her. Always with a habit for art to calm her nerves, his exotic looks had inspired her curiosity.

Perhaps beyond the appearance itself, the origin of the Flightless mystified Vata even further. Hailing from a nation that had already abandoned belief in the Zaam a century earlier, both she and Eta marveled at the evolutionary possibilities of how the Flightless had come to be.

And, most importantly, how they were not truly flightless. Although recent generations had seen the Flightless gene diluted to where the majority was now born without flight or even wings, Hak had long ago caught the interest of the Kano science division as perhaps the final winged person on the Plane.

Before their marriage, Hak had told Vata that he had flown once. He'd stayed close to the ground, gliding only three meters above its surface for about half an hour. Yet he had flown.

And Vata had been mesmerized when he demonstrated once for her on the eve of their wedding.

The second time he flew in her presence was to rescue her from a rogue palm cat. His heroics had ended there, however.

Their relations had proven painful. After numerous medical examinations, the discomfort was determined to be psychological. Still, Hak always treated her kindly, and made life a trifle easier with his attentive skill in teaching the Tabir language to the children of Ayam.

While Vata knew intellectually that her children were not inherently malicious, she could never quite shake the frustration over the privileged lives they had led—education, martial training, and parents who hadn't wandering hands.

Ara's disability, however, struck a thorn in her side like no other. Despite his impressive visage, his clumsiness along with his tendency to both read and write separate words as one continuous string had proven a challenge for even Hak to manage.

Once Hak had fallen to the disease, Ara's crown only served as a reminder to Vata of how the beauty of her late husband had attracted an Ayam native right into Hak's arms.

An Ayam *whore* who had no doubt been unfaithful to her own husband, if she had even been married. No one could tell with these savages. Though Inad had gotten one thing right—the sickness spread through intimate relations. Relations and blood exchange.

If growing up at her father's mercy had taught her anything, Vata knew the morbidity surrounding relations. Evidently, Hak had needed those sensations more often than she could provide.

He paid for it dearly.

Through the haze of half-sleep, Vata saw again, clear as day, the scene play out before her eyes.

The fever had struck Hak suddenly, matting down the feathers of his crown in a moist, sweaty clump. The muscle aches and violent cough began soon after, and then the immense fatigue.

Maru had visited them then, but Vata already knew how the disease spread. She had always known, ever since Eta's head scientists provided her with the first vial for the initial Pricking ceremony.

Even after Maru had confirmed his status as Cursed, Vata had prepared her pistol.

For the sake of respect, she joined Maru in helping Hak into one of the extra hardgrass cages that they had been building increasingly sturdier every day. A barrier between the beasts and the unafflicted to give the ill at least some chance of remaining in Ayam society.

After all, they lived normally again with each sunrise.

But perhaps the area in which she most resembled Eta, Vata retained her resolve. Her mind had made up.

Once Maru had departed with a healing prayer, Vata waited about an hour until the wisewoman and the other villagers would be far away from this clearing deep in the jungle where they kept the hardgrass cages.

That night, no other cages had been constructed in this corner of the forest. The dark canopy swayed as the insects and frogs began to sing in the trees and along the riverbanks.

When one of the chief's warriors offered to stand guard, Vata had shooed him off. He had left swiftly, no doubt all too glad to take leave of the Tabir's presence.

Soon enough, the agonized groans of Hak's first transformation joined the forest's peaceful night time melody.

Vata still recalled the crystal-clear image of Hak's moist, light-bronze flesh peeling away to reveal silver scales, teeth breaking free as his hideously elongated jaw soon tore wide open, full of newly grown, deadly sharp fangs. Yet his feathers remained intact. The crown of a majestic bird with the face of a monster.

His wings lay limp against his back, hidden away from her in the shadows.

As he turned his hideous, hungry face toward her, she aimed her gun squarely at one of the beast's pupiless silver eyes and pulled the trigger.

That night had been the one and only time that the chief's family had interacted with Vata's children prior to the wedding between Inad and Telo. The then chief had promised to keep Ara and Inad safe and occupied while Vata did what had to be done.

More recently, what both intrigued and terrified Vata all at once, was the growing number of villagers now infected back on Ayam. She could only wonder how long her refuge on the small island would remain untouched.

Perhaps Eta had guessed as much regarding Vata's reason for ordering Inad sent here. Perhaps Vata had, in fact, sought the safety of her children as well as her own.

But discipline would always come first. Inad and Telo both had to learn that Tabira dominated, and her daughter in particular must understand that Vata controlled their nation's stronghold on Ayam. A marriage to the chief meant absolutely nothing where civilized peoples were concerned.

As attached to the natives as her children had grown, Vata knew that at this rate, the Ayam would not last much longer.

Still, that was hardly her concern. If they refused to denounce the Zaam, that was their mistake. After all, Tabir scientists had synthesized the plague, same as the automobile and the data cube.

No matter how this had all happened, it had been mortal people of the Plane—not gods—who had achieved these wonders.

And yet…

Vata nearly clenched her fists at the idea of Eta keeping this secret from her. Did her older sister also know of an antidote that could keep Vata and her children safe? Another piece of cryptic knowledge to which only Eta and whichever other participants in the Illumination were privy?

Just then, lightning struck the skies outside, and Vata tore herself awake, sitting up in a cold sweat.

Still in a stupor, dazed from half-sleep, she marched into Eta's quarter across the hall.

When the traditional doorknob gave with a turn, Vata thanked the absence of one of those fancy palm pads. Access denial would not have had the desired effect.

Eta was already sitting up in bed, her face pale in the soft light of the megalith from the window. If it weren't for the storm clouds outside, Vata suspected the first glow of dawn would already have graced the plains.

"I need you to tell me," Vata demanded in an almost strangled whisper, halting just short of the bedpost.

Eta simply stared back, communicator in hand. A few moments passed, and Vata noticed the glazed over look in her sister's eyes.

"Really, Eta? That Garo grass? Again?"

"It dulls the stress of these types of unexpected encounters," Eta prompted hazily. "What is it now, Vata?"

"You've no right to keep it to yourself any longer," Vata fumed. "How long before I die, before your niece and nephew become a meal on that jungle rock? How long will this mission go on with me in the dark as to what we are actually dealing with? About how the pathogen even exists in the first place? How all of this was made possible in under *thirty years*?"

"The Illumination, you mean," Eta replied.

It wasn't a question.

"I will not follow blindly any longer," Vata said through gritted teeth. "I am no longer that little girl. By hiding the truth, all you're doing now is signing my death sentence."

Eta's gaze flitted downward to her communicator before returning swiftly to her sister's narrowed hazel eyes.

"I've just received a call," Eta began, and Vata opened her mouth to demand they return to the topic at hand, "The governor of Garo was killed. Burned to death. His ashes were discovered on the floor of his home."

Vata paused before speaking again. "How do they know it was him?"

"The local courier received a service request from the governor less than an hour before he discovered Par's front door unlocked and the ashes inside. The security camera outside his doorway was broken, so the Kano couldn't track who entered or left that night. No one has heard from the governor since."

Vata exhaled slowly. "Could it be the Lasha?"

"Fire is not their weapon of choice. Typically, the Garo favor the flame, and Samed has reported that Lir just experienced a fire demonstration outside of their main temple."

Vata went very still. "It's him, the tree thing. He's avenged the Lirians by killing Par."

"We've had no trouble from him ever since he went to live in Lir," Eta said quietly, "Nasin, crone that she is, is not dense. She knows better than to order him to do something that would rouse Tabir suspicions, and Samed has already stated that the Kano officers stationed all around the Lirian citadel never saw anyone exit between the event of the terror attack and Par's death."

"Then it was someone within Garo..." Vata reasoned. "Speaking of Nasin, why haven't we ousted her yet? She's been in power for how long now? Besides, rumor has it that she is, in fact, mentally unfit."

Eta fought the urge to laugh out loud. "You have this on good authority?"

"Her brother's wife had mentioned something—years back. Before Hak and I went to live on Ayam, and Nasin's family came to visit Tabira. Father was still at the Capital Center."

Eta knew they couldn't risk ousting a democratically elected politician who was viewed as somewhat of a miracle for having taken in two lost children.

The Mak returned to the matter at hand. "Vata, contrary to what you may believe, Samed's brother, Joleh, is the only source I have as to the Illumination. He was the only one to ever provide this knowledge, and our scientists spent months experimenting before we actually successfully implemented any of the designs."

"Joleh never mentioned how he came about such knowledge?" Vata remained skeptical.

"Oh, he's said plenty." Eta sighed, reclining her back against the headboard behind her. "From the depths of a prison cell. None of us on the Oligarchy ever paid heed to the ranting he began spewing."

"Yet you decided to invest time and der in these rantings of a madman?"

"The madness didn't begin right away," Eta clarified. "You know that before he took up with the boy, Joleh was a respected officer, relentlessly determined to participate in the scientific wing of the Kano. His brother, Samed, excelled in this area, of course. It was thanks to officers like them that Tabira has long exceeded the other nations in terms of industrialization.

"Though when Joleh actually began providing exact instructions for certain advancements which our people had only begun to brainstorm—drawings for automobiles, designs for the circuitry of data cubes, blueprints for cellular manipulation to cure illnesses as serious as the growth disease…even the development of the Ayam pathogen—we began to take note. Although Samed denied knowing the source his brother had used, Joleh soon began repeating a name over and over. Never a religious man, as no Tabir has been for generations, this seemed odd."

Lightning flashed outside, followed closely by a low rumble of thunder.

"Religious?" Vata asked. "What was the name?"

"Echil."

Vata pursed her lips. "The Zaam."

Eta nodded. "The Zaam that Tabira has held for decades to have never existed."

Vata concluded, "The Zaam that we have committed to wiping out an entire nation for its belief in them."

A stretch of silence ensued, as the clouds burst and the downpour finally began outside.

"What do you believe?" Vata finally asked.

The Mak sighed. "I've always marveled at such a long-harbored faith in a single class of deity across all of the known Plane—even a nation as far-flung as Ayam."

Another flash struck the skies outside, the only light apart from the glow of the megalith behind the Capital Center.

"So what now?" Vata equal parts hated the fact that she was again turning to her sister for the answer, and also utterly chilled by this creeping feeling that something she had never wanted to conceive of being true might as well have materialized before her.

"Tomorrow I will arrange a mediation assignment between Garo and Lir," Eta stated, turning off her bedside lamp. "For the moment, both nations seek repayment for damages committed by the other."

"But if the Lir didn't murder the governor…" Vata began in the darkness.

"For now, all we can do is continue on as we have," Eta replied. "Keeping the lesser nations in line while we get to the bottom of the bigger picture. Your children definitely take after you—especially the girl. Such gall—ferocity, really. Do let me know when you and yours wish to return to the colony. We have greater trouble stirring than misbehaved children."

"Then you are truly ignorant to any sort of cure for the pathogen?" Vata hissed, wanting nothing more than to have her daughter standing here so she could strike her once more. "Or do you simply not care if we fall to the plague?"

"You took the assignment knowing full well what the measure of enforcement would be if the locals refused to accept denouncement. I know just as little as you on that front. The scientists are working daily to find an antidote. In the meantime, simply stay on your small island. The afflicted cannot swim, just as they cannot climb. You know this better than anyone."

Of course. Because an afflicted Ayam seeking revenge wouldn't possibly think of taking a canoe to the small island, hiding out until dark, and then killing the Tabir.

Following a few moments, Eta still sensed her sister's lingering presence in the dark. "Good night, Vata."

***

Inad's first reaction upon waking was to cough and sputter, clearing her lungs of the sudden onslaught of hot water.

Eyes flying open, Inad threw her arms around her naked torso, bending over as far as she could to conceal her lower regions, despite her wrists being currently chained to the wall behind her. Her dark curls hung loose over her shoulders, soaking locks irritating the dull ache at her nape.

Now her head joined her nape in a dull ache that had stung with the near-scalding spray.

"Another hit!" called a male voice from outside the silica-enclosed area that she now realized surrounded her.

Moments later, scalding water again filled her mouth and stung her eyes, hotter than the first blast.

"That should do it," the same voice announced. "It's already nearly sunrise, and she's exhibited no changes."

Half a second of silence, and Inad nearly yelped when a deluge of lukewarm air pummeled her from above, lasting for about one minute straight.

With that, a burly man wearing a white suit of a strange material entered the small area and grabbed her shoulder. A tech, it seemed. His apparel matched the four walls beyond this translucent cage.

Powerless to hit him, Inad could only struggle awkwardly, haphazardly kicking out with her right foot.

"Quit fussing," barked the man irritably. "You're clean. Good thing, too. Wouldn't want to feel the sterilization chemicals."

"Sterilization?" Inad could barely form words as she continued to cower for modesty.

"You're not afflicted," the tech returned curtly through his sanitation mask. "Now be quiet."

Inad let out a dry laugh. "If I were afflicted, everyone in this room would be dead, and no amount of hot air or water would save you."

The tech gripped her arm again with one hand as he unlatched her wrists from the wall.

Yanking her free, he stepped in closer. "What did I say about keeping quiet?"

Still in a somewhat primal state of mind from her earlier descent into savage intimidation tactics, Inad instinctively spat on the transparent surface of the tech's hazard mask.

Spittle falling easily from the reflective front of his mask, the tech wordlessly wrenched Inad from the strange tank area.

As they strode through the narrow space of what appeared to be a lab area, Inad feared the worst. Though it was quieter here than outside, every noise made her want to jump from her skin.

All around, people in long grey coats hurried to and fro.

Had they brought her here to experiment on someone whom they believed to have had recent contact with infected people? Or had her mother simply sent her here to endure excruciating and invasive procedures as a form of punishment for disgracing a strategic union?

Also, where had they taken her brother?

Inad's thoughts were interrupted when the tech released her momentarily, tossing a dark green smock and trousers at her.

"Put these on," he snarled. "Unless you want all the men to see you in the natural. And if you try to run, there's a guard stationed at every entrance and exit."

"Men?" Inad willed the shake from her voice.

"Prison's co-ed," he replied flippantly. "Most of the guards are male too, and don't take kindly to being spit on. Just a warning."

So they *had* been sent to prison. At least that meant she might see Ara soon…

After donning the scratchy uniform as quickly as possible, Inad wanted to growl as the tech again grabbed her wrist and pulled her through the next doorway.

The rancid smell of the dank air struck her senses even before the taunting shouts that promptly increased as soon as her escort began push-guiding her down an even narrower corridor.

The passageway was filled with barred cells on each side and from above.

Men and women alike wearing the same dark green uniforms yelled curses from all directions. The entire way, Inad kept her focus firmly on her feet.

Following the ascent up one of the three levels, the tech shoved Inad into a cell in the center along the right wall, and promptly swung the metal door shut, securing the lock with keys from his trousers pocket.

Lab henchman and guard, it seemed.

He'd had keys this whole time, and she hadn't thought to try and wrest them from him. Inad wanted to slap herself. Although she'd no way of knowing if an escape attempt would have worked, she was already now feeling the confinement of the consequences.

Inhaling as slowly and silently as possible, Inad stole a gaze around her, noting only one other person in the cell.

Another female, perhaps no older than fourteen. Her short hair was arranged in a messy Tabir-style braid atop her head.

Possibly thinner than Inad, she sat huddled in one corner on a thin mattress, not bothering to sit on the bench provided on her side of their cage.

There was also a bench on the opposite side of the cell. Next to the bench lay a mattress on the floor and what looked like a small metal bowl with high edges.

When the shouts from the cells around them died down with the dimming lights, Inad allowed herself a sigh of relief.

Then the darkness came.

Inad took a seat on the unoccupied bench and drew up her knees, leaning back against the wall.

Her stomach rumbled loudly. Not an unfamiliar feeling.

"We won't eat for a few hours," the other girl spoke in a whisper, just loud enough to hear across the small space, and Inad instantly glanced over, eyes roaming in the darkness.

"It's fine," Inad replied simply in a tone just as low.

"What are you in for?"

Inad dearly hoped this girl wouldn't want to make small talk till dawn.

"My mother sent me for not obeying her orders," Inad answered truthfully.

The girl hissed. "Your mother must have some influence."

"Why are you here?" Inad asked, steering the conversation away from herself.

"I worked in one of the factories," the girl said. "My little brother was becoming ill, so I was feeding him my rations. A guard told us to split them. When I refused, he tried to take some bread from my brother and I kicked him between the legs. Men can't stand that."

Inad said nothing. It always seemed to come down to food.

"What's your name?" Inad's cellmate asked.

"Inad."

"I'm Erme. You have an odd accent."

"I haven't been in Tabira long," Inad replied. "I'm tired now. Good rest, Erme."

Surprisingly, Erme left well enough alone and rose to lie on her own bench, arranging a mattress and blanket from the corner.

Inad followed suit and just about fell onto her own bedding, stifling a groan at the ache in nearly every limb.

A dreamless sleep followed moments later.

***

Officer Samed stared blankly at the gray powder on the floor of Governor Par's home.

Giving the courier, Yote a brief side-glance, the head Kano tried once more to clarify the situation.

"Yote, you've called me here to look at a pile of dirt?"

“No, officer!” Yote protested in shoddy Tabir. “I told you. Someone has set the governor alight!”

“Did you see this happen?” Samed asked dully, humoring the wiry Garo by squatting to examine the ash more closely.

“Governor Par called me to make a delivery,” Yote rushed. “When I came, I found only this. The governor is missing. No one has heard from him for more than a day. Has he called you, officer?”

“…no,” Samed relented, rising up. “Very well. We will see to the issue.”

Exiting Par’s home, Samed contacted Mak Eta on his microcommunicator. “Pleasant day, Mak. Governor Par appears to be missing. He hasn’t been responding to attempts at contact, Treasurer Belim’s and mine included. Orders to proceed?”

A pause before the Mak’s lucid, deep tone sounded from the other end.

“The disproportionate actions from Lir have gone on long enough. First Lasha Nasin will be removed from position as head of the Lirian advisory. I will send a Tabir representative promptly.”

No, that wouldn’t work. Although Samed couldn’t say for certain where he found the gall to stand up to the Mak, there was a first time for everything.

What he knew for certain was that a forced resignation of the Lasha would give the Evaporation a notion of Tabir support for terrorism.

Still, he had to approach this diplomatically.

“Mak Eta, if I may... We have no reason to believe the Lirians had anything to do with this. I found no evidence of a water attack… In fact, there is no body, only ashes, suggesting a small fire inside the governor’s home.”

“You mean to say the Evaporation is to blame?” Eta probed.

“They are terrorists, Mak,” Samed replied frankly. “Tabira cannot support terrorism. Removing the Lasha from power would suggest that we encourage the Evaporation’s methods. That said, I do agree that the time has come for Kano to represent the sole law enforcement in this region. With your permission, I would dissolve the Lirian police force for good. Without their aid in Lir proper, the Lasha’s advisory will have far fewer resources at their disposal.”

“Very well,” Eta decided. “Clever thinking on your part, Officer. Call for Captain Kari’s resignation by Lir’s nightfall.”

Withdrawing the communicator from his pocket, Samed prepared to inform Governor Belim that the Kano investigation into the disappearance of former governor Par had drawn to a close. Following eight weeks of nothing apart from a pile of dirt as evidence, the case had officially ended.

Officer Samed could not recall an uncannier instance of a person vanishing into thin air. Though he would never admit his apprehension to Eta, the unprecedented lack of control he felt at his first cold case gnawed at the back of his mind. If the Governor *had* somehow been burnt to an identifiable crisp and the Lirians were somehow responsible, Samed was determined to control border activity beyond the simple three-meter wall currently acting as barrier. The time had arrived for the local Kano unit to upgrade to land mines.

Later, he resisted the urge to roll his eyes at the sheer indignation on the face of the man before him.

"Just what right do you have to dismantle Lirian police presence from our own territory?"

Captain Kari, final member of the Lirian police force, refused to go down lightly.

"Captain," Samed tried gingerly, "I give you my word that I am only following orders. The Central Oligarchy of Tabira has decreed that the Kano will operate as the sole law enforcement in both Lir and Garo."

"I see." Kari dared a step toward the Kano officer, hand sliding gradually to rest over the gun at his belt. "Officer Samed, just how gullible do you think I am? Tabira seeks to weaken our only defense against the Garo threat. I thought you didn't take sides."

"Garo has never had a police force apart from the Kano," Samed stated stoically. "They are getting along fine."

"Why would they need police when their own people are the terrorists? Lir has never developed an army, and now you want to dissolve our law enforcement…"

"Remove your hand from your weapon, Captain," Samed requested coolly, fingers resting over his own larger handgun.

Kari's hand fell stiffly to his side. "So Tabira truly does support Garo."

"We remain neutral, as we always have," Samed returned. "Kano forces disrupt terror operations where they arise, and we quell unfair advantages in superior technology."

"The Lirian forces only carry out deluge attacks on points in both territories associated with terrorist activity," Kari insisted through a jaw set in frustration.

"Such retaliatory attacks have frequently resulted in a great amount of collateral damage," Samed answered pointedly.

"Collateral damage cannot always be avoided…"

"Kindly explain to me the need for an air raid following an attack carried out by two individuals," Samed interjected.

"The Kano prohibit all Lirians save for First Nasin and her advisory from entering Garo," Kari bit back in earnest. "Air raid is our only available method to catch the cowards once they've run back across the border."

"One might question your utilization of air raids at all, given the Lirian experience during the Cleansing," Samed responded icily.

Now he had gone too far.

Captain Kari clenched a fist before replying. "I suppose you would know all about conducting such attacks, *Officer*."

In the next moment, the young Lirian captain's muscles tensed as Samed suddenly stepped forward until he was standing directly over Kari, gun drawn and pointed idly at the floor.

"You listen to me, Kari," Samed seethed. "For years, the Kano have looked the other way while Lirian technology evolves closer and closer to weaponry. If you don't wish for me to alert the Mak of an official discovery regarding this technology, I suggest you resign quietly and cease all contact with Nasin and her council."

Kari pursed his lips, every fiber of his being itching to draw his own weapon as fast possible and shoot this arrogant Tabir where he stood. "How will I feed my family?" Kari appealed to a sympathy plea as an embarrassing yet genuine last resort. "I have a wife and two young boys."

"I will convene with Mak Eta regarding compensation for your family until you can secure a new line of work," Samed replied calmly.

Kari resisted the furious lump that threatened to rise in his throat as he refused to break Samed's gaze. "Officer Samed," he managed in a tight voice, "the Garo like to play the role of the underdog. They play the victim in order to garner sympathy."

"As you just did by mentioning your family," answered Samed easily.

"I *have* a family," Kari spat. "You do as well, if memory serves?"

"A brother, yes." Samed seemed like he didn't like where this conversation was headed. "Why is that relevant?"

"I see." The captain shook his head. "The Kano whose brother kept a child hidden for years, for who knows what revolting purpose..."

Samed's face went white just before flushing a subtle pink.

"My brother's actions have nothing to do with Lirian law enforcement. The Mak's decision stands. Lir will no longer have a police force. Now turn in your weapon."

Extending his right hand, Samed stood his ground.

Pulling the gun from its holster, Captain Kari gave a final shred of consideration to shoot Samed, then thought of his family and fired the remaining two diamond bullets at the wall behind Samed without a word.

Moments after the weapon clattered to the ground, the Lirian formerly known as Captain Kari turned and strode out of Samed's local office quarter.

***

"Why won't you look at me?"

That high voice was beginning to grate on Kel's nerves.

"Look." Kel still didn't spare a glance away from his current nervous task of tidying up a perfectly organized den. "You don't want to be here, do you?"

"Mother says I will see her one day soon," Unno replied, alternating between watching Kel work and fiddling with her small cup of tea.

Kel changed the subject. "Are you happy with the tea? Have you finished?"

"Yes, thank you," said Unno. "When will we train? Nok and Father always spoke of great glory."

Kel's blood ran cold. Nok. This girl had been Nok's younger sister.

"Your brother fought in the Evaporation?" Kel asked, just to be certain.

"Yes. He fought and died for our land."

By the Zaam, this girl spoke well for one so young.

"Your age?" Kel prompted.

"Ten years."

Now, Kel did stop and look at her.

"I know, I'm small." Unno quirked a half-smile. "Nok said it's because we don't eat enough with the Lirians blocking imports from Tabira."

A pause.

"And what makes you want the glory?" Kel attempted to make conversation as he joined her at the small table beside the den sofa.

"For the Zaam, of course," replied Unno hurriedly. "Though I would see Tabira first. Will we ever visit Tabira for training? Or perhaps on a mission?"

"No need," Kel said gruffly. "Training will last two weeks. Then you will carry out your mission in Lir."

"The Lirians," Unno said thoughtfully. "Why do they want this land? It's barely got enough food, and water is always hard to find."

"Water is scarce only because the Lirians use their technology to keep it for themselves."

"They don't share." Unno seemed to agree. "So can't we go to Tabira and learn how to make our own water? The Lirians learned from the Tabir, didn't they?"

Kel sighed. "Yes. The Tabir favor the Lirians, while pretending not to take sides."

"If I could," Unno began excitedly, "I would move to Tabir for schooling and show them how Garo are just as worthy."

"But you are a girl," Kel interjected matter-of-factly.

"Girls can visit other places." Unno eyed him sharply, and the Evaporation's leader wondered how a frivolous young man like Nok had gotten on with such a precocious sibling. "The governor's language woman does."

"Ah, Lan." Kel nodded, willing away the simmering revulsion that arose upon thoughts of Belim. "She is married to a very important man."

"Father often speaks about the science of healing," Unno continued. "But he just works with herbs. I want to do more. I want to learn how water works. Fire can't get us much further."

"The Zaam created fire for the Garo." Kel nearly cut her off. "The flame is our weapon."

"Yes, I wear its symbol every day." Unno fiddled with the fire pendant about her throat. "A gift from Mother—from the temple. But we can have both. Why not use fire *and* water as weapons?"

"It's a victorious path." Kel was beginning to feel quite simple next to this ambitious girl, whose mind clearly didn't muddle so easily from the late hour. "Light as the blade. Such power ensures that we will pass into the Realm of Joy."

"So Mother will come along with us for the mission? She will join us in the Realm."

Unno's question brought Kel straight back to attention.

"Why do you ask that?"

Unno's eyes were bright. "She says I will see her soon. Once I've completed the mission."

Kel nearly choked on his tea. Deki would have likely scoffed.

Outside, the final temple call of the day sounded through the approaching dusk.

"Unno…" Kel realized that was perhaps the first time he had uttered her name aloud. "Your mother meant that you would see her one day when you both pass over. When you are both gone from the Plane."

Unno seemed to ponder her next question. "Is this mission like Nok's first was?"

"Yes," Kel nearly whispered.

The gaze with which Unno fixed him next was perhaps the most child-like he'd seen from her yet. Her murky amber eyes shone softly in the light of the megalith that ghosted through the den window.

"On this mission…I will die?"

Kel said nothing, staring down at his nearly untouched cup of tea.

Chapter Thirteen

"Yes, Mak. Understood." Turning off the communication line on her desk's surface, Nasin clenched her fists to keep from crying out in frustration.

"What's the verdict?" Rohem asked gently, approaching from the doorway. "Have they blamed us for the governor's death?"

"So far, it seems not." Nasin replied coolly. "Eta didn't mention culprits, only that she's had enough 'childlike skirmishes', and has unilaterally chosen to play peacemaker."

Rohem frowned slightly.

"I'll need you and Thia to go see Gether for a check-up." Nasin began typing a communication to Oria. "You two handle yourselves well, but I want to make sure you're in optimal condition for this assignment."

"Nasin, please don't stall." Rohem stepped forward. "What is the Mak planning?"

After a brief pause, Nasin set down her communicator and glanced up at her ward. "She's requested that we bring along a Garo on this excursion."

"You can't be serious," said Rohem in a tone louder than normal. "How does she expect…"

"Their agreement to escort us overseas is contingent upon this term," Nasin explained.

"*Escort* us?" Nasin and Rohem both turned to face Thia, who had just entered with Oria close behind. "We don't need an escort. All we need is the means to fly!"

Oria spoke up then. "Thia, you can't pilot a massive glider, and that's what we need to cross the Teal Sea. The engines of anything smaller won't suffice."

"And seeing as our generous neighbors blew up our last fully functioning glider," Rohem continued, "we'd be out of luck anyway. Especially now that Tabira won't trade us anything unless we make friends. So which Garo are we bringing along?"

"Lan," Nasin stated simply, "the interpreter. Belim evidently wants an emissary who can gather linguistic knowledge from Ayam to bring back to Garo."

"Well," Oria said glumly, "I can't see her having the gall to try and take out either of you. She seemed quiet enough when I went to see Par."

"You're staying here, then?" Thia prompted Oria. "At the base to keep an eye on the informants?"

Oria nodded. "I'll be making rounds with Samed."

Later that afternoon, Gether finished his physical work-up of Thia.

Beside them, Rohem tried his best not to mope over the postponement he would need to make on his apprenticeship.

"Looking good, as always." Gether put away his examining lights. "When do you expect the change?"

"Sometime next week," Thia replied, dropping off the edge of the exam bed. "The day varies."

"Right. Make sure to get as much rest as possible, Thia-*tha.*" Gether turned to Rohem. "And you too. Fortunately, health hazards shouldn't pose too much risk for you two, especially seeing as both the Mak and the island chief confirmed the pathogen only spreads through blood transfer and intercourse. Just make sure to wear knee-high boots. There are likely to be various venomous crawling species on the ground in the jungle. When you come back, we'll be in for many sleepless nights with rounds at the hospital. We're still setting up the second hospital and getting more and more cases in from both Lir and Garo every day, so the patients keep piling up."

Rohem scoffed. "It might help if they'd use some der on building their own hospitals and sending their own people to train in Tabir medicine rather than sending all their sick to us and blaming us if they don't make it."

"If I were a believer, I'd doubt even the Zaam would have the power to make them stop seeing us as monsters." Thia shook her head as she and Rohem took their leave.

"Take care now." Gether embraced Thia briefly. "Your light shines on me."

Several hours into the night, Rohem's communicator buzzed.

"Arin has completed three straight night rounds this week, and I'm afraid he's too worn out to safely assist tonight. I'm sorry your first assignment as apprentice arrived with such little warning," Gether stated blearily over the communication line. "Though these situations often do."

"On my way," Rohem replied, clipping off his communicator.

The Garo treasurer, Belim—or stand-in governor, as it were—had just called in on behalf of a couple. The wife had been in labor for nearly thirteen hours and had begun bleeding at a concerning rate. Proving beyond the capabilities of Garo's still makeshift medical facility, Belim had contacted Nasin and Samed for transport across the border.

Samed had escorted the man and his wife through the checkpoint that separated the two territories. Once at Lir's hospital, Gether had already prepared a bed.

Once Rohem arrived, he immediately set about fixing a line of anti-infection and coagulation serum to halt further bleeding, along with pain medication.

"Careful with the anesthetic," Gether cautioned as he examined the woman below her abdomen. "Forty drips per minute will suffice. There's a good chance she has never had this treatment, and we don't want to shock her system."

Rohem had to wonder if his hands were actually sweating beneath his thin gloves. His heart was certainly beating quickly as a lightning bird, relief growing as the woman's loud sobs gradually ebbed into soft whimpers.

Until, not a half hour later, her whimpers were joined by the shrill cries of a newborn.

"The bleeding seems to have ceased." Gether took a deep breath, examining the tiny infant. "And this little girl looks just fine. Lady, how are you feeling? Shall I bring your husband?" Gether addressed the woman in clipped Garo, though the mother, it seemed, was contentedly sleeping at the moment, all vital signs steady.

"She's still out," Rohem stated. "Let's cut the medicinal line?"

"I'll do it," the doctor said. "Take her for me, please? And bring in the patient's husband from the waiting area."

Holding this tiny being in his hands felt positive, no doubt about it. And yet, strange. She had stopped wailing, eyes still closed against the harsh, new light of this world.

No time to ponder now. Rohem turned to summon the little girl's father.

Even as the middle-aged Garo man followed Rohem into the delivery room and took his daughter into his arms, he glanced surreptitiously at the medical apprentice. Enough of Rohem's features were visible beneath the sterility mask to be recognizable. At times, Rohem wondered how much the common Garo were privy to the propaganda of their leaders.

***

Finishing up her evening prayer, Oria turned from her quarter's shrine at the knock on her door.

"It's me," Thia murmured, stepping softly into the room. "I'm not disturbing anything?"

"Prayers were finished," Oria replied. "How are you feeling about the mission?"

Thia shrugged. "As ready as we'll ever be. There comes a point when you just have to go for it, no matter the outcome."

"It's amazing," Oria said. "How you keep such faith and yet believe in nothing."

"I don't believe in religion," Thia pointed out. "Doesn't mean I don't believe in faith. I do have faith, Oria. Nasin bringing you here—bringing Rohem here. That was a miracle. My father surviving to become a doctor months before the Cleansing, in time to help establish our first medical facility—*that* was a miracle. You surviving the Cleansing. A three-year-old. All miracles. And we did it all either by ourselves or through helping each other. No powers from above, unseen for so long they've been lost to legend. Just us."

Oria kept her eyes averted.

"I respect your skepticism," Oria finally answered. "Though my faith in the Zaam keeps my family's memory alive. Those I lost and my grandmother who still lives, but likely not for much longer."

"Her ailment has worsened?" Thia asked.

Oria nodded.

"Well, I'll let you rest now." Thia turned to go. "I just wanted to check on you after the attack on the temple."

Oria averted her gaze. "It...it just felt too close to the air raid on our temple in Tabira during the Cleansing. But I am fine. Thank you."

She smiled genuinely, turning for bed.

"Thia—" Oria began again.

Avithia turned back expectantly.

"Does the killing bother you?"

Thia gnawed thoughtfully at the inside of her cheek before settling on the most honest answer. "Every time. But it's either them or us. We try our best to avoid civilians, as we always have. I personally have never harmed an innocent Garo, and I don't plan on ever doing so."

Oria nodded mildly, averting her gaze.

"Good sleep, Oria." Thia smiled, turning toward her own quarter.

"Dream easy," Oria returned quietly. "May Echil protect you both."

Once Thia had closed the door and stood alone out in the narrow corridor, she sighed. Although she, Nasin, and Rohem had always remained neutral regarding the existence of a higher power, Thia almost felt as if denouncing the concept entirely strode too close to the stringent atheism of the Tabir.

She would never wish to sound like them, especially not after what had happened to Oria's family back in Tabira. And yet…believing in the Zaam felt all too similar to the Garo. Even if they truly did appear to worship fire rather than an actual supreme entity in recent years.

Yes. Safest to remain neutral. That was always part of what made conversation slightly smoother with Rohem than with Oria.

At the thought of Rohem, Thia's eyes swept over to his door, which remained slightly ajar.

Though she knew he didn't quite sleep, he rested at night along with Thia and the others.

Lifting a foot to take a step toward his door and reaching for the handle, Thia halted. Somehow this time, his shirtless visage from their last sparring session by the pool popped unbidden into her mind.

After all these years, now she was suddenly considering his physique…damn the situation with Walar for muddling her thoughts.

Shaking her head, Thia turned for her own quarter.

"Avithia." Nasin's voice sounded just gently enough to avoid making Thia start. "You're up late. Is everything all right?"

"Fine," Thia replied, barely above a whisper.

Nasin looked her over, clearly not convinced. "What's bothering you?"

Thia stood her ground. The sight of the Lirian beggar bothered her. May as well get this over with.

"When I went to apprehend the fighters at the reservoir by the border," Thia began carefully, keeping her voice low despite Oria's closed door and the fact that Rohem could likely hear them perfectly through his open door, "I saw a beggar."

"How close were you to Garo territory?" Nasin asked, a hint of worry in her dark eyes.

"That's the point," Thia cut in. "The man was clearly a grass addict, and he was Lirian."

Nasin paused for half a second, and then nodded curtly. "Some of ours find themselves in the unfortunate situation of addiction. Such individuals typically abandon their families and take to the streets by choice, scavenging what they can from across the border."

Thia voiced the first question that came to mind. “The Tabir have never allowed unsupervised trade since erecting the border blockade. Why don’t the Kano arrest these addicts for loitering?”

Nasin sighed softly. “The Kano realize that Lir cannot afford to house these people, leaving the responsibility to Tabira—a burden they also refuse. To arrest the beggars would admit to there being a problem…”

“But there *is* a problem,” Thia insisted, still keeping her voice low. “We shouldn’t have to depend entirely on Tabira to care for our own people. Can’t we put some of the temple funding toward providing shelter for these beggars? They’ll have no chance if they’re just left at the border to be tempted by Garo to smuggle stuff.”

“The beggars have chosen their way,” Nasin replied with cool serenity. “I pity them, but the families must come before the individual. Every family unit maintains a home. Many of those families with young children belong to Lir’s religious sector, and they visit the temples three times daily. You know this, Thia. We must respect the values of the faithful.”

“Why?” Thia asked, tone rising slightly. “Because they revere the Lasha?”

Even when Nasin’s eyes flashed, the younger Lasha didn’t drop her gaze.

Following what seemed an hour-long staring bout, Nasin spoke. “Pleasant night, Avithia.”

Turning on her heel, Thia made sure to depart the scene first.

***

That night, Rohem struggled to find even a hint of rest.

Even sitting by the rear exit of the compound, every atom in his body seemed to be on edge, jittery from the experience earlier this evening.

Witnessing firsthand how Gether saved both mother and child had been simply indescribable. Certainly, Rohem had read about the birthing process and memorized quite thoroughly the procedures such as surgery to heal burn wounds and injury by gunshot, yet somehow, the risk of such a beautiful thing as bringing new life to the world astounded him most of all.

He had first considered a career in medicine not long after witnessing the first couple of Avithia’s changes. Back in early childhood, the gender change had been significantly more uncomfortable—almost painful.

After living alongside a person who underwent such a process on a semi-regular basis, Rohem soon reflected back on the daily suffering of many homeless children back in Tabira. Those working in the factories and begging on the streets. Those like the orphan Hazur with whom Rohem had collaborated while on the run from the Kano, following Joleh’s imprisonment. Many of these street children fell ill after rationing the meager scraps they could find for their younger siblings. Then there were those who simply failed to find shelter during the cold season, and succumbed to the elements.

Others faced a more sudden, yet still brutal death.

His mind turned to Hazur. All bright smiles with a bounce in his step. He was quick on his feet, always insisting on racing Rohem as they climbed through windows to take what they needed from the shops. Even though Rohem had no need to eat, he would make sure Hazur was fed—even though the boy preferred to snatch his own food. Always the competitor, much like Avithia.

Then the automobile had appeared from around the corner, and just like that, Hazur never ran or climbed again.

First, Rohem had failed in intervening quickly enough to pull the boy from harm's way. He had been too preoccupied with snatching a slice of bread from a street stand, unaware of just how far Hazur still had to catch up.

Then, try as he might, the boy's wounds were too grave. The energy transfer, which could usually perk him up after a fall, couldn't touch his pain.

Rohem shook his head of the memory. That boy he had pulled from the temple fire had the same bright look in his eye as Hazur. Medicine surely rendered miracles, no doubt, and yet Rohem intended to use all available assets to protect the innocent.

Even the abilities many viewed as fearful.

His mind had made up several years ago. He would commit to saving lives. His failure to rescue Hazur had steeled his resolve. Nasin's bringing him to Lir had seemed a miracle in itself. He would not let such a gift go to waste. After completing his medical education, he was determined to return to Tabira and help others like Hazur and the nameless boy from the temple.

Moreover, tonight had provided his first real taste of the urgency involved in medical practice. Once again, his skin felt prickly all over, this time enhanced with languid warmth throughout every limb.

After opening his nightshirt, he decided to take a walk and cool off in the brisk air.

Strange. Heat had never made him so restless—never before tonight and that time he'd nearly touched the megalith.

Once he had walked about five meters away from the compound, Rohem's gaze immediately rose to the megalith beyond the city wall, its light nearly drowning out the softly twinkling stars and frozen flame in the dark sky beyond.

The tingling again began rippling across his skin as he sauntered in bare feet through the narrow streets and eventually used his remote key to unlock the gate. The next step he took bathed his path in the gentle light of the immense tower before him.

No going back now. Gamma, pure electricity, whatever these structures were truly made of—he could bear it. Anything to staunch this *hunger* that started at his core and now gripped every centimeter of his flesh.

Breath now coming in labored pants, Rohem raised his left hand and pressed his palm outward toward the glowing surface.

He didn't stop until the steady sensation of exhilaration and power filled him once again.

Somewhere, he idly wondered if this is how Joleh's friends used to feel when…

No, he would not think of that. Not anymore.

And then, the light seemed to be all around him, swallowing him whole. Yet, he wasn't afraid…

"*You are safe.*"

The words flowed through his mind more than they reached his ears. They had no voice, he simply *registered* the thoughts as naturally as taking a step forward.

He almost didn't care about the origin of the ethereal message. Only this indescribable strength that flowed through his very being.

Until he felt a furtive pressure engulf his open hand, and this strange, wonderful feeling surged to the point at which he might have forgotten his own name.

Not realizing he had closed his eyes, Rohem glanced around, feeling another presence materialize before him.

All around, the now impossibly iridescent bright light shimmered like a never-ending waterfall. Like the fabled Oasis of several Lirian legends. The sheer beauty of the bizarre glowing essence reflected the indescribable sense of ever increasing exhilaration he felt inside.

He felt as if he were riding a wave over the entire Plane itself.

Eager to see just how far this power extended, Rohem tested the mind speech again.

Are we inside the megalith?

The other presence seemed to send a signal then. Emotion? Perhaps mirth. All at once, Rohem realized that the light before his eyes seemed to pulsate with the emotions of the other entity.

"*Megalith—the people of the Plane call it so. You have initiated a cerebral connection by touching its surface.*"

"*You are in my mind...*"

At Rohem's question, the presence seemed to smile, a pulsating current through the rich blue-white light, as the pressure on his hand spread throughout his entire being. Glancing down, he now saw how the shining fluorescence around them seemed to have encased his entire body as well.

The sense of pure, undiluted power resembled nothing he had ever experienced. Both physical power and unblemished clarity—he never wanted to let go.

The indescribable haze of pleasure spread from his consciousness to the tips of where his limbs would normally have been, to his central core and below, culminating in a colossal wave of ecstasy that seemed to wash over him again and again...

All at once, the endless world of light vanished back to dimly lit night, as Rohem found himself standing on the sand beside the megalith. His breaths came even heavier than before.

"We can also speak as you are accustomed," stated the person who now stood before him, drawing a hand from the space between them. The entity with whom he'd just...frankly, the words escaped him. Judging by the hair length, he assumed he was looking at a female.

All conscious thought temporarily stagnated as soon as Rohem registered her appearance. Though the voice sounded relatively normal, the being before him looked utterly...*anomalous*. While the base tone of her face shared his own dark brown, no fewer than three overlapping, rotating spheres intersected her forehead, eyes and lips at asymmetrical points. Even in the soft glow from the megalith, the circles seemed to cast a subtle luminescence.

After several moments, Rohem realized she had spoken in Lirian. Her voice was low, muted, though not meek, with the subtlest trace of an accent. She wore a dark grey outfit that covered her from throat to feet, identical shirt and slacks seeming to flow as one, culminating in what appeared to be boots.

The odd uniform contrasted sharply with the glowing intricacies of her face and hands. Silky black hair nearly as long as Oria's shone softly in the gentle light.

Although Rohem's limbs still tingled, the same leaden sensation as that previous night had set in once more. An unprecedented feeling of satiation.

The logical half of Rohem's brain took this opportunity to pounce.

"What was that? Who *are* you?"

"A strong sense of curiosity." An almost mirthful intrigue graced her dark gaze, pupils giving off the faintest hint of blue. "Impressive."

Rohem remained silent, glancing to the megalith and then back at the woman before him.

"You've grown up among the Lirians," she stated plainly. "Before that, you lived in Tabira. You have no idea how many times I wanted to reach out, to speak to you. Through the light and as we are speaking now."

Despite the relaxed stupor that had set in, Rohem's patience was growing thin. This person seemed to have at least a general idea of his entire backstory, while he still knew nothing about her.

"I asked who you are."

After a brief pause, the woman spoke again. "Those who have raised you know me as Echil."

Any leftover heat seemed to drain out of Rohem at the speed of lightning, replaced by an ice-cold chill that settled in his gut.

"The Zaam…and the megalith."

"We call them the rises," Echil replied, that curiosity in her eyes growing, although she made no move to approach him.

If Rohem had to describe her expression, he could almost call it one of fascination.

"Rises," he stated simply.

"Yes." That rich voice never increased in volume, yet remained clear as the brisk night air. "The solar rises. Together, the five rises form a network which maintains the Field above the Plane."

"What does the Field do?" Despite his hesitation to believe any of this, a part of Rohem desperately feared that he would soon wake up from the first dream he'd ever had.

Only he never slept.

"It's an electromagnetic field," this allegedly living form of Echil explained. "I am familiar with your understanding of science, in particular physics, biology and basic astronomy. So I will tell you plainly. Together, the Field and the rises harness the full power of our star—of the sun."

"Solar energy," Rohem stated. "We are eons away from achieving the ability to draw power directly from our host star. We still rely on petrol, taken from the fossils of animals driven to extinction…"

"To fuel your technology, yes," Echil interjected gently. "Such is the first stage. Then comes the adoption of solar energy to fuel life itself. Everlasting life."

The photosynthesis process he had reasoned while speaking with Gether.

"You use solar power to prevent the aging process and enable instant cellular regeneration. How?"

"The Plane ones believe in the magic of the gods," Echil casually evaded, sauntering up to him ever so slowly. "Our host star has power all its own. Energy to fuel countless eons of civilization. With that advantage followed an end to destitution and all conflict over resources."

"But...but how was I able to touch the meg…the solar rise?"

Echil's slight smile transformed into a full-on grin as she raised a hand to ever so softly touch his cheek. "The healing, the fact that you don't bleed, the strength, the power you draw from sunlight…"

"No…" Rohem suddenly felt as if the very ground had fallen away beneath him. Idly he noticed that the bizarre overlapping circles also graced the back of her hand.

"The people of the Plane—I had a great part in teaching them verbal speech. Today, the distinct nations that congregated around each of the five rises have taken to speaking evolved variants of our language. The original tongue of the Plane. The language of the Zaam. Of your people."

Reality struck Rohem like a crude splash of cold water to the face—the abundance of the number five.

The time system used by the entire Plane prior to the Illumination. Five-day weeks, five-week months, five-month years, five nations, all worshipping these beings called Zaam in some form or another for millennia.

Staggering backward, the last thing he noted was the being before him tilt her head slowly to one side, mirroring the exact quirk for which Avithia frequently teased him when they were children....

Then he turned and ran back toward the city gates.

Once inside Lir proper, Rohem took a deep breath to steady his racing heart.

Giddy dizziness and a flurry of questions overwhelmed his mind.

If the Zaam had always, in fact, existed, were their seemingly wondrous abilities simply a result of inconceivably advanced technology?

And to think, observant Lirians such as Oria had spent countless years avoiding technology as much as possible, strongly distinguishing such advancements from the perceived mysticism of the Zaam…

And why Echil? Who was she, truly?

How often did the other Zaam walk the Plane? How many of them were there all together?

Even after years of knowing he was different, this new revelation seemed simply unfathomable. His mind felt close to exploding.

After approaching the home compound, Rohem's nerves still raged. Rest wouldn't come easily tonight.

As he passed the wooden pen outside the compound, Rohem took note of a low sound—a deep, strangled groan.

A strained noise that to his currently hypersensitive hearing sounded closer to a roar.

Yeni had been ill with age for the entire past year, her belly sac unable to retain as much water as her system required.

Entering the pen quietly so as not to startle her, Rohem took a shaky seat beside the large animal. Her gentle breathing had a lulling rhythm that he'd always found oddly relaxing.

Leaning a shoulder gently against the lukewarm fur of her thick neck, Rohem closed his eyes and recalled the day that Avithia and Oria had first taken him to see Yeni and her mother.

The first animals he'd ever laid eyes on besides the rare stray hound in Tabira. He'd since come to enjoy the horses' presence immensely. Sentient, and yet they could not speak. No judgment, no cause for violence or cunning.

Yeni's mother had passed years ago, leaving Yeni as possibly the last dunehorse on the Plane following the great famine that had swept Lir throughout the past one hundred years.

He knew the Garo had once kept steppehorses, though word had it that the Opal had taken them all for their own use, leading to the extinction of the species once the Tabir took control of the region north of the steppe.

Crouching down to caress Yeni's side, Rohem caught his own reflection in the contents of her water trough. From the depths of his eyes to random areas on his cheeks and forehead, a subtle dark blue glow seemed to emanate.

Stroking her soft pelt, Rohem realized how utterly relieved he felt at the sheer normalcy of this moment. He touched Yeni and she gave nothing in return. No spark or mystical sensation, only the soft sound of normal life in its old age.

Her breaths were truly ragged this night, suggesting why she had been groaning. Moreover, the skin beneath her fur held considerably less natural heat than normal.

Her blood was beginning to thin and slow as well.

No. He refused to think of Hazur.

Pursing his lips, Rohem kept his eyes closed and focused on transferring the vestiges of warm energy he'd gathered during his terrifying yet wonderful encounter.

Just to make her more comfortable while he rested tonight at her side. In turn, he soon found that the energy provision settled his mind as well—enough to rest, at least.

Yeni gave a slight huff in response and nosed against his neck, settling down peacefully.

By the first light of morning, her breaths had ceased.

APEX FIVE

Chapter Fourteen

After seeing his sister stunned with that strange weapon, Ara wanted to kick himself for not trying harder to resist his own restraints.

What cowards these Tabir already seemed to be. First things first, find Inad and escape.

Ara had only seen his father fly twice before his passing.

The first time had been as a display for the locals during the first months of their stay on Ayam. Though Vata always insisted that Inad had been too young at the time to remember, Ara recalled the event in bits and pieces.

The second time had been to rescue Vata from a palm cat that was stalking her dais on the mainland. This event both Ara and Inad remembered vividly.

One of the Ayam women had been offering Vata a freshly picked honey melon. Their mother had refused curtly, convinced that the fruit hadn't been washed properly. No sooner had the native woman's eyes filled with fear that Inad and Ara heard the hiss from behind them.

Dropping the piece of fruit and grasping both small children roughly by their shoulders, pushing them to the nearest trunk with rope ladder not two meters away, the Ayam woman shoved first Ara and then Inad ahead of her up the tree.

Behind them, the palm cat began to circle the closer pray—Vata.

Although palm cats were known to climb trees on occasion, they usually avoided areas with more than one native person. The fact that this animal simply yowled and continued to advance on Vata suggested it to be a rogue, for which previous encounters with Ayam spears held no concern.

Once up in the tree, the initial shock passed and both children began calling for their mother. Once the woman had hushed them, they simply watched the beast below prowl closer and closer to Vata, who still sat rooted to the spot.

And then, their father had dropped from the canopy and swooped in to pluck their mother from the jaws of a creature about to lunge.

Even to Ara's faint memory, Hak's wingspan had been magnificent. Bright blue colored throughout with streaks of green and red, he had never witnessed anything so colorful, aside from the rainbows that sometimes graced the sky over the canopy following a rainfall.

This past warm season would make already twelve years that he had been gone from the Plane.

Ara wasn't as simple as he felt certain many suspected. He knew the reason behind his mother's sour disposition toward him. In fact, he often placed himself in her shoes to try and understand why she might compare him to his father. It all made sense. She missed Hak greatly. Though perhaps even more so, she had despised her husband for his affair.

They truly were opposites, Hak and Vata. Hak had always been gentle and lighthearted with the children—particularly Ara, assuring him that his difficulty in reading and writing was nothing to be ashamed of.

Vata had a fierce light, a fact known to all who crossed her path. Ara had decided long ago that if his mother regarded both him and his father with scorn, she must have her reasons.

Still, prison for Inad struck Ara as taking it a step too far, even for their mother. He only wished he'd had a chance to see where they'd thrown Inad amidst all the chaos of these three levels of cages. Metal cages they were, far sturdier than the hardgrass enclosures currently used to confine *onn* beasts.

He had to wonder why his mother had never sent for a shipment of such cages to the islands. Though somewhere in the back of his mind he understood Vata's need to realize her mission. The mission to strip the Ayam people of all belief in the Zaam, no matter what it took.

At such moments of doubt, Ara tended to self-console with the memories of their mother before their father's death. Though always strong-willed and impatient, Vata's eyes had never held the disdain for him they always seemed to throughout the years since losing Hak.

Still, pondering over his mother could wait. Just then, Ara only wished that his father had taught him how to fly, as well any tips on carrying capacity. Although on that day Hak had only flown with Vata the short distance to the nearest tree dwelling, the fact that their father had managed the weight of a person with solid bones boded well for Ara carrying Inad.

Crossing the sea would be a whole other matter entirely…

Ara's thought train halted at the sound of a raspy voice.

"Hey you, what's with the hairnet?"

Ara glanced around in the shadowy stillness, momentarily taken off guard by the voice coming from his otherwise empty cell, until he realized the person had spoken from the next cell over. A lanky, yet muscled man in a sleeveless shirt that looked like it hadn't seen a wash in a while.

Instinctively, Ara bit his tongue. As it was, he considered it a miracle that his hair cover had withstood the onslaught of hot water they'd used to detoxify him…

Then, remembering that his mother wasn't around to chide him, he assumed her demeanor instead.

"Hiding something you wouldn't want to see."

"Is that right?" The other prisoner's eyes seemed to gleam in the shallow stream of light from Tabira's megalith that graced the windowpane. "Mysterious one here. Hey Tike, we've got a new one."

"Dressed all funny, aren't you?" remarked the younger inmate. Tikeh.

"Don't mind him," the first said. "I'm Chomad. Tikeh and me sometimes get restless at night. Odd sleep habits."

"Some of us get naps after each meal," Tikeh harrumphed, turning over on his bench. "You have kitchen duty. Unlike those of us who are called in every time the toilets need cleaning."

"Anyway," Chomad continued, turning back to Ara, "what's your story?"

For the first time, a cage made Ara feel brave. What did he have to lose?

"Have you heard of the Flightless?"

"Sure," Tikeh scoffed after a moment. "Those bird people on that island. They're apparently famous with the natives. Not me though. Chomad and I worship the Zaam only. No half-animals."

"The Zaam…" Ara stated. "But you're Tabir, aren't you?"

Chomad barked a laugh. "That's what landed us in here. Two Tabir who dared to keep the faith."

"So you are friends then?" Ara asked.

Tikeh quirked a grin at Chomad. "Special friends."

"Took him a while to grow on me. We take turns bribing the guards," Chomad put in.

"Or trying," his cellmate chuckled. "The one who comes around here at night is a Concealed officer. He won't accept any pleasure favors."

"Concealed?" Ara asked after a pause.

"Prison speak for an undercover religious Tabir who joined the Kano to avoid penalty after the Illumination," Chomad explained. "There are likely a lot of them out there. Funny thing—one of the other inmates actually took first notice when we overheard him talking all quiet on his speaker to the Mak. Something about being worried the disease over on the colony would harm her sister's children. It's no secret that the Mak's sister's kids are Flightless. Only a person of the faith would give a hound's end what happened to those—if there are any left, that is."

After one final glance around the dark corridor of cells, Ara took this opportunity to pull off his hairnet, releasing colorful quills that shone even in the soft light from the window.

"There are."

The men across from him simply stared for a moment, mouths agape.

Tikeh spoke up. "Who threw you in here again?"

"My mother," Ara stated truthfully. "To punish my sister for not marrying the chief of the Ayam colony."

"Keep it down, you two," Chomad shushed them. "And you, put that cover back on your head. It's for the Concealed only."

"It's real," Ara assured him, even as he secured the hairnet back atop his crown. "Which guards keep the faith?"

"We'll point him out," Tikeh said. "Plenty do, though the one on this floor works the night shift. He'll be around…"

That was when that brutish horn sounded again, and two guards appeared from the lift moments later.

"Neither of those," Chomad hissed in Ara's direction before taking a seat on his bench and pretending to busy himself reading.

When the guards stopped at Ara's cell, he took a seat as well. Within the next moment, he realized the presence of a woman between them. A woman carrying a bundle.

"New cellmate," grumbled one of the officers, unlocking the door to Ara's cage and nudging the woman inside.

Even after the guards had departed, the two men in the adjacent cell, as well as the woman with the swaddle, kept silent.

As soon as the bundle whined softly, Ara's suspicions were confirmed. She was holding a baby.

Moreover, she looked terrified.

Feeling guilty, Ara decided to try and ease her nerves as best as possible. If he couldn't help Inad at this moment, he at least intended to be of some use.

"Where are you from?" he asked.

Not looking him in the eye, the woman replied meekly, "The old quarter. Do you know it?"

Ara nodded. "My aunt works at the Capital."

"Why would you be in prison, then?" The woman did spare a glance this time.

"My family isn't very happy with me at the moment," Ara replied honestly. "What's your young one's name?"

"Rela," she answered after a moment. "And I am Kamra. I suppose I should be thankful that they've caught us and the worst is over."

"The worst?" Ara frowned.

"The waiting to be caught." Kamra averted her eyes once more. "What's your name?"

"Ara. And you're right, as long as we lay low, everything will be just fine. The worst has passed."

***

Once outside the gates of Lir, Oria stopped to catch her breath.

Glancing at the glowing digits on her wrist timer, she smiled. She had finished her evening jog in under an hour this time, and that had been *after* covering the entire inner city.

Taking a brief break and slowing to a brisk walk, Oria reflected on the recent atrocity at the Lirian temple. She had never before been so close to a fire, seen the men burning, the smoke stinging her eyes.

Even from several meters away, she had seen it all. Now, she could still picture clear as day their peeling flesh as they howled prayers in sheer agony…

Somewhere in the depths of her mind, a voice that she hated to acknowledge wondered if maybe her foolish rashness toward Par had somehow started the domino effect of first the terror attack on the temple and then the Garo governor's death.

Of course, her grandmother's comments on the matter didn't help Oria's guilt at all. No more than the older woman's tendency to voice every thought on how Oria's weight diminished her marriage prospects did wonders for the latter's self-esteem.

These days, intelligence mattered just as much as faith. Intelligence and the protection of Lir.

She only dreaded how the Garo may retaliate next—and how her people were expected to simply lay down and take it, never permitted by the Kano to venture into Garo territory, even to defend Lir.

Tightening her hair band, she sprinted the last few steps to meet Nasin and the others outside the base.

No more knee aches either. Definitely an improvement.

Only moments later, Rohem appeared seemingly from nowhere.

"Took one of the terror tunnels." He quirked a teasing smile at Oria's questioning glance.

"Did you sleep outside the gates again?" Thia asked. "We're all sad over Yeni, but we need you in one piece for this mission."

"I'm here in one piece," Rohem shot back, glancing sideways at Oria.

If she hadn't known better, she might have thought he actually looked...*tired.*

As soon as Thia had engaged Nasin in conversation, Rohem spoke. "Oria, what's the significance of your hair? It's length, I mean? The religious meaning?"

Frowning curiously, Oria replied, "The archaic accounts say that Echil appeared with such a hairstyle when she walked alongside us on the Plane."

Just then, a rise in volume of Thia's speech caught their attention.

"Lir really should have started engineering massive gliders long before now," Thia huffed as they waited at the base for the arrival of the Tabir escort. "Where is the interpreter, anyway?"

"Lan should be here any minute," Nasin replied.

"Kano aircraft survey the Teal Sea daily," Rohem regarded Thia's previous question. "It's officially Tabir airspace. No Lirian glider would make it to those islands."

"It's not enough that they have officers on our border and in charge of our prison," fumed Thia. "These people want to police the entire Plane!"

"So we essentially have no idea what to expect on Ayam," Oria said bitterly. "Seeing as no Lirian has actually been there. All the informants have gathered is what they've picked up on the streets in Tabira, which is barely more than what we hear in the news anyway. A *mysterious* illness that's spreading quickly. How do we know they're not sending us into a trap?"

"I would suspect the same," Nasin replied, "if we hadn't been the ones to request the expedition."

"We'll have our communicators on at all times," Rohem put in. "And Ayam has access to Network connection. Oria, if you find something in any of your research, we know you'll reach out."

"Of course." Oria squinted against the harsh morning sun, then noticed the figures emerging from the short distance between the gates and Lir's megalith. "I think the Garo have arrived."

Surely enough, the treasurer and stand-in governor, Belim himself, had come to greet them, approaching side-by-side with his wife, Lan.

While Nasin and Oria had observed Lan while the Garo had served as interpreter during diplomatic discussions, Thia and Rohem seemed both taken aback by her light coloring.

Delicate features concealed in gold paint, both had to marvel slightly at how closely the guise matched her sand-colored hair. She wore her locks partially braided, presumably to keep them from being marred by paint.

As always, Belim wore the face of a politician—no paint.

“First Lasha, apologies for the delay.” Belim regarded Nasin with a smile so full of charm Oria wanted to gag. She hoped for Thia and Rohem’s sake that he wouldn’t be joining them on this mission.

“Governor.” Nasin nodded politely. “Lan. The escort should be arriving momentarily.”

In fact, the low faint rumble had already announced the approach of the great glider from beyond the dusky horizon.

The ground crew was thankful for the great megalith, which shielded the city wall from most of the dust storm that was kicked up as a result of the massive machine touching down onto the dunes.

As the arrival of the glider grew to a near-deafening rumble, Belim stepped surreptitiously away from his wife and whispered softly, just loudly enough for a Lasha to detect. “If either one of those freaks harms Lan, you’ll have an enemy in Tabira to the west and Garo to the east.”

Right. As if Lir weren’t already at war with Garo, Nasin thought.

Several sharp barks distracted Belim from his menacing stance.

Garo and Lirians alike turned to see the Tabir pilot step down from the glider, holding tight to the leash of a hound.

Though she’d never admit it, Oria was grateful that the animal didn’t growl any further beyond the first few barks.

“Let’s get going.” The pilot wasted no time. “You can load all cargo into the hold back there.” He pressed a button on the inside panel of the exit he’d just taken, and a large wall of metal lifted up toward the rear of the glider. “If my hound smells anything strange in the cargo, that item will not come along.”

Although the hydroblaster was currently folded to half its normal size, Oria saw Thia glance rapidly at Rohem, who carried the concealed weapon on his shoulders as if it were a massive backpack.

As luck would have it, the blaster passed the test.

Once Lan and Belim had said their farewells, the Garo woman embarked the glider first. Behind her, Thia followed like a scorpion on a watchful prowl.

"Stay calm," Rohem hissed once they had all boarded and he took a seat beside Thia in the second row of seats behind Lan. "You saw Nasin pat her down out there."

"I wouldn't put it past one of them to conceal a weapon on the inside," Thia grumbled, staring straight ahead.

Rohem just raised his eyebrows as the glider engines began rumbling once more.

Soon, their attention was drawn to the sand falling away below as the glider lifted into the sky.

Thia was busy admiring the view of the megalith from this height, when Rohem took notice of a whimper. Lan was clutching both arms of her seat, trying apparently with all her might to conceal her fear.

"Guess she's never flown a small glider," Thia mused quietly.

"Their women aren't even permitted to drive automobiles," Rohem pointed out.

By now, the glider had leveled out. Every few minutes, the slightest dip would elicit another muffled gasp from Lan.

"You want to keep her company?" Rohem asked playfully under his breath. "Distract her before she has a heart attack?"

Thia crossed her arms. "I'm not going over there. You can feel free."

Rohem stood up carefully despite another dip of the glider.

"Watch my back." He smirked at the Lasha beside him.

Settling in beside Lan, Rohem soon realized the Garo might take a while to notice that he'd joined her.

"Everything looks so different from up here," he spoke gently.

Glancing slowly sideways, Lan replied, "– the physics of this just seems all wrong. So many issues could arise with the mechanics."

Rohem had to admit, he was taken aback by both her fluency in Lirian and her generally eloquent speaking style.

Right, time to take her mind off the tremors.

"Avithia and I fly these gliders all the time back at that base—smaller ones. Definitely less steady than this one. We'll be fine. The pilot knows what he's doing."

"Women—piloting," Lan remarked, her voice seemingly a bit smoother. "I'd just like to drive. It would be so much easier to make the trip to Lir on my own for meetings."

"I've never seen you during a discussion between Nasin and the Garo leadership," Rohem said.

Lan turned to him then, not boldly but not shyly either. "At how many talks would Par allow your presence? Or the other Lasha—"

"Thia," Rohem finished for her, when he swore he could feel the namesake bristle two rows back.

"Avithia," Lan stated. "Even the faithful one, – the intelligence officer. Though she holds her ground well."

"Nasin taught us well." Rohem smiled.

"The island will be fascinating," Lan said, almost wistfully. "I can feel it. Although it's a shame they likely won't have shrines."

Rohem paused thoughtfully before replying. "The Ayam are arguably the most faithful of the four nations. I am sure they have their own ways of worship."

"…I suppose you're right."

After a moment of silence, Lan leaned back against the headrest.

"Feeling a bit better?"

"Hmm," Lan returned. "I drank some herbal tea for relaxation. Belim felt I might need it. He always says women worry too much. This is one situation where I'd agree with him on that."

Rohem made to rise and return to Thia, when Lan set her right hand on the armrest, her pinky finger brushing his forearm ever so slightly.

She was warm. Nowhere near as warm as Echil's touch had been, but quite pleasant. Normal.

Rohem smiled again.

Thinking again of Echil, he couldn't help but marvel at the accuracy with which people of faith seemed to have captured the…entity's form in their figurines. Right down to the hair length, emulated by pious women like Oria and Lan.

Different from the ear-length style of Nasin, Thia, and even Eta, as he could recall. Different, yet pleasing.

As Lan's breathing steadied beside him, Rohem glanced past her out the window beyond.

The wispy strands of white clouds against the rich blue backdrop brought up so many questions, he nearly had to look away.

How could he even explain any of this to Nasin and the other wards?

Rohem continued to watch with silent fascination as they rose to unprecedented heights, far above anywhere he and Avithia had flown by glider.

From all the way up here, the Plane no longer appeared flat, but curved…

Just how much didn't he know about this world in which he had grown up?

Moreover, was their glider flying through the Field at this very moment?

Chapter Fifteen

If one good fruit had grown from Telo's encounter with his new bride, it had been Inad's revelation of how the Curse spread.

The chief now knew beyond the shadow of a doubt that the illness indeed passed through relations—and the Tabir woman had known. Perhaps her mother had informed her, or perhaps Inad had figured it out on her own.

Idly, Telo fiddled with the shelled marriage necklace about his throat.

Whether Vata truly kept such secrets from her daughter as Inad claimed, Telo had no way of knowing. He only knew what he had to do.

What action he and his warriors must take to save their people. A quest on which they should have embarked long ago.

Vata had run away like a coward, leaving a simple decision for Telo. He would not wait twenty suns. By the next sundown, they would go to war. The Ayam would band together and face the *onn* beasts.

For the past five suns, all men upwards of ten years old had begun training to defend themselves, if caught outside and below after dark. Soon, they would finally gain stronger weapons as well.

"Chief Telo," his head warrior Dato informed, approaching Telo from where he waited surreptitiously behind the trunk of a large palm, pretending to survey the women washing clothes. "The leader of the Tabir warriors has left his group. He is visiting a tree now. About five meters from the wisewoman's home."

"Very good." Telo nodded curtly. "The men are assembled?"

"Yes, Chief. By your home, just as planned."

Not wasting another moment, Telo puckered his lips and elicited the warrior's cry. Taking her cue, one of the women, Palu, dropped her basket and started screaming.

Make a scene. Cause a distraction. Behave as savages to stall the Tabir.

As Dato darted off to feign an assault on Palu, Telo activated his communicator and shouted, "Come now! Several men are attacking a woman! We need backup!"

Within the next several moments, he could already hear the Tabir officers approaching, as he ran in the direction of Maru's dwelling.

Officer Doreh took a deep breath of fresh, humid air.

Only two days and already the forest seemed far quieter without the head colonist and her children. Particularly Vata. Whereas even highly esteemed officers such as Samed over in Lir shared regional control with the rightful territorial leaders, Doreh now held complete authority in Ayam.

Of course, there was the Chief. While many Tabir such as Vata and the Mak didn't even tend to regard even the Ayam ruler as an actual person let alone a powerful figure, Doreh had to admit inwardly the young man's intimidating presence. Not that he would ever let this wariness be known…

Yet, neither Telo nor any of the other natives had caused him and the troop any trouble. It had been blissfully quiet. In fact, for the first time in years, Doreh's homesickness didn't plague him so strongly.

Surely enough, Telo spotted the lead Kano officer, Doreh, crouching in the dirt, just in time to alter the angle of his arrival so that the soldier wouldn't see him and have time to draw any weapons before the chief could get close enough.

The head officer didn't even know what had hit him until Telo had the dagger—Inad's dagger, as it were—at his throat.

Feeling the slightest shift of Doreh's hips, Telo pressed the bone blade against the soldier's flesh until a drop of blood ran along the dull white edge of the weapon.

"Try anything, and you die," Telo hissed, feeling around the man's pants, currently pooled about his feet, and withdrawing a handgun with his other hand.

In a smooth second motion, he knocked the communicator from Doreh's ear. "Put back your pants now. And stand up."

Lips pursed and face blanched with humiliation and anger, Doreh pulled up his pants and turned to face the Ayam chief.

Stepping on the tiny communicator with his bare foot, Telo aimed the gun and held the dagger slightly raised. "You will take me to your weapons," he stated coldly.

"You're not happy with your *spears*?" sneered Doreh.

With a single click, Telo prepared the trigger with his forefinger. "I want to see the guns. *All* of them."

"We'll have to take that canoe of yours," the Kano deadpanned, realizing he truly wasn't avoiding this one.

As it happened, the guns were stashed on the small island, beneath Vata's makeshift throne. How fitting.

Before the light even dropped behind the Great Stone, the inevitable skirmish erupted.

Doreh made a mad dash to alert his men, who began shooting, only to miss the warriors who had already scattered into the dense brush. Once their artillery ran out, Telo and his warriors incapacitated the troop with both their spears and the newly acquired guns.

Only Doreh survived, dashing away into the jungle.

Dropping out of and from behind trees, the Ayam warriors regrouped around the base of Telo's home, where they began to practice fighting form with the Tabir gun as well as the mighty spear.

The rest of the day passed like the flight of a watermoth.

Telo had been sitting at the lip of the Maw now ever since the sun began its descent behind the Great Stone. Part of him itched even now to wait for the flute's song, warning the people of the approaching dusk. To stay seated where he could so easily lean forward and see which happened first.

Even from up here, he swore he caught a faint whiff of rotting flesh…

Maru often encouraged afflicted Ayam who approached her to end their lives here. Unable to bring herself to poison them slowly with the lethal *laka* herb, the wisewoman instructed those who wished to die before another transformation to step off the lip of the Maw.

Even now, perhaps Telo could glance down and see all the corpses of the beasts who had wandered too far and their victims who had joined them—or perhaps the chief would lose his balance and fall into the abyss himself. To join his mother and father…

The Zaam would sooner fall from the skies.

Telo glanced up, the first faint stars emerging as the glow of the massive Stone gradually replaced the sun's receding rays.

Just then, the communicator around his neck chirped.

How he despised these machines he had to wear whenever the colonizers were away. He truly had no mind to speak with Vata or any of her fools this morning.

"Yes?" he barked.

"It's Vata. I'll arrive by tomorrow morning." She cut the line from her end.

Thank the Zaam that had been brief. She'd better have Inad in tow. Telo also wondered where Ara had gotten up to. Knowing Vata, she likely felt them both deserving of some cruel whim she wanted to enact.

And well, even if he couldn't have Inad and her brother safely back on the island just yet, he would ensure Vata's acquiescence to return them once Telo demonstrated the true strength of the Ayam people.

The people who had raised Vata's children.

Sighing, the chief fought the urge to lean further over the edge and glance down. No one knew for certain the actual depth of the Maw. He thought perhaps that would be the only advantage of one of those flying machines.

For tens of hundreds of days, the Ayam had flourished in these jungles without ever rising above the canopy. Quick of step and with a sure light, the chief and his warriors had surmounted all obstacles, from meat scarcity to flooding during the rainy season, to dangerous predators.

Until the arrival of the people from across the Great Water. Ever since the Curse spread, the entire village had spent their days hurrying to rebuild dwellings up in the treetops rather than on the ground. While some Ayam had always lived above the ground, today they knew only the canopy after nightfall.

Yet today, his men had proved ample strength during practice. Even Finu, usually more content to help Maru with her herbal remedies, had taken up his spear.

For a woman, or so his younger brother claimed. Telo had to admit any woman who could resist Finu's charm long enough for the latter to actually feel obligated to flaunt his warrior light impressed him.

As if on cue, Finu sat down with a thud beside the chief, spear in hand.

"I knew I'd find you out here," Telo's brother muttered breathlessly.

"Did you run here?" asked Telo.

"No." Finu began to pick at the dull end of his hardgrass spear. "Just easily winded today."

"You're out of practice from all your herbal lessons with Maru." Telo almost smiled. "You belong with us. With the warriors."

"Ako actually says she admires my interest in the healing craft." Finu grinned, the waning sunlight illuminating his brown eyes.

"Ako," Telo scoffed. "Ako is married, Finu."

"Why should we accept the Tabir custom of one partner?" Finu quipped. "Besides, her man ran off. Nearly two suns ago."

"Ah. And when did you last see her? Have you granted her the name of keeper?" Telo teased.

"She…is shy. Coy as a *tan* bird. But I like the mystery…"

Without warning, Finu doubled over, clutching his front, spear rolling to the side.

"Finu, Brother," the chief started, "what's gone wrong? Do you have pain?"

In response, Finu let loose a rasping cough, blood splattering the soil of the ledge before him.

Nearly leaping back, Telo felt the blood drain from his face instantly. The heart pain and coughing with blood. The first signs of the Curse.

No. Zaam, please. Please, this could *not* be happening. He could not lose anyone else!

"I...I had suspected." Finu took a rattling breath, his lips bright red in the orange glow of the sunset. "So tired."

Finu's voice dragged Telo back to the present moment. "You and Ako…"

"Only once, this morning." Finu tried to steady his breathing, all the while clutching at his chest. "Her man left, then she disappeared before I woke again for the day…and as today went on, I grew so tired. You were right, Brother. Love spreads the Curse."

Wide-eyed, Telo simply stared at his brother, face fixed in a horrified grimace.

"Y-you know what you must do." Finu's teeth chattered as he struggled to get to his feet, grasping his spear in hand.

As Finu held out his spear to Telo, the chief resisted the urge to toss it back in his brother's face.

It was a chief's duty to protect his people—both the innocents who remained healthy and those who had fallen to the Curse.

In the case of the fallen, to save meant to end one's suffering.

"Quickly," Finu urged, turning his head to hack and spit out more blood. "Before my skin grows hard."

Unbidden, seemingly endless flashes of Finu's face throughout their time growing up flurried through Telo's mind.

The little boy with black hair that wouldn't flatten, the way he'd spoken back to their father on many an occasion, his love of climbing…

No. Perhaps Telo was a coward, but there was no honor in killing a member of one's family.

Snatching up Finu's spear from the ground, Telo grasped his brother roughly by the wrist and darted away from the clearing of the Maw into the dense forest.

After several dozen footfalls of Finu coughing violently and moaning in agony, they came to one of the hardgrass cages. Possibly the same one in which Vata's husband, Hak, had perished to her gun before having the chance to fight his way free as a beast.

"This will never hold," Finu remarked through shaky breaths. The skin of his face had turned ashen, his eyes red-rimmed.

"It will give me a head start." Telo shoved him inside and tied the flat grass strip around the stalk of entrance and side. "You stand a greater chance of surviving until morning."

Telo set his jaw. A warrior never ran from danger...yet, as much as it pained him, turning his back now may be the only way to survive and save his people. The Ayam chief did not miss the look of sheer panic in his younger brother's eyes before Finu dropped to his knees with another coughing fit, this time crying out from the pain.

As the sun's final rays gave way to the steady glow of the Great Stone overhead, Finu's shoulder popped out of its socket—and Chief Telo ran, feet running so fast they seemed to glide over the soil.

Telo could not sleep that night. His thoughts raged like a violent thunderstorm. Every snap of a twig or cry of a night creature brought the dew drop-clear reflection of Finu's face right to the forefront behind his closed eyes. Only one choice remained – to sequester all those infected to the small island.

Telo prepared to allocate all available weapons to each Ayam they could, children included. For years, the people from across the sea had brought nothing but destruction. Even when Tabir themselves fell ill, they couldn't even be trusted to deliver a cure for the disease they had unleashed. Though he had to admit, Inad seemed as thrust into this as he was. He couldn't deny her the right to return home, should she make it back. Aside from her and her brother, however, any Tabir not be permitted back on Ayam. The people would not fall. Instead, they would grow strong enough to rid the ugly mark of the true monsters—the Tabir.

A sharp sound from right beside is head took him by surprise. The communicator.

"Vata," Telo managed just barely above a whisper. "Not now. Tomorrow hasn't even arrived…"

"This is Mak Eta, Chancellor of Tabira. Vata's sister."

Any other day, that voice and title may have brought him to fuller attention. Not today.

"Yes, Mak."

"Chief, a glider will arrive by morning on your side of the Plane. We have sent an emergency crew to assist with the situation on the island."

"Crew?" Telo sat up. "From Tabira?"

"No," Eta replied. "I assume you are aware of the other regions. Lir and Garo. Backup will come from these nations."

"Do you wish to destroy the Garo and Lir as well?" Telo asked pointedly, the fatigue clearing from his tone.

"They are aware of the danger," Eta returned sharply. "The glider will not arrive on Ayam until after dawn. We aim to help, Chief."

"Vata will be coming with them, then?"

"No," said the Mak. "My sister has set off from Tabira."

"And her daughter? My wife, Inad. And her brother?"

"Time will tell."

The communication line cut.

***

Both Erme and Inad awoke along with all three levels of inmates to the blaring horn.

A commotion followed closely by song. Inad sighed and rolled over, covering her eyes with the corner of her thin blanket. The Tabir national anthem, apparently sung by the Kano guards.

From the vast plains to the desert
The mountains to the palms
Out across the great sea

Tabira Tabira,
Through both darkness and light
There is no peak we cannot reach.

Short and sweet, thank whatever dwelt beyond the Plane.

Breakfast came soon after, and Erme ate sparingly. Inad refused any.

"Still not hungry?" Erme asked, spooning some soupy eggs into her mouth.

"Why is breakfast served in here?" Inad evaded the question.

"So we can get to work faster instead of taking up time in the kitchen. The meal hall is for supper only."

"What animal do these eggs even come from?" Inad wanted to know.

"Plaincow." Her cellmate shrugged. "They breed them on farms around here for either their eggs and meat, or burn them for fuel. You are far from home, aren't you?"

"Across a sea," Inad murmured, sitting back against the wall as her stomach let out another loud rumble.

"...not the Teal Sea?" Erme glanced at her wide-eyed.

"From the island colony itself." Inad didn't look at the other young woman.

"A-are there any other Tabir out there?"

"Besides my mother and brother, a few Kano officers, yes," replied Inad.

"How long are you in for?" Erme asked.

"However long my mother wishes," Inad answered bitterly. "My brother's here too. I have to find him."

"What does he look like?"

Inad thought for a moment, realizing he would certainly be keeping his crown concealed. Might this Erme actually be willing to help her search for Ara? Could she trust her? She did appear to be just another prisoner. Inad likely had little to lose...

"He wears a hairnet," Inad finally replied. "He was born with a misshapen head that my mother tells him to hide."

"I never knew my mother," Erme mused, finishing her chunk of bread and setting down the plate through the bars of the cell. "My little brother, Borad, probably saw me as an annoying parent though. The factory was really all we knew. There, all the children were treated the same, so we had to look after each other. Big machines, easy to get hurt."

"What did the factory make?" Inad ventured.

"Textiles. Clothes and such."

Inad chuckled. "You don't need factories to make clothing. On Ayam, all of the women make group events of weaving together fronds from all manner of plants. Even the houses are made from tree parts."

"Tree houses." Erme smiled almost wistfully. "Are there fearsome large cats like in the news stories?"

"Yes, once…"

Inad stopped short when Erme winced and clutched her chest, lying down on her bench mattress.

"Is everything all right?" Inad asked.

"Of course it is," came a male voice from behind her. "Little miss princess here just doesn't want to do her chores. It's the kitchen, sweet thing. Not exactly a hardship. Unlike you—"

The newly arrived guard glanced at Inad.

"New girl. Time for your first day on the job. Shower and toilets. Let's go."

With a glance back toward her cellmate, Inad nearly shivered at how quickly Erme's face had gone ashen, her lips turned a subtle shade of purple.

The eerie resemblance to Braku's early symptoms of the Curse had Inad on edge instantly.

"What's wrong with her?" Inad hissed to the guard, once they were out of earshot. "She looks ill."

"Nothing catching," the guard said nonchalantly. "Chemical poison. We see it in most of the inmates that come from the factories. Fake chemicals used to color clothes are toxic when they're fresh. Enough time breathing and touching the dye would poison even a beast the size of a plaincow."

Once the door opened, the smell hit her first. Rank, sour, and something stronger that turned her gut. Like fresh droppings.

"Toilets are backed up, and we only have a few others come on duty each day. Inmates are spread thin. Happy working."

The guard gestured to the corner where a stick with odd strands of grassy material seemed to sprout from the end. The stick sat in a metal basin.

Holding her breath in increments as long as she could muster, Inad ignored her rumbling stomach and tried to focus on the virtue of silence.

She had to find her brother.

***

The setting sun over the Garo steppe left in its wake faint starlight and white skyflame.

Kel crouched behind a shrub, waiting for Edo to leave the herb shop. He'd be taking out the next shipment by Tabir rail, if their business still continued as smoothly as last Deki had reported.

Damned Lir couldn't control every centimeter of the area—not when the Tabir wanted tube access through to the steppes. Fortunately for his family, Edo was the only herbalist the Tabir trusted enough to provide rail access. Escorted, of course.

Kel had always trusted Deki's sister. She had a keen eye for numbers and assessing profit. Lucky that Deki had an intelligent woman in the family, particularly given his own predilections for the narcotic grass. It amazed Kel how few Garo men even had the opportunity to pass through the Lirian checkpoint and study in Tabira—and yet still, males remained superior in every way.

Never before had the records told of a female Evaporation fighter. Never a female, and never a child under seventeen.

Which brought him right back to the small girl who now sat inside his house, praying by the shrine.

Tsal was a mother. Perhaps that was all he could hope for now in terms of a confidant on this matter.

"Pray until I return," he had instructed Unno. "Echil will ensure a strong flame for your mission to see Nok again."

Such a strange thirst for knowledge she had. Especially for a female. The son of grain tillers, Kel hadn't ambition for the sciences. The Evaporation had always provided a fulfilling enough life mission for him and his three elder brothers. They had given their lives valiantly, and he had taken up the role of cause leader in their honor.

Once the automobile had driven out of sight, Kel approached the house and knocked lightly on the door.

"Who comes?" called the voice from within.

"Kel," Tsal stated flatly, opening the door just a crack, thoroughly concealing the knife she kept for safety. He could only detect its presence from the crinkle of the shirt fabric over her hip. "Haven't seen you around here since we heard the news."

Kel nodded. "Just laying low. I was...held in questioning about the murder."

"As always." Tsal looked like she wanted to roll her eyes. "Those Kano suspecting fellow Garo. As if we're savages. Come on in."

Once Kel had entered, he took a slightly stiff seat on the sofa by the hearth.

"Still harboring the knife then?"

Tsal made her way over to the small kitchen behind the shop counter.

"A shop that sells grass would be just as much at risk for robbery in Lir as here," she stated simply.

In one of the two other small rooms, he could hear quiet chattering.

"Kids in for the night?" he asked casually.

"They're always a bit energetic whenever Edo makes a run. I've told them to settle in." Tsal fixed them both some tea, as the patter of gentle rain began outside.

"How have you and Edo been holding up?"

Tsal scoffed. "Edo never had patience for Deki's love of the grass, no matter how much that grass increased our profits ten-fold beyond any strictly medicinal herbs we sell here."

"Don't you ever worry the Kano will discover that you sell the grass? Aren't they always monitoring who boards the rail tube?"

Tsal glanced seriously then at Kel. "Really, all that time spent with Deki and you think anyone besides Edo uses the tube? Anyway, it's other Garo wanting the grass who worry us most."

Kel frowned, perplexed.

"Those Garo without Edo's privileges have always traveled by strait." Tsal deadpanned, as if it were the most obvious route.

"There are ships that cross the Strait?" Kel asked. "Kano ships?"

"Hardly." Tsal chuckled then. "The Kano have always felt themselves too good for ships. They consider them primitive. Outlaws and refugees man these ships, mostly. Garo trying to escape the occupation and make a life in Tabira."

"So they are pirate ships," Kel stated pointedly.

"Yes," Tsal replied once she had begun a fire at the hearth and took a seat in the chair across from Kel. "Tabira may have aircraft at their disposal, but they still rely on ships for transporting cargo across the Strait."

Kel worded his next statement carefully, keeping his voice low. "I've always been...*interested* in Deki's source."

"Surely, Deki has revealed his sources." Tsal stirred her tea. "Being as close friends as you were."

She fixed him with that stare of hers. The gaze that had always raised Kel's suspicion that she knew he and her brother had been more than just friends. Though he hadn't the heart to tell her the events surrounding Deki's death. Better she just believe the cover story, that he'd been taken out by a fellow grass handler.

After a pause, Kel asked, "How do Garo handlers make it past the Kano by the checkpoint into Lir?"

"The same way you do," she replied simply. "Tunnels. The old ones though, closer to the megalith and away from the outer Lirian base. The Lasha haven't come running to fill them in yet."

"They might not even know of their existence," Kel chortled. "Those tunnels are from the Opal days, nothing to do with the occupiers of today."

"I still wonder why they left at all." Tsal shook her head. "If their land meant so much to them. After all, *we* stayed, and the Opal tried to destroy our people as well."

Tsal's comparison between the Garo and Lir brought to mind a clear image of Unno just then.

"Tsal," Kel began again slowly, "what if—what if you had the chance to go study business in Tabira?"

Tsal quirked a brow. "You mean at one of their universities? The Mak has been assuring Par, and now even Belim, for months that an agreement is underway."

"I mean if it were possible right *now*," Kel cut in.

"As a woman, it wouldn't be easy. I'm sure Edo would have something to say. Though if it helped with the books for the shop, I'm sure I could sway him. I mean, who are we fooling? All that time spent in Tabira clearly helped the Lir gain the upper hand once they returned. Why do you ask?"

Glancing furtively over at the doorway to the other room, which now stood ajar and emitted no more sounds from within, Kel dropped his voice to a whisper.

"Before Governor Par passed…he sent me on a new mission. A mission which Belim has now taken charge of overseeing. I have a ward."

"Only one ward?" Tsal seemed perplexed.

"Yes," Kel replied. "A child. A girl. Ten years old."

After a lengthy pause, Tsal took a thoughtful sip of tea and averted her gaze. Then she raised her eyes to meet his again. "Men of the Evaporation never refuse a mission."

"As surely as the Zaam watch over us." Kel nodded. "However, the records hold no prior instances of either women or children giving themselves to the Realm of Joy in the name of the Evaporation—and certainly not for any other purpose."

"Surprising that Par would have thought up such a quest," Tsal remarked. "After what happened to his own daughter."

Kel said nothing.

"Will you see it through?" Tsal asked bluntly. "Seems like you might be having second thoughts."

Carefully dodging her question, Kel stated, "She is a woman of purpose. She wishes to learn the sciences."

"A will like that shouldn't go to waste, if you ask me." Tsal shook her head. "Have you ever thought her curiosity—and even her age—might come of use some other way?"

At Kel's horrified expression, Tsal waved him off. "For Zaam's sake, I would never suggest such a thing. I have children of my own. Still though, the innocence of children can put people off their guard. What if you were to use...what's her name?"

"Unno."

"What if you were to use Unno to ease the selling process?" Tsal's dark eyes almost glittered in the lamplight, half of her painted face cast in shadow.

"You mean have her at my side so people take pity on me?" Kel asked.

"You and her, of course," Tsal answered. "I've used Ike and Ani for such purposes many a time, even right at home here in Garo."

Kel thought carefully. "So if I could use the tunnels to take Unno out of Garo and avoid the Kano, we could hop a ship across the Strait to Tabira."

"And a child plus the grass are sure to win you some der, even in that godless nation." Tsal looked decidedly pleased with herself.

"But..." Kel frowned. "The Zaam's will. For Garo's freedom."

"The will of us all, trust me." Tsal rose, taking both of their empty tea cups. "But you're more likely to get further with a sweet-looking child at your side—and who knows, if she does somehow end up winning you enough der, by the time she's old enough, she might even be able to study the sciences in Tabira. Just make sure to start schooling her in the Tabir language now so she'll be able to handle herself over there. For now and the future. There are ways to carry out the Zaam's will besides early entry into the Realm. The likes of you and I are too old by now. Though, if we could have a Garo—a *female* Garo, at that—pioneer our nation's learning of higher technology, we could at least have a chance at rivaling the Lir and their water machines. At the very least, this Unno can draw in a lot of money for more of our people to afford that Lirian hospital."

By Echil, this woman had a strong mind.

Despite the elation he could already feel growing, Kel feared the first obstacle. "I don't have any grass to start with…"

Smiling wryly again, Tsal turned to open the uppermost cabinet by the kitchen window.

"Deki always kept some stashed up here. Who better to have it than you."

"And the Kano still buy that it's a healing herb?" Kel asked incredulously. "The grass has been outlawed in Tabira for years."

"They're police," Tsal scoffed, "not scientists. Though Edo has reported stories of a science wing of the Kano over in Tabira. Suppose the goons over here are just all brawn. Besides, the grass does heal in its own way. It clears the mind of pain."

Indeed, Kel had first met Deki around six years ago while visiting Tsal and Edo's shop. His last remaining brother was on his way out after a flame demonstration on the Lirian border, and Kel had sprinted the some thirty meters to retrieve the strongest pain-numbing herb. The shop's official owners had been out at the time, with Tsal and her young children tending to the herb patches while Edo made a product run. In their place, Tsal's brother and jovial assistant, Deki, had assured Kel that this herb would soothe his brother's burns until his passing.

Ever since his last surviving brother perished, Kel's yearning for a familial bond had somehow been satisfied by something different, and yet every bit as deep. A stable kind of comfort from which the spark never died. A comfort that kept him visiting the herbal shop week after week simply to speak with the herbalist's brother.

Love.

Forbidden love—of the ugliest kind, according to Garo law. Yet he would not have exchanged the sensation for anything. If only the Realm of Joy would provide a contentment half as sweet.

Once Kel had taken the paper bundle, Tsal continued in a low voice, "With the first temple song tomorrow at dawn, meet me here outside the front door. Edo will still be on his run, but the ships come and go all the time from the Strait's shores. The Kano fall short there as well. They think they're all freighters from Tabira, when it's usually Garo holding Tabir stevedores at knifepoint to pose as their cover. Some of the pirates are even Tabir themselves. Come with the girl, and I'll show you to the tunnels."

Turning to leave, Kel chanced to ask, "Why are you telling me all this? Helping me go against the wishes of the leadership?"

Tsal smiled. "I loved my brother. And he cared for you a great deal."

"What took you so long?" Unno demanded bluntly as soon as Kel stepped foot back inside his flat.

"Pack whatever clothes you brought from the prison," Kel answered. "The mission starts now."

Chapter Sixteen

Thia jerked awake, torn from a hazy stupor by a jolt of turbulence.

The last thing she remembered before drifting off were the Garo steppes gradually giving way to the higher, snow-capped mountains and cliffs of the since deserted Opal territory. Within the half-hour that followed, they had continued on eastward, taking to the skies over the sea…

Glancing groggily to her right, she slowly made out the empty seat beside her in the dull interior lighting of the glider.

The rumble of the huge engines had quieted to a droning hum.

Eyes roaming over the seats in front of her, Thia's gaze settled on the peak of Rohem's dark curls, just visible from where he sat—beside Lan.

Inwardly, Thia berated the sting of possessiveness that chewed at her core. Though she knew he didn't actually sleep, he was likely just resting there and keeping the Garo woman company. So she wouldn't have hysterics.

Sighing, Thia tried to focus on the small window to her left. The wing of the giant glider was just visible from here—about as long as a palm trunk, perhaps even longer. Every five seconds or so, white lights flashed at the tip.

The skyflame was nowhere to be seen from this angle.

Beyond the wing, the deep blue-black of night gradually took on the golden hue of dawn. Thia took another breath, this time of relief. She'd never admit it, but pure night without even the glow of the megalith presented an unprecedented sort of unease.

The tidbits of news from Tarel's and, more recently, Oria's investigations had used to analyze the situation in Ayam suddenly seemed very scarce. As if they were going in blind.

Without warning, a sharp chill pricked at Thia's spine, the fine hairs on the Lasha's nape standing on end.

Perhaps the proximity of a Garo coupled with the fact that they were virtually headed into an unknown situation had taken its toll—but Thia's senses had gone into overdrive, images of the scorched cement temple walls flooding her thoughts. Like a singed round log with a flat top, the ruined house of worship had stood amidst its decorative surrounding beds of blue, black and orange flowers burnt to a cinder. Even the trunks of the adjacent palms were streaked with black.

Thoughts turning to Lan, Thia struggled fruitlessly against the deluge of memories from the afternoon her mother was killed, caught in the petrol explosion set off by Garo terrorists at Lir's central market plaza.

Her father's face—she could still picture clear as day his expression of sadness and fear. Although the years had muddled plenty of other memories, and she remembered taking a time back then to process exactly what happened, she recalled Gether's face.

Over the ensuing days, she had eventually come to realize that her mother wasn't coming back to them. If it weren't for the few photographs they had kept, Thia likely would have forgotten her face by now. The face of one of the two people who had helped her through the first years of the change. Through those initial years of life.

Thia regretted not having brought along the photograph of her mother she normally kept in the wave pendant Oria had given her for her seventeenth birthday—the same year she had met Walar, ironically enough. The year she had officially obtained the title of Second Lasha and Nasin's backup, should strategic planning for Lir-Garo relations need to fall on someone other than the First.

Though as much as she wished to keep a reminder of her mother on her person, Thia soon concluded that the memento was safer at home with Nasin and Oria.

Should anything go seriously awry with their mission on Ayam.

The glider dropped several meters. From two rows back, Thia could make out a rustle as Lan shifted in her seat.

The Lasha nearly scoffed. The Garo woman was probably still floating on that grass from earlier. Relaxation herbs, indeed.

At the thought of the grass, Thia willed away the rising frustration she felt toward her most recent conversation with Nasin. The idea that her lifelong mentor might actually enjoy being worshipped left a disturbing taste in Thia's mouth.

Still, while their spat hadn't included the most ideal of parting words, she couldn't afford to dwell just then. Such was a discussion to revisit upon their return to Lir.

Upon landing on the vast open beachfront, multiple lights shone from several of the nearest jungle trees, marking the entrance to the village. Behind them, the waves lapped gently at the shore, the white sand still faintly glowing in the fading light of Ayam's megalith.

From the sound of it, their pilot had spoken via communicator with the chief himself rather than a Kano officer or some such ground operator, as she knew the process typically worked on Tabir airfields.

As the pilot, his hound, and the three passengers disembarked, the warm, moist air struck Thia first and foremost.

There was water in the air here. The distant rumble of thunder promised more to come.

Closing her eyes briefly and taking a deep breath, Thia approached the pilot.

"We're going straight to the chief?" she asked. "No Kano patrol?"

"Seems not," replied the pilot. "You should be relieved."

The Lasha might have snickered, were her nerves not still on high alert.

"I understand the Mak and her sister both entrust many Ayam affairs to the chief," Lan spoke up.

"Thanks for filling us in," Thia quipped.

Rohem just kept silent, falling into step between the Lasha and Lan as they followed the pilot over to a tree with an immensely wide trunk, its bark and upper branches strewn with electrical lighting that glowed in the dusky shadow of the canopy.

Climbing down from what Thia soon realized was a rope ladder, a young man dropped to his feet at the base of the tree before them.

Shirtless and barefoot, he wore half-trousers that reached to his knees. In his right hand, he held a spear made from either wood or bone. Thia couldn't tell which. Hair pulled up atop his head, his dark locks and brown eyes differed little from Nasin's or her own, his skin perhaps a shade lighter.

The hound let loose a brief growl that faded to a whine as its master tugged on the collar around its neck.

"Bright morning. I am Dato, first warrior of the Ayam," he spoke in halting, thickly accented Tabir. "Chief Telo will see you."

Thia wondered if the chief had instructed his first warrior to say this. Surely, Chief Telo spoke Tabir.

"Do we climb up?" Rohem asked, his voice standing out amidst the morning silence.

In truth, the jungle seemed alive with animal sounds. However, such noise still paled in intensity compared to the city life of Lir.

"The chief comes," Dato answered.

Moments later, another young man around Thia and Rohem's age descended the rope ladder, landing gracefully beside Dato. Like the first Ayam man, he wore his hair in a taut bun. He also stood with his chest exposed, his own cut-off trousers secured with a belt of rope.

"I am Chief Telo," he stated, without even the hint of a smile. His faint accent suggested years of schooling in the Tabir language. "Thank you for making this long journey."

Their pilot wasted no time. "Chief, where are Vata and the Kano?"

"The Kano are attending to matters of the illness that plagues us," Telo replied smoothly, "Vata will return from Tabira by midday."

Then, to Lan, Thia and Rohem, "Welcome, arrivals of Lir and Garo. We are pleased that you saw a fruitful journey. Names, please?"

"Avithia Getherka. Called Avithia."

"Lan Belimte. Called Lan."

"Rohem Nasinka. Called Rohem."

The chief's gaze lingered briefly on Rohem's face as he stated his name. This Ayam man clearly did have an impressive knowledge of Tabir. No doubt he was pondering the meaning of Rohem's name—'tree thing'.

Thia seized the task at hand. "The forest is beautiful. We are humbled to assist your people with the troubles they face."

Rohem followed up. "How long has the sickness afflicted your nation?"

"Just over twelve years," Telo replied.

"I will use my medical training to help in any way I can," Rohem continued.

Telo nodded, eyes moving to Lan, who still had yet to speak.

"I am interpreter and language specialist for the government of Garo," Lan stated in a steady enough tone. "I wish to gather knowledge of the Ayam language to share with my nation."

"Very good." Telo turned, starting on the worn dirt path away from his tree. "The women are just finishing the morning meal. After we eat, we can speak of the risk our nation faces."

***

For the days that followed, Ara went about his chores—kitchen, as it turned out—berating himself for having been so reckless in revealing his crown to two other inmates on his very first night in such a perilous situation.

His mother would have struck him at least once.

Miraculously, none of the guards had approached him yet. In fact, Tikeh had even pointed out to him the guard who evidently kept the faith. A lanky officer who worked the night shift. Chomad had applied to join the Kano, and assured Ara that all officers were trained to fly a glider.

Then there was his cellmate, Kamra—a woman of about thirty, with her seven-month-old infant. As it turned out, Kamra had been imprisoned for selling herself on the street.

"To feed my baby," she had insisted, even when Ara hadn't asked.

"What about your husband?" Ara asked.

"We don't marry in Tabira," she had answered. "You're a foreigner?"

"Yes." Ara had left it at that.

"My partner worked in the automobile factory. He enjoyed the grasswater too much. One night, he never came home. They found his body destroyed on the railway the next morning."

And that had left Kamra and her baby to fend for themselves.

Ara had never even considered selling oneself. It seemed odd that someone would be willing to pay for that.

"Can you work?" Ara had asked. "Back home, my sister teaches children to read and write."

"I never learned to read or write," Kamra had replied simply.

That had taken Ara aback. His mother had always spoken of Tabira as a place with educational opportunity for everyone.

Making sure his hairnet stayed firmly in place, he ignored the dull ache of the feather roots bending in on themselves beneath the wiry material.

"We are safer here," Kamra went on. "They feed us."

As a mother herself, Kamra worked alongside the other mothers of infants in a makeshift daycare.

During his next shift, Ara took a chance.

Acting on impulse for the second time since arriving to Tabira, Ara snagged a small jar to collect some foul-smelling but dark colored meat juice from the kitchen.

Once back at his cell, he tugged out a feather from his crown with a grimace. From there, he dipped the quill in the brown liquid and wrote up the Tabir character system on the wall space beside his sleep bench.

For several days thereafter, whenever Kamra wasn't resting between shifts and meals, Ara helped her voice the characters, and even began to write out certain words to help her sound them out.

Whenever he asked himself why he was doing this, the rational part of his brain always responded that he was looking to pass the time until he could either make it down to see Inad or catch that guard during his shift. After all, it did bring to mind afternoons of tree art with the children back on Ayam.

In the back of his mind though, the pride over being the more literate one for once threatened to spring forth.

It wasn't like his mother insisted. He wasn't completely useless with characters and learning.

The food preparation wasn't so complicated. The other inmates kept their heads down just as he did, and the day passed without much incident.

The main difference that struck Ara between Tabir and Ayam meal customs was the type of meat consumed. While back on Ayam, the largest beast they consumed was the palm cat—and that already not for some years—the Tabir evidently ate plaincow, a large beast at least the size of three grown men. He had seen images here and there during searches on the Network, and yet never had he *smelt* such an acrid stench of meat.

Holding his breath, Ara struggled to keep his chin down so that the neckline of his dark green prison uniform shirt stayed balanced over the bridge of his nose.

"The collar will keep slipping down," came a voice from beside him.

He glanced over to see a slim girl preparing a frying pan, onto which Ara then placed the meat he was flipping with his flat paddle.

He hadn't even taken notice of those around him. This girl appeared quite young for prison. Her face was ashen pale as well, as if she might be ill.

"Seems so." Ara quirked a smile. "Are you feeling all right?"

"I used to work in a factory," replied the girl. "Long working hours with little sun. We all get pretty pale. I'm Erme."

"Ara."

"Inad's brother?" she asked casually yet softly, oiling up the pan.

Ara halted mid-flip. "...You've met my sister?"

“We’re cellmates,” Erme said. “She told me to keep an eye out for the man with the hair piece. They put most people under sixty either in the kitchen or toilets. I figured it was only a matter of time before one of us ran into you.”

“How is she?” Ara wished he’d just skipped to asking if Erme had any idea where in the Plane’s name Inad was working.

“She doesn’t eat much.” Erme frowned, removing her gloves. “I’m off shift now. We’re on the second level, mid-section.”

Just then, a young man poked his head over the counter.

“Factory girl, make sure to actually *cook* the meat this time.” Then he glanced over at Ara. “Nice head piece.”

With that, he ducked away again.

Frowning, Ara looked to Erme.

“Just ignore him,” she muttered, keeping her head down. “Okad likes to stir up trouble. He thinks he’s a big deal in here because he got put away for a violent crime instead of self-defense or keeping the faith, like most of us.”

Ara kept silent.

With a final furtive glance over the counter—likely to check if the coast was clear of Okad--Erme turned and left.

Ara returned from his shift to find Kamra finishing up nursing her baby.

“Another lesson before supper?” she asked, eyes bright.

Ara smiled. He would find Inad, and they would soon be out of here. Until then, he planned to play the teacher for as long as possible.

APEX FIVE

Chapter Seventeen

Seabirds called out the first signs of dawn, their sharp cries running parallel with the hint of golden rays on the horizon over the eastern steppe. Already, the sky had begun to brighten, the approaching sunlight dappled through the dark, craggy branches of the leafless trees scattered across Garo's flatlands.

Right, Kel thought. *If seabirds fly this close, we can't be that far from the Strait.*

Needless to say, the proximity of their route hardly eased his disposition regarding Unno—whom he had hours earlier provided face paint supplied by Tsal for the girl to conceal herself as a newly chosen bride.

As for Kel, he wore a commoner's sun cap—abundant enough to not arouse suspicion, and a sufficient way to hide his own identity. As men of the Evaporation were known for avoiding sun caps and relying solely on the paint for protection from the harsh sun, his chances of being recognized would hopefully diminish.

"The water will be glorious," Unno whispered loudly as Kel studied the sloppily drawn map Tsal had made up for them. "We'll walk there?"

"It will take about an hour," Kel replied. "Hopefully we won't meet many others along the way. Just keep your head down, and do not speak unless spoken to. If anyone asks?"

"We have left the faith and Garo to escape the Lirians," Unno answered. "And I am the widow of your close friend killed in the war with Lir, now engaged to you. Because members of the Evaporation do not wed, but after giving up the faith, you are no longer a fighter."

"Yes, yes." Kel brushed her off. "But the second part will only be necessary if someone recognizes me."

"The Lirians might," mused Unno. "Let's hope those tunnels aren't guarded by any Lasha or Kano."

Kel wanted to bite his tongue. Was this girl *trying* to raise his nerves?

Deki likely would have laughed it off. He'd always gotten along with his own niece and nephew well and enjoyed looking after them while Edo and Tsal both had to tend to the shop.

Unno and Kel walked in silence for a bit. Apart from the occasional seabird shriek, the new dawn remained silent. Kel heaved a sigh of fresh morning air.

The silence didn't last long.

"What's it like on a ship?"

"I wouldn't know," Kel returned flippantly. "Never been on one."

"Kel." Unno nearly smiled. "I'll stop asking questions."

By some miracle, they traveled the rest of the way to the tunnels in sweet quiet...

Which inevitably left Kel alone with his own thoughts. Arguably just as insufferable.

Once again, sweat beaded on his forehead as Deki's death replayed itself in Kel's mind. Now that he was technically abandoning the Evaporation as a government-backed initiative, he tried not to focus too much on how much they would be depending on profit rendered from the grass Tsal had given him.

Moreover, he wondered who might be appointed to lead the Evaporation once Kel's desertion became apparent. Kel had only been selected by Par some ten years ago, following nearly another decade of relentless commitment to the cause.

Best not to fret over such matters any longer.

Thoughts returning to money and basic survival concerns such as eating, Kel also owed Tsal a great favor in return for the water supply she had provided them. Even just the one sizable canister could be split between Unno and Kel, while the rest could be mixed with bits of the grass...

Grasswater—while forbidden among members of the Evaporation and severely discouraged among the Garo at large—the beverage sold abundantly in Lirian dance houses. Somehow, Kel doubted that even elite Tabir were immune to the temptation of grasswater.

It wasn't until Kel spotted the first mark on the map that his heart began to race.

There it was, the nearly imperceptible mound in the firm steppe soil that should reveal the tunnel—when hacked into about half a meter.

This mound also marked the closest to the Lirian border he had ever tread while above ground.

"Stand watch," Kel instructed his ward.

Pulling his digging tool—the rarely used traditional Garo sparring weapon, the *tso* blade——– from his belt, Kel drew back his arm and began to chip fervently at the seemingly solid side of the mound.

"These used to be used only during the most honorable battles," Kel murmured between hacks. "Now, since the Kano have labeled them a terror weapon, we can't even use them in duels among Garo. The Lirians make all the rules."

"That's what we're going to change," Unno replied, keeping her face turned away, forearm shielding her face from the dust. "Enough talking and more digging."

For some reason, Kel had more inclination just then to laugh than to scold the girl for her impertinence.

Not ten minutes later, the sun had barely risen halfway above the steppe, and the two Garo refugees made their way into the cool, dark tunnel.

***

Telo showed the new arrivals to their nightly lodging—adjacently located vacated dwellings of unwed Ayam who had fallen to the Curse.

Thank Echil he had succeeded in a steady greeting, many thanks to Dato. His chief-second always provided welcome support, even when Telo had woken him at the break of light to tell the news of Finu.

As he struggled to focus on helping the newcomers settle in, the chief's stomach burned with nerves. Still, he took every opportunity to glance this way and that in search of his brother.

Had Finu made it through the night? Had he thrown himself into the Maw, upon returning to normal?

"Only Vata goes to the small island," Dato explained to Rohem, who inquired about the other piece of land across the narrow strait, just visible from beyond the black megalith that stood at the edge of the mainland.

"What about the Ayam?" Thia pressed. "Doesn't it belong to you as well? Have you tried quarantining the ill on the small island? Perhaps Vata could move to the large island…"

Dato glanced at Telo then in earnest, silently requesting assistance in interpretation.

"A fine idea," Telo mused genuinely, "Tell me, you are the chief of 'strategies', as the Tabir say?"

"Yes," Thia replied. "Martial strategies and weapons. Rohem is in medicine."

After a pause in which Telo and Dato looked to Lan, the Garo woman decided it was safe to speak again.

"I am…chief of language. I have come to study the Ayam language and bring knowledge back to Garo. In turn, I hope to spend time with your children and instruct them in the basics of Garo."

"A change from Tabir might be good." Telo nodded, "Very well. You and Rohem will work with Maru." He glanced to the elderly woman who now approached. "She speaks enough Tabir to communicate. Avithia, you will work with Dato and myself in training with weapons."

“Do the Ayam tribes have wars with each other?” Thia asked.

Following a brief pause in which the nearby stream rushing suddenly seemed deafening, the chief spoke. “The Tabir tell you little. The Ayam have not fought each other for more than twenty years. We have united as one people.”

“Under Tabir instruction?” Rohem prompted.

“Only if that was their purpose for turning our people into monsters with the Curse.”

“Curse?” Thia frowned.

“The sickness,” Dato clarified.

“Monsters?” Lan asked.

“Every night, the illness turns those who are sick into flesh-eating creatures, the *onn* beasts,” Telo elaborated. “*Onn* is the Ayam word for ‘cursed’. When the sun rises again, they turn back into Ayam.”

“You do not know this? No one tells you?” Dato asked in Thia’s direction.

Glancing furtively at Rohem, Thia seemed to communicate a look of...was it fear?

“Why do you think we told the machine not to land before first light?” Telo inquired, his gaze flitting in the pilot’s direction.

Perhaps these newcomers truly hadn’t any idea of the horrors into which they had stepped.

“So that is why you require weapons training,” Lan reasoned.

“We have trained on our own just fine,” Telo replied, not unkindly. “Still, you and Rohem’s strength and knowledge of different weapons will help us in this war.”

“The war,” Rohem deadpanned. “To oust the Tabir from Ayam? Where are all the Tabir again?”

“Clever.” Telo smiled admiringly as if Rohem were a child who’d just made an impressive discovery, rather than a man near his own age. He was piecing together the story. “We have cleared the Tabir from the area for now. They will not ruin this war to take back our land. To rid our people of this Curse spreading further.”

“You’ve killed the Kano stationed here,” Thia stated rhetorically, not sounding like she necessarily took issue with the concept.

“Their leader still hides in the trees,” Telo sneered. “We are searching for him. Coward.”

Dato chose that moment to interject. "We do not kill only to kill. Our people must live again."

Rohem seemed to ponder something, hands still calmly folded behind his back. "How does the Curse spread?"

"By the bite of a beast or a lick from its burning tongue," the chief answered gruffly. "And when people lie together."

"And how long is the incubation period?" Rohem asked, and then clarified following Telo's narrowed eyes. "How long before an afflicted turns?"

"As soon as the next night comes," Telo answered.

Just then, Dato glanced to the pilot at his right. "What do you have?" he asked harshly, stepping forward, swiftly confiscating the microcommunicator that the Tabir man was attempting to stealthily switch on by his ear.

Nodding at Dato, Telo surveyed the group of arrivals. "We thank you for your help. If you help us and bring no further threat, we will show you only kindness. You have my word as chief, shone upon by the Zaam."

***

When Erme told her cellmate the good news, Inad could scarcely believe it. Ara was close by!

"I've told him where we are," Erme explained. "He seemed hushed enough, so I expect him to lay low."

"He will." Inad nodded fervently. "How are you feeling?"

Erme shrugged. "Finishing shift always feels nice. Time for rest. How are your chores coming?"

"The smell." Inad wrinkled her nose. "And the cleaning thing—that stick with the sprouts at the end."

Erme giggled. "The mop, you mean?"

"Everything truly works better when you let the soil take care of the waste," Inad decided. "I'm headed back to wash up now for the night. Then thankfully, that's the last of the toilets I'll be seeing until tomorrow."

"I'll join." Erme followed Inad before the loud speaker called lights out.

The whole way to the washroom, Inad hoped beyond hope that Ara wouldn't search her cell area only to find her gone. She couldn't miss him. They had to find a way to escape. If possible, she would bring Erme along.

The three of them. Not truly belonging anywhere. Simply free.

Down at the toilets, Inad was just finishing cleansing her face with the cloth she rewashed daily when she heard Erme groan slightly beside her.

Glancing toward the door, Inad realized that a man had just entered. She had seen him before, around the kitchen. He appeared perhaps several years older than Ara. Not thick or slim, his presence gave off an air of confused haughtiness.

Looking around at first, he soon fixated on the two young women at the washbasins and snickered.

"Factory girl, make a new friend? Haven't seen you around here."

His gaze settled on Inad.

"I've been fortunate enough not to see any men at all in here till now." Inad returned to cleaning her face as Erme busied herself washing her hands.

"It's a shared area, new girl," replied the man. "I'm Okad."

"Thinks he owns the washroom before lights out," Erme murmured under her breath. "All because he tried to jump his own sister. It's what landed him in here."

"Erme likes to whisper when she lies," Okad said a bit too loudly. "About owning the washroom, that is. The other part is true."

Even as Erme looked like she wanted to head for the door, Inad stood her ground, wringing out her face cloth. She wasn't going to let some pervert order her around.

Okad continued, his voice still a shade too loud. "In any case, it's lights out. Time for you ladies to move along."

"I'm shaking from fear," Inad muttered, just loud enough for the young man to hear.

She didn't look at him, just finished washing her cheeks and forehead.

Drying her hands on her uniform, Erme made for the exit. Once she'd passed Okad and realized Inad hadn't moved, the younger woman glanced back.

"Inad, please come," she urged.

“Better listen to your friend.” Okad smirked.

“What if I don’t?” Inad was truly growing tired of people telling her what to do, when to speak, how to eat. Enough was enough.

“Hm, a little skinny, but I’m not complaining.” The words were followed closely by a firm squeeze of Inad’s backside.

Inad barely had time to turn around with a snarl before the soggy brush end of the mop smacked Okad over the head with a spray of water to his face.

“You…” Okad reeled on Erme just as the three inmates turned to see the Kano officer standing in the doorway.

“Lights out was half an hour ago,” the officer stated rigidly. “Follow me. All of you. *Now.*”

Even Okad didn’t protest. As Erme passed gingerly by the guard, he smacked her on the ear.

“And you, don’t *ever* let me catch you striking a fellow inmate again. Or I will finish the job he started back there with the new girl.”

That was it.

Inad saw red, her hands instinctively grabbing the miraculously still intact mop from the washroom floor. Drawing back with all her might, she grasped the wet brush end and used the momentum to smash the wooden end against the guard’s nose from behind.

After that, everything happened in a blur.

Through the rush of adrenaline and her painfully thudding heart rate, Inad idly registered Okad staring and following obediently as the guard with the now bloodied face grabbed both her and Erme by the upper arms.

His grip would leave bruises, and yet Inad’s endorphins numbed the ache to a dull itch.

It wasn’t until Inad was shoved into a large, cold chamber that she took notice of her surroundings.

How had they gotten here? She vaguely recalled the guard pulling them down a stairwell. Had her rage really muddled the memories between the washroom and their journey here?

Glancing around, Inad realized that Okad had left their company somewhere upstairs. Instead of sitting beside her, Erme stood beside the guard.

Please, no. He wasn’t going to hurt Erme—not because of Inad!

In the center of the room stood a meter-high platform with a glass tube three times that size feeding into the ceiling above, dwarfing both Erme and the officer.

"Please." Inad despised the sound of her own voice begging. "If you must punish someone, it should be me! Just get it over with!"

"Vata's daughter?" The guard mused almost gleefully, the area around his nose relatively clean of blood. "As much as I'd like to have you my way, the Mak would have other ideas."

Inad considered bolting for the door, but she couldn't handle the thought of abandoning Erme. The girl was barely more than a child…

"As luck would have it," the guard went on, "this little slave here has no powerful family watching out for her."

In another situation, Inad may have scoffed at the idea of either Vata or her aunt actually watching out for her.

Now she just stood transfixed, as if her feet had molded to the floor beneath her.

Making a final dive for Erme as the guard pulled her onto the platform before them, the Kano officer turned and backhanded Inad so hard that dark spots momentarily clouded her vision.

Stumbling backward, Inad fell to the hard cement ground. Watching helplessly, a cold fear icier than the day she'd been wed to the chief gripped her spine. Before her, the guard opened a child-sized panel at the front of the glass tube and heaved a barely struggling Erme into the encasing, shutting the small door moments later.

Just watching her cellmate start to squirm, Inad wanted to flinch at how cramped that space must feel. The urge to panic was becoming harder to resist, as Inad struggled to steady her breathing.

"You see, inmate," the guard turned and looked Inad straight in the eye, "we do things a little differently in Tabira. We're not savages. We only *tame* them."

In the next second, the Kano pulled a lever to the left of the door handle. The glass tube filled from top to bottom with what looked like water, until Erme was floating and wide-eyed, limbs flailing and bubbles escaping her mouth in silent screams.

"And neither the Mak nor your mother said anything about watching."

After what seemed like an hour, the guard pulled a second lever below the first one and the water vanished through a pipe inside the platform that stood below the tube. Inside the cylindrical, silica-based walls, Erme fell to her knees, gasping for air and sobbing frantically.

Turning her head to the side, Inad hacked to resist the bile that threatened to emerge.

By the fourth fill-up and emptying of the tube, Inad vomited the meager meal she had eaten hours earlier.

Barely able to catch her own breath and hating herself for it, Inad steeled her body against the limp form of Erme that the officer shoved into her arms.

"Clean that up," the guard barked, as Inad struggled to clear the mess beside her with the face cloth from her smock pocket, while supporting a barely conscious Erme with her other arm.

Beneath her fingers, the girl's hands felt frozen to the touch, her entire body shaking subtly. The water in that tube must have been *frigid.*

If she'd only screamed louder, been stronger—no, this still would have happened. Who was she fooling? She was just as powerless here as she had been on Ayam. Her dire mistake had been striking an authority figure without even considering the consequences.

Erme's torture was all on Inad. She had acted rashly and angered the guard, a move eerily similar to something her mother would have done. At the thought alone, a hot spike of rage settled in the pit of Inad's stomach.

The entire walk back to their cell, Inad envisioned herself as a mother palm cat nursing her injured young. Taking advantage of the darkened, empty corridor of cells, she removed her own uniform top to help dry off Erme from her soaked hair to her dripping hands and freezing feet.

Feeling the eyes of the approaching guard on her, Inad rose from her knees to help a violently shivering Erme into the cage, whose door would inevitably close on them.

It wasn't until the guard had fastened the padlock and departed that Inad glanced back out through the bars and saw Ara staring at them both with sad eyes that shone in the light from the small windows overhead.

Chapter Eighteen

"So it infects data cubes, but it's still called a virus?" Oria asked perplexedly.

Samed smiled. "It's a program that self-replicates the same way biological viruses do," he explained. "Another similarity is stealth. A computer virus changes its shape too quickly to be detected. That makes it difficult for computer users to deploy our own programs to track down malicious actors and eradicate them from our part of the Network. If left unchecked for too long, the satek within will be corrupted as well."

Oria sat back with a sigh, running her fingers through her long hair. Behind them, the spinning fan on the windowsill provided little relief against the returning heat of the warm season.

"I thought you were just going to show me how to use the Network to check for Tabir archives," she muttered. "Not give a lecture on computer illnesses."

"The signs of a virus are important to recognize," Samed continued. "If you don't annihilate a threat actor right away, the attacker who detonated the virus can easily gain access to all of your files. Once the satek are affected, the entire system crashes. Imagine a Tabir politician with special sympathy for the Garo's plight browsing all the intelligence you've gathered on Evaporation militants."

"I write down many of my findings by hand." Oria challenged.

"Your first mistake there was even telling me that in the first place. For all you know, I could be one of those politicians."

"You don't know where I keep my files." Oria surprised herself at the swiftness of her reply.

"They're physical files, not even encrypted or on a password-protected data cube," Samed retorted. "It would only be a matter of time."

"Encrypted?" Oria frowned.

"Hidden with a special code," Samed explained.

Oria raised her eyebrows as she looked over at him briefly. "Like your hidden purpose to dismantling our police force," she stated gently.

Pausing, expression unreadable, Samed's eyes flitted from her back to the monitor.

"Nothing was hidden there. Tabira's government has long considered Lir's power over the Garo as disproportionate. The choice lay between dissolving your police or removing your First Adviser."

Oria pondered this.

As she sat back in her seat, he glanced sideways at her. Though she didn't return his look, she was surprised at how his eyes on her didn't unnerve her. Perhaps it had something to do with the fact that his gaze didn't linger. He simply seemed to want to check on her digestion of the material.

Not that she had any way to know he was telling the truth. Though surely, the Mak could remove Nasin from power if she wanted to…

Thoughts returning to the present, Oria had to marvel inwardly at the current company.

She knew her grandmother would likely lock herself away in the temple for a week at the notion of Oria sitting so close to a Tabir—and a Kano, at that.

Now thinking of her grandmother, Oria took notice of the hour on the cube monitor before her. "It's already three hours past midday." She stood up, slinging her bag over her shoulder. "I must visit my grandmother. Thank you for the lessons, Officer Samed."

"Please, just Samed," the officer insisted as Oria took her leave.

The drive to her grandmother, Yasit's, home fortunately lasted under ten minutes. Still, by the time she exited the dunemobile, sweat beaded her forehead. They really needed to speak with the Lirian engineers about installing fans for vehicles.

Somehow, as she ascended the several steps to Yasit's modest house, Oria suddenly found herself wishing she could continue lessons with Samed. He had a stern, almost cryptic nature about him, and yet he either didn't notice or refrained from mentioning anything about her appearance. As much general distrust as she had grown up harboring toward the Tabir, she could appreciate such decency from Samed as an individual.

"You're late." Yasit stated the obvious as Oria entered the front quarter to find her grandmother on the sofa.

"Please pardon, grandmother," Oria replied, gathering up the empty teacup from the small table in front of Yasit. "I was working and lost track of time."

"Working, indeed," Yasit huffed. "If you took your proper place as a templewoman, you would be close by. Less worry about being late."

"Grandmother," Oria answered politely, rinsing the teacup at the washbasin in the small kitchen area, "we've discussed this. I can easily observe the faith and work outside the templehood."

Yasit scoffed. "Your husband would never approve of you working anywhere outside the templehood. And intelligence, at that? So close alongside those godless Tabir brutes?"

"We don't actually have to work that closely with the Tabir," Oria said. "Mostly we stick to our own resources."

Yasit hummed in reply. "You remember this evening?"

Drying off the cup and replacing it on the shelf above the counter, Oria turned to face her elder. "Of course, grandmother. How have you come by Leker?"

At that, Yasit smiled again. "A wonderful man and careful guardian of the word of the Zaam as salvaged in the last Sen. His father has served at the templehood his whole life. I have told him of your eligibility during our services these past months."

Oria smiled back good-naturedly. "I will dress for charm and decency."

Yasit smiled then, revealing worn teeth. "I keep your mother's evening wear in my bedroom closet. Though, I doubt they will fit you."

Oria bit her tongue instinctively.

"I have been tr-exercising."

"Also becoming to men, I am sure," Yasit answered sarcastically.

"Grandmother," Oria struggled not to grind her teeth, "what can I do? I exercise to shrink my figure. I cannot help if men don't like this. They don't have to watch me exercise."

"Those *brothers* of yours do," Yasit remarked. "I expect you're used to it by now."

"Avithia is a sister half the time," Oria retorted, knowing full-well that her grandmother wouldn't dare insult a Lasha. "Men of the faith need not concern themselves with my training. Can I get you any more tea?"

Yasit ignored her granddaughter's last question. "Or you could eat less and there would be no need for such training."

And there it was. Gut-wrenchingly similar to Governor Par's phrasing, in fact.

"I prefer to eat healthy and exercise," Oria stated coolly. "Now if you are quite well, I will go change. I have brought my own outfit for this evening."

"Just please leave off the spectacles," her grandmother called after her as Oria left for the sleep quarter to change.

Taking as long as possible to shower, Oria made an unusually long affair of combing out her dark red hair before even painting her eyelids with soft blue powder and spreading honey on her lips for color and sweet scent.

Every minute she spent back here shortened the time she'd have with Yasit before their guest arrived. As much as the knot in Oria's belly gnawed at her in thinking of their approaching visitor, hopefully the Zaam would show mercy and silence her grandmother with the young man present.

Needless to say, the core of her restlessness stemmed from her need to cast aside marriage concerns for the more pressing matter at hand—terrorism.

The loud knock from the front area jerked Oria from the welling urge to bite her nails. Taking care not to trip over her nearly floor-length sunset-colored skirt, she strode past Yasit on the sofa and opened the door.

He was…short. At exact eye level with Oria, in fact. And stocky, dressed in the traditional religious garb of matching off-white smock and trousers.

"Hello," deadpanned the man before her, all ruddy-faced and beefy limbs. "I am Leker."

After a brief pause following the palm-to-chest greeting, Leker brushed by Oria and entered the house, to which she steeled herself with a smile. "Please come in."

Following a brief introduction, whereby Leker introduced himself formally to Yasit, and Oria offered him tea, the young man refused both beverage and seat.

"There is plenty of tea at the temple teahouse."

He made for the door. "My parents send their regards."

After directing the last bit at Yasit, Leker turned to Oria. "Come along."

With that, he was out the front door.

Halfway through her tea, Oria wanted to bolt from the very room. Was this sort of forced formality common in spending time with men? Surely, Thia and Walar hadn't begun with such an…*uncomfortable* vibe.

Trying her best not to stare, Oria found herself perplexed by this man's tendency to compulsively wiggle the fingers on his left hand.

Still, this oddity at least served to give her a focal point besides the urge to nod off at the lulling melody of the stringed *ket* instrument steaming in from the adjacent temple.

Tuning back into Leker's nearly half hour-long monologue, Oria willed herself to pay attention and engage. Not that he seemed to need any words from her end.

"…and that was when I decided I wanted to remain in the templehood. So many family gatherings, and our path is chosen for us. Instead of years wasted in school, we have the chance to pursue the most glorious profession there is—service to the Zaam and rediscovery of the Great Oasis."

By the time her table companion had begun to perspire from the stuffy room, Oria hoped he had finished as she took her final sip of tea.

No such luck. Suddenly, Oria found herself longing for Samed's lessons in data cube viruses. Truly, Lir's temple had just been attacked, and Leker hadn't even mentioned the incident. At least politics would have been a subject where she could have chimed in.

Leker concluded, "And of course, while I service the Zaam, you would continue the family line. This way, the gods will never be forgotten and the Tabir will not succeed in wiping faith from the Plane. The Tabir declare we can have no army, so we will create a league of worshippers instead."

He looked at her in dire earnest, and she wanted to crawl under the table. Even with faulty vision from having left off her spectacles, she could make out the drop of sweat about to fall from the tip of his nose.

"Oria, as a daughter of the templehood, what do you say? Join me. I will lead prayer at the temple while you make and train our children to serve the Zaam."

By some miracle, Oria caught herself before her jaw stayed unhinged for too long.

Once back at the compound, she relished in the serene silence. Nasin hadn't yet returned, and Oria took this moment to breathe a sigh of relief.

Following a brief glance around the empty front room, Oria felt the sudden urge for fresh air.

Stepping outside, she fastened her thick blouse closer to her torso against the cooling dusk and set off down the quiet street.

Shops lined each side of the road, with only the occasional dunemobile disturbing the quiet evening.

Just beyond the city gates, the megalith rose high in the gold-tinted sky, its luminescence already superseding the subtle glow of the white skyflame arc overhead.

"Pleasant evening." Oria greeted the dunemobile mechanic as he exited his shop for the night.

"Thought the faithful ladies couldn't speak to strange men," the machinist—Shenir, she believed he was called—chuckled, not unkindly.

"Some of us do," Oria replied smoothly, avoiding the urge to finger her pendant.

His ability to make out her wave charm despite the darkness impressed the young Lirian.

"I expect training with the First Adviser calls for certain reformations," Shenir surmised. "Do the primary classes still all instruct in religion at every school?"

"Yes," Oria replied tightly, well aware that her grandmother's stubbornness had led to that particular occurrence. "Do you have young children?"

"A girl about to start school with the next warm season," answered Shenir. "As far as I'm concerned, she should develop her own opinion. I've never believed in the Zaam or magical water or any of that. I don't think our schools should sway these children a certain way. I've heard that it's a growing sentiment among the resettled Lirians. Is Lasha Nasin aware?"

So this man recognized Oria. She could work with that.

"I will pass on your sentiment to the First Lasha immediately." Oria smiled.

"I hope so," Shenir opened the door to his dunemobile, "Especially considering those faithless folks who cannot secure jobs tend to turn to the grass. I gather the pious don't approve of such vices—and yet, what choice do the godless have? It's readily available on the streets, despite the blockade with Garo. Venture closer to the border and you'll find plenty of beggars, many who can no longer afford home rent due to their spending on the grass. They're pitiful—red eyes, all weepy and sick. Children my daughter's age shouldn't be seeing that. The Lasha should put some of her efforts in protecting temples toward more room in schools and controlling the import rate of that sludge."

Thinking back to Rohem's statement regarding Nasin's attestation of a zero percent homelessness rate in Lir, Oria swallowed hard.

Nevertheless, the citizens responded best to a confident representative.

"Once again," Oria returned evenly, "the First will hear of this growing concern. "Pleasant night now."

Truly, she had to wonder if Nasin herself ever faced such encounters with everyday citizens. She truly hoped so. Although she wanted to believe the good of regular Lirians mattered to Nasin as much as the security of the Lasha minority, Oria had her doubts at times. After witnessing Nasin enlist several Lirian officers and even a Kano to arrest a Garo man last year for yelling threats against the Lasha while attempting to climb the concrete blockade, she preferred to think that the first Lasha invested as much effort in allocating funds for both the temples as well as schooling, so non-religious Lirians could find work. Although she knew most of Lir's educational financing stemmed from Tabir Cleansing reparations, she suddenly found herself curious as to how many handouts actually trickled down to the ordinary middle and lower class citizens of school age—as opposed to specialized professional programs, such as law and medicine.

Passing on swiftly down the street, Oria pondered the conundrum of representing regular Lirians— a portion of the population that seemingly fell further out of touch with their faith as the years drew on.

While she doubted she'd ever lose faith, she admired the audacity of those who questioned the majority in any situation. In the case of Lir, the faithless had fast become that majority, and yet Oria resolved to uphold their right to a lack of belief. If she and Nasin agreed steadfastly on anything, it was the duty of a politician to defend freedom of belief at all costs.

In any event, she appreciated the danger of both extremes— while the faithless could riot in their ambition to eradicate religion from the Plane, she faced firsthand the relentless need for order harbored by the faithful. In fact, she had only just admitted to herself how dangerously close the need of the pious Lirians to control women treaded to the Garo habit of smothering their own female population.

Of course, questioning the religious way had never seriously occurred to Oria. After all, the shadow of her family's murder hanging over her grandmother's strict lifestyle did tend to hinder Oria's willingness to think critically in regard to the faithful faction of Lir.

Oria had no doubt that her love for prayer and time spent at the temple with other families of faith would never diminish. At the same time, however, her first actual introduction to a would-be suitor from a religious background and the accompanying outlook on women's roles in society turned her gut.

She respected her grandmother— she truly did. Yet Oria's mind had made up. There would be no marrying off for the sake of reputation. Her path would remain in intelligence. She would continue work with Samed under Nasin's Advisory. The Zaam needed a regular Lirian to embolden the nation against its enemies.

***

"Here we are." The wisewoman, Maru, set a wooden platter of crisp meat and dark yellow fruit slices before the arrivals from Garo and Lir.

Dato looked at the pilot who was pretending to sit at a short distance from the rest of them, letting his hound sniff around.

As it approached, Thia made sure to slide the bundled hydropweapon away from its curious muzzle.

The animal's dark grey fur lay matted down from the humidity.

"Dog." Dato smiled. "The Tabir Vata had one many years ago. When Tabir first came. Just a baby."

"Did he die of age?" the pilot asked.

“The palm cats found him,” Dato replied with a shake of his head.

Maru took a seat between Lan and Rohem.

“What is this?” Thia tried to ask as politely as possible.

“Tree snake and…melon of honey. *Ur* fruit,” the elderly lady settled on the words.

Lan paused mid-chew. “The snake here is edible?”

“Surely not all serpents of the Plane are venomous,” Rohem pointed out with a smile.

“Perhaps only those in our region.”

“Poison snake is on the ground, not tree,” Dato explained through a half-full mouth. “All the ground snakes are gone.”

“Gone where?” Lan asked.

“The Cursed ate them,” Chief Telo stated matter-of-factly.

Breaking the tense silence that followed, Thia dug into her meal— with her fingers. It felt oddly liberating, if she were honest. Although the Lirians had adopted the Tabir custom of eating with utensils, somehow tearing into her food with her hands didn’t feel so out of place— especially when Lan, despite her neat hair and generally proper appearance, took to it with such vigor.

Rohem, of course, joined them out of good grace. “Very sweet,” he remarked of the fruit. “The *ur* melon grows on the trees?”

Maru smiled, lining her cheeks and forehead with deep wrinkles. “On our palm trees.”

“How fortunate that many palms grow here,” Lan observed.

“Vata noticed the same,” Telo remarked, still slicing his own fruit. “She often insists that Ayam use the palm tree as our national symbol— alongside Tabira’s sun. Even though we have no desire to trade with the other nations.”

“Lir’s is water,” Thia put in, then added haltingly, “and Garo’s the flame. All natural elements like a tree.”

Telo glanced at Thia with an unreadable expression.

“Water for the Lasha,” he stated. “Vata has also spoken of your kind. A gift from nature.”

“You’d be smart not to trade beyond the forest,” Thia settled on.

Pursing her lips, she ignored Lan's surreptitious gaze out of the corner of her eye, and continued eating.

As they neared the end of their meal and more villagers began walking through the area carrying out morning duties, Rohem made sure to avert his gaze.

Glancing around, Thia realized why. How hadn't she noticed that the women here did not cover their chests? While they all wore a thick belt of palm fronds down below, the bosom remained exposed.

Eyes flitting surreptitiously over to Lan, she saw that the Garo woman too seemed to be taking great care to focus on her food rather than their surroundings.

Well, Thia certainly wasn't complaining about the scenery. In fact, she had to admire this untouched aspect of Ayam culture.

"Your women don't cover their chests," she stated bluntly, idly gesturing at her own clothed breasts.

Beside her, Dato tried unsuccessfully to conceal a snort.

Telo neither smiled nor frowned. "For years, they did hide their top and bottom. Since Vata left, we have begun to return to our customs from before the Tabir arrived. The jungle is hot. Man and woman can walk as they please."

"As it should be," Thia remarked. "The forest truly is beautiful during the day."

"Night also has beauty," Dato put in, finishing his last slice of *ur*. "Dark comes and the small spiders jump to stay warm."

"Jumping spiders?" Lan asked inquisitively.

"The eggs jump to stay warm after sundown," Telo explained. "You can hear them after nightfall during the cold season."

So this was also their cold season. The water in the air must hold the heat of day.

At this, Rohem stood up with his platter. "How do we clean these?" he asked of Maru.

"I will take…" she began, reaching for the platter.

"No, please, I've got it," Rohem returned curtly. "I'll just wash it in the stream?"

Maru nodded, averting her gaze.

As soon as Rohem knelt by the streambed, Thia joined at his side.

"The first warrior Dato talked about training the children to use guns for self-defense," she murmured simply. "We'll have to make sure that doesn't happen. The adults should learn how to use them, but children are out of the question."

Once finished scrubbing the platter, Rohem set aside the flat wooden plate and ran a hand through his dark curls.

"None of them should even need those weapons," he muttered. "The Tabir should have found a cure. Though considering they're the reason the Ayam fell ill in the first place, that's clearly not an option. So much for Nasin's plans to use the plague as a bioweapon. It's lethal beyond anything we've ever seen, and spreads too easily. It just seems strange…"

Avithia said nothing, gaze settled thoughtfully on Rohem.

Somewhere nearby, a shrieking sound like laughter signaled the presence of an exotic jungle bird.

He went on. "The fact that the afflicted are normal during the day, and only change at night…seems to suggest a correlation with exposure to sunlight."

Thia frowned. "You mean…when it's taken away, the disease affects them. You think your heat emission could help?"

"It's never been that powerful." Rohem shook his head. "But there must be a way the solar energy can be preserved and transferred, even after dark…"

Thia could tell he wasn't sharing everything. "Is there something you're not telling me?"

***

The trip through these tunnels was...different.

About half the size of the tunnels normally used by the Evaporation for missions to the Lirian border, these narrow crevices barely fit Kel, even when he was crawling on all fours.

"Not much longer now," Unno spoke, also crouched over as she trudged along ahead of Kel, map in hand.

She held a small candle-lit lantern up to the parchment in her right hand.

Kel was glad he'd never truly feared small spaces. Only now his knees had begun to cramp, and the once cool air had grown thick and musty.

"Just keep quiet," Kel managed through labored breaths. "We don't want…"

"There's the end, up ahead!" Unno hissed, cutting him off.

At least she'd kept her voice low.

Sure enough, Kel glanced up to see the smudge of light nearing as they approached.

The stones here were looser than he had expected, giving away after only about five hacks from his *tso* blade.

After about fifteen more meters, Kel gently pushed Unno to the side and poked his head out ever so carefully.

Pulling the front of his sun cap down over his eyes, he glanced around furtively before withdrawing back inside the tunnel.

"We've reached the port," he reported. "I'll go out first to make sure it's all clear."

Crawling the last quarter meter out of the crawl space, Kel stood and dusted himself off.

Overhead, the sun had reached midpoint in the sky, the frozen flame still faintly visible amidst the rich blue horizon.

A flock of screeching seabirds completed the seascape, complete with a fresh, salty breeze. Directly ahead, not twenty kilometers, the dock held about three modest ships with grey sails.

"So this is the sea?" Unno asked mildly, emerging from the tunnel mouth behind him, still holding the lantern and folded map. She blew out the candle inside the lantern.

"The Strait," Kel corrected. "The sea is far larger."

Unno pushed the map into the pocket of her tunic. "So what now? How do we know which ships are safe to board?"

"None are safe," Kel pointed out. "But we want the freighter ships, with grey sails. So we're in luck."

"Right." Unno took off by his side, making sure not to walk ahead of him. "So you are my husband now. Let's go."

"Stay silent," Kel warned her. "Your Tabir is still very basic, and no one can know we are fresh arrivals from Garo."

"But they'll notice your accent," Unno stated.

"I've given up the paint," Kel returned, though the very fact pained him. "Any Tabir aboard must think us Garo who have given up the faith."

As they neared the dock, it soon became evident that the port was a bit more crowded than upon initial glance.

Fortunately, the two Kano officers present stood conversing with a freighter captain some fifty meters to the left.

Taking Unno by the forearm, Kel strode up to the freighter closest to them and glanced around once more. By some miracle, no one had called them out just yet. He supposed they did a better job blending in than he would have thought.

"You there. State your boarding purpose."

Kel shut his eyes. He'd hoped too soon. The voice had spoken in fluid Tabir.

Turning around, Unno went to open her mouth. When Kel tried to cut her off, the other man stopped them both.

Thank Echil, he wasn't Kano. He wore no beige uniform, and instead of the neat cut of an officer, had his hair pulled back in a matted, oily bunch.

"You have a child. Are you war refugees?"

Suddenly, this whole husband-and-wife plan seemed like a very risky ruse to pose to a people who deemed themselves morally superior. May as well cater to their beliefs that an age difference beyond five years between spouses was unthinkable.

"Yes," Kel returned. "My daughter and I are refugees from the war with Lir. The water people have killed her mother, and now we have given up the faith for a secure life in Tabira."

"Are you Kano?" Unno asked in halting Tabir, and Kel wanted to smack the back of her head.

Too late.

"No." The man almost looked like he wanted to smile. "I am just the freight captain. Very well, both of you stand still. Have to keep my cargo weapon free."

He then proceeded to pat down each of the Garo refugees. He didn't check their feet. Kel thanked the Zaam again that Unno had the grass hidden in her shoe.

Once he'd surprisingly calmly confiscated Kel's *tso* blade from his belt, the man took a step back.

"I'm Malur. Welcome aboard." The captain smiled, and a moment later Kel noticed that he had withdrawn the two der bills from Kel's pocket.

The only money they had brought along.

Right. That answered the question of payment. This freighter simply had to be a pirate vessel.

Now they just had to pray that these pirates had a love of the grass— or, at the very least, the willingness to trade the herb.

Ara swallowed at the sight of the pale girl draped over his sister's shoulder.

As Inad gently laid the young woman onto one of the bench mattresses in their cell, he recognized the unconscious figure as Erme, the kitchen worker.

Perhaps this could help sell his story. Although he only had the word of the other inmates Chomad and Tikeh that the guard at his side would even blink an eye at what Ara was about to reveal, he had little to lose.

"I'll take it from here," the night shift officer reported to the guard who had escorted Erme and Inad.

If Ara had ever believed in the Zaam, he would be praying now with all his might that this officer was, in fact, religious.

Best to warm him up a bit, just to be safe.

"May I ask your name?" Ara asked once the other guard had departed.

"No. Why have you brought me here?"

"My sister is sick," Ara insisted. "The girl on the right."

The guard squinted in the dim light from the megalith outside.

"She looks thin, not sick."

"The other one, then?" Ara tried. "They have both been unwell for a week now."

"You, girl." The officer walked up to the cell, and Inad shrank back, despite shielding Erme with her body. "What happened to your cellmate?"

Inad paused for a split second, glancing at Ara with a hollow gaze. Even in the shadows, the chapped lips and dark circles beneath her eyes stood out.

"They tortured her," Inad managed shakily.

"The water tube?" The guard wasted no time.

Inad nodded slowly.

"The one penal tactic we learned from the Lirians," the officer mused. "She's alive?"

"Barely," Inad replied.

"Make her comfortable, and get your rest for chores tomorrow. Let an officer know when she dies," the man said. "One less mouth to feed."

At that last bit, Ara's mind had made up.

When the guard turned to take him by the arm back to his cell, Ara reached up and removed the hairnet.

"Please," he fixed the officer with a look as desperate as he could muster, "my sister and I are the last Flightless. Vata is our mother, and she has imprisoned us for being who we are. She doesn't accept us anymore. Yet the Zaam call to us."

Ara swore he could *feel* dozens of eyes on him, as the other inmates watched the scene play out in the dark. At the sight of his colorful crown, their faint gasps seemed to echo from all around.

Would the guard draw a pistol and shoot him right here in front of everyone? After all, they were all prisoners. Then they would have two fewer mouths to feed—and Inad would be alone.

No— he could not think like that.

"Wearing disguises now? Where'd you get the art supplies?" The guard bristled, closing the distance to Ara and plunging a hand into the feathers atop his head.

Grasping hold of several white quills, the officer tugged, and Ara's hand shot over his own mouth to stifle a cry.

Through the haze of sudden pain, Ara made out the look of surprise on the guard's face as he examined the feathers' bloody roots.

The officer then drew his handgun so fast that Ara's own gasp came a moment after those of the other inmates.

"If any of you breathes a word of this encounter," he hissed lowly, turning in a circle as he aimed the weapon, "I will take out this entire level myself."

"Please," Ara stammered again. "What do you want? Anything to get us out…"

Without a word, the guard grasped Ara by the shoulder and began pulling him past the row of cells toward the empty, dark officer's quarter at the end of the floor.

Shoving Ara inside the small space, the guard shut the door quietly and then turned on Ara.

"How long have you been in here?" he seethed with wide eyes.

"Like I said," Ara replied cautiously, his scalp still throbbing slightly where the quills had been wrenched out. "About one week. It's hard to keep track of time in here."

"You came from Ayam?" The guard was looking more and more...was it frightened? Perhaps just shocked. "And now wish to return?"

Seems he was finally beginning to realize the truth of Ara's words.

"Yes," Ara steeled his gaze on the other man's eyes. Never relent. "My sister and Erme— and myself."

"The other one has been here for some time," interjected the guard, "She is Tabir."

"She is *dying*," Ara protested, "You said it yourself, one less mouth to feed. We can leave her here in Tabira, but just not in this place. Not where she may get tortured again."

The guard looked down in thought for a split second, and Ara took the opportunity.

"I'll ask again," he spoke with as much authority as he could muster. "As a Flightless, I wish to know the name of the Tabir with whom I am speaking."

A pause.

Ara fought the urge to pace with anxiety. He hadn't hidden in the bathroom on this level until after dark for nothing.

"Yimeh," the guard murmured gruffly, bringing Ara back to the urgency of the situation. "I still don't see why two Flightless would be in prison."

Glancing at him earnestly now, Ara decided on half-truth. "Our mother is not Flightless and does not believe in the Zaam. But Inad and I do. They speak to us every day. So we must return home to Ayam, the last nation whose people still remain fully faithful."

Ara willed back the tears of frustration.

"Can't fly there yourself, hm?" Yimeh asked skeptically.

Pulling the thin cloak from his shoulders, Ara swiveled around to show the guard his wings that bulked against the rope restraints.

"I could release my wings," Ara conceded. "Against my mother's wishes. But I likely wouldn't be able to make such a journey myself, let alone carrying my sister. The Zaam, in all their radiance, have not graced us with such strength."

"I can pilot you out," Yimeh finally answered, avoiding Ara's eyes "I can have the glider back before my next shift begins. It will be a small glider, used for surveillance runs. Aircraft control keeps tabs on the massive gliders."

Ara could scarcely believe their fortune. "Yes, of course, Yimeh. The Flightless thank you."

"Why doesn't your sister have quills or wings?" Yimeh asked, making Ara stop short, though it was a fair question.

"Our mother had her wings and quills removed as punishment for not lying with the man that was chosen for her."

Once again, honesty. In part, anyway.

"Right." Yimeh harrumphed. "This way. Keep in front of me. The lift has security cameras. Lucky there's a stairwell. And put the hair piece back on."

Holding the cold pistol to Ara's back, Yimeh ushered him back down the corridor.

Once there, he continued holding the gun on the young Flightless as he unlatched Inad's cage with the other hand.

Ara pursed his lips as he watched his sister emerge from the cell, half-carrying a still very weak Erme.

Either most of the other inmates had gone back to sleep or decided it wise to keep quiet. The officer Yimeh's procession out of the prison continued in silence.

The air pad outside sat about a fifty-meter walk from the beach and dock.

"You can leave her here." Ara stopped at the sound of Yimeh's voice before realizing the guard was addressing Inad.

"Please…can't we take her?" Inad shifted her weight beneath Erme, who was now glancing around groggily.

"She's already dying," Yimeh said. "The toxic chemicals in the textile colors they work with in the factories. "We have many like her in the Capital prison. Let her rest now in the fresh air. I will start the glider. When you hear the engine start, come immediately."

Kneeling down, Inad gently helped Erme take a seat on the moist sand.

Squeezing Erme's hand, Inad looked her directly in the eyes.

"I will come back. I promise, I will come back..."

Erme began shivering then in the sea breeze, taking a deep breath. "It's fine," she managed shakily. "I've...I've never been this close to the sea. Is this how the water looks from Ayam too?"

The violent cough she let loose then chilled Ara. Somehow, he doubted this girl would live long enough to be taken back to prison.

Inad didn't let go of her former cellmate, the look in her eyes screaming fear and dismay all at once. Even in the still dim light of pre-dawn, her ashen cheeks held barely more color than the girl she held in her arms.

When Inad spoke again, her voice was barely above a whisper. Soon Ara realized she was actually singing softly. He recognized the lullaby that Maru sang to the young children back home.

"As the bird sings,
So the palm cat growls
The river flows and the trees grow.
For all this life, we give thanks
To the Light."

Trying his best not to panic at the thought of leaving this child out in the open, Ara focused on the horizon. Already the sun had risen halfway, like a bright pathway to salvation leading from the shore across the sparkling blue expanse.

Kamra and her baby. This escape scheme had all happened so quickly, he hadn't had a chance to say goodbye...

In any case, even if Kamra and her baby would be safer behind bars than out on the streets, Ara was immensely relieved that Erme could breathe freely again, even if for a short while.

By the time the lyrics ended, the buzzing rumble of the small glider sounded from over at the air pad. From where Ara stood, he could no longer tell if Erme still breathed as Inad softly laid her to rest on the darkened sand, the tide licking gently at her bare feet.

Studying her still form, Ara berated himself inwardly for even suggesting bringing such an ill person back to Ayam. Though the forest still held beauty by day, the canopy had become a death trap after dark.

As much as it pained him, the girl deserved to go peacefully rather than in violence. With a shaky breath, he turned and followed his sister off the beach toward the air pad.

Once they had ascended the short stairwell into the small glider, Ara frowned at Officer Yimeh's glum expression.

"We will have to be very careful," he grumbled, turning toward the controls as the door closed behind Ara and Inad. "An automated reply went out to all officers on duty today. Just an hour ago, a massive glider departed for Ayam."

"Mother," Ara stated stoically, removing his hairnet to release his crown at long last.

Beside her brother, Inad drew a shaky breath and steadied her gaze toward the window. A definite improvement from the cargo hold, she struggled to focus on the scenery as they lifted away toward the rising sun. She had witnessed a girl younger than herself die - more than merely die. She had watched as Erme faded right before her eyes...all because Inad had acted before thinking. Just like her mother.

Telo's punishment seemed to pale in comparison to the horror of life in her parents' homeland. For even the briefest of moments, she had attempted to take his life. A chief to whom all remaining Ayam looked for hope from the misery *her* people had brought. Who on the Plane was she to attack him without reason? He had not even made to approach her yet…

The sudden wave of longing for the warm rainforest air and Maru's kind instruction nearly overwhelmed her. As much as she had longed to escape the fate assigned to her by her mother, never had she imagined what darkness existed in the world beyond her birthplace.

And now they were returning to Ayam, and she would see Telo again. She couldn't deny the realization that reuniting with Telo seemed far preferable to facing her mother again. While not having directly killed anyone besides their father upon his affliction, her mother had willingly ruined the lives of hundreds. As much as Vata's unpredictable outbursts and relentless belittlement of Ara had always gotten on Inad's last nerve, she simply couldn't stand the thought of standing idly by their mother's genocidal mission any longer. If it came down to Vata or Telo and the islanders with whom she had grown up, Inad would choose the Chief.

Chapter Nineteen

"You *touched* the megalith?" Thia bristled.

Or at least she seemed angry. Rohem couldn't be sure.

"Yes, and I'm fine." Rohem held up his hands, palms out.

"Well, no surprise there, but…" Thia leaned in. "So it didn't hurt, at all? Was it hot, cold…?"

Rohem laughed. "It was…incredible."

"How so?"

Putting words to the experience would prove challenging in itself. Not to mention, Rohem wasn't even sure what had occurred, and also didn't know how many details he wanted to share— even with Avithia.

"…I just felt...a lot of power. Like I could do anything. And…"

Thia looked at him expectantly, and the next words just tumbled out.

"And waves."

"Waves?" Thia prompted. "Like the sea?"

"Waves of feeling," Rohem clarified, "They just kept coming, over and over. I couldn't focus on a single thought. Only this pure…"

"Pleasure?" Thia finished wryly.

"I think so." Rohem frowned. "Why are you smiling?"

"That sounds like a climax." The Lasha nearly grinned now. "You know, the reason for all the noise with Walar."

"I-I mean, I don't know…" Rohem stammered until Thia cut him off.

"This happened from just touching the megalith?"

"Partially." Rohem suddenly wanted to change the subject. He didn't want to bring up Echil just yet.

"So you were alone?" Thia probed.

"You know, let's just forget it," Rohem decided. "It was strange."

"Sounds like it was a good strange." Thia's eyes were bright. "Was that your first time? Feeling something like that?"

Rohem closed his mouth after realizing it had been open slightly. To his utter relief, Thia let up.

"We can drop it if you want, Rohem. Just please know I'm here for you. Though I'll be honest, the fact that the megaliths can be touched...is interesting."

"Please don't go trying it out," Rohem groaned.

The wisewoman Maru chose that moment to interrupt their conversation by the stream.

"Avithia, Rohem, come now," the elderly woman summoned them. "Avithia, you go with Dato and the chief. Lan, Rohem, come with me."

Just as the latter two made their way toward Maru's dwelling, another young man burst out from the foliage to the right of the tree trunk, nearly colliding with Lan.

Rohem took in his bloodied appearance with immediate concern.

"You're hurt," he said instinctively, hoping immediately afterward that the man could understand Tabir.

"It is not my blood." The other man brushed him off in a thick accent, sprinting forth to embrace the chief.

Ever since the man had appeared in the clearing by Maru's home, their pilot's hound had started barking. Just now, the bark gave way to a vicious growl. This time, its owner didn't bother to silence the animal.

Within moments, Dato held the tip of his spear to the young man's throat from behind, shouting something in Ayam.

The man covered in blood grinned and pivoted with alarming speed, knocking the weapon from the first warrior's grasp.

Maru opened her mouth to speak as Telo drew a pistol from the pouch at his rope belt and fired a shot into the air.

Several children scurried behind their mothers, who stopped short in their chores, glancing toward the chief.

Lowering the gun slowly, Telo spoke in Tabir. "Finu. Brother. Please step away now."

So this was the chief's brother.

At that, Finu turned back toward Rohem. “My brother does not understand,” he insisted in Tabir, approaching Rohem. “The blood is of animals— small birds only! This is not a Curse, but a gift. We can stay away from the village by night and be strong by day. Strong and *alive*. We are all Ayam!”

Rohem thought that this Finu seemed almost manic.

“That is no life,” Telo uttered stonily. “You would risk us all.”

“They are speaking Tabir for our benefit,” Lan whispered to Rohem in fascination. “What incredible language skills.”

“What seems to be the trouble?” Thia asked irritably from nearby Dato, her own handgun not far out of reach at her belt.

“The Curse has taken him,” Telo stated.

“And now I am a monster, yes, brother?” Finu seethed, closing in on Telo again, this time in anger.

This had to stop. Rohem suddenly saw a brilliant chance to test the science of this disease— here and now.

“Wait.” He stepped forward, holding out a hand between the chief and his brother. “Please. Listen, we still have much to learn about this Curse, but…from what I see, you only turn when the sun goes away. What if that didn’t have to happen? What if we could keep the sun for you through the night?”

Telo’s eyes narrowed. Surprisingly, Finu seemed more tempted. “Would I still be strong?”

Rohem glanced back in earnest. “Yes.”

“Chief,” Maru spoke up, her croaky voice gentle amidst those of the three men. “We try tonight?”

“Why should I trust you?” The chief’s eyes narrowed further, yet he didn’t move from his spot by the trunk of Maru’s home.

“Because I am a doctor, a healer,” Rohem replied calmly. “And because I have lived my whole life watching the destruction the Tabir have brought. We are of Lir. When we walked in Tabira, they killed many of our people simply for keeping the faith. Our science is not theirs. We want only to improve, not to destroy.”

“Rohem, please,” Thia began in Lirian, “not the energy transfer…”

Cutting her off swiftly, Rohem continued, "I will join Maru and Lan for the rest of the afternoon. When the sun begins to set, Finu can join us back here at this place. We will hold the sun's power for Finu."

Lan's mind was reeling.

When it came to the Ayam culture, the sheer richness and simplicity all at once excited her like nothing before.

Their day-to-day activities seemed so...*quiet.* No automobiles, no prayer song - the occasional sound of a crying infant the only noise to permeate the bubbling stream and insect noise.

Prior to the Tabir's arrival, this island truly had been untouched.

And their language, harsh to her ears and yet rhythmic. Already, she had taken note of several Ayam terms:

Onn for 'cursed'.
Ur for that sweet yellow fruit that grew on Ayam palm trees.

Jotting down what Maru was saying now, Lan resolved to hold onto her small notepad for dear life. Despite having had a personal Tabir instructor under employment of Belim, she had never spent more than several hours in Tabira at a time, and could hardly believe that she would spend an indefinite period of time on this largely unexplored island.

"*Man-AH-fata.*" Maru grinned warmly with a raised hand, palm facing inward toward her own face. "This is morning greeting."

"Why the hand gesture?" Lan asked curiously.

"We cover face from the light of the other," Maru explained.

Lan nodded. An acknowledgement of the other person's presence and understood as light, in reverence of the Zaam, just as in Garo.

"And the high-pitched sound in the middle of the word?" Lan ventured. "The *ah*?"

Maru smiled again. "Tabir say this is part of Ayam that other languages do not have."

A phonological isolate. Fascinating. Though she loathed to consider the prospect of returning home to the same old routine just then, Lan couldn't help but wonder if Belim could be convinced to accept some of these villagers as refugees in Garo. If enough linguistic information was gathered during this trip, she could streamline the interpretation process to ease the transition.

Glancing over, she checked on how Rohem was getting along. Still busy using his medical tools to carefully examine the children, as their mothers stood by watchfully.

Lan chewed her lower lip.

The men of Garo strove for strength and made a point to show off their power. Although she knew well of Rohem's reputation for nigh insurmountable physical prowess, she never would have guessed to observe him now. In fact, he tended to the children with downright gentleness.

And his skin tone…

For the first time in as long she could remember, she no longer felt like the odd one out on account of her appearance. He was as dark as she was light.

Shaking her head, Lan returned her focus to the wisewoman's words. Though it seemed the elderly woman had evidently taken a break from schooling to grind up some paste in a wooden bowl.

"Green fish," Maru interpreted, seeing Lan's stare. "*Kaha*. For children when they fall and hurt. This also helps when blood comes to woman."

"Is it a paste?" Lan asked, then further clarified, "from the insides of the fish?"

"Ah, yes." Maru nodded with a smile and resumed grinding with the long, rounded rock she held. "You put on the skin of belly or other hurt part."

"Can I help?"

"*Sana*. Thank you," Maru replied. "The women by river have more fish."

"*Sana*…is thank you?" Lan surmised. "Maru, how should I tell them I want to help?"

"*Bako*," Maru answered. "They understand. Your face…is very beautiful. Shines like the sun."

The gold paint.

"*Sana*." Lan smiled.

Time to wash her outer skirt before tomorrow. A good excuse to join the villagers in their activities at the river. Taking a deep breath, the Garo sauntered over to the group of women chatting by the streambed.

"*Bako*." She held out her hands.

The women smiled shyly, yet gestured for her to assist with gutting the pile of fish already collected at the water's edge. Though she hadn't participated in such a craft before, she found it oddly calming, the stench not as repulsive as she would have expected.

Once Lan had grown accustomed to the careful shredding and pulling of the slippery flesh between her fingers, she found her attention drawn back toward the women and children who had begun congregating around Rohem by Maru's home…

A quick movement atop one of the branches of the thick tree trunk caught her attention. Not a moment after registering the man crouching in the tree with a handgun aimed straight down at Rohem and the several children near him, Lan cried at the top of her voice in Tabir to alert Maru as well, "Rohem, in the tree above you!"

Lan hadn't long to ponder whether Rohem even had a gun for self-defense, when the man in the tree started and fell from the tree, landing several meters from one of the children, head hitting the firm soil with a sickening crunch. As Rohem looked about to retrieve the gun from the ground, Maru got their first, stooping gingerly grasp the weapon. Lan stayed rooted to the spot. The elderly woman looked quite strange holding the firearm.

"The Kano chief," Maru stated blandly, as Lan approached them once again. "Will not frighten the children again. Come, we will move to Chief Telo's home. When men return, they take body to Maw."

So this man was the Kano Telo had mentioned running off when the Ayam warriors ambushed. How strange he looked, staring up into nothing, mouth slightly ajar…

"Thank you, Lan."

She glanced up to see Rohem, smiling.

Once they had all gathered by the chief's home well away from the Kano Doreh's temporary resting site, Rohem examined the children while Maru buried the handgun in a shallow spot by the base of the tree to provide the Chief. When she joined Rohem and the children, the medical apprentice glanced up with a smile.

"They are all very healthy." He remarked.

Truly, he hadn't felt so elated in a long time. The relief of finding all of these children in strong health despite the pathogen ravaging their people was indescribable.

"They eat well." Maru smiled back. "Girls make food with mothers, and boys learn to fight with warriors."

Just then, one of the women stepped forward and gingerly took Rohem's right hand, sliding a white-shelled armlace onto his wrist.

From nearby, Lan observed with a tentative smile. In that moment, a sense of joyful peace filled her. A man had perished without honor right before her eyes, and yet the beauty of this place still overrode any discomfort over the matter.

"Thank you…" Rohem glanced up at the young mother whom had gifted him the simple piece of jewelry.

"That is payment," Maru explained. "For healing."

"You barter?" Rohem asked.

The wisewoman nodded. "No need for the paper money."

"Them staying healthy is all the payment I ask for." Rohem stood, glancing up briefly at the megalith that was just starting to glow with the first signs of the sun's retreat.

Telo approached them then.

"Chief, all is good?" Maru asked in Tabir.

"Finu will join us soon," replied Telo, leaning against the tree trunk with a spear under one arm.

"Are they all like that?" Rohem ventured. "Strong, I mean? Even during the day?"

"All that have come back to the village." The chief nodded. "When it first takes them, they bleed and grow very weak. And then by the next day, they are like my brother was today. Full of power and even joyful. Many times excitable and quick to violence."

"But they cannot rejoin the community," Rohem stated.

"Those whom are not killed in self-defense by our warriors fend for themselves by day," Telo replied.

"And what of those whom you've had to put down?"

Gazing briefly at the megalith that stood high above the canopy, Telo beckoned to Rohem. "Follow me."

Unlike the arid dunes of Lir or monotonous planes of Tabira, the jungle sang with natural life.

All around, Rohem pushed aside giant leaves and narrowly avoided spider webs the size of his entire body, the silk glittering in the soft light with tiny dewdrops.

The beauty extended deeper than the visual novelty of lush green and other vibrant colors. The manner in which the natives tended to their children with both discipline and gentleness struck Rohem as particularly unique. Ayam youth clearly learned not only skills for surviving with highly limited technology, but also how to hone their martial craft.

All afternoon, he had observed the mothers gathering fruit and fishing with their daughters, while sons accompanied their fathers to trap snakes on the ground and repair tree dwellings.

Meanwhile, two groups of ten boys trained under Telo and Dato in the art of spear fighting. All in all, Rohem had to admire how these people simply continued their days, despite the grave danger that loomed each night.

If these people were uncivilized, then he didn't think he held much regard for civilization.

Following several offers to carry the Kano Doreh's corpse, Rohem had surrendered to the Chief's insistence on transporting the body himself to the apparent resting place of the deceased. After they had traveled about thirty meters along the stream and through the adjoining brush, Rohem covered his nose instinctively against the putrid stench.

Although many years had passed since he had last smelt the odor—indeed, not since his on the streets in the poor district of Tabira—he still recognized it as clearly as air.

Decaying flesh, accentuated by the clouds of gnats hovering all around.

Focusing on the path ahead, Rohem stopped directly behind the chief. They stood at the ledge to a drop off. An immense, yawning crater in the soil spanning about twenty meters across.

"That smell…" he finally murmured.

Telo nodded. "This is the graveyard for the fallen."

"Your people dug this crater?" Rohem attempted to peer over the edge.

"Please, don't look," Telo placed a hand on his shoulder. "You could fall in."

Too shaken at the moment to argue, Rohem relented and stepped back, glancing down when his right foot caught on something...

What appeared to be a translucent strip of thing material lined in jagged off-white bones lay draped over the front of his boot.

"The beasts shed their skin to return as Ayam," Telo said simply.

Rohem stepped aside swiftly, the skin and…teeth falling to the forest floor.

"We did not create the Maw," Telo went on. "It has existed here for as long as the Ayam have, maybe longer."

"Then you've always placed your dead here."

The chief nodded again, hoisting the limp form from over his shoulder, the body tumbling into the massive pit before them."Come, we must return now. My brother comes."

Upon reaching Maru's dwelling, Rohem and Telo didn't have to wait long.

Thia and Dato had reconvened at the tree as well.

Just as Lan and the other women set the final large bowl of fish by the fire Maru was now igniting, Rohem sensed movement behind him.

Turning sharply, he squinted at the foliage from whence they had come.

Nothing.

Telo's voice brought his attention back to the gathering before him.

"Finu," the chief murmured.

Suddenly, the area where they stood beneath the canopy seemed very dark. Rohem had to wonder how much time they had before Finu's symptoms would present.

The chief's brother strode up to Rohem all of his own accord.

"Let us see if this works." Finu looked like he was concealing a snicker. "*Healer*."

From high overhead, thunder rumbled in the distance.

"The rest of us will retire to the trees," Telo informed Rohem. "The other beasts will wake soon. The Mak has told of your power. The Cursed may look like us during the day, but by night they have the minds of a hungry animal. Can you fight many predators at once? Creatures with tongues that burn?"

"Yes," Rohem replied calmly, despite Thia's horrified gaze burning into his peripheral vision.

"Very well," the chief answered. "I will watch from up in Maru's home. Dato, Lan, Thia, please return to your trees now."

All around them, the women and warriors had already cleared away to take shelter for the night.

Even the pilot hoisted the hound under his arm and joined Maru in her tree hut.

Lan looked as if she wanted to approach, when she stopped short at Avithia charging forth to take Rohem in her arms.

"You can do this," she hissed by his ear.

Following a brief yet bone-crushing embrace from Thia, Rohem soon found himself standing alone beside Finu.

Somehow, he had to wonder whether Thia had been referring to his ability to help Finu or to fend off multiple afflicted Ayam, or perhaps both.

Following the ascent to his home, Telo glanced around at the slight disarray that still remained. His attempt to obtain the Tabir weapons had distracted him from daily tasks such as cleanliness.

No matter. Soon enough, they would see through this plague. The Zaam would show the path, and the Ayam people would follow.

Though the nightly song of insects had already begun, Telo nearly gasped when the communicator at his throat chirped.

"Hello?" he grunted.

Static. He waited.

"Telo." Inad.

Telo froze momentarily before replying back cautiously. "Inad. Are you with your mother?"

"No," her voice sounded strained through the choppy buzz, "But she is returning to Ayam."

"Are you well? Where are you?" he asked under his breath, completely still as he gazed out at the dark forest from his home entrance.

"It doesn't matter," came quiet Inad's reply. "My brother and I are coming home."

Telo frowned in the shadows. "Home...to Tabira."

Inad's answer was barely audible. "To Ayam."

The communication ended. Wherever she was, Telo had to assume Inad hadn't possessed access to a communicator code chart. Then she had memorized his code. The chief couldn't recall her voice ever sounding so mild, an odd source of calm at a time when his worries raced for his brother and their people.

Apparently in good health and separate from her brutal mother, his wife was coming home. After believing them all dead, Telo had laid eyes on a palm cat. By Echil, there was hope. The Ayam would survive, and he would lead them.

Solemnly, Rohem prepared his examination tools once again and listened to Finu's vitals.

All normal.

"Cold." Finu cringed slightly at the metal chest scope used to assess breath and heartbeat.

"My apologies," Rohem replied, casting a glance up at the immense tower through the trees. The...solar rise was nearly at full illumination.

The sun must have just set.

That was when Finu wrenched away from Rohem's instrument, falling to his knees with a hoarse shout.

Resisting the urge to back away, Rohem knelt by Finu's side.

"Take my hand. Now," he stated as solidly as possible.

Grasping Rohem's hand, Finu gritted his teeth against a violent tremor that ran through his entire body.

"Hold on as strong as you must," Rohem urged, securing his fingers around Finu's.

Without another thought, he closed his eyes momentarily to begin the energy transfer.

"Talk to me, Finu," Rohem encouraged, trying to distract the Ayam man from the pain. "What have you been up to today?"

"I train w-with a stick," Finu stammered, now doubled over but with a tinge of mirth to his tone. "Telo has my spear."

In the next moment, Finu gripped Rohem's hand so hard that it actually did hurt. Still, the energy flow only increased.

"What…what are you doing?" Finu suddenly relaxed a bit. "That feels…very good. Warm. Like the sun…"

Rohem only concentrated harder, pursing his lips together.

"The Zaam…" Finu continued, lying back on the ground, still clutching Rohem's hand. "They must give light to Ayam."

At the mention of the Zaam, Rohem glanced furtively at Finu. The Ayam remained the most religious of all the nations. He was simply praying, nothing more.

"Is there a temple you visit here in the forest?" Rohem asked gently, keeping the energy transfer steady.

"Temple?" Finu frowned up at Rohem, his eyes more clear.

"A house of worship."

Finu smirked. "We...we do not need house for worship. We pray to the Great Stone."

Rohem followed Finu's gaze up to the megalith's glow, dappled softly through the leaves onto the soil around them.

"Do you…touch the Stone?" Rohem asked.

"Never," Finu replied, struggling to a sitting position beside Rohem. "Only close."

A brief pause.

"I also trained as healer." Finu spoke up again. "With Maru."

"A healer *and* a warrior?" Rohem observed. "Impressive."

Finu chuckled. "Not a good warrior. That is my brother."

Rohem took notice of the subtle patter of rain that had begun all around them. Yet they remained dry.

"Is the canopy so thick that it blocks out all the rain?" Rohem asked, perplexed, looking up into the dark treetops.

"Not rain." Finu ran a hand through his shoulder-length hair. "Spider eggs. The rain comes soon."

Rohem licked his lips pensively, increasing the energy flow ever so slightly. The sound was truly quite soothing.

The sky now appeared pitch black through the leaves above.

"How are you feeling?" Rohem asked Finu, re-securing his fingers around Finu's, whose own grip had finally relaxed.

"My body," Finu examined the fingers of his other hand in fascination, "it does not change. I am Ayam."

"You have always been Ayam," Rohem assured him mildly.

Just then, another thought occurred to him. Foolishly late.

"Do you still see and hear the same while changed?" he asked, keeping his language as simple as possible for the other man.

Finu grinned. "Do not worry. The *onn* beasts do not see or hear like us. They only see when we move."

Motion sensing. Incredible — in a disturbing sort of way. Best to stay as still as possible in that case.

Lightning flashed overhead. Moments later, a thunderclap preceded the large pellets of rain that began falling through the canopy.

"The air here is so fresh…" Rohem began again in an attempt to make conversation.

Finu cut him off with a shout loud enough to make Rohem start.

Bending over again, Finu clutched at his chest with his free hand. A cold chill shot through Rohem.

Before his eyes, this young man was transforming.

Despite the increased fervor of the energy transfer, Finu's tears joined the rivulets of rain running down his face as his mouth opened in a silent scream.

From the tree above, the hound's vicious barks sounded amidst the heavy rainfall.

Holding on as if for dear life, Rohem stayed rooted to his spot beside the chief's brother. In part, he wasn't sure he could tear his eyes away. From both sheer terror and morbid fascination.

Finu's nails dug sharply into the flesh of Rohem's palm, as his open mouth elongated to roughly twice its normal length. No muzzle like an animal, just a grotesquely long jaw.

In the pale light of the megalith and the hanging lamp fixed to the entrance of Maru's home, Rohem could only watch helplessly as the taut skin around Finu's mouth began peeling away.

Beneath his normal face, the raw pink flesh beneath momentarily gave way to dark grey bumps that shone with the rain.

Scales.

The only features that remained untouched by this re-growth were his shoulder-length hair and his nose, which maintained the appearance of a skinless skull's nasal cavity.

Idly, Rohem registered the barking of the hound in the dwelling above growing ferociously louder.

One by one, Finu's teeth popped out with slow streams of dark red blood that poured down his chin onto his bare chest. Rohem nearly froze as multiple needle-like fangs grew instantaneously to replace the fallen teeth, just as the scales completed their rampage over what used to be a man's face.

Finally, the chief's brother's eyes rolled back, glinting silver replacing white and dark brown.

Beneath his fingers, Rohem steeled against the sensation of a rough, moist undulation against his own hand as the scales spread, the bipedal monster reaching peak height at a half meter above the man whose form it had consumed.

For a fleeting instant, Rohem considered snapping Finu's neck just to put him out of this misery. He abandoned the thought as quickly as it had come.

No. He *had* to attempt to reverse this.

When Rohem unleashed as powerful a blast of energy as he could muster, the creature before him let loose a deafening, rattling roar.

For the first time, he was witnessing a life form mutating right in front of him. And he was helpless to prevent it.

Only when jaws as long as his entire head snapped at Rohem's face did he release the now scale-covered limb with a rapid heat blast and dash off into the dark jungle.

"Did you hear that?" Lan hissed, clearly trying to hold her voice steady.

Thia's stomach lurched. Less at the fact that the Garo had insisted on following her into this tree hut so as not to be alone, and more because she feared for her best friend— her family.

The Lasha didn't speak. Never in her life had she heard anything remotely close to that sound. Like the bellow of a monster both agonized and enraged.

"I should be out there with him." The words tumbled from her lips before she realized she'd spoken them aloud.

Lan waited a breath before replying. "He will be fine. He's very strong."

"You've only just met us," Thia replied, gentler than she had intended. "You wouldn't know."

Lan kept silent, knees drawn up as she sat toward the far back corner of the hut.

"I'm going down," Thia decided, kneeling to push aside the fronds at the dwelling entrance. "You stay here."

She shot the last part over her shoulder, as the Garo woman made to follow her.

"You wouldn't stand a chance out there." Avithia tried to make her words cutting, before noting that it likely only made her seem concerned for Lan's safety.

She supposed that, as someone with physical gifts, she did have a sort of moral responsibility toward Lan— if that only involved steering the older woman away from reckless decisions that Belim would later blame on Nasin. Such responsibility helped calm Thia's nerves when the Garo had followed her into the tree.

"Be careful." Lan's soft words barely registered over the pounding in Thia's own ears as she hoisted the folded hydroblaster onto her shoulders and descended the rope ladder.

Despite the still relatively modest four liters in the tank, Thia remained confident that the enhanced pressure of the deluge should suffice to knock a group of at least fifty men off their feet with a single blast. Such force would certainly slow even a beast as deadly as the Ayam purported the afflicted became by dark.

As soon as Thia hit the ground, the smell of fresh blood hit her full-force. Rohem didn't bleed...

Of course. Surely, these creatures bled when they transformed.

Navigating in the general direction from where the roar seemed to have come, the Lasha soon found herself at the other empty dwelling Maru had pointed out. The electrical tower used for Network connection throughout the two Ayam islands flanked the empty tree house, its apex reaching just above the canopy.

Once she tracked down Rohem, perhaps the two of them could take shelter here...

Ducking through leaves as large as her torso, Thia nearly jumped when a hand grasped her shoulder.

Spinning around, she stopped just short of striking Dato in the face with her fist.

"Avitia." He spoke lowly in skewed pronunciation of her name, holding his hands up to calm her. "It is me. Please come up. It is not safe here."

"I have to find Rohem..."

"The healer?" Dato asked with a quick glance around. "He runs by this tree where I hide. Only short time past. Toward the Great Stone."

"He left the forest?" Thia was confused— until she recalled his experience at the megalith. Could he somehow use it to draw more power?

Activating the communicator at her ear, she paged Rohem.

Static— the same as when she had tried not an hour ago.

"He can go to small island," Dato assured her. "Across water. No *onn* can swim there."

"Small island?" Thia asked.

"Where Vata lives," Dato explained. "Sister of the Mak. We have boats at the water. Now Vata is in Tabira and Kano gone, so many women with children sleep on small island."

She had to at least know he was alive.

"Rohem!" Thia called as loud as possible. "Can you hear me?"

Silence.

Nudging Thia gingerly with the hand that held his spear, Dato urged her toward the tree dwelling before them. Thia started forward, withdrawing her pocket communicator cube as it buzzed.

A text message in Lirian, from Rohem.

"I am safe. Stay in the trees."

"Come," Dato urged her again. "We will be safe up high with your weapon and my spear."

"These are my belongings," Thia returned sharply. "My only weapon is my gun."

"Vata talks of your water weapon." Dato almost smiled. "This is good. We can use."

So the Tabir had surmised about the martial aspect of hydrotechnology after all.

Sighing heavily, the Lasha begrudgingly followed the chief's first warrior up the trunk of the vacant dwelling.

Chapter Twenty

Kel couldn't decide which was worse, the sickening rock of the ship or Unno's incessant clinging to his arm as they sat together in the tiny cabin below deck.

Although both had tried to make the most of the fresh air above deck, the choppy waves that had begun preceding the approaching wind and rainfall soon caused Unno such a fright that she'd started whimpering, eyes moist.

When Kel had asked what she was afraid of, she'd just stared at the gradually rising waves around them, the silent tears escaping down her cheeks.

Kel had understood. Following years of intermittent deluge air raids by Lirian police claiming to pursue Evaporation fighters, many a Garo child had learned to fear large quantities of water.

As ill as he felt down here, he hoped that Unno's lament stemmed more from seasickness than terror.

"It shouldn't be much longer," he assured her, swallowing fervently as the vessel dove over another sharp hump.

"If you feel ill, try some of the grass," Unno whispered, though they had secured their own corner of the cabin. "I still have it safe in my shoe."

"Can't risk wasting the goods," Kel replied, bracing himself with a palm against the wooden wall beside them, as he kept his backside firmly planted on the bench beneath to keep from sliding off with the next roll of the sea.

"It might be better not to, you're right," Unno pondered. "Nok enjoyed the grass too much."

Kel glanced over at Unno, stroking his chin lightly and focusing on the growing stubble to distract himself from sickness. "Your brother?"

Unno nodded. "You know he worked as an herbalist's apprentice before joining your mission. He would steal from the shop. I found him one morning about six years ago, sleeping and with little breath. He'd passed out outside during the cold season and nearly frozen to death. He only had several meters to walk, and he could have made it home. After that, father insisted that he join the Evaporation."

What a sight to witness at four years of age. For all Kel knew, Nok could have even been working for Edo.

Kel hummed. "I only knew him for a short time. He was always…enthusiastic. The cause is a good means of direction for the aimless."

"Reminiscing about the good old days back home?" came a voice from the cabin entryway.

It was the captain, Malur.

“I took a break from the rainy upper deck,” he explained, sauntering inside the small space to take a seat on the bench across from Kel and Unno.

The rainwater dripped from his clothes all over the cabin floor.

“The storm is still going?” Kel asked.

Malur nodded. “So what’s Garo like? Do you really pray three times a day at the temple?”

“The temple or the home shrine,” Kel answered.

May as well let the beard grow out. No need for piety where they were headed. Suddenly, the idea of defying the holy word of the Senti scripture and never wearing the paint again seemed very strange—and at the same time, entirely worth it to leave behind his former identity that had failed to prevent Deki’s murder.

“But we left religion,” Unno followed up in halting Tabir, almost as if she had read Kel’s thoughts. “When your neighbors kill you, faith goes.”

“Ah, the Lirians?” Malur smirked. “They’re also religious, aren’t they? I never finished much school. The Mak and the Oligarchy started charging around two decades ago, and agricultural workers like us couldn’t afford studies. But I’ve heard on the streets that Lirians worship water like you lot worship fire. Word also gets around about that Evaporation from Garo who’ve made the passage to Tabira. Seems many do fear the Lirians.”

“There are some Lirians who live entirely off water,” Kel interjected then. “It is unnatural.”

“Ah.” Malur’s eyes took on a glazed look. “Bet it makes the women’s skin soft…”

Kel nearly cringed. “Certain Lirian women…don’t always remain women.”

The captain frowned then. “What are you getting at?”

“The water creatures are strong creatures who can live for many lifetimes,” Unno added.

“Tell me, Captain,” Kel put in. “Tabir women— they always stay female, don’t they?”

Now Malur looked utterly confused.

“You’ve never heard of the Lasha?” Kel asked disbelievingly.

“I come from Tabira’s third class, poorest of them all. Those not at sea are on the stage acting in spectacles for the first class, without a chance to travel over the Strait. As I’ve said, we have no access to schools even today, and those street broadcasts only show what the Mak wants us all to see. If you can't read, the broadcasts are the only window to the world beyond Tabira."

"Then…I take it your Evaporation targeted these water people?"

"Yes," Kel answered firmly. "They call us terrorists because we resist their occupation of our land. Don't you have a purpose behind your looting?"

Malur snickered. "We loot because we *can*."

He reached inside the crossover front of his vest and withdrew Kel's *tso* blade, the triangular weapon glinting softly in the dim gaslights of the cabin.

"Speaking of which..." He grinned again. "This will make a pretty addition to our collection. It is a weapon, isn't it?"

"Yes," Kel replied curtly. "Used to strangle an opponent from behind."

"Attacking an enemy from behind. How valiant." Malur stood and replaced the *tso* blade inside his vest.

Kel bristled. How dare a *pirate* insult the Garo way of battle? Still, best to keep a low profile, at least until they safely crossed the Strait.

"Come out whenever you like. We're having fresh fish. After supper, we should be reaching Tabira in the next hour or two.

Still feeling too nauseated to eat, Kel chose to try and sleep off the remaining time they had before arrival.

As Unno curled up once more on the floor by Kel's bench, the former militant leader touched her shoulder.

"Please, take the bench to sleep. We will arrive soon."

Within the next hour, the storm calmed in time for the dawn of a new day, as the ship docked in Tabira. A fresh start in a new land and, Zaam willing, a second chance at freedom for the Garo.

***

Rohem couldn't say what had enticed him to sprint to the megalith. Only that once he arrived, he fell to his knees, utterly drained from the energy transfer with Finu.

In particular, the surge of heat he had unleashed as a barrier between himself and the beast had taken the most out of him.

He'd heard Thia call out a short while ago, and then silence. He could only hope his text communication had gone through. Even if all Tabir presence on the island had fallen, the Network connection should still be active, so long as the electrical tower their engineers had constructed still stood.

Behind him, the clattering of jumping spider eggs sounded in the trees, coupled with the rainfall. Gazing up at the glowing structure above him, Rohem drew a deep breath of salty sea air, curling his toes inside his boots as the droplets fell upon his face from above.

The guilt washed over him like a tidal wave from the vast watery expanse beyond the megalith.

He opened his eyes.

No, not megalith. Solar rise.

He had access to unimaginable energy— the power of the sun itself, and yet, he had failed to carry out his role as a doctor. As a healer.

For what seemed like an eternity, Rohem remained on his knees, unable to take those final few steps to enter the rise. The shame ate at him like a hungry scorpion, and he wouldn't allow himself the powerful escape available to him in that radiant obelisk.

As a rasping rattle sounded from somewhere deep in the foliage behind him, Rohem shut his eyes again.

He could hear the thing approach, almost *sense* as it emerged from the canopy onto the shore where he now sat.

Clenching his fist in preparation for the final heat blast he could manage, Rohem rose and whirled to face the creature—

And found himself staring at a tall, vaguely man-shaped blackened cinder that crumbled to a pile at his feet moments later.

Immediately behind the fallen beast, Echil held Rohem's gaze with a subtle smile, that deep blue tinge gently illuminating the small area between her eyes.

Rohem swallowed hard. Had that creature been Finu?

Flustered, he blurted the first response that came to mind.

"I had him."

"Your energy levels are depleted," Echil replied nonchalantly, stepping over the pile of ashes as if it were a flattened mound of dirt.

As during their previous encounter, she wore that same strange grey uniform, long dark hair pulled back over one shoulder.

Rohem faltered for a moment before retorting, “Are you going to invite me back inside the meg…the solar rise?”

“It’s understandable that you would be skeptical.” Echil sighed, keeping an appreciated half-meter distance from Rohem. “The rises provide the most direct energy source. Still, fusion is possible without them.”

“Fusion?” Rohem was at a loss. “I know only of nuclear fusion, the theoretical process that takes place in the sun’s core.”

Echil smiled then. The expression seemed almost bitter.

“The Tabir would have this information,” she mused. “Though, yes, fusion does take place at the sun’s core. Hydrogen atoms burn so hot that they transform instantaneously into helium.”

Rohem crossed his arms. “Are you about to tell me that the Zaam are also made of hydrogen and helium?”

Echil smiled again, this time with mirth. “You asked previously after your ability for spontaneous regeneration. You are a scientist. As you know, energy is neither created nor destroyed, only transferred. Zaam biology consists of two states— a bioform comprised of the same natural organs possessed by seedlings for long-term activity outside the rises, and a plasmoform, a state in which bioatomic satek assume control and conduct solar energy to convert the bioform into ionized gas—plasma.”

Seedlings?

Rohem’s head was spinning. This felt like a lecture at the medical academy. Plasma he had learned about as a high-energy gas—though very rare, if ever, present on the Plane, save in the form of lightning. Still, to have an entire alternate form of existence that he’d never even realized…

And satek? He had only ever read about these on a theoretical basis, mainly for the curing of diseases. A form of microscopic artificial intelligence that, as far as Lir knew, even Tabira had yet to scratch the surface of developing.

And these satek must be truly infinitesimal, if they could meld not only with biological cells but atoms as well. Not to mention there had been no trace of any abnormalities on Gether’s scan of Rohem’s body.

Somehow, assuming he and Echil represented the typical Zaam bioform, Rohem wondered if the prolonged absorption of direct sunlight could account for their dark skin tone.

"So…what is fusion?" Rohem probed, noting how she still hadn't answered his question.

"The rises and satek are made of the same solar-absorbent material, single crystal silicon. As the plasmoform is our natural state of existence, time spent outside of the rises has our satek constantly seeking to achieve balance with other plasmoforms. The way, our ion charge will level out and the photon energy achieve a high electromagnetic wavelength. This balancing process allows for instant non-verbal communication and can be quite…pleasurable. Even overwhelming."

She fixed him then with a soft gaze, a hint of mischief in her dark eyes. Instantly, Rohem recalled his conversation with Avithia regarding climax, and shifted uncomfortably. Time to steer the conversation elsewhere.

"Why are you here?" he asked. "Do you frequent all the rises?"

Stepping forward and placing a gentle hand on his shoulder, Echil transported both of them through the Field to the uppermost atmosphere, stopping only when they reached the highest point before the Void. To Rohem's knowledge, not even the most durable Kano aircraft braved these heights. As they stared down upon the Plane, the entire surface appeared dark, save for the illuminated spherical peaks of the five solar rises surrounding them.

From this height, Rohem could just make out a pattern he had only seen drawn on maps - a captivating ring of luminous white circles. Soon enough, he even became aware of the panoramic perspective from which he viewed everything. It was as if he could see the Plane's surface far below, the gleam of the rises and even the stars above without a single pivot.

Through their plasmic connection, Echil registered Rohem's utter awe and even a hint of fear. Not wanting to overwhelm him again, she returned them to the Plane, to a thick branch at the top of the Ayam jungle canopy, about a meter from the solar rise.

Suddenly realizing that he now sat naked, Rohem glanced around frantically, crossing his arms over the front of his thighs.

"Calm yourself." Echil nearly laughed. "Only the trees see us up here."

"We can use the rises and Field to travel anywhere on the Plane within seconds." Echil plucked a yellow fruit off the short branch of the adjacent palm tree, smiling slightly at Rohem's befuddled expression as he sat beside her. "Over time, the satek accumulate and store enough energy to transport a plasmoform directly through the Field, regardless of our distance from the nearest rise. The lightstreams observed by seedlings throughout the millennia are the visible manifestation of such transport."

"Why haven't I discovered the plasmoform before now?" Rohem probed quietly.

“When you made physical contact with the solar rise, your satek were re-activated to the necessary degree,” Echil returned plainly.

“The blue glow…” Rohem absentmindedly raised his fingers to his left cheek, recalling the subtle light he had seen that night after nearly touching the megalith the first time.

“The satek appear blue when beneath the surface of bioflesh, and enable instant cellular regeneration upon injury, even when dormant.” Echil replied. “Our plasmoforms are much brighter, like the rises themselves.”

Glancing back at the younger Zaam, she took a generous bite of the fruit, savoring the rare sweetness that came with eating in this form.

As the juice dribbled down her chin, she giggled quietly, using her other hand to deftly catch the escaped droplets.

Biting his lower lip, Rohem averted his eyes from her exposed form, though her now loose hair covered most of her front and what he could see appeared oddly dark and uniform. The dappled light from overhead cast soft shadows over the curve of her left cheekbone.

“No need to hide,” Echil cooed, as he attempted to pivot his torso slightly away from her, despite the fact that the darkness from the canopy shielded most of his own body. “Such modesty is highly primitive. Traveling in plasmoform renders common clothing obsolete. No apparel can withstand such temperatures, only the skinsuit, also fabricated from the satek.”

After a pause, Rohem raised his eyes to hers once again. Then the shadows weren’t playing tricks on him - unlike him, Echil remained clothed in the dark grey outfit. From somewhere deep in the foliage behind them, a low rattle echoed through the darkness.

“What did you mean by ‘seedlings’?” Rohem finally asked.

Echil paused briefly and turned to gaze up at the solar rise through the tree leaves before speaking again.

“The seedlings are what we call those with whom you grew up. The people of the nations surrounding each of the five rises.

“Long ago, before the rise of the nations, there was a storm. A devastating meteor shower that took the Zaam by surprise. Immense pieces of rock rained down for days on end. The Field remained intact, of course. Yet we were forced to move many operations underground and off the Plane while the surface replenished itself. Fortunately, our underground tunnels had long been equipped for such a catastrophe. Before the storm, we had secured in our underground laboratories several animals from each of the large species as well as birds.

“Over time, we bred the large animals to repopulate the Plane. We also engineered beings, modeled after ourselves but with wings and hollow bones like the birds of the Plane. These creatures served us well, surveying the landscape from high above to report on air and soil quality, so that we could assess the returning fertility of the land. Over four-hundred years passed before the Plane became habitable once again for natural life."

The Flightless were the first seedlings—Mak Eta's niece and nephew as well as their father's entire line had been engineered.

Rohem frowned. "Such advanced technology, and you had to breed scouts? No automated surveillance?"

"Life forms provide more genuinely nuanced feedback," Echil deadpanned.

"No nation holds records of such an event, nor any meteor sightings," Rohem pointed out, focusing again on the subject of this alleged storm.

In the next instant, Echil transported them both back to the solar rise.

"This was before the time of the nations." Echil's eyes never moved from his face. "Though only the Zaam, with our plasmic nature can access it, the Field extends from the Plane's surface out to our sun. Together, the Field and the Star Unit have guarded you well against such threats from the Void. Still, even we had never faced such a disaster."

She glanced up toward the still dark sky.

"The white flame—what the Ayam call the night clouds," she said softly, indicating the skyflame. "This is a remainder of the storm. The last pieces that now orbit the Plane just beyond the Field's barrier. By night and day, they move all seawater across the land. Such is common elsewhere in the Void. In time, the remnants will become spherical as they mold to the shape of the Plane's gravitational orbit. Right here on this island is that great pit the Ayam people call the Maw. I recall clearly the moment the rock fell and created that crater."

"And what about the Lasha? Are they the result of genetic breeding as well?"

Echil glanced sideways at him. "No. For as long as we have studied the process of evolution, natural anomalies remain that we did not catalyze."

He found some comfort in the fact that two people with whom he spent much of his life had not also originated from exterior interference.

Returning to the topic of the five nations, Rohem was determined to tackle one question at a time. "When did the nations come to be?"

"Within the centuries that followed, we reseeded the Plane with life forms much like ourselves. We taught them the verbal language we had used before coming to rely largely on the Field and fusion for communication. Zaam individuals have not possessed personal names or even regularly spoken language for millennia. However, the seedlings required such a rudimentary form of communication, given their lack of a plasmoform."

"Seedlings don't possess the satek," Rohem reasoned. "That's why they die of sickness and old age."

"You catch on quickly." Echil glanced back at him with a half-smile. "Our satek draw power directly from the sun, replacing the need for sleep as well as any other form of nourishment. From cellular regeneration upon injury to eradication in the instance of unchecked growth, we are invulnerable to illness. So long as we have access to solar energy, we are indestructible."

In that case, Tabira's cure for the growth disease must utilize satek with the similar capacity to target wayward cells.

"Why do you have a name?" Rohem wanted to know. "If you no longer have use for spoken language?"

"*Ich el* is the term for 'good' in our original tongue," Echil replied. "Over time, as the seedling nations developed their own languages from ours, they came to associate the name Echil with symbols such as hope and positive omen. As I was the Zaam who walked most often among the early seedlings teaching them language and how to hunt and gather food, they modeled their idols after my form. When we eventually instructed them in literacy, they began developing stories and laws compiled as a sacred text, surviving today among the Garo as Senti and Lirians as Sen, the seedling renditions of 'sent', the verbal Zaam term for 'truth'."

How quaint.

"Then the name of your species is Zaam?"

He wasn't remotely ready to refer to them as *his* species.

"Just as we have no use for personal names, nor do we designate our race as a whole," Echil answered. "Similar to the development of my name, the seedlings began calling us Zaam from nearly the beginning. In our verbal language that we passed on to them, the word means 'light'. Every night, the seedlings looked to the solar rises as a beacon of light in the dark. A way to hunt and stave off predators."

Your light shines on me.

Suddenly, the origin of that declaration of devotion shared between both Lirians and Garo became clear.

Rohem almost laughed. Possession of these satek could have saved Hazur as well as Oria's parents and Avithia's mother—not to mention countless others over the past generations.

For centuries, the different nations had viewed each other with suspicion and sometimes, even disdain—despite the fact that they originated from the exact same source.

"So you engineered a new species far weaker than yourselves, without the added benefits of cellular regeneration or longevity," Rohem stated. "Why?"

"Because we had the scientific capacity to do so," Echil returned matter-of-factly.

So in the face of Tabira's years-long effort to dissuade faith in favor of technology, the Zaam themselves represented the most advanced technology in known existence. Echil's nonchalance toward the creation of life chilled Rohem more deeply than even his encounter with the *onn* beast. Speaking of which, had the Zaam insight into curing the deadly pathogen?

Moreover, had Echil been watching him his whole life? Had the recent sensations of being followed both here and back in Lir been her all along? If she'd truly seen him grow up, why had she waited twenty-three years to show herself?

"If I am Zaam," he began again as steadily as possible, "why was I raised among...non-Zaam? Am I part...*seedling*, as you say?"

Echil's expression grew stormy. In the shadows from the trees, those spheres seemed to glow even brighter. "No," she deadpanned. "You are pure Zaam. As you know, Zaam lack the means to breed with seedlings. We cannot even procreate with each other. Your growing up among the seedlings was a mistake. One that I deeply regret."

"Why you?" Rohem wanted to know, deciding at the last moment not to question why his face didn't share the same...attributes as her own. "Are you the only Zaam left on the Plane?"

"I have remained the most frequent visitor to the Plane for the past twelve millennia since the storm." Echil nodded. "Though it was because of my recklessness that Joleh got a hold of you."

Twelve millennia.

Rohem stilled. "You knew Joleh?"

"He seemed the perfect pastime. A male feeling inadequate in a society ruled by females. Living in the shadow of a younger sibling. Not naturally blessed with the gift of scientific understanding and yet hopelessly eager to learn. Having taken advantage of their naturally fertile land and industrialized to an impressive extent by then, Tabira had all but progressed beyond the need to worship us as the other nations still did. Joleh presented the ideal subject."

"Then your relationship wasn't...intimate?" Rohem nearly cringed at his own question.

Echil looked like she could have scoffed. "No. Seedlings can make good pets. Like that Tabir pilot and his hound. Nothing more."

"Then it's all about ego for you," Rohem stated pointedly. "Play god over those you created to soothe your wounded pride over the destruction caused by the storm."

"I respect your honesty," Echil replied. "You see, the Tabir had managed to develop the basic automobile, weapons like the gun as well as succeeded in constructing large buildings and simple medicines capable of curing non-lethal pathogens. Though it was the knowledge that Joleh provided that allowed them to reach their current level of advancement."

"You just handed over all that information? To one commoner?" Rohem ventured skeptically.

"No." Echil cocked her head. "I saw in him a desire for challenge. Like you and me, Joleh aimed to push the limits for the goal of technological achievement. I hinted to him the nature of the Zaam. How we are not born, but harvested in the rises. How a Zaam develops as the result of fusion between embryonic cells and bioatomic satek. Information from which his people were so far removed he never could have devised a similar method of creation. But I trusted him too much…"

When Rohem didn't reply, Echil continued. "Following the storm, some Zaam retreated underground, far below each solar rise. Beyond anywhere the seedlings could detect.

"Still, most took to the Void in the pursuit of star exploration. However, the very occurrence of the storm didn't sit well with me. For centuries beforehand, the Star Unit we had established around the Field had kept out all threats of impact from the Void."

Rohem was trying and failing to contain his excitement. Until tonight, all he had occupied his time with were matters of the apprenticeship and affairs of state. Yet these beings had been exploring the stars for centuries—even *millennia.*

The glaring difference in scale nearly overwhelmed him.

Still, he detected a note of foreboding in her tone. He pretended not to notice that look of fascinated curiosity in her eyes that had reappeared since their first encounter. Something about the face and even the voice before him seemed eerily familiar, and he pushed it from his mind.

"Something penetrated the Star Unit?" he spoke up.

"I saw the need for an alternative method of procreation, should the solar rises become unavailable to us." Echil again skirted his question. "As the lead scientist at the time, I devised the practice of sporing."

"Sporing." Rohem frowned. "As in plants?"

He suddenly recalled his own comparison to his dependence on solar energy as akin to photosynthesis.

"As well as bacteria and fungi, yes." Echil nodded. "As Zaam, our physical prowess increases the longer we exist and accumulate sunlight over time. However, we only age if we do not re-enter the solar rises after the sun sets each day. Each night we do not recharge within the rises, our bioforms age by one day. My hypothesis held that if a single Zaam could spend days on end with direct exposure to solar power from only the sun itself, the ions in our plasmoform would become so excited that both satek and cells would split off in multiples, resulting in a new individual. My proposal to the rest of our people was immediately rejected as too controversial. Still, I conducted the experiment with myself as the test subject."

After another pause, Rohem ventured, "So did it work?"

"Yes." Echil nearly grinned, white teeth contrasting with her dark skin. "You are proof of that."

Rohem froze where he stood. From the darkness beyond the solar rise, the waves crashed as the hint of sunrise peaked over the watery horizon.

This being before him— he still couldn't bring himself to consider her a woman, even in his own mind—was what to him? A sibling, parent...*clone*?

Still, that burning question remained, and he would not let her avoid it any longer.

Closing the distance between them, Rohem resolved to assume as intimidating a posture as possible.

"What was Joleh's part in all of this?" he asked as icily as possible, eyes boring into the Zaam who stood at his eye level.

All around them, the rain slowed to a gentle drizzle.

Echil smiled serenely and turned toward the approaching sunrise, the warmth of her expression reflecting the first glowing fingers of dawn as she reached back and gently took his hand in hers.

Already, his skin was tingling from her touch coupled with the nearness of the solar rise before them.

"Why tell you when I can *show* you? Come, a new day approaches. Let's rise with the sun."

As Rohem joined Echil in plasmoform, all hesitation and rational thought gave way to the most intense euphoria he had ever experienced.

The waves of pure, unadulterated bliss blended seamlessly with the sequence of imagery that followed, as the being called Echil relayed her message.

For the first time in centuries, a radiant white lightstream accompanied sunrise in the skies over the Plane.

Echil had to admit, she found the pure innocence radiating from her progeny to be impressive. His sensitivity to the novelty of fusion triggered in her a response both protective and intrigued. Even the most basic mode of communication practiced by their species for millennia must strike him as worlds apart from anything he had ever undergone.

His memories alone had clarified for her the unpleasant truth that, despite being compelled for the first years of his existence to please the seedlings with his energy, he had yet to experience the reception of such energy.

Now, she could finally show him what he had been missing. What a gift— wildly intelligent and with powerful resolve.

A sincerely beautiful new life form—and all hers.

After waiting for the initial nirvana to subside for Rohem, the elder Zaam answered the most pressing question she had registered from his end.

"*No cure exists for the pathogen the Ayam nation calls the Curse.*"

Rohem's reply resonated through her as a current of pulsating, raw emotion.

Guilt, misery, and immense disillusionment.

"*How can we keep it from spreading further*?" Rohem's next question arrived shortly thereafter.

Echil wasted no time. "*Only when all the afflicted are eradicated will the illness end.*"

Surely, the only way forward pointed to indefinite quarantine of the infected. Nevertheless, the battle to survive this pathogen would persist.

"I will support the Ayam in their struggle." Rohem's emotions emanated deep indignation and determination.

"*The affairs of seedlings are no longer any concern of the Zaam*," Echil replied.

"*Just how is that?"* Rohem pressed. "*When you are the ones who created them? Why do you have so little faith in these people?"*

"Have you learned nothing from the Ayam affliction? The seedlings have proven more dangerous than capable when exposed to advanced technology," Echil answered calmly. "*As I've mentioned, Joleh showed both ambition and curiosity.*

Following several seedling years by my side, I confided in him my theory on sporing. I will never forget his expression of pure reverence and intrigue. He asked to assist me in any way he could.

Carrying out an unprecedented experiment in only the presence of a seedling proved exceedingly reckless on my part. The Zaam's rejection of my concern over our species' preservation clouded my judgment.

Our balance of bioatomic satek and cellular makeup is quite fragile and complex to maintain. As it happened, the sporing process highly complicates this balance, sending the participant into a deep catatonia. This state lasts until the progeny re-assembles from plasmic state to adapt outside of the rises, manifesting as an infant bioform. By the time I awoke, Joleh was standing over me, holding you in his arms."

Shock reverberated over their joined consciousness.

"*Joleh was there from the beginning?*"

"*He joined me as lookout while I absorbed the sunlight from the highest hilltop in Tabira. A place near enough to the solar rise that seedlings would not approach. When I came to and tried to take you back, I realized I had weakened to the capacity of an infirm seedling. I could not revert to plasmoform, and could barely stand in bioform. As soon as I grabbed Joleh's arm, I released what little power I had remaining, hoping it would faze him. He cried out from the burns, but would not yield you and ran. It was still night by then. By the time the sun rose and replenished my health, Joleh had long gone.*"

His realization as to the source of Joleh's scars traveled over their connection.

Echil knew Rohem could sense her remorse and humiliation roiling in waves, mingling with the ethereal iridescence of fusion.

"*When I asked what it would take to have you back, he requested all the knowledge of the Zaam,*" Echil went on, "*I didn't give him everything, of course. A wise decision, as he did not fulfill his promise to return you to me. In the end, the Tabir went on to erect their capital atop that hill. Meanwhile, Joleh went mad and received no credit for any of the knowledge he'd provided Tabira.*"

The fusion path relayed to Rohem Echil's sheer frustration in not regaining the physical strength to take him back from Joleh by force.

"*Then you gave Joleh the knowledge for the Curse as well?*" Rohem probed.

"*That I presented directly to Joleh, shortly before his first imprisonment,*" Echil replied. "*A vial of serum that could defeat any enemy. I extended the token as a peace offering. A final touch that I meant him no harm. If he only persuaded his connections in the Kano science wing to test the substance on an animal subject, the outcome would not disappoint.*"

"*What is the pathogen comprised of?*" Rohem wanted to know. "*Is it also dependent on solar energy?*"

A deluge of pride erupted from Echil's end.

"Impressive deduction. Yes, the pathogen is composed of injected satek and, like ours, cannot be removed once they enter a host. However, as the seedlings fully developed without embryonic fusion, the bioform treats them like a virus and, when deprived of solar exposure, the satek mutate the host into a reptilian semblance of the primordial creatures from which we all evolved. With their next intake of sunlight, the satek regenerate the seedling from its mutated state. When existing separately from a Zaam, these satek are constantly seeking new bioform hosts. Therefore, also similar to a pathogen, they transfer upon exchange of blood and other anatomical fluids."

Echil anticipated Rohem's next statement.

"Then you hoped the people would destroy themselves, with Joleh to blame," Rohem stated rhetorically.

"He shouldn't have stolen you," came the matter-of-fact reply.

Rohem continued, "*Why didn't you come for me following the return of your strength*?"

Echil conveyed her defensiveness through a subtle spike in their connection.

"*We warned the early nations never to touch the rises. We never wished their race harm—after all, we created them. Still, many fancied themselves brave and didn't follow our advice. They melted within seconds of contact.*

"*Still, we favored their survival as a fledgling species. In order to maintain the balance of power, Zaam are prohibited from using our plasmic abilities to kill a seedling. Observant Zaam can use the Field to detect our heat signature making direct fatal contact with a seedling life form. As I had told Joleh that the penalty for conducting an experiment in the face of opposing consensus was eradication, he used the threat of exposure as leverage. That if I made to force him or even kill him, I would cease to exist as well.*

"As for the possibility that I might collect you when he kept you hidden during the day, he threatened to shout to the skies that I had spored—and as other Zaam do occasionally frequent the Field, the risk that they would hear was present."

"Then Joleh is gone. That's why you came out of hiding. Yet you didn't kill him." Rohem was clearly striving to remain emotionless.

"The burns he sustained from our encounter gradually spread to his mind," Echil replied evenly. *"His own madness destroyed him."*

"*So you feared your own people enough to leave me among strangers*?" Rohem stated icily through their connection. "*You…an indestructible entity, worshipped by thousands for eons*?"

More memories—accompanied by shame—surfaced from Rohem's end. Memories from the time he spent in Tabira.

"*And for this, I apologize,"* Echil answered. *"I cannot begin to express the pride I feel at your ambition and intellect. Only fellow Zaam can truly appreciate what you have to offer. You can be free of all that now. We can exist separately from both the seedlings and the others of the Field. Come with me."*

A surge of bitterness channeled through their joined consciousness, momentarily jarring Echil's senses. The flurry of images—faces and experiences both cheerful and scarring—registered more clearly than ever.

Among these flashes, several individuals stood out. The older Lasha, Nasin. The younger, Avithia. The faithful Lirian, Oria…among others.

"I will fight for these people," Rohem seethed. *"*My *people. They don't wish to hide me like some failed science experiment."*

Echil bit back a spark of indignation. *"The seedlings. You believe you are one of them?"*

"As you've stated yourself, I grew up among those you call seedlings," Rohem returned. *"They have given me more than the Zaam ever could."*

Upon Echil's extension of an increase in fusion power, Rohem resisted the temptation with all his will.

Reluctantly, she released him.

Tearing frantically out of fused state, the newest Zaam found himself back on the beach of Ayam, standing alone and bare by the glinting black megalith, facing the fully risen sun.

Glossary of People, Places and Things

SETTING

The Plane: The world on which our story takes place

Megaliths: Five megastructures of unknown origin, spaced out across the Plane, each extending roughly 30,000 meters into the sky. Each of the five nations of the Plane developed around these structures.

Zaam: Mysterious entities worshipped by the majority of nations across the Plane. Though religious people among the nations associate them with the five megaliths, proof of the Zaam's existence has never been confirmed or recorded.

Echil: An androgynous maternal figure and the only remaining unique face of the Zaam in all religion and myth across the Plane

NATIONS & CHARACTERS

Tabira
Religion: None
Symbol: None
Mak Eta: Chancellor of Tabira
Vata: Eta's sister, leader of Tabir colony on the jungle island nation, Ayam
Ara & Inad: Vata's children
Hak: Vata's husband †
Samed: Tabir intelligence officer of the national Kano police force, stationed in Lir
Joleh: Samed's brother, also a Kano officer. Imprisoned for leading a rebellion against Mak Eta.

Kano: The brutal Tabir police force

Opal
Symbol: Mountain peak
Have since been wiped out by the Tabir; used to dominate the Plane's northeastern region, subjugating both the Garo and the Lirians. They had fair skin, light hair and light eyes. Lir ended up migrating to Tabira to escape the Opal. The Opal megalith still stands to the north,

overlooking coastal cliffs, dense forests and intricate cave systems. As the Opal intermingled with Garo before being conquered and assimilated by the Tabir, some Garo still have light features.

Lir
Religion: Worship the Zaam through the symbol of water (value water, as a desert-dwelling people); most Lirians have returned to the Lir homeland from Tabira
Symbol: Wave
Nasin: Political leader of Lir, mainly in terms of defense and trade. She is one of two currently living Lasha, people with a rare genetic mutation granting enhanced physical strength and the ability to sustain on only water for weeks as well as to alter biological sex. As Nasin has Chosen female, she no longer undergoes the change.
Avithia: The other of two currently living Lasha, ward of Nasin. Avi is the male form. Thia is the female form.
Oria: A young Lirian intelligence officer who lost her parents in the Tabir Cleansing of Lirians. As her mother was a respected Lirian priestess, Oria maintains her belief in the power of water.
Rohem: For the first seven years of his life, he was held captive by both Officer Joleh and the Tabir Capital. Before that, his origins were unknown. He has the ability to absorb and exert extreme heat, does not bleed, eat or sleep and possesses physical strength that possibly exceeds even that of the Lasha
Gether: Avithia's father and head physician in Lir
Officer Kari: The one remaining officer of the small, restricted Lirian police force
Yasit: Oria's grandmother, also highly religious and critical of Oria's work in intelligence
Walar: One of the few younger Lirians whose family remained in Tabira after the Cleansing

Garo
Religion: Worship the Zaam through the symbol of fire
Symbol: Flame
Par: Governor of Garo
Kel: Head militant in the Evaporation (freedom fighter initiative)
Belim: Treasurer of Garo
Lan: Wife of Belim, head linguist and interpreter for Governor Par. She enjoys traveling and learning about other cultures. Her fair skin and green eyes reflect her Opal ancestry.
Unno: Sister of a former freedom fighter and first female, child freedom fighter

The Evaporation: Freedom fighters who set themselves on fire in groups to stage protests as well as use small bombs to resist what they view as the Lirian occupation

Ayam
Religion: Worship the Zaam; refer to their megalith as the Great Stone
Symbol: Palm tree (eventually)
Telo: The new young chief of Ayam
Maru: Wisewoman of Ayam
Dato: Telo's first warrior

Finu: Telo's younger brother

BACKGROUND TERMS

The Cleansing: A three-day-long, genocidal air raid by the Tabir government on the Lirian quarter of Tabira

Concealed: A Tabir who secretly still practices religion

The Curse: Pathogen spread via blood exchange and sexual intercourse, unleashed upon the Ayam by Tabira to penalize them for refusing to give up belief in the Zaam. Curse causes infected people to transform into reptilian, acid-spitting beasts every nightfall.

Flightless: Term for evidently genetically engineered beings with hollow bones and wings. These days, the few remaining Flightless rarely even have wings and typically cannot fly. Inad and Ara are the last remaining Flightless. Vata uses their presence to persuade the Ayam natives to trust her, as they resemble the jungle birds, which impresses the locals.

Grasswater: Addictive sedative taken from a grass grown in Garo. Safer when diluted with water.

Great Stone: Ayam name for their megalith

The Growth Disease: Cancer

Hydrotechnology: Lirian devices used to harvest water from beneath the desert sand; recycled water used to provide for households and as ammunition in waterblasters

Illumination: Tabira's adoption of unusually advanced technology, swiftly leading to the nation's majority giving up religion

Lasha: A genetic mutation that only appears among Lirians. Evolved after centuries of harsh treatment under the Opal and Tabir and then wandering the desert to return to Lir. Only one Lasha is born per generation. One Lasha possesses the strength of five grown men, alter their sex every seven weeks, and can survive weeks without food as long as they drink just a bit of water.

The Maw: Massive crater in the Ayam forest floor, used by the Ayam as a mass gravesite

Satek: Microscopic artificial intelligence utilized for many purposes, primarily medicine

Tso Blade: A traditional Garo blade with a triangular shape used to strangle an opponent from behind

Made in the USA
San Bernardino, CA
18 July 2019